FINALITY

A METAPHYSICAL SCI-FI NOVEL

MARCUS MARTIN

 HYPERSONIC PRESS.

First print edition 2021

Book design by Marcus Martin

ISBN 9781913966034 (hardback)

ISBN 9781913966041 (paperback)

ISBN 9781913966058 (ebook)

www.marcusmartinauthor.com

CHAPTER ONE

I t was the screams that woke Michael up. A series of gut-wrenching cries from his neighbor's front yard. He raced downstairs, joining his younger sister in staring at the spectacle next door.

Their neighbor was prostrate on the lawn, with his arms wrapped around his wife's legs. He was shaking as he wept, repeating the same guttural cry, begging her not to go. She was immaculately dressed - like she was going to a job interview. In her hand she clutched an old-looking brown envelope. Michael could just make out a neat signature and a faded Ministry stamp on the front.

The couple had lived next door for as long as Michael had been alive - almost eighteen years. They were a little older than his mother, Val, but not *"old*-old" like Grandfather Amal. Michael had always thought of them as youthful people; active, fashionable, sociable. But here they looked broken; the creases on the man's brow had become trenches. His once-glossy hair looked ashen, his mouth ragged. His clothes were muddy and grass-stained.

His wife could have been carved from marble, such was

her resolve. She stared straight ahead, unflinching, but her cheeks sagged, as if gravity had called in all of its debts at once. Her polished black shoes twinkled in the scattered morning sun.

Amidst the man's wailing, Michael's front door slammed shut. Through the netted curtains, he glimpsed his mother hurrying upstairs. Across the street, neighbors were appearing on their doorsteps and at their windows, watching with pity and shock.

The husband's wailing petered out into a whimper. Kneeling down, his wife gently prized his fingers from her calves. The man craned his neck and stared at her with bloodshot eyes and sodden cheeks.

"Please... Don't go," he stammered.

She took his head in her hands.

"I will always love you," she whispered.

She forced a fleeting smile and kissed his forehead once. Her eyes were misting but she blinked the tears away before they could fall. Swallowing, she stepped away from her husband.

He curled into a ball and wailed with unfettered anguish as his wife marched to the end of their path, and onto the sidewalk. She kept her head perfectly level and set off for the great dome rising from the center of the city. She was clutching the envelope so tightly her knuckles turned white.

Michael and Sophia watched in silence as the woman shrank from view. With bowed heads, the rest of the street returned to their homes. But the desolate husband continued weeping on his lawn, clutching his sides in disbelief.

Michael's front door opened once again and his grandfather stepped out, brushing crumbs of toast from his lips. He ruffled Sophia's hair and nudged her back inside. Being on the cusp of teenagehood, she'd normally have scorned such a gesture of affection, but the events of the morning had unsettled her. She hurried in without a word.

Michael was about to follow her, but his grandfather intervened with a warm smile and a firm pat on the shoulder. He spun Michael around and steered him to the edge of their garden.

"You're almost eighteen now, you need to be ready to face these things."

He gave Michael's shoulder a squeeze, then led the way into their neighbor's yard. Amal knelt beside the weeping man and gave him a consoling pat. "Come on, pal," he cooed.

With a tilt of the head, he beckoned Michael closer. They scooped up the man like a wounded soldier and led him inside. They deposited him on his sofa, where he curled into a ball and sobbed.

"Time for a cup of tea," winked Amal.

He gave Michael an encouraging smile and stepped away, busying himself in the couple's kitchen. Michael hovered awkwardly by his weeping neighbor. Tears streamed into the cushion under the man's head. Michael snatched a clutch of tissues from the counter.

"Here," he muttered.

But the gesture was futile. The man was clearly incapable of resolving his leaking nostril situation without more direct assistance. Indeed, he seemed barely aware of Michael's presence at all.

Michael gingerly swiveled the man's legs and sat beside him, dabbing the mucus away, and drying the man's cheeks.

Amal returned with a laden tea tray. His rummaging had yielded several packets of biscuits, too.

"What should we do?" whispered Michael.

Amal reclined into a comfortable chair and blew across the top of his mug.

"Be here. That's all that matters today."

Michael scrutinized his grandfather's expression. Behind the reassuring twinkle and all-weather smile, he saw a flicker of something uncharacteristic. Sadness? Empathy? No - it was more specific than that. It was déjà vu.

CHAPTER TWO

Kelsey paced outside the principal's office like a caged animal.

"How much longer is she gonna be? Are you people even allowed to do detentions on Saturdays?"

"It's not a detention, and she'll call you when she's ready."

"Intervention, detention, same difference," shrugged Kelsey.

"Take a seat," urged the secretary.

Kelsey examined the brochures on the mottled counter, then rearranged them face down.

"Do you mind *not* doing that?" snapped the secretary.

"I'm helping. No-one wants to see that ugly bitch Lisa on the cover."

"Lisa is my niece."

"I can see the resemblance."

Before the secretary could reprimand her, the principal's door opened. A stern voice summoned Kelsey in.

She blew the secretary a kiss then strode through, heading for the principal's vacant chair.

"Don't even think about it," said the principal.

Kelsey rolled her eyes and slouched onto the adjacent couch, helping herself to an apple. Beyond the sealed office windows, a zeppelin hovered above the playing fields. Figures were descending from ropes and winches, practicing a rescue drill.

"Where are your Ministry guardians?" said the principal.

Kelsey shrugged. "Probably in the bar. Or a police cell. Dead, if I'm lucky."

"I rather wish they were here for this meeting."

"And I *rather wish* my real parents weren't meth heads but there we go."

"Is that true?"

"If you'd bothered to read my file you'd know."

"I confess, when you transferred here, I didn't have time to digest all the particulars of your, uh..."

The principal trailed off, blushing as she flicked through a dense binder.

"My crappy life?"

"Your journey to us."

"You gonna keep pissing my Saturday up the wall or can we get on with whatever this is?"

The principal set the binder aside with a sigh. Folding her arms, she leaned forwards.

"I'll keep this brief, then. You have ignored every warning, skipped detentions, fought and intimidated other pupils and parents, and rejected all our help. You've even shirked the remedial classes we put on for your benefit. Everyone appreciates you have difficulties at home, but we've reached a point where your behavior is impacting-"

"I thought you said 'brief'?" interrupted Kelsey.

The principal's face soured.

"Miss Bailey, with regret I am forced to expel you permanently. The Ministry is being notified as we speak, and they will liaise with your guardians henceforth."

"Good luck with that," snorted Kelsey. "So what now, on to the next dump of a school?"

"Because this is your third expulsion, you're no longer eligible for mainstream education. You are being transferred to a residential correctional school. See it as an opportunity."

Kelsey glared at the woman.

"Would you send your kids there?"

The principal blushed. "My kids aren't a danger to society."

Kelsey balked. "Society's a danger to *me!*"

The principal's door opened and the Head of P.E. entered. A gray garment hung over his arm. The material looked thick and coarse, and buckles ran down one side. Kelsey's stomach churned as she realized what it was.

"Don't be alarmed, Kelsey, this is perfectly routine. If you comply, we'll keep the straps loose."

The principal stood up and waved her broad-shouldered colleague through.

"It's just a precaution until the Ministry get here."

Kelsey sprang to her feet and backed away.

"You can't do this to me," she cried.

"In a way, you've done this to yourself," sighed the principal.

Jaw clenched, the Head of P.E. unfurled the straitjacket and approached Kelsey.

"Leave me alone, I'm not crazy!"

He lunged for her, but she spat in his face. The man recoiled, cursing, then whipped out a spit hood and dived towards her.

Kelsey couldn't match his size and strength, but she was several decades nimbler. She leaped over the desk and grabbed every loose item within reach. Hurling the lot, she forced the pair to retreat. Within seconds, the despairing educators had fled to the front office, as paperweights and textbooks crashed against the walls.

Alone and panting, she searched for escape. The principal had locked the only door, and was yelling through the keyhole.

"Kelsey, we need you to put the jacket on! The Ministry will be here any minute, we'll be in trouble if we've not followed regulations. They'll subdue you with force, you don't want that!"

Kelsey's eyes moved to the ceiling tiles above her. Standing on the desk, she pulled herself up into the dusty ventilation shaft. It was narrow and rusty, like much of the school.

There was a glimmer of light several yards away. As she clambered through the vent, the metal groaned beneath her. Realizing what was happening, the principal rushed into the office.

"Get outside, don't let her leave!"

But it was too late. Kelsey was gone, and running for her life.

CHAPTER THREE

Several hours had passed since Michael and his grandfather scooped their bereaved neighbor off his lawn. The man had howled himself into an exhausted stupor, leaving them to keep vigil until his sister arrived from out of town.

As the two siblings reunited in tears of grief, Michael felt like an intruder. By contrast, his grandfather was enthusiastically instructing the newcomer on the care needs of the house's various pot plants. Michael intervened and dragged him to the door, offering the neighbor an awkward thanks for the tea as they left.

"Barring our abrupt departure, you did well in there," said Amal.

The old man patted Michael's shoulder and set off along the sidewalk, in the opposite direction to their house.

"Where are you going now?" groaned Michael.

"You have questions, I can see them on your face. They're better discussed out of the house. Come."

Michael flopped onto a cushioned booth at the ice cream parlor. His grandfather eased himself into the opposite side, with joints creaking like a floorboard.

"You did two good things today," said Amal.

"Two?"

"You helped your neighbor in his hour of need. And then you bought your old pops some ice cream."

Michael rolled his eyes while Amal chuckled.

"Should I come back?" said the waiter.

"No, we're ready to order. I'll take the salted caramel sundae please, extra sauce," said Amal.

"Are you trying to bankrupt me?" said Michael.

"I can't impart valuable life lessons to you on an empty stomach," insisted his grandfather.

"What about you, young sir?" said the waiter.

"Just a scoop of vanilla, thanks," winced Michael.

As the waiter left, Michael ducked his grandfather's gaze.

"Come on boy, out with it," urged Amal.

"When Father died..."

"Was it like that?" said Amal.

Michael nodded. His grandfather gazed out of the window and smiled at the afternoon sun.

"I'm surprised you haven't asked before now, although I suppose your mother didn't help things," he mused. "When your letter comes, you have a choice to make. And so do the people around you."

"What choice did Father make?"

"The wrong one. I knew your dad well; he'd been with your mother for a decade. He was there for me when your grandmother passed. Which is why I never understood his final actions."

The waiter returned and plonked two very different

servings before them. Amal clapped his hands and shoveled a mound of ice cream into his mouth. Pain shot across his face. He slapped his jaw with agitation, laughing in discomfort.

"Brain freeze!" he groaned.

Michael pushed his solitary scoop around the bowl.

"Did he die... badly?" said Michael.

His grandfather loaded up another brimming spoonful.

"He was always such a thoughtful man. A devoted father and husband, and a popular man in the community. He had his whole life to plan that moment, and yet..."

Amal trailed off, returning to his sundae.

"Yet what?" said Michael, snatching his grandfather's bowl.

"You should try some - the sauce is incredible."

Michael scowled at him.

"We've avoided this conversation for twelve years. Indulge me a few more mouthfuls of ice cream, there's a good lad," said Amal.

Tutting, Michael released the bowl and watched his grandfather tuck in with childish zeal. Amal devoured the lot, then leaned back in his chair, with a hand on his belly, and immense satisfaction across his face. Pointedly, Michael handed him a napkin. The old man mopped the sugary carnage from his face and sighed, wearily. He placed both hands on the table, as if earthing himself, before looking Michael in the eye.

"You only get one chance to get death right. It's a moment you've known was coming since the day you turned eighteen. Given a second chance, I *know* your father would have acted differently. But there are no second chances in life, Michael. Certainly none in death."

"I don't understand. Did he *do* something?" said Michael.

His eyes were wide, his heart fearful. In all these years, it had never occurred to him that what had happened might have been his father's fault. His mother had refused to talk about the topic, hiding behind his younger sister whenever Michael raised it. Eventually, he'd stopped trying, and chose to settle for the sanitized narrative his six-year-old mind had created.

"Your father meant well, Michael. He meant the best, of course he did. He loved the three of you more than he could ever express. But that love led him to make choices I would never have imagined. He regretted it so bitterly, his final act was to shield you from the truth."

Amal drummed his fingers across the table then snapped them down decisively.

"But that was a long time ago. You're nearly eighteen, and you'll soon be walking the same path as the rest of us. How can we expect you to avoid such grave mistakes without knowing what they are? At the same time, I don't want you to stop loving your father. What he did has to be contextualized. Are you sure you're ready?"

"Like you said, Pops, I'm nearly an adult. Whether I'm ready or not, I need to know," quavered Michael.

There it was again, that look of weary pity he'd seen in his grandfather's eyes so many times before, hiding beneath the soft, wrinkly smile.

"So be it," said Amal.

The parlor door swung open and Michael's mother, Val, marched in with his sister in tow.

"I thought we'd find you here. What are you two talking about?"

Val smiled politely, but her tone was direct. She fixed Amal with a fiery glare.

"We were discussing Michael's father."

The smile vanished from her face.

"With all that's happened today? You think that's appropriate?" she snapped.

"I think it's important."

Val scanned the room, flitting between her father and the other customers. She was a woman of composure and stately dignity. It was rare that Michael saw his mother this flustered, and it made him uncomfortable.

"Mum, Granddad was telling me about Dad's-"

"I'm sure he was doing nothing of the sort. Your grandfather knows better than to disrespect his memory like that."

With blazing eyes, she took a seat and thrust a menu into her daughter's hands.

"What flavors do you want, sweetie? Sophia finished all her homework, so we've come out for a treat," she explained.

"Did Michael finish his too, Grandpa?" asked Sophia, eyeing up Michael's ice cream with curiosity.

"No, he didn't. In fact, Michael should be getting back to it now," snapped Val.

Michael rose with a heavy sigh, accepting defeat. At least he didn't have to pay for his grandfather's ice cream now.

"We'll talk later," whispered Amal.

Michael trudged home, gloomily. His grieving neighbor was still curled up on the couch next door. The man's sister was making phone calls beside him, surrounded by coffee cups and beer.

Michael toe-punted the gate open, adding to the scuff

marks around the base. He climbed the stairs to his bedroom and flopped onto the bed, staring at the calendar opposite.

Three days to go. His throat felt dry, and his head felt light. He wasn't ready to choose his death.

CHAPTER FOUR

The front door was wide open. Litter lay strewn across the yard, and there was shouting from inside. Something smashed, followed by an angry yell. Kelsey edged along the dirt path towards the dark hallway. She didn't bother trying the switch; the lights hadn't worked in months.

Squinting into the darkness, the familiar stench of the beer-soaked carpet greeted her. More crashing from the kitchen. Someone was throwing plates. Footsteps hurried towards the doorway. Kelsey retreated just in time as a bottle flew past her shoulder.

"What the hell?" she yelled.

Her foster father tripped over the front step and tumbled down before her. A scantily-dressed woman of similar age leaped over him. She hobbled away on one shoe, clutching a pile of clothes to her chest.

"Come back here, you whore!"

Kelsey pressed herself flat against the mobile home as her foster mother erupted from the house. The woman was the size of a car, and held an armful of crockery, which she was hurling at the retreating woman. Out of ammo, she turned to her philandering boyfriend and gave his backside a thorough kicking, while schooling him on the virtues of monogamy.

"Darlin', it ain't like that, you know me darlin', I swear, she was lost is all," protested the man, yelping at the blows.

"Stacey, that's enough, people are looking," yelled Kelsey.

"I'll say when it's enough!" puffed her foster mother.

The woman dropped to her knees, crushing her partner, and pounding him with her mallet-sized fists.

"Darlin', come on, you know me!"

"Yeah, Tony, I know you're a cheating jackass!"

"Stacey, that's enough, he's said sorry," urged Kelsey.

She grabbed her foster mother's shoulder but Stacey lashed out, elbowing Kelsey hard in the face. Kelsey staggered back, gasping in pain. Blood gushed from her nose.

"Bitch, you broke my nose!" she yelled.

Stacey lurched towards Kelsey, panting.

"What d'you call me, girl?"

Kelsey raised a hand in surrender, as the woman's shadow engulfed her.

"I clothed your ass, fed your ass, and this is how y'all repay me?" fumed Stacey. "Was you givin' him a piece too? Y'all laughing behind my back? We'll see who's laughing now!"

Grabbing Kelsey's hair, Stacey dragged her inside and threw her to the filthy floor. Kelsey winced as her bloodied hands landed in strands of fur and feces.

"I'm sick and tired of y'all disrespectin' me," snarled Stacey.

As Stacey raised her tree trunk foot, shards of porcelain burst across her head like a snowball exploding.

"You miserable waste of space," yelled Tony. "Charlene was the *only* good thing I had goin' on, and your fat ass gone ruined it!"

As Stacey stormed towards her partner, Kelsey seized her moment. Fleeing to her bedroom, she scraped her hands clean then shoved a tampon up each bleeding nostril. She filled a bag with clothes, grabbed the meager savings hidden in her bedpost, then fled for the alleyway.

***

The bus reached its terminus and the driver kicked Kelsey out into the driving rain. Spotting a grimy cafe across the way, she made a beeline for the bathroom, bracing for an ugly reflection.

Astonishingly, her nose wasn't at the ninety-degree angle it had felt like, but Stacey's titanic chicken wings had managed to blacken one of her eyes too. Gingerly, she tugged the tampons out of her nostrils, then cleaned the dried blood away.

There was an agitated knock at the door.

"Toilets are for customers only."

"I'm a customer," Kelsey snapped.

She quickly switched out her bloodied top for a clean one, then washed the crimson stains from the sink.

The knocking grew louder.

"Just a minute already, god! You wanna come change my tampon yourself?" she yelled.

The man apologized and hastily retreated. Kelsey nodded to her reflection in approval. Technically, she hadn't lied - not that lying bothered her – but she liked to congratulate herself on the occasions where it wasn't required. Grabbing her backpack, she prepared to dart for the exit. But as she stepped into the filthy corridor, a crushing realization set in.

She had no place to go.

"So, what will it be, *customer?*" said the owner, startling her.

Kelsey regrouped and fixed him with a demanding stare.

"I want a job."

He eyed her up, disdainfully. "We're not hiring."

"Your bathroom's filthy, your tables need cleaning, and I can make better sandwiches than those wonky pieces of crap in your cabinet."

"This is your first interview, isn't it?"

"I thought I'd start at the top."

The owner considered for a second, then laughed.

"One trial shift. Speak to a customer like that and you're out, understood?"

Kelsey nodded, barely masking her astonishment.

"ID card," said the owner.

"What?"

"I can't hire you without an ID card. You don't have it with you?"

"No, I've got it," said Kelsey.

She fished it out of her pocket and held it up, covering the date with her thumb. The owner plucked it from her hand and swiped it through the till. The machine whirred and spat out a receipt. Tearing it off, he examined it with a frown.

"That's weird. Let me try again."

As he repeated the motion, the till swallowed the card. It churned out a fresh message, this time in red ink.

"Uh, just a moment, I need to check something," said the owner.

He slipped away through a beaded curtain into the pantry. Kelsey heard him spinning the number dial on a phone.

"Yes, hello, it says to call this number and quote code '4-M-1?' I see. Of course."

He hung up and sidled back to the counter, with an unnerving smile.

"Uh, please, how rude of me, I didn't offer you any refreshments. Tea? Some cake, maybe? It's a - er - tradition for new employees."

Kelsey's stomach rumbled. There'd always been food at her last home, but it was rarely hers to eat. To an empty belly, those wonky sandwiches looked pretty good.

She sat behind a greasy table and stared out of the window while the owner prepared her dish. Absent-mindedly, she probed the swelling around her eye, while her head swam. Where the hell was she going to sleep? Her math teacher had always been kind, but Kelsey had no idea where the woman lived. It wasn't like she could drop by the school to find out.

As the minutes drifted, her attention returned to the café. Something wasn't right. The sign on the door had been flipped around and the tables were clearing. There was no sound of a kettle boiling, and her food had yet to materialize. She glanced out of the streaky window and her heart froze. A police officer and an automaton were pulling up outside.

"What have you done?" she cried.

"I'm sorry, I was just following the Ministry's instructions!" protested the owner.

Grabbing her backpack, Kelsey darted for the fire escape.

―――――――――

Trash bags clanged into a dumpster, waking Kelsey with a start. Sleep-deprived and shivering, she emerged from her cardboard cocoon. If it was winter, she'd have perished. This wasn't a sustainable plan.

Wincing at her stiff back, she peered into the dumpster and surveyed the canteen menu. Supermarkets were reliable places for dumpster-diving; piles of edible food, fractionally past its sell-by, all there for the taking.

Assuming, of course, it wasn't contaminated. Kelsey recoiled as the stench of rotting fish wafted up. Time for Plan B.

She smartened her hair, tucked in her shirt, and approached the storefront. Casually, she browsed the fruit aisle, deftly slipping apples into her pocket before moving on. At the bakery, she picked up a croissant, devouring it on route to the toiletries' aisle, where she sprayed herself with deodorant. As she smuggled the remaining aerosol into her bag, a hand landed firmly on her shoulder.

"This way," growled a security guard.

Kelsey protested her innocence as he marched her to the security office. He emptied out her bag and pockets, uncovering the range of items she'd amassed. At least he couldn't take the croissant back.

"Where's your ID card?"

"I lost it yesterday."

"Too bad, because no ID is an additional felony," continued the guard. "You've gone for the classic supermarket crime, where you buy one, get one free."

"You can count. Well done. I can see how stringent security guard school must be."

"It beats jail. The police will be here to collect you shortly," said the guard, with a sadistic smile.

"Can I at least have a coffee or something while I'm stuck here?" said Kelsey.

"Certainly, ma'am. Would you like almond milk or soy? Brown sugar or white? Kiss my ass or eat it whole?"

Laughing, the guard departed, locking Kelsey in the holding room alone. She slumped her head against the table. At least it was warm.

The police station lobby was clad in emerald green tiles and dark wood panels. It could have been beautiful, were it not for the metal benches, underfoot drains, and hollering cries of the inmates.

"Name?"

The staff sergeant was a bored-looking woman with a center parting and thick, square-framed glasses. She hadn't bothered looking up from her paperwork, so Kelsey didn't bother replying.

Irritated by the delay, the woman's head snapped up.

"Are you deaf, girl?"

"You have lovely eyes," said Kelsey.

"I'm aware of that. Name?" snapped the sergeant.

"And your hair is divine."

Kelsey kissed her fingers away from her lips as if praising a bowl of pasta.

From the corridor beyond, an inmates' argument had escalated into a fight. The sergeant scowled as an alarm sounded.

"Fill this out and lose the cheek, or you'll be in with them."

She slapped a clipboard across the counter. Kelsey's bravado faltered as the sergeant grabbed a baton and marched off towards the yelling.

Accompanied by her arresting officer and automaton, Kelsey took a seat.

"I can't fill it out like this," she said, raising her handcuffs.

"You can fill it out fine," grunted the officer, before turning to his automaton colleague. "I'm going on my break. You watch the punk."

He slouched off, yawning, leaving Kelsey to answer the registration form. She snorted and set about it with sarcastic relish.

What is the reason for your visit:
I won the lottery.
How long do you expect to stay with us:
Play your cards right and maybe I'll spend the night.
Are there any mitigating circumstances:
No, I was born this way.
Is there anything we can do to enhance your stay:
A Swedish back rub wouldn't hurt.
Dietary requirements:
I only eat blue M&Ms.

Only after littering the page with such responses did Kelsey see the footnote.

Your answers will be referred to a judicial panel and may impact your sentencing.

"Crap, crap, crap," she muttered.

The pen wouldn't let her modify anything she'd written; the ink only flowed into blank fields. Kelsey groaned and tossed the clipboard to the side.

The staff sergeant whistled to the automaton as she returned.

"Yo, tin can, take the punk to cell nine."

The sergeant took Kelsey's bag, while the automaton ushered her on. Dragging herself off the bench, Kelsey trudged through the hallway, stopping abruptly as she reached cell nine.

"Uh, this can't be right," she said, puzzled.

The door was made of thick frosted glass, glowing with soft white light. The automaton held its palm to the sensor and the door buzzed open.

The room was domed like the inside of an igloo, only it was perfectly smooth. As Kelsey stepped inside the pristine white space, the door snapped shut behind her, sealing her in alone.

With a mechanical creak, the floor jolted. Kelsey staggered back as the circular wall appeared to rotate. She spun around, trying to get her bearings, but the wall was indistinguishable from the floor. Disoriented, she fell to her side, quickly scrambling onto all fours. The room was spinning faster. With each rotation, the doorframe faded further until it too was gone.

As the room settled, she rose to her feet, swaying.

"Hello?" she called out.

The sound was completely flat; there was no reflection whatsoever. Similarly, there were no shadows, no joins in the wall, no silhouettes beneath her feet. Light seemed to enter the room from all angles. Kelsey felt her pulse rising.

"Can anyone hear me? I need my stuff. It's got my medication in it!" she cried. "Did you hear me? Let me go or you'll regret it, my mom's a big deal in the police!"

As she yelled, she grew light-headed. There was something about the lighting and the soundscape that were causing her brain to trip out.

Hungry, exhausted, and defeated, she slumped to the floor. But as she touched the ground, an electric shock lashed out. She sprang to her feet, nursing her posterior, seeing no trace of the cause. Carefully, she lowered herself to the ground, only for another shock to send her leaping back up, stinging her palms too as she scrambled. Surrendering, she leaned against the wall instead.

"Son of a bitch!" she yelled, rubbing her arm.

She kicked the wall in frustration, triggering a shock to the foot. This sent her sprawling onto her hind quarters again, where the floor shocked her once more.

Dancing with pain, she yelled in frustration, shaking out every part of her body to try and numb the tingling of her overloaded nerves.

Whimpering, and clutching her sides, Kelsey shuffled into the middle of the brilliant white room and stood, trembling, as tears rolled down her cheeks.

"What do you mean you didn't ask? It's your *job* to ask!"

"She didn't have any ID, and there was an incident with some other inmates. I got distracted."

"So you put her in an infinity chamber? Are you trying to get us both fired?"

Kelsey sat in the police community liaison room with a blanket wrapped around her shoulders. Clutching a cup of heavily-sugared tea, she stared at the mahogany table, while the station supervisor bellowed at his staff sergeant.

Two days had elapsed since her arrest. An automaton sat beside her in silence, bearing its fixed, neutral expression. The supervisor dismissed his junior and took a seat opposite Kelsey.

"Ms Bailey, my profound apologies for the misunderstanding with your accommodation."

Beneath the veil of kindliness was a palpable fear.

"My colleague failed to notice that you were technically a minor at the time of your incarceration, and thus should not have been placed in such quarters," he continued.

Kelsey took a long, deliberate sip of her tea.

"If you wish to lodge a complaint, we do have a procedure for that, but truth be told it's an arduous process. Lots of paperwork, I'm sure you've got better things to do. Perhaps we could chalk this whole incident up as a mutual learning curve?"

Kelsey looked the man in the eye.

"Shouldn't I have a lawyer or something?"

The supervisor shifted uncomfortably, twiddling his walrus-like moustache.

"In normal circumstances, ma'am, you would indeed be entitled to a lawyer, but the thing is, see, you're no longer being charged. You were a minor when you absconded and committed the shoplifting, but your criminal record is expunged when you reach adulthood. So, as of today, there are no charges for us to pursue."

He sat back and folded his hands, admiring the elegant solution like they were old friends catching up.

"So... I can go?" said Kelsey.

"Absolutely."

"Wait, you said I *was* a minor. I'm not anymore?"

Sheepishly, the supervisor produced two documents from a folder. One she recognized as her ID card, which had been confiscated in the grimy cafe. The other was a creased white envelope. It bore her name in Ministry typeface and faded black ink.

KELSEY BAILEY

Taking it in her hands, she turned the envelope over, revealing a scrappy, handwritten fragment.

Emmeline Bailey xxx

Her biological mother; the woman lost to a life of drugs. Her handwriting was smudged and shaky, perhaps added in haste when both the letter and Kelsey were being taken away forever.

The rough, creased paper weighed heavily in Kelsey's hands. She looked at the supervisor, realizing what the envelope meant.

"Happy eighteenth birthday, Ms Bailey. The Ministry is expecting you."

CHAPTER FIVE

"Now remember," said Val. "As soon as you touch the envelope, you're committed. There's no going back; the Ministry forbids it. Think carefully before you choose. Your whole future will be in your hands."

"Quit pressuring him," grunted Amal.

"Smile, dummy!" giggled Sophia, snapping away like the paparazzi.

"Hush darling, be nice to your brother, it's a big day for him," soothed Val.

"He's scared of robots!" cheered Sophia.

"Am not!" snapped Michael.

Amal steered Sophia away to take photos of their extended family, who had traveled up for Michael's ceremony.

"Someone at school said you can't look them in the eye," whispered Michael.

"Nonsense," replied Val. "The custodians are here to protect us. Just be respectful and show them you love the Ministry."

"Relax, kiddo, you'll do great," winked Amal.

Val finished running the lint roller over Michael's blazer and presented him to the crowd.

"My boy's going to be a man!" she declared.

As a cheer rang out from the assortment of aunts, uncles, and cousins, the clock tower chimed eleven. Michael cringed, hating the attention his unwieldy clan was drawing from the clusters of other families waiting in the square.

"Go, go - you mustn't be late," urged Val.

There were tears in her eyes. She gave him a final, rib-breaking hug, then shoved him towards the stone steps and buried her face in Amal's side.

Since childhood, Michael had been taught that this day was a gift; that it embodied the greatest virtues of their civilization. So why was his mother looking so concerned, and why was Amal comforting her?

He climbed with trepidation. The building was an imperious marvel; a vast dome framed by two tall towers with spires stretching into the clouds. The Ministry's maxim was inscribed around the dome in large, repeating, gilded capitals:

REGULATING LIFE TO LIBERATE LIVES

As Michael climbed, a young woman was descending the steps. She had tanned skin, multiple earrings, and a rebellious attitude to shirt-tucking. Michael glanced back to see her welcoming committee, but there wasn't one — the only group waiting below was his own whooping circus.

Cringing, Michael hurried upward, hoping the attractive girl wouldn't think they were with him.

Inexplicably, his hand chose to do a mini wave. "Hey," he mumbled.

The woman held up her middle finger and passed Michael without smiling.

He hastened toward the green archway on top as the clock ceased chiming. The copper frame had oxidized long ago, but the polished marble surrounding it looked new.

Michael presented a white envelope to the clerk. It was worn, and somewhat dust-stained. The clerk pulled out the brief document within. It bore Michael's name and date of birth, and his parents' names, all printed in the Ministry's standard typeface eighteen years ago.

She posted the letter through a bronzed chute, then beckoned Michael through a turnstile. Michael's mouth fell as he stepped into the grand atrium of soaring archways and elaborate masonry. He'd seen nothing like it.

He hesitated in the middle of the lobby, his feet straddling a marble sun and moon.

"Quickly, please, we have many people to see today," urged the clerk.

Michael glanced back at the turnstile. What if he ran? What if he refused to go?

The clerk cleared her throat, as if reading Michael's mind.

"I wouldn't try that. Come on, place your hand over here."

She led him to a font made of white marble infused with black veins. The block was hip width, and came up to Michael's lowest rib. The stone was cold to touch, and perfectly smooth from the generations of hands that had passed across it over the centuries.

"Michael Hadley, the Ministry sees you and welcomes you to recite the creed," said the clerk.

Michael hesitated, nervously.

"A copy of the scripture can be provided if you would rather-"

"No, I know it," interjected Michael.

He let out a deep breath and closed his eyes.

"We, the citizens, ask that the Ministry,
Born of the wisdom of our ancestors,
Bears the burden of our mortality,
So that we may live most freely,
Within the confines of impermanence.
I hereby vow to protect this gift,
Cherishing all consciousness,
Accepting all consequence,
And returning in love, and gratitude,
On the day I so choose.
This is my fate and it is my own,
In good faith I do make this vow."

Michael opened his eyes. The clerk nodded curtly and placed one hand across her chest.

"The Ministry hears you, Michael Hadley, and shall receive your burden."

"I am unb-"

"Not yet, kid. You gotta go up there first," said the clerk, pointing to the tower. "Come along, they're waiting."

She led him to an elevator at the base of the tower. Its brass buttons gleamed beneath the flickering gas lanterns overhead. An automaton stood in the threshold, occupying half of the narrow doorway. Michael squeezed inside, awkwardly.

"This one's level twenty-five, six B," said the clerk, remaining in the lobby.

The automaton punched a button and the grate rattled shut. The clerk crossed Michael off her list and returned to the desk, while the elevator rose with a clatter.

Whereas Michael was enjoying a flood of relief, having not fluffed any lines of the creed, the lad beside him was an anxious mess; sweaty, trembling, hyperventilating.

"Relax, friend, that's the tricky part over with. We made it! They're going to ease our burden now. The Ministry loves us," said Michael, earnestly.

"You think?" laughed the boy.

Michael looked at his feet, blushing.

"You don't get it, do you?" continued the boy. "This is it. The beginning of the end."

"We're only choosing a letter, it's not a big deal," muttered Michael.

"And what if it's got today's date on it? You'll never leave this building again!"

The elevator shuddered to a halt, and the gilded grate clattered open. The automaton turned its mechanical head to face the boy, then pointed into the hallway. With a moan, the boy departed, and the elevator continued upwards.

Michael's head swam, mulling the boy's words as they climbed. *What if I choose today?* Fear took root in his mind.

The doors re-opened, and the automaton raised a silent finger, pointing Michael left. It was a far cry from the splendor of the atrium. The deserted corridor was narrow, the red carpet faded and worn. Nervously, Michael set off.

Each room had a small window cut into the door at eye-level. The rooms were circular, and the walls lined with mailboxes from floor to ceiling. The boxes were identical; neat metal flaps wide enough for an envelope and tall enough for a lock and name card to be fitted to the front.

An automaton was depositing a letter into one of the mailboxes. Opposite it sat an eighteen-year-old boy with a garland around his neck, who was fidgeting with the hems of his tracksuit.

Michael jumped as the door beside him opened. A young woman stepped out, smiling.

"It's not so bad once you're in there," she said, as the

elevator chimed open to collect her. "I am unburdened!" she declared, with a satisfied sigh.

She was gone before Michael could ask any questions. He edged towards the room she'd vacated. Inside, the automaton was feeding two letters into a chute. A puff of black smoke and soot billowed out from it. The machine twisted its head and fixed Michael with a piercing stare. He gasped and backed away, hurrying along the corridor until he reached his appointed room.

Six B. An automaton sat behind a table with a serene look fixed on its face. It stared unblinkingly at the opposite wall, with its hands folded across the table. Michael turned the handle and stepped inside. The room smelled of old metal.

Turning to face him, the automaton gestured to the seat opposite. The chair was stiff-backed and heavy. Michael shunted it closer to the desk, then sat with his shoulders hunched and his hands tucked under his legs.

"Um, I'm here to choose my-"

The automaton pulled open a drawer and produced three blank envelopes of identical proportions. It laid them out before him, then sat up straight with its hands clasped.

As Michael regarded the envelopes his head felt light. He tried to remember his mother's advice. *Be polite. They're there to help you.*

"Um... which should I...?"

The automaton gave no reply, staring serenely through him.

Michael's hands were clammy. He reached for an envelope then froze, arm outstretched. He longed to seize the envelopes, tear them open and see what was written inside. But he knew it was pointless. The letter would be inscribed in symbols only the Ministry could read; it wasn't for him to know. His job was to blindly choose one fate and live with it.

He glanced at the custodian's face, searching for a clue. Was this the right one? Was this his destiny? Michael moved his hand to the next envelope along. Was it just his imagination, or did the automaton's eye twitch? Was that a sign? He reached across to the third envelope. Was that a tilt of the head? It was almost imperceptible - but he knew to look. His mother had told him to look.

Inch by inch, he lowered his hand towards the third envelope. His mind whirred as he tried not to imagine the different dates written in each of them. Was his fate to be decades? Years? Months? A bead of sweat trickled from his brow.

His heart pounded. His fingers trembled. A rushing sound filled his ears. Snatching up the pen, he scribbled his signature across the central envelope.

A weight evaporated from Michael's shoulders. It was done. Sighing with relief, he opened his eyes and smiled. But the automaton looked agitated; its neck was twitching and it was avoiding his gaze. Silently, it rose from the desk and took Michael's signed envelope.

"What's wrong, what are you doing? Stop - I've changed my mind," stammered Michael.

Ignoring him, the machine glided to a mailbox on the far side of the room. Michael staggered around the desk, hurrying to catch up.

"Wait, I want to change it, I want to-"

Catching up, he grabbed the tip of the envelope. The automaton froze. With a shudder, its marble eyes rolled back, flickering. A hatch popped open, revealing a cavity in its throat.

"No, not that, I'm begging you! Just listen, please!"

A shrill alarm resonated from the cavity. Michael wrenched off his blazer and stuffed it into the machine's neck, trying to smother the signal and cover its eyes.

As he snatched back the envelope, a sharp blow knocked the wind from his lungs. The force of the machine's punch threw him across the room, into the opposite mailboxes. Michael scrambled to his feet, groaning, bracing for another attack.

The signed envelope had fallen from his hands and lay on the floor between them. The automaton ripped the blazer from its throat, flooding the room with a tinny klaxon din.

As it glided towards the fallen envelope, Michael darted past the machine back to the table. He snatched another envelope and threw himself at his mailbox.

The machine's alarm turned to a piercing scream as it saw him holding another letter. As its broad metal body bore down on him, Michael thrust the new envelope into his mailbox.

The machine crashed to the floor, twitching. As its eyes fell still and its siren failed, a public address system sounded from the corridor; the alarm was spreading.

His brain raced. He grabbed the two remaining envelopes – the blank one on the desk, and the signed one in the machine's hand. A cloud of smoke and soot puffed out as he thrust them into the incineration chute. Grabbing his blazer from the floor, he raced from the room.

"Security to level twenty-five," repeated the public address system.

Michael pounded the elevator button until the doors slid open with a ding. The automaton bell hop stared at him serenely as he leaped inside.

"Ground floor, hurry."

The machine obliged. As they plunged, its head twitched like an egg timer being set and sprung in rapid succession. The elevator shuddered to a halt and Michael sprinted across the atrium. The clerk stared at him, ashen-faced, as he pushed his way through the turnstile and into the open air.

Michael scrambled down the steps, two at a time, so fast he was almost falling. His family's excitement turned to fear as he hurtled towards them. His portly uncle intervened, catching him before he wiped out Amal's frail figure. Val pushed through the crowd and seized Michael by the shoulders, staring him in the face.

"Michael, what happened? You look drained."

"It's done, Mom. Let's go," he replied.

"Did you get the words right?" asked Amal.

"Uh, yes, Granddad. Come on, let's *go* already."

"You hear that, everyone? He is unburdened!" declared Amal. "Time to celebrate!"

The group roared in approval. As Michael cajoled them onward, he glanced back at the Ministry. Atop the cascading marble, a metallic figure glided out from the Moon Tower. Its head rotated smoothly until it fixed its expressionless eyes on Michael. Extending a strong, shiny leg forwards, it began to descend.

CHAPTER SIX

Kelsey's stomach rumbled as she approached the city's principle nursing home for the elderly. Homeless, sleep deprived, and still bearing a black eye from Stacey's elbow, she crossed the brick driveway. It wasn't a place she'd ever visited before, but it promised hot food, empty beds, and low security.

"Good morning, miss, can I help you?"

"It's madam, actually," snapped Kelsey.

It was still her eighteenth birthday. She wasn't expecting cards or flowers, but people were damned well going to start recognizing her as an adult.

The receptionist's face soured.

"We are unburdened," said the woman, bowing her head with the formal greeting.

"May we use it well," said Kelsey, bowing in return.

It was the first time she'd ever invoked the Ministry blessing legitimately. The recognition that came with it felt good. Although, as the receptionist glared at her, Kelsey made a mental note to be less cranky in how she extracted respect from people. After all, she needed to charm the woman if she was going to get inside. And right now, charm was even more of a stretch than usual, given that she'd just spent the night in a blindingly bright infinity chamber, and was now functionally homeless.

As if sensing Kelsey's ruminations, suspicion crept across the receptionist's faced.

"So, *madam*. Who are you here to visit?"

"My, er, aunt."

"Does your aunt have a name?"

"It's... uh... Agnes."

"You'll need to be a little more specific than that, *ma'am*. We've got multiple Agni here."

"Um... Agnes... Lather...ly..." stumbled Kelsey.

She was far off her A-game. Brazening into places was usually her forte, yet this was not going well.

"Sorry, *ma'am*, but we don't have any residents by that name."

"Oh, er, then try... Agnes... Maples... It's her maiden name."

The secretary nodded with a venomous smile and scanned the index.

"Alas. No one by that name either."

"Um... Maybe it's wasn't Agnes after all... Maybe it was... Julie?"

The receptionist beckoned Kelsey closer, glancing around with a conspiratorial flash.

"I get it, hun," she whispered. "You're cold, you're hungry, you're just looking for a bit of warmth and comfort."

Kelsey's heart fluttered in panic, but the woman was smiling at her softly.

"Uh... it's only temporary... If there's anything you can do..." stammered Kelsey, regretting her initial rudeness.

"Of course, sweetie. I can call the manager over, and have you barred from the premises, or I can call the police and have you arrested for fraudulent trespass. Which would you like me to do first?"

The secretary's smile tightened, her pupils narrowing as the venom crept back into her face. Kelsey leaned back from the desk. Glaring at the woman, she backed away with her hands raised.

Turning performatively, she waltzed to the exit, taking care to "trip" into a fragile vase of daffodils on her way out.

Ignoring the receptionist's fading consternation, Kelsey marched around the side of the complex, livid. The gall of that woman! Speaking to her like that. Outrageous.

As she trudged, she cursed her sleep-deprived mind for making such rookie errors. She'd broken rule number one of bluffing entry to anywhere: project confidence at all times, and never show weakness.

The nursing home was a grand complex, like a stately home on steroids. The red-bricked mansion was situated in a sweeping woodland estate, overlooking luscious trees, a duck pond large enough to be a lake, and an array of ornate water features.

Kelsey skirted the building, searching for the goods entrance. Sure enough, after a few quirky annexes and extensions, she found a metal door propped open, with a pair of kitchen porters leaning against it, smoking.

"Morning, chaps. I'm late, I know, I know, my bad, long story," said Kelsey, ignoring their puzzled looks and brazening her way inside.

Not hesitating for a moment, she marched down the corridor, being sure to continue forwards without so much as flinching in case the pair were watching. The key, she reminded herself, was to always look like you knew where you were going; like you had some place to be.

Unfortunately for Kelsey, keeping up this façade meant continuing straight past the kitchens, where tantalizing scents of lunch wafted into the corridor. She could double-back later, she assured her rumbling stomach. She just had to find a place to lay low first; a store cupboard, or a resident's room, then take it from there.

The corridor ended in a T-junction with no signs. Kelsey swept right, sincerely hoping she wasn't making a beeline for the management office.

A pair of voices reverberated from around a corner, headed her way. Kelsey diverted swiftly through the first doorway she found.

As the door clicked shut behind her, she immediately regretted her choice. The sight that greeted her was a far cry from the nursing home pamphlets, and definitely not something the public were ever expected to see.

A warehouse stretched before her, several football pitches deep. Floor to ceiling it was lined with row upon row of bunks, each illuminated by caged overhead lightbulbs.

The bunks were crammed in, with only enough space for a person to squeeze between side-on. Each bunk held an iron lung; a large cylindrical chamber of pressurized air roughly four feet across, and six feet long.

Every machine seemed to breathe in sync, filling the hall with an echoing, mechanical wheeze. Poking out of the ends of each cylinder were pairs of bare feet of all sizes.

The voices from the corridor behind her were getting

closer. With no choice, Kelsey squeezed between the berths and weaved her way further into the strange warehouse.

She didn't have time to marvel at the thousands of sleeping heads poking out of the cylinders all around her. She had to hide before she got busted.

The door to the warehouse swung open and two workers entered, followed by an automaton. The workers wore purple scrubs, and were carrying buckets and rags, each with a towel slung over their shoulder. They squeezed their way past the unconscious, wheezing bodies, stopping a few rows ahead of Kelsey's hiding place.

"This is us today – stack nine, row eleven, berths CC through CX," declared one, checking a roster.

"You heard her," said the other, to the automaton.

The machine clicked its head from one worker to the other, then glided to a nearby control panel. Kelsey cowered lower as it approached, cursing herself for not spotting the interface when she'd picked her space to hide.

There was something unusual about the automaton's appearance; whereas Ministry machines were usually near-spotless, this one had a blemish in its bodywork. A blue stain dappled half of its brass forehead, stretching down its cheek to taint patches of the enamel discs on its jaw and neck. It looked like a chemical spill, or a birthmark, incongruous on the otherwise immaculate machine. From the scratch marks around its face, it looked like there had been numerous attempts to erase the stain.

The tainted automaton punched in a series of commands, then tilted its head upward. Kelsey followed its gaze. Her mouth dropped as the entire stack of berths in front of her rotated from ceiling to floor, like the shelves in a supermarket reordering themselves.

The berths clicked into their new positions, and the workers sidled up to the nearest pair.

"Time to hold your breath," chuckled the first.

The metal cylinders clicked open like steel coffins, revealing skeletal-thin bodies inside each. The workers placed oxygen masks over their wards, then set about sponging the exposed bodies clean.

"How old do you reckon this one is?"

"Dunno. Hundred, maybe?"

"Nah, it's gotta be more – look at the toenails!"

"Ew. I hope you're planning on trimming those."

"Not my job, amigo. I sponge. It's someone else's job to trim."

"Ooh, my one's got a tattoo."

"No way, your person's a transfer!"

"A what?"

"They're from the old facility. It's where this crusty lot were kept before this place was built."

"But this place is, like, super old."

"Right?"

"Dayyuummm," whistled the worker. "So this brother's gotta be a solid two?"

"At least."

"There's nothing to him. Dude's just skin and bone."

"Stick around as long as this fella and let's see how you look," chuckled the other, returning to their patient.

Kelsey peered out from her berth, determined to glimpse the ancient human inside it. The man was naked, and of tiny, child-like stature, save for the copious amount of wiry pubic hair and wrinkles. His skin had turned pale gray in the chamber, and was so loose he resembled a lump of elephant hide more than a human.

Kelsey's eyes tracked to the tubes affixed to the man's

stomach. One in, one out. Each led to a chemical tank on either side of the man's berth.

As her stomach rumbled, she turned to the berth immediately beside her. The tubes passed out through small perforations in the hull, connecting the person inside to the tanks on the outside. The external chemical tanks were themselves plumbed into a broader network of pipes spanning the entire warehouse.

Kelsey traced the two fluid tubes. One was clear, presumably the feeder tube; while the other was murky brown, presumably the soil pipe. Placing a hand against the feeder, she twisted the tube away from its tank.

Clear liquid trickled onto the floor below. The pitter-patter was masked by the mechanical wheezing of the hall, and the workers' own sloshing in the rows ahead. Placing her tongue against the tank, Kelsey gulped in the nutrient-rich fluid.

"Eugh!" she cried, spluttering and retching across the floor. The liquid was utterly rancid.

"What was that?" said a worker, sharply.

"I think someone's in here!" replied the other.

A set of purple scrubs weaved swiftly towards her.

"Hey, you there! What are you doing in here?"

Kelsey sprang from her hiding place, launching herself into the row behind. But the automaton was gliding across to intercept her. The pair were closing in like pincers, while the other human covered off her original entry point.

With no other option, Kelsey ducked and weaved further into the giant warehouse.

As she ran, she randomly punched buttons on each control panel she passed, setting off mechanical conveyor belts in all directions. Rows of tubed, sleeping humans descended from the ceiling, while others shifted horizontally like a baggage carousel.

The workers cursed her, demanding she stop running, as they tried to pick their way through the mechanical assault course.

Spotting a doorway up ahead, Kelsey dived through it. Still retching from the fluid, she stumbled forwards, pushing through two more sets of doors until she found herself bursting into the center of a grand atrium.

It was radically different to the warehouse from which she'd just come. This was a beautiful conservatory, with a high glass ceiling, chandeliers, and a regal carpet.

Hundreds of elderly residents filled the splendid parlor, which overlooked the lake. Some snoozed in the luxurious armchairs, while others sat about talking, knitting, or selecting delicacies from the tea trolleys being wheeled by automatons.

Kelsey straightened up, hastily smoothing her appearance. Suppressing the nausea, she pressed on, smiling politely at the elderly onlookers as she raked her sweaty hair into place.

An automaton twitched, as if detecting her incongruously fast movements in the soporific parlor. She slowed to an agonizing shuffle. Her pursuers could burst into the room at any moment, and every instinct was telling her to run. But if she triggered the automatons in here, the game would be up. She had to hold her nerve.

The machine relaxed and continued serving tea to a table of wrinklies, while Kelsey strolled calmly through the chamber, searching for someplace to hide.

If these residents were here, she reasoned, then their bedrooms must be unoccupied right now. It would be a start. From there, she might find one that's totally unoccupied.

The mahogany doors up ahead swept open. Two automatons glided in backwards, wheeling refreshment trolleys with them.

Kelsey pivoted away, knowing she couldn't risk a direct confrontation. As slowly as she dared to move, she altered course, keeping her head held high in an attempt to project entitlement.

A humbler, pine wood door beckoned. She was yards away from it.

"Stop her! Hey!" came a cry from behind.

The worker in purple scrubs had burst into the parlor. All eyes fell on Kelsey, as ripples of unease spread across the residents.

Kelsey darted through the pine doorway and immediately scaled the flight of stairs before her. She bounded upwards, taking them three at a time until she was two storeys up.

She emerged, breathless, into an elegant corridor lined with striped wallpaper and oil paintings. It resembled the accommodation level of a luxury hotel.

There was no time to admire the décor - the worker's shouts echoed from the stairwell, joined by other voices in the mushrooming search party.

Rushing across the corridor, Kelsey tried door after door but they were all locked. She rattled the handles desperately as her pursuers' voices grew louder.

As the stairwell door burst open, so too clicked the door in her hand. Kelsey dived inside, sealing it behind her. She leaned against it, breathless, trying to listen over her thumping heart.

"Which one did she go into?"

"How should I know? I was behind you!"

"God dammit, fetch the master key!"

Kelsey crept back from the door, thinking fast. Going door-to-door, it would only take them a few minutes to find her.

If they chased her again, there was no way she had the energy left to outrun them. She wasn't after an exit strategy; she needed a hiding place. A good one. Somewhere she could bed down and recover.

Kelsey peered at the elderly woman sleeping beside her, who was rigged up to feeding tubes, but not a respirator. Kelsey snatched the footnotes and skimmed them. The woman was comatose, apparently. Was this one of the many Agnuses here? Her chart bore no name. It merely said *Ministry Aware*.

Lying across the woman's bed was a tray on stilts, bearing an untouched bowl of porridge. Still reeling from the rancid warehouse fluid, Kelsey leaned over and took a cautious spoonful. It was cold, but delicious.

She scoffed the lot down in seconds, feeding her ravenous appetite. As her brain danced with endorphins, she briefly forgot all about the workers tracking her down until the door handle dropped down with a click.

Kelsey froze, clutching the empty bowl to her chest. She was ready to throw it, if needed. A brass hand pushed the door open and the automaton glided in. The blue stain across its face was even more prominent in the patient's room.

The machine lingered in the threshold, looking from Kelsey, to the bowl, and back.

"You found anything yet?" came a call.

"Nope – you?" came the reply.

Doors slammed in the corridor as the workers closed in.

The automaton gazed at Kelsey for a moment, then retreated, closing the door. Kelsey listened closely as the workers passed by.

Sighing with relief, and unable to explain what the hell had just happened, Kelsey slumped against the wall and closed her eyes, exhausted. Perhaps she was safe for a few more hours.

———

A tap at the door jolted her awake. Her neck was cramped from sleeping in a squat. The door rattled once again.

Kelsey froze, watching fearfully as the handle clicked down. The tainted automaton glided in with a lunch tray, placing it before her.

Kelsey accepted it, suspiciously.

"Er... thanks?"

The automaton stared blankly at her. The machine was definitely weirding her out, she'd never known one to behave this way before.

But the scent of hot food clawed at her nostrils, swiftly dispelling her misgivings. Kelsey perched at the foot of the woman's bed and shoveled the mashed potato, gravy, and tagine into her mouth.

Food spattered her clothes and the sheets around her, but she was too hungry to care, devouring the lot within seconds.

As Kelsey set the fork down with a satisfied clatter, a portly man appeared in the doorway, flanked by an imperious looking woman.

Kelsey jumped up, startled. The automaton seemed indifferent to the humans' arrival, and stayed gazing at her from the doorway.

The two humans barged past it, cursing the lump of metal.

"Damned machine. Look – it's brought her food!"

"I'm sick of this thing. It's been defective since day one. Send it back to the Ministry, we're well due an exchange," snapped the woman.

She stepped before Kelsey and glared at her, sternly.

"And you are?"

"I'm here to see my-"

"Drop the act, kid, I wasn't born yesterday."

"I'm not a kid," snapped Kelsey.

"Excellent, in which case I'll be calling the police. Bernard, apprehend the intruder."

"Yes, boss," grunted the man.

"Wait!" yelled Kelsey. "I have a proposal..."

CHAPTER SEVEN

As usual, the restaurant was doing a roaring trade. Overpriced, and under decorated, it was the nearest eatery to the Ministry, thriving off of hungry dignitaries and celebrating families.

Michael sat hemmed in between his sister and his grandfather at an embarrassingly large table for his embarrassingly large family. Ninety percent of the noise in the restaurant was coming from his visiting relatives.

The waiter battled his way around the table collecting orders, reaching Michael last. But Michael's appetite had vanished; he was pre-occupied by events at the Ministry. He attempted to wave the man away, but Val was having none of it. She leaned across and loudly ordered a main with two side dishes for the birthday boy. Michael sank lower into his chair.

"I want another drink - give me a hand," said Amal, rising.

"Can't the waiter-" began Michael.

His grandfather gave him a telling smile, then slid out

from the bustling table. With legs like lead, Michael followed him to the bar.

"What's eating you?" said Amal.

Michael swallowed hard, too scared to confess what he did. He couldn't evade his grandfather's gaze forever, though.

"Pops, what was your eighteenth like?"

His grandfather chuckled, then took a sip of his scotch.

"You mean back in the stone age?"

Michael forced a chuckle, but his chest felt hollow.

"From what I'm told, kiddo, the ceremony hasn't changed at all since my day. You go in, pick an envelope, they put it in your vault, you leave. Frankly, I found it anticlimactic. Is it different nowadays?"

"No, that's how it was for me too," blurted Michael.

He snatched his grandfather's scotch and necked it, then spluttered in dismay.

"How can you *drink* that stuff? It tastes like feet!"

Michael pawed at his tongue with a napkin, grimacing. His grandfather chuckled and ordered a replacement.

"It takes many years of practice to pretend you like the taste. Eventually, your brain stops fighting back. That's when you know you're an old man," chuckled Amal. "Hey, you know you can talk to me if something's bothering you?"

Michael nodded while swigging water, spilling it down his chin.

"It's normal to feel weird after your eighteenth, lots of people do. Throw it over your shoulder, you did great. Believe me, if you didn't, we'd know about it. Hey, our entrées are coming. Ooh, nachos!"

Amal patted him on the back and ambled back to the table. Michael's stomach churned. He ran to the restroom, burst into a cubicle and dry heaved over the pan. After a moment, he climbed to his feet, rinsed his mouth out, and made to leave. But as he pulled the door open, his heart skipped a beat. An automaton was standing at the far end of the restaurant, by the main entrance. A waitress was pointing it towards Michael's table.

Michael rushed back to the cubicle, locked the door, and climbed onto the toilet seat. With his knees hunched close to his chest, he listened keenly. A customer came and went. Footsteps. Flush. Wash. Gone. Then another customer. Footsteps. Flush. Gone. Then a pause. This time the lavatory door opened but there were no footsteps. Just the squeaky rumble of rubber wheels on tiles.

The automaton's shadow edged further into the bathroom. Michael held his breath as the first cubicle banged open. Then the second. A startled customer yelled in fright, fleeing as the machine continued. The third cubicle crashed open, then the fourth. Michael's was the only one left. A shadowy arm reached towards his hiding place.

The restroom entrance swung open.

"Do you mind? Customers are complaining," snapped the manager.

The shadowy arm halted its outstretched position before Michael's cubicle.

"And are you gonna fix those doors?" she added.

With a rubber squeak, the machine pivoted and glided out, followed by the manager.

Michael climbed down from his position, crept to the main doorway, and peered out. The automaton was hovering in the middle of the restaurant. Its head rotated three hundred and sixty degrees as it scanned the room. It had a peculiar blue stain across its face and neck, a blemish Michael had never seen before in a Ministry machine.

Hurrying back across the bathroom, he shunted the window open, and leaped out. As he darted across the parking lot, the automaton glided out of the restaurant. Its head twisted, zeroing in on Michael. With eyes locked on its target, the rest of the machine's body rotated into alignment to follow.

The automaton leaned forwards and sped towards him. Michael ran faster, skidding into the side of his car and dropping his keys in his panic. As he fumbled on the ground, the machine closed in. He hauled the car door open and started the engine.

"Michael? Yoo-hoo, Michael!" cried a voice from across the lot.

Two car doors slammed shut in quick succession. His auntie waved at him excitedly, while his uncle followed, looking altogether less keen.

"You're not leaving, are you? We're so sorry we're late, it was the traffic, you know how it is," she crowed.

A bell rang from the university's tower. The automaton stopped in its tracks. Michael paused too; door open, engine running. His auntie followed his gaze.

"Is that thing after you Michael boy? Are you in trouble? Lighten up kid, I'm joking! God, the look on your face."

The automaton cranked its spine back into a bolt upright position and pivoted its body towards the university. Its marble eyes lingered on Michael for several moments, before it turned its head too, and glided away towards the ringing bell tower.

CHAPTER EIGHT

Kelsey loaded the last dish into the industrial washer and slammed the casing down with a sigh. She'd been on her feet since the crack of dawn, and her body ached from the constant movement.

An adjacent machine bleeped, signaling the end of its program. She cracked it open and stepped back from the plume of steam that billowed upwards. There was no time to let the dishes cool, not if she wanted a half decent sleep cycle.

Donning a pair of oven gloves, she stacked the steaming crockery onto trolleys, ready for the breakfast shift.

She glanced at the clock overhead and cursed. It was five to midnight, and she was running behind.

She hurried over to the one dirty dish on the side counter; a pasta bowl containing scraps from the residents' dinners. Snatching a spoon from the cutlery rack, she ate as she walked, hastening through the back corridors of the nursing estate to the laundry rooms.

She only managed half the plate before having to stow

the rest by her bedside and turn her attention to mountains of dirty linen all around.

Kelsey leaned over the rim of a huge drum, balancing precariously across her midriff as she stretched for the chain dangling in the middle.

The laundry machines were like giant mixing bowls. They were designed for automaton operation, and tailored to their size and strength. But, the manager had insisted, the Ministry didn't see the nursing home as a priority, and had allocated several of their laboring automatons elsewhere. Thus, it had fallen to Kelsey to load and unload the huge swirling buckets.

On the first night, she'd worried she wouldn't be able to sleep with the sound of the clattering launderettes all around her. But she'd been so exhausted, she was out like a switch being flicked.

Instead, just three nights in, she'd grown to welcome the humming tanks and rattling tumble dryers. The only time she heard them was when it was bed time; the most precious part of her interminably long days.

Exhausted, she polished off the rest of her dinner scraps, then lay her head down on the mattress, letting sleep wash over her.

Exactly two and a half hours later, the *beep beep beep* of a completed machine woke her again. Bleary eyed, Kelsey dragged herself over to the machine, hauling on the chains and dragging the damp, spun-dry load out of the washer, along a pulley, and into the neighboring dryer. Several more machines beeped in succession, and Kelsey did the rounds. Thirty minutes later, every machine was churning a fresh load, and Kelsey was once more horizontal.

This all happened again at 5 a.m, after which she would

get only a further thirty minutes' sleep before it was time to assist in the kitchens.

By 10 a.m., the breakfast rush was over, she'd devoured a fresh batch of scraps, and had several liters of black coffee flowing through her system.

Kelsey checked her schedule and hurried upstairs to the residential quarters – it was time to change the guests' bedding.

She was warm, fed, and safe. Sleep deprived, sure, but you can't have it all. This wasn't exactly her dream scenario, but it was only temporary, and it beat being on the streets, too scared to sleep. Besides, it was no worse than the foster homes she'd endured growing up. Plus, if she got more efficient at the routine, she reckoned she could probably get up to six and a half hours' sleep each night.

Kelsey stripped a set of damp bedsheets from a mattress so stained it looked like marble. As she prepared to lay the fresh sheets on, a cry sounded from the corridor.

"Please, Mom, I'm begging you!"

Kelsey approached the hallway. The voice was coming from the room opposite. Two voices, in fact. The first woman, who was becoming increasingly desperate, and an older voice, which moaned incoherently. Both were growing louder and more agitated.

"It's me, Mom, *me*, why can't you-"

The woman broke down. Her guttural sobs formed a haunting duet with the older woman's wailing.

As the door swung open, Kelsey locked eyes with the emerging woman. She was dressed for an office job, presumably heading to work. Her eyes were red from crying, her face soaked with tears.

"Four years, *four years* since she used my name, or even recognized me at all!" cried the woman.

Kelsey didn't know what to say, but soon found the woman's face buried in her shoulder, heaving with tears.

"I'm sorry, it's not fair to... None of this is fair," sniffed the woman, breaking off abruptly.

Stifling her sobs, she disappeared into the stairwell, leaving Kelsey alone in the hallway. The elderly woman's moans rang out into the corridor, laced with confusion and fear. Through the doorway, Kelsey could only see the outline of the woman's feet beneath the bedsheets, but the anguish in her voice told of the human inside.

Kelsey was about to approach, to try and offer some comfort, when a metallic clicking startled her from the side.

The blue-stained automaton glided towards her. It stopped in front of the door and locked eyes with Kelsey. Its body rotated to face the distressed woman's room, and without breaking its stare, drifted backwards into the room.

The door closed quietly, muffling the woman's voice. Her moaning settled down in waves, like a puppy being soothed back to sleep.

Kelsey returned to her work, fitting fresh linen, aware that she had to get through three corridors before the morning was up.

As she finished the pillow cases, an alarm rang out. Kelsey clapped her hands over her ears, trying to mute the piercing sound. It was as loud as a fire alarm, but the pulsations were different. She peered into the corridor; a red bulb was glowing above the sealed door opposite.

The manager burst out of the stairwell and rushed into the old woman's room, with two workers in tow.

"Call a code! Get the crash cart in here right away! Oh god, not today, not today, please god," the manager begged.

The workers sped about frantically, one calling for an ambulance, while the other smashed open a wall cubby and grabbed the crash kit.

"She doesn't have a letter. Somebody tell me how the hell this is happening when she doesn't have a letter!" screamed the manager.

"I don't know, boss, I don't-"

"Clear!" cried another. "Again!"

Electrical shocks rang out from the room and the old lady's feet twitched beneath the sheets.

"Again!" yelled the manager.

"Clear!" cried the orderly.

"Again!"

As the team tried in vain to resuscitate the woman, the manager hurried to the door. Locking eyes with Kelsey, she slammed it shut.

———

Fourteen hours later, Kelsey dragged herself out of the kitchen, chowing down a half-eaten bowl of scraps, and heading towards her nightly laundry duties.

As she wended her way through the corridors, something peculiar caught her eye. The light in the manager's office was on. She'd been trying to corner the woman all day to discuss her remuneration, but hadn't seen her since the incident.

As she reached for the door, it swung open.

"Steady," said a woman, several years her senior.

The stranger wore a dark blue trench coat, and sported a tightly-bound red ponytail. Whereas Kelsey looked utterly haggard from a long day of toiling, this woman looked positively spritely for midnight.

The woman glanced at Kelsey's dinner medley and raised an eyebrow.

"Looks tasty," she quipped, before disappearing down the hall.

Knocking, Kelsey entered her boss's office. For the first time, the manager looked as tired as she did.

"Bailey. What is it?"

"Uh, hey boss, I was thinking maybe we could discuss my pay? I could use an advance so I can put a deposit down. You know, rent a place, stop living in the laundry room, that sort of thing."

The manager's head snapped up and she glared at Kelsey.

"Do you seriously think you're in any position to be making demands?"

"No, not at all, I was just-"

"One snap of my fingers, girl, and you're out on the streets again, so how about some gratitude?"

Kelsey bit her lip.

"Sorry boss. Tough day, huh?"

"What's that supposed to mean?"

"I mean with that old lady dying upstairs..."

"I don't know what you're talking about."

"What? The woman from this morning – she had a heart attack or something, you were trying to revive her? I'm guessing it didn't work because when I went back in later, her bed was empty. That sucks, I'm sorry for your-"

"Once again, Bailey, I have no idea to what you are referring. Whatever you *think* you saw, you must have been mistaken. Am I clear?"

"I... Yes, boss."

"Good. Take a seat."

Kelsey sat, awkwardly, with the bowl of scraps balanced across her green scrubs. The manager swiveled round and retrieved something from the shelf behind, returning moments later with a decanter and two glasses.

"You drink?"

"It's not really my-"

"Nonsense, Bailey, everyone drinks. Here," insisted the manager, pouring two generous measures. "Welcome to the mad house."

She chuckled and downed the drink, slamming the glass on the desk with a "woooeee".

Reclining in her chair with a sigh, she immediately poured herself a second glass, while topping up Kelsey's untouched portion.

"You wanted to discuss pay, Bailey. Let's discuss. You work what, fourteen hours a day?"

"It's more like seventeen at the mome-"

The manager cut her off short, leaning forwards and punching numbers into a calculator.

"So, at standard basic rate that's... Then multiplied by three days gives us... OK.... minus the expenses for uniform, of course... Not to mention the vase you broke in the lobby... Oh, and the wasted fluid in the warehouse... Then there's room and board to deduct... Which leaves us with..."

As the manager finished tapping, her face fell with exaggerated disappointment. She slid the device around to show Kelsey the outcome.

"But... that's a negative number?" gasped Kelsey.

"I'm afraid so. Believe me, I'd love to give you an advance," said the manager, necking more of the liquor, "but you need a positive balance first, and by my calculations you're several weeks away from that."

"But I'm working every hour of the day!" protested Kelsey. "There's no way I can physically-"

"Hush, hush now. I'm sure we can come to some sort of arrangement, pretty thing like you. You got all kinds of... options."

As the woman ran her finger around the rim of her glass, Kelsey's stomach churned.

"You're not seriously suggesting what I think you're suggesting..."

"That depends on how badly you want to get off the streets, and into a lovely new apartment," shrugged the manager. "I can make it happen for you. Think of it as a win-win."

Kelsey's face dropped.

"I'm not... That's not what I-"

"Oh come on, don't be such a prude. Are you seriously telling me it's not something you've done before? Girl like you?"

"What the hell is that supposed to mean?"

"Many people would take that as a compliment, you know? Look, it doesn't have to be all at once. I'm a patient soul. We can go steady, bit by bit. Make a game of it, even."

The woman stood up and slunk around the desk, approaching Kelsey's seat. She placed her hands on Kelsey's shoulders, and dug her thumbs in, massaging her tender back.

"I give as much as I take, Bailey, that's what you've got to understand about me. It's not in my nature to be selfish."

The woman's thumbs pressed tenderly and rhythmically into Kelsey's shoulders. Her lips were close to Kelsey's ear, her voice soft and breathy, making the hairs on Kelsey's neck bristle.

"Our little arrangement could be something really quite special," she whispered.

The woman's hands slipped over Kelsey's shoulders and down towards her breasts. At the same time, she leaned in, kissing Kelsey's neck.

With a scream, Kelsey leaped from the seat, shoving the manager backwards, and fleeing the office. She ignored the woman's calls for her to come back and to talk things through.

The manager's pleas quickly turned to curses and threats. Kelsey raced from the building, away from the grand red bricks, and vanished into the chilly night.

She traipsed the streets of the city center, constantly moving to keep herself warm and out of harm's way. Dawn was only two hours off; if she hung in there a little longer, she could find a bench to sleep on under the protection of daylight.

She shivered, drawing her arms in closer. Could she really survive like this? Constantly walking to stay warm, trying to avoid trouble from the police, or from other street-dwellers?

Being broke and homeless went hand-in-hand, and Kelsey knew that if she didn't find a way of getting money soon, the situation could become permanent. Growing up, she'd seen it happen multiple times. Of course, getting money meant finding a new job come first light.

But the last manager's advances had left Kelsey shaken. The woman's vengeance would surely follow her to any interview in the city. People like that woman were always interconnected, after all; forming an impenetrable ring of managerial nepotism, wrapped around the city's neck like a choker, keeping a tight leash on the workers below.

Kelsey's childhood had hardened her, given her a certain resilience to situations like this, but what always gotten her through was the firm belief that as an adult, she would do better. She would fix her life. And yet here she was; alone, and more afraid than ever.

She needed a way out; an exit strategy from the indelible stain of chaos on her reputation. She didn't care what the work was - *anything* was better than living like this.

As she passed an electrical store, a flickering light caught her eye through the security shutters. On the sepia display screens, the weather forecaster was issuing a dust warning and demonstrating how to wear a face mask correctly.

The feed cut to a reporter at the quarry. Beside her was a site supervisor, clad in a hard hat and a dust mask. Behind them were rows of mining machines, carving ever deeper rings into the earth's crust. Nearby were the workers' quarters; dozens of temporary cabins stacked high.

Kelsey peeled her eyes away from the screen and looked to the hills beyond the city. Faint wisps of dust blew off the ridges of the quarry, rising like ice vapor in the cold moonlight. In her pocket, her thumb ran over the single coin she'd found on her night walk. It was just enough money for a one-way ride. Clutching the coin firmly, she set off for the bus station.

CHAPTER NINE

Michael's alarm blared out. It was 6 a.m. and he'd been asleep for all of ninety minutes. The continuity screen flickered across the TV as he jerked out of bed. Rushing downstairs, he pulled open the front door. It was lashing down with rain and utterly frigid. Were mornings always this cold?

Snatching the key off the rack, he darted to the end of the lawn, not bothering with a rain jacket. His hands trembled as he fumbled with the latch. "Come on, come *on…*" he muttered, forcing the key in. He wrenched the flap open, revealing an empty cavern.

Sighing with relief, he slumped against the mailbox. His eyes followed the pipe into the ground, where it disappeared beneath the grass and roads, and joined an invisible network leading back to the Ministry.

A clicking noise pricked his ears. Across the road, a neighbor was locking her box back up. Unlike Michael, she looked bitterly disappointed. He caught her eye but she turned away, bowing her head in shame until she'd disappeared inside the house. He remembered when that couple had moved in as newlyweds ten years ago. They used to be so lively, so sociable, yet this was the first time he'd seen her in months.

Michael traipsed back inside, squelched upstairs, and put on dry pajamas. As he slumped into bed, relief washed over him, and with it, precious sleep.

He awoke some hours later, cursing. Now he was running late - even later than normal. He threw on clean clothes, an intoxicating amount of deodorant, and hurried out of the house. Miraculously, the school bus was still on his street; he could make it if he ran.

But he didn't want to make it; the bus would be stopping by the Ministry. His grandfather's words rang in his ears. *If you did your letter wrong, we'd know about it.*

His family didn't know yet, but the Ministry did. An automaton had already traced him to the restaurant, and it was only a matter of time before they tried again. Michael had to keep a low profile until he could figure out how to undo the damage.

Setting off at a brisk march, Michael tucked into a side street and began the long, arduous detour around the Ministry building.

It took him two hours to reach school, through a mixture of jogging and marching. By the time he arrived he was drenched in sweat, and his stomach was rumbling. Signing himself in, he waved away the secretary's words about consequences for punctuality, and slid into his history lesson.

"Mr. Hadley, you're late, and, dare I say it, wet. For a man due to graduate in a matter of months, this bodes ill for your career prospects. We are unburdened?"

"Yes, Ma'am. Uh, I mean, *may we use it well*," mumbled Michael, bowing as custom dictated.

"Indeed," continued the teacher, with a raised brow. "Did we forget something else today, Mr. Hadley?"

Michael looked around the room in dismay, surveying the rows of pupils in black funeral attire. His peers were snickering at him, pointing at his regular clothes with mirth.

"It's Tribute day," sighed Michael.

"I would call this a poor tribute, Mr. Hadley. What would your ancestors say, if this was your way of paying respects for their sacrifice? Your classmates know the important of their heritage, yet you see fit to beat your own path, it would seem? That must require a special kind of arrogance."

"It's not like that, Ma'am, I just... forgot. Obviously I know it's a big day."

"'Big'? *Big?* It's Tribute day, you ungrateful wretch! We're commemorating the darkest day in our city's history."

"I know, I know. A small group of mentally unwell individuals challenged the benevolence of our Ministry. They marched on Ministry Square with burning torches and burned the vellum creed."

The teacher considered this nugget of information, sliding her round glasses higher up her piggish nose.

"I'm glad to see you at least did your preparatory reading," she mused. "And do you know what happened then?"

"The fire... spread?" asked Michael.

He hadn't exactly *finished* the reading...

"It engulfed the entire Ministry, the very heart of our people!" exclaimed the teacher. "But that small band of renegades, while they succeeded in destroying the fabric of the building, they could not destroy the spirit of its people. As the cowards fled, believing their work to be complete, our ancestors formed dozens of human chains, ferrying water to douse the flames. It was a truly historic act of societal union."

The teacher took a beat to regain her composure, having become somewhat animated in her recitation.

"Ahem. Can anyone tell Mr. Hadley what happened next?"

"Thanks to the people's unity, the building was saved," said a girl in the front.

"It wasn't saved dummy, it burned to the ground. They *rebuilt* it. Using stone," chimed her neighbor.

"Indeed they did," said the teacher. "But what of the vellum creed? Mr. Hadley, when you went to the Ministry for your recent ceremony, did you see such a document?"

"No, Ma'am. Just a marble font."

"And could you read the inscribed creed?"

"Uh, sort of? I think it's mostly been rubbed away over the years though."

"Can anyone correct poor Mr. Hadley? It would appear that history, like punctuality, is not his forte."

A boy from the middle chimed up. "The ancestors didn't write it down. Not like the old one, at least. They decided the safest place for the creed was in the hearts and minds of every citizen in the city. Our people committed it to memory, so that it can never be lost or destroyed again. The stone font is a symbol to remind us of our ancestors' fortitude."

The teacher smiled like a smug cat.

"It's amazing what can be learned by those who turn up on time and do their full homework, wouldn't you agree, Mr. Hadley? Take your seat. Now, can anyone tell me why our school celebrates tribute day a week before all the others? And for a bonus point, what year that tradition began?"

Keeping his head down, Michael hurried to his seat. The teacher continued a Q&A with the class's keenest, while chalking up that week's homework on the board.

"Don't worry pal, I hear it's all bollocks anyway," muttered Hamish, Michael's go-to partner in crime for talking in class and failing assignments.

"You mean Tribute day?" whispered Michael.

"My brother told me it's a lie. He said there was no wooden Ministry building, no vellum creed. Even the fire bit's made up."

"But the uprising?"

"That bit's true. But he says it was suppressed by the automatons, with people fighting alongside them. Apparently, the only thing that burned was the bodies of the dead revolutionaries piled up in the Ministry Square."

"But what happened to their-"

A cane cracked down on Hamish's desk.

"Principal's office. Now," snapped the teacher.

Michael and Hamish jumped, neither having seen nor heard the hawkish woman approaching. She loomed over Hamish with an eviscerating glare.

"I didn't mean to cause trouble, Ma'am, I was just goofing around," said Hamish.

"Not. Another. Word."

The teacher's voice was low, and quivering with such rage as if she might strike him at any moment. Hamish glanced at Michael nervously then packed his bag and left the room.

Michael watched his confidante leave. This was devastating. He hadn't even had a chance to tell Hamish about what really went down during his Ministry visit. It would have to wait.

The teacher's voice fizzled into nothingness as the class resumed. Michael's mind immediately drifted back to the Ministry's mail room, reliving the moment he challenged the automaton. Was it dead? Could those things even die? He couldn't ask without arousing suspicion. Those things were basically sacred. If you broke the mutuality pact, there were consequences. He couldn't so much as breathe a word to another living soul without invoking the wrath of the entire city, human and metal alike.

Lunch was over in a flash. He devoured a mini mountain, then napped against the table until the bell rang. As he and thousands of other pupils headed back to class, there was an excited buzz ahead. A teacher was calling for students to make way.

Michael's heart skipped a beat. Gliding through the sea of students was an automaton. The same one from the restaurant. Its tainted face bore the same rigid smile as it rolled through the crowd.

Michael thumped his friend's chest. "Cover for me, Doug!"

With that, he turned and threw himself against the tide of people.

"Dude, where are you going?"

Michael ignored his friend and pushed harder, fighting his way back towards the canteen.

"Hey, watch it!" complained a girl, as he barged through her group.

"Michael?" said his sister, baffled.

"Sophia, your brother's a weirdo," said one of them.

"Oh my god, don't *even*," she said, rolling her eyes.

As Michael reached the canteen doorway, he cast his head back. The machine had spotted him. Sprinting across the food hall, he kicked open the emergency exit.

Michael raced across the sports field towards the woods. To his horror, the machine was sprinting across the turf after him.

Whimpering, Michael tore through the trees, tripping over gnarled roots, and covering himself in mud as he tumbled down an earthy embankment. Scrambling back to his feet, he ran with all his might. The machine was falling behind - moving more cautiously over the uneven terrain. Michael pressed his advantage and staggered onto the road beyond.

Without a moment's hesitation, he ran out in front of an oncoming pickup truck. The driver blared his horn and screeched to a halt.

"Are you insane?" cried the contractor.

"I'm sorry, it's an emergency," said Michael.

He pulled open the passenger door and jumped in before the man could object.

"What kind of emergency?" said the contractor, sternly.

"I'm being bullied. Please. I just need to get away, they already beat me up once," said Michael, checking the rear view mirror.

"Want me to deal with them?" said the contractor.

"No! I mean, no thank you. I just need to get to town. I'll figure it out from there."

The contractor grunted and they set off. Michael pretended to listen to the man's lecture about standing up to bullies as they entered the business district, where a lengthy traffic jam brought them to a halt.

Michael's eyes fell on the wing mirror and his heart froze. The automaton had caught up and was weaving through the tailback. Michael fled the truck, running away from the traffic jam and making a beeline for the metro station.

Leaping the turnstile, he descended the escalator two steps at a time. The platform was all but deserted as he skidded out and sped to the far end.

Metal footsteps rang out from the escalator. Michael ducked behind a pillar and waited, praying the machine would pass him by, as his heart pounded in his ears.

The automaton's steps halted as it reached the platform, giving way to the squeaking of its wheels. The machine paused sporadically, each time letting its head click in rotation.

Michael's pulse quickened as it wheeled closer. It was just yards away now. Michael's muscles quivered with adrenaline.

The automaton discovered Michael's pillar and locked eyes with him. With a cry, Michael surged forwards, pushing it as hard as he could.

The machine toppled over the platform edge, landing on the tracks with a clang. The machine was splayed on its back, its fingers twitching. It tried to rotate its head to look at Michael, but its neck was broken.

A rumbling noise echoed from the dark metro tunnel. Michael was about to flee when something caught his eye. Clasped in the automaton's hand was a glass rectangle. Bursts of color shimmered through the glass, revealing symbols as Michael moved. They looked hauntingly familiar.

Michael leaped onto the tracks. Someone entering the platform saw him and screamed. The sound of running footsteps and cries for help filled the air.

The approaching train's headlights bounced off the tracks. Michael prized the glass token from the machine's hand, then hauled himself onto the platform.

"It fell! I tried to help it, but it's too heavy," cried Michael, dragging himself up.

Michael raced past the alarmed onlookers and up the escalator. Screeching brakes and crunching metal drowned out the sound of his footsteps.

Emerging onto street level, he staggered into a side alley to catch his breath and examine the stolen object. It was the size of a matchbox. Something was suspended in the glass itself; a vitrified wafer, less than a millimeter thick. The symbols glimmered as he tilted it in his hands. What did it mean?

He peered back at the metro. To his relief, the machine was absent, as were the platform people. His gaze drifted to the curved pyramid on the horizon; its golden bricks rising above nearby office blocks. Michael slipped the glass into his pocket and set off at once. They might have the answers he needed.

He approached the university warily, sticking to back streets. The pyramid was opposite the Ministry building, connected by the great square. He was loath to get so close, but he needed answers fast. He hastened towards the imposing gold entrance and pushed through the rotating door. Golden light bathed the interior, filtering through the translucent bricks.

A stern receptionist peered up from behind her spectacles.

"Yes?"

Michael pulled a stray leaf from his hair and hastily wiped his muddy hands against his even muddier jeans.

"Uh, I'd like to speak to someone about an artifact," he said.

Was that the right word? He had no idea.

"Are you trying to sell something illegally? We're not interested in that sort of business."

"Nothing like that, I'm doing some research – a, uh, personal project."

"Carolina Mesorsky is professor of historical artifacts. You'll have to make an appointment, she's extremely busy. It may be weeks before she can see you, though. Months, even."

Michael took a prospectus from the front desk and said he'd mull it over. Leaving the dazzling gold atrium, he crossed the street. Hidden from the Ministry, and obscured behind some parked cars, he set up camp on a bench overlooking the university entrance.

It was a long wait, but as 5 p.m. came, so too did Professor Mesorsky; a spitting image of her own starchy prospectus portrait.

Michael set off after her. To his horror, she was heading for the great square. He had to intercept her before they got near the Ministry.

"Uh, Professor? Professor Mesorsky, excuse me!" he called, jogging over.

She looked at him warily.

"Forgive my appearance, it's been a rough day. I need to ask you a question," panted Michael.

"Make an appointment with my secretary, I'm rather busy at pres-"

"I think I've found an artifact. It's a piece of glass; only small though, it would fit in your hand. It's got symbols embossed on the side, and they glimmer in different colors when you tilt it in the sun."

The professor's face fell.

"Is this a trick? I don't know how you learned of such things, but I am not prepared to discuss this further until I do."

"No trick, I swear. Please, I just need an opinion."

"I can't advise on something I've never seen." she snapped.

With that, she turned on her heel.

"Wait!" called Michael.

He shuffled closer and drew the glass block from his pocket. The professor gasped and took it in her hands, marveling at it.

"It's still intact," she said, in awe. "Where did you get it?"

"Found it," said Michael.

"You're lying, but perhaps it's better I don't know the full picture. These glass slices aren't artifacts, they're called 'sequelae'. Consequences, in other words. They're linked to an individual's being. Their health, their life, and so forth. So much of what we are is stored in these forbidden capsules. Our lives are constantly changing, and so too are the capsules we are made of. Something must have changed upstream in this person's life, causing their sequela to be released."

"I don't understand," said Michael.

"It means the person's in danger."

"The person?"

"These blocks are unique. The symbols relate to an individual citizen. And the citizen on this block is in trouble, that's for sure," she said.

As the professor crossed into the grand square, Michael snatched the glass from her hand.

"Careful with that! You shouldn't even have it. Wait, where are you going?"

"I can't let them get me, I can't!" cried Michael.

"What's your name?" she cried.

With the glass clutched in his palm, he vanished into the rush hour traffic.

CHAPTER TEN

With a jolt, the cable lowered them down the shaft. Sodium bulbs glowed at ten-meter intervals. Kelsey fidgeted nervously with her protective overalls. The darkness rang with activity; hundreds of hammers striking rock. After several minutes of descent, the cart shuddered to a halt.

"This is us," said her supervisor.

They stepped out onto a short, rocky platform, which gave way to a dark tunnel carved into the stone. Caged lamps hung overhead, connected by a long, orange cable that sagged periodically, dusting the hard hats of workers passing by. Smaller corridors branched off from the main tunnel in diagonal strips, like the branches of a pine tree.

Workers ferried rocks from the side passages to the main tunnel, where a central conveyor belt took them to the central shaft. A pulley system covered in hooks busily exchanged full buckets for empty ones, whisking rubble away to the surface, while keeping the workers busy below.

"It grows in layers. This seam's pretty good, you can start down here."

Kelsey's supervisor indicated for her to grab an empty bucket and follow him into one of the branch tunnels. None of the other miners paid her any attention. Their backs were turned, driving hammers into the rock.

As they walked, Kelsey tweaked the fabric mask on her face, trying to keep the dust out. The air was so hot and thick that sweat trickled over her lips. Mist formed in the corners of her goggles with each breath she took, compounding her mounting claustrophobia.

They reached an unused cubby; out of sight from the main passage.

"This is you."

Kelsey stepped inside. The cubby was just deep enough to fit her body in, if she stooped. The rock was pockmarked and uneven, blighted by chisel marks.

"Make it three times deeper this week," said the man, straining over the clatter. "Work until you hear the bell. Then come to the surface and eat until you fall asleep on your plate."

He gave her a thumping pat on the back, then disappeared into the gloomy corridor, shouting instructions to the other workers.

Kelsey looked at the dark, solid rock face before her. Taking the hammer and chisel from her belt, she set to work.

Hammers clattered in the darkness. Kelsey wiped a sleeve across her sweaty, dust-covered brow. Her hands ached from chiseling, but that was a constant; there was no sense of time in the mine. For all she knew, there could be hours left to go.

The miners' dorms were at the edge of the quarry. Each of the past six days had finished with a perfunctory, high-calorie hot dinner, followed immediately by sleep. But it felt like no sooner would she lay her head on the pillow than the whistle would sound, calling them back to work.

The miners' sole luxury came every two days, when they were permitted twenty minutes of UV treatment. They would sit on wooden benches in the tank room, wearing only black-tinted goggles and underwear. The ultraviolet light stimulated vitamin D production, allegedly. Kelsey didn't know if that was true, but she relished the break from monotony, even if it was just an opportunity to sleep in a different position.

"Yo, thirty-two, keep it moving," called the supervisor.

Kelsey shook herself out of the UV daydream and hacked away at the rock. Chunks of grey and orange rubble fell to the ground, bouncing off her steel-capped boots. As she gathered them into her bucket, one piece caught her eye. It had a crooked, shiny seam, like a glassy vein. The sliver featured a sunburst pattern, with golden flecks.

"Finally! I was thinking this cubby might be a dud. Keep it up, thirty-two, we all get a bonus if you hit the quota," cheered the supervisor.

Kelsey tossed the chunk into her brimming bucket and crawled out of her cramped, squatting position. She heaved the load onto her shoulder and stood up, wincing as her aching muscles straightened out.

Staggering along the branch tunnel, she entered the main corridor, taking care to avoid swinging hammers and laden buckets. With a grunt, she dropped her load onto the conveyor belt and watched it disappear with the others, hoisted up by the pulley.

She caught her breath for a few precious seconds, then

grabbed an empty bucket and shuffled back to her cubby. Being at the furthest end of her tunnel, it was barely illuminated by the single lamp serving their branch.

When she returned, her supervisor was still there, studying her cubby with a hand-held lantern.

"This is even more promising than I thought. When I come back, I need to be standing here, not squatting. Pick up the pace, thirty-two, this could be the richest seam on this level. I'll see you get a bonus. Fail me and I'll put someone in here who *wants* the rewards, while I drop your ass to the lower levels. Got it?"

Kelsey nodded, fearfully. From what the other workers had told her, the lower levels were a fate worth avoiding. The air was so thick with dust they could barely breathe down there, even with the masks. They needed lanterns on their helmets just to see the tools in their hands. It was not a place she wanted to be. Taking her tools into her blistered palms, she set to work with zeal.

When the lunch whistle sounded for her level, she kept working - asking a colleague to bring her a sandwich on her way back. It wasn't technically allowed, but her colleague was willing to bend the rules in exchange for a cut of the food. Kelsey knew she risked inhaling a lot of dust, eating down there. But she figured that was better than inhaling ten times more if she got demoted to the lower shafts.

As she hammered away, a huge chunk of rock fell from the wall. She leaped back as it landed where her feet had been. Lining the freshly exposed rock behind was a huge strip of the glowing sunburst mineral. Cerebrium. The most valuable commodity in the nation.

Kelsey glanced around. There was no one else about, just distant hammering from lower-level miners, whose lunch was later.

She could pocket it if she wanted. Even a small amount of the ultra-rare mineral would be enough to set her up for years. She could escape that dreadful place.

Her heart sank as the fantasy ebbed away. Yes, it was the most valuable commodity in the city, but there was only one buyer: the Ministry. Even if she smuggled some out, no one would dare buy it from her for fear of being thrown in an infinity chamber.

Shouting echoed from the levels above. The hammering had stopped and the voices sounded urgent. Kelsey climbed out of her cubby into the branch tunnel to listen. Were people running?

An alarm sounded and the ground shook. Buckets tumbled off the distant conveyor belt. As Kelsey raced for the exit, rocks crashed through the end of the corridor. The tunnel was caving in.

Shock waves ripped through the mine. Kelsey dived into her cubby and curled into a ball as rocks rained down from the ceiling.

When the tremors finally subsided, Kelsey tried edging backward out of her cubby, but boulders had piled up behind her. She called out into the darkness, but her voice was smothered by the rocky swaddling.

As dust swirled around her tiny space, all she could hear was the muffled siren, hundreds of meters above ground, echoing down to her ears through an impossible labyrinth of debris. With her nose up against the rock face, she was trapped. And she was fast running out of air.

Kelsey tried to regulate her breathing as panic rose through her. She was churning out carbon dioxide in a space no bigger than a coffin.

Placing her palms against the rock face, she pushed away. The unyielding rubble behind her bit sharply into her back. Panting, she probed the area by her feet, kicking her heels back until they found a weakness. As the rocks fell away, others tumbled down to take their place, cutting her ankles as she recoiled just in time.

Kelsey quivered, contemplating her choices. Stay put and suffocate, or keep kicking and risk getting her leg crushed by fresh rock fall, then suffocating in agony.

She chose the latter, kicking hard and fast until she'd punched a permanent gap in the rock behind her heel. Widening it, with difficulty, she forced her other leg through.

This freed up just enough space in her pitch-black cubby for her to twist her torso onto the opposite shoulder. As her skin scraped against the jagged rock, she saw a glimmer of light. Some of the primary tunnel must have survived!

Wriggling her way out backwards through the clearing she'd made, Kelsey focused desperately on not dislodging the rocks above her.

The coarse ground scratched her stomach to shreds as she shunted her body backwards, finally emerging into a clearing several meters wide. The tunnel ceiling was intact in this section. Clambering to her feet, she gulped in some of her new oxygen allowance.

Light glimmered through cracks in the wall of rubble before her. This time there was no way to burrow under it; she would have to find space on top.

She placed a tentative foot against the lowest boulder,

wobbling as she transferred her full weight onto it, and climbed inch by inch until her helmet struck the ceiling.

Suspended above the ground, and crouched in a climbing-squat, she extended a hand towards the top layer of rocks, pulling them away like Jenga pieces. She cleared a space just big enough for her torso, but it left her legs dangling on the outside, scrambling for purchase.

Lying across her bleeding stomach, she heaved at the boulder ahead, trying to clear space to crawl forwards.

Without warning, it broke free. The force of the release flung Kelsey backwards. Rocks cascaded down, sealing the gap she'd created, and halving her precious glimmers of light.

Kelsey dragged herself against the side of the tunnel and hugged her knees, gasping in pain. Her arms and hands were covered in cuts from the fall. She called again for help, but there was no reply.

Her mouth was parched, and her body exhausted. A fog was descending on her mind. As the last of her strength faded, she stared at the slits of amber light spilling through the rock wall, before she fell limp against the stone.

A warm breeze struck her cheek and Kelsey came to. She had a splitting headache. Her heart sank as she remembered where she was.

Walls of rock and rubble extended around her in all directions. Yet there was a new current of air.

Groaning, she climbed to her feet. She had no idea how long she'd been out. Pressing her hands to the rock wall, she felt for the breeze. She pulled down her mask and feasted on the fresher air.

Liquid trickled down the wall beside her. Kelsey sniffed, then tested it, discovering to her joy that it was water.

Pressing her tongue against the rock, she let the water drip into her mouth. The amount was meager, and the flavor faintly metallic, but the relief was immense.

As she drank, the floor trembled. Kelsey cowered flush against the wall as aftershocks sent rubble tumbling from the mounds beside her.

When the shaking finally settled, a gap had opened up. The mound ahead was sloped now - tapering away at the top just wide enough for her to try squeezing through.

Kelsey didn't waste a second; the next aftershock could come at any moment and rearrange things again, sealing her in forever. Scrambling up the mound, she dragged herself through the narrow crevice.

The mound was much deeper than she'd expected. The shafts of light reaching her were reflecting off strips of cerebrium within the debris, getting far further than they should have in an ordinary quarry.

She moved one limb at a time, testing each rock's load-bearing capacity before committing. But as she reached the far edge, she realized she had no plan for the descent. Kelsey was staring face-forward at a drop as high as her, with a rough landing below, and no room to turn around.

The only option was to try climbing down like a gecko, without breaking her neck. She slithered over the lip of the mound, trying to control her descent using her trembling arms.

She tugged her trailing leg but it wouldn't budge. Something had snagged against the ankle of her jumpsuit. Suspended, blood was pooling in her head.

If she didn't free herself in the next few seconds, she

knew she would pass out. Jerking her leg desperately, she tugged until the rock tore through the fabric, freeing her leg, but slicing through her muscle in the process.

The momentum sent her careering over the edge of the mound, causing a cascade. Kelsey landed in a heap amidst the rolling rubble. Her wrist felt fractured.

As she nursed the wound, inspecting it beneath the dangling ceiling light, a sound caught her attention. Muffled voices, coming from the tunnel. Someone was shouting instructions.

Jumping to her feet, she limped towards the sound, croaking for help. As she picked her way through the boulder-strewn corridor towards the main tunnel, an almighty crash sounded from above. She cowered, clutching her face mask as a dust cloud billowed through the tunnel.

The electric lights flickered out completely. Kelsey dropped to all fours and crawled forwards. She could hear the voices shouting again - she was getting closer to the edge of the tunnel, but there was no sign of the elevator shaft.

Her hand suddenly plunged downwards, meeting no resistance. She slumped forwards, landing hard on her chest, with one arm dangling into the pitch-black abyss. Among the echoing noises, her spinning mind pieced together the final numbers of a countdown.

Kelsey jerked backwards just in time. With a deafening buzz, a drill pierced the rocks obstructing the shaft. Boulders tumbled through the darkness with a crunch. Kelsey squinted as a powerful search light swung from the tip of the corded drill.

"Over here! Help!" she croaked, waving desperately as if it could see her.

She ducked as the juddering drill swung precariously. It powered down and retracted back up the shaft. Kelsey peered upwards as the light dwindled with it, imploring her rescuers to come back.

As the drill light disappeared, two smaller lights appeared either side of it, getting closer. Rescue workers were abseiling into focus.

The extraction was a blur. Kelsey was vaguely aware of a harness being fitted to her, and the cord being pulled taut. She tried not to look into the black void below as they winched her to the surface, but the journey was slow, and fraught with obstructions.

A sea of arms hauled her over the lip of the shaft and onto the gangway. Someone forced an oxygen mask over her mouth, but Kelsey's world was flickering out.

As the medical trolley rushed forwards, her brain registered one final sensation: a pair of cold, metal hands, pinning her down.

CHAPTER ELEVEN

Michael crept inside and slipped off his shoes. Beside the coat rack was their census portal, a small, rectangular wooden unit with brass plaques on the front and six card slots on the top. At the end was a snow-globe-shaped counter, displaying a number card with the total number of occupants in the house.

His mother's card was nestled in the slot above her name plaque, and two along from that, his sister's. Michael's eyes lingered on the furthest slot, which was empty, as always. The Ministry had replaced the original plaque with a shinier one bearing the inscription *Guest 3*.

Michael punched in and the snow globe tally updated. He tiptoed towards the staircase.

His grandfather's voice resonated from the kitchen. Halting, Michael peered around the door frame and listened. His mother was there too, speaking in hushed tones.

"The boy's adjusting, that's all. It's common after visiting the Ministry," soothed Amal.

He was doing the washing up at a glacial pace.

Michael's mother was beside him, chopping vegetables like a machine.

"Something's up," she said, shaking her head. "He's not been himself since his birthday. You saw how he was at the meal, all jumpy and distracted. I think he's freaking out. I've always said eighteen's too young, especially for a boy who grew up without... you know."

She tipped the carrots into a pan of simmering water.

"Give the boy a chance, he needs a little time, that's all," said Amal.

He took a clean plate from the rack and absently submerged it in the dirty dish water.

"He looks exhausted *constantly*. It's not healthy. I've tried talking to him, but he's shutting me out, so I've made an appointment with the doctor," said Val, unscrewing a jar of tomatoes.

"Why?"

"What do you mean, 'why?' My boy's been rattling around the house at all hours of the night, he's barely eating, he's picking fights with his sister, it's not right. You know the school called today? He didn't show up until lunchtime. But I saw him leave this morning, so where the hell did he go?"

"You think he's hiding something?"

"Maybe. Something's upsetting him, that's for sure."

"So, you want to medicate him?"

"I want to help him."

"Then talk to him."

"You've seen me trying, and he doesn't respond. It's time for a professional opinion. There must be something that can take the edge off until it all blows over."

"You mean until he accepts his choice?"

Val ignored the question. Lifting a pan of lentils off the hob, she carried it to the sink, nudging Amal aside.

"Can you grab a sieve?" she asked.

Amal ambled across to the stove and picked up the pan of simmering carrots. He gasped in pain as the metal scalded his bare hands. He dropped the pan with a clatter, drenching the floor in steaming vegetables and boiling water.

"What the hell!" cried Val, rising onto tiptoes to avoid the flood. "Oh god, Dad, are you OK?"

She steered her father towards the sink and held his hands under the cold-water tap.

"What happened?" she asked, concerned.

"I don't know what I was thinking. Boy, that hurts."

Michael had instinctively sprung forwards, completely forgetting his cover.

"Pops, are you OK?"

Val glared at him from the sink. "Michael! Have you been eavesdropping? Don't just stand there gawping - grab a mop and help clear this up."

While Michael cleaned the mess up, his mother set a timer for Amal to run the cold tap over his hand. It lasted ten minutes, eight of which Amal spent insisting he was fine.

Keeping a low profile, Michael made the most of his mother's distraction and avoided troublesome questions about his absences.

Val was juggling Amal's injury, making dinner, and helping her twelve-year-old daughter, who had appeared with a homework question. When the phone rang, she was brisk.

"Yes?" she said, snatching the cream handset from the wall.

A weary cloud settled across her face.

"I understand. I'll be right there."

She hung up with a heavy sigh.

"I have to go. There's been an urgent incident and they've assigned me to the case. I'm sorry everyone, it can't wait. There's ointment in the bathroom cupboard, it will soothe the burn once the timer's up. Michael, see that everyone eats, then set up the guest room for your grandfather. Oh, and Michael I meant to say, Hamish came by with his family this evening while you were out. I think he wanted to say goodbye - they seemed to be in a hurry. I didn't know they were moving ouf town?"

"Neither did I" replied Michael, aghast. "Did they leave an address?"

"I'm afraid not honey. They seemed anxious. Look, I don't have time to go into it but I suggest you ask at school? I've got to fly!"

Val gave Sophia an affectionate squeeze, then prized away the clingy child's arms and hurried out. Michael felt a lump in his throat as he watched her go. His mother hated work invading their evenings, but as sole breadwinner, and given her line of work, she had no choice.

After a subdued dinner, Michael helped his grandfather up to the guest bedroom and massaged ointment into the old man's burned hands. They were red raw, and starting to blister. How had he been so careless?

"My own stupid fault," chuckled Amal, as if reading Michael's mind.

Michael could see through the brave face. Amal was shaken by the incident, and exhausted. Michael dug out some of his dad's old pajamas and helped Amal to change. A chain caught his attention.

"What's this?" said Michael, holding it to the light.

Amal strained his eyes downward to focus on the chain around his neck.

"That? It was an anniversary gift from your grandmother. Forty years. It reminds me every day of the love she brought to my life. You know, we used to joke that-"

"No," interrupted Michael, "I mean, what are those symbols on it?"

A sense of dread was sweeping across him, as he took in the unmistakable pattern.

"It's my name, written in *eterna*. It's the old language of our nation - don't they teach you anything at schools these days?"

Michael let the chain fall from his fingers. It jangled against his grandfather's collarbone.

"Lighten up kid, it was only a joke."

"I... I should go. Good night, Granddad. I love you," said Michael.

Amal looked at him, baffled at Michael's meek tone.

"Pancakes for breakfast?" he called.

Michael hurried to his room, sealed the door and drew the curtains. Pulling the glass sequela from his pocket, he shone it under his desk lamp. The symbols were unmistakable. It related to his grandfather.

Michael sank onto his bed as guilt swelled within him. Whatever was coming was his fault, and his grandfather would be the one to pay.

CHAPTER TWELVE

Kelsey passed through the security scanner and collected her suit jacket from the luggage belt. A clerk beckoned her forwards, checking her details.

"You'll be in courtroom C. Take a seat along the hall."

Kelsey crossed the polished atrium and waited for her counsel to arrive. The wall featured a mural of automatons and humans conquering a mountain together with a shared flag. The flag featured a human eye, housed in an automaton's metal casing. She'd never seen anything like it. Beneath it was a line of symbols. She recognized the style from her eighteenth birthday, but had no idea what they meant. Sweeping through security, her lawyer joined her.

"How are you feeling, honey? The outfit suits you, I'm so glad. You look the part."

Kelsey frowned. She didn't get why this woman was being so nice to her, especially given her own unrelenting abrasiveness. Ever since their first meeting at the hospital two weeks ago, this lawyer had been all honey and roses. Kelsey had met her type before. Purveyors of transactional affection; Ministry officials who pretend to be your best friend, then the minute you're off their to-do list, it's like you never existed. But this woman seemed different.

"It must feel strange, being back here," said the lawyer.

She poured them each a glass of water.

"At least my parents aren't here. They can't ruin it this time," Kelsey snorted.

"Do you remember much of the building?"

"Not really. I was only a kid. I remember it was quiet inside. Until Mom started yelling, of course."

The lawyer opened her brief case and showed Kelsey an array of large print photos revealing the severity of Kelsey's injuries from the tunnel, including a wrist X-ray, broken ribs, and a torn calf muscle.

"They're gonna say I already looked like that," said Kelsey.

She pointed to the photographed black eye above the cut on her cheek.

"And we'll prove them wrong," said the lawyer, brightly.

"You can't know that. Why do you always talk like everything's gonna be fine when it's not?"

"I'm an optimist by nature, Kelsey, but a realist by trade. Trust me, you'll be fine."

Kelsey snorted. "Heard that before."

"Not from me," smiled the woman.

"Oh my god, ditch the fairy godmother act already. Just because I'm your latest charity case doesn't make us best friends. I want a lawyer, not some washed-up mom. This is business, so let's get it over with, then you can go back to whatever it is you normally pretend to care about."

Her lawyer took a dignified pause, then revealed photographs from when Kelsey was arrested. Kelsey's lip soured as she confronted her own mugshot; it should never have been her in that cell.

"I look like a criminal," she groaned.

"To human eyes, maybe, but the judges don't see like us. They see the bigger picture. And that's what we're showing here," said the lawyer.

"Whatever."

The woman's wristwatch chimed. "It's time - let's go."

The courtroom was smaller than Kelsey remembered. Three automatons sat behind an elevated judging panel at the end of the room. Seated on their left was the defense; Kelsey's mining supervisor, several directors, and their Ministry-appointed lawyer.

Kelsey and her own Ministry lawyer took their seats on the right. A clerk collected documents from both sides and placed them before the central automaton judge.

A thick, neatly-folded silk band covered each judge's eyes. The left-hand judge's was yellow, the right-hand judge's was red, and the central judge's was a fusion; two thinner bands stacked.

The central judge opened the prosecution file and read the contents using its fingertips, before circulating it to the other automatons. It extended an instructive hand to the prosecution panel, and Kelsey's lawyer rose to her feet.

"Your honors, we are seeking compensation from the city mining corporation, whose gross negligence caused significant injuries to my client, both physically and psychologically. She has been unable to work since, and is dependent on a Ministry hardship loan pending damages from her former employer. That loan expires today, hence we are seeking an urgent decision."

The central automaton rotated its head to face the defense. It extended its arm, and the opposition lawyer rose to his feet.

"Your honors, this is brazen opportunism. The prosecuting individual has no job prospects, no abode, and is seeking to place blame on her former employer for a lifetime of poor decisions."

Kelsey jolted in her seat, incensed, but her lawyer restrained her. The prosecution automaton looked up from its reading and tilted its head at Kelsey, like it could see her despite the blindfold.

What followed from across the chamber was a brutal depiction of her life to date. They had her school reports, testimonies from her previous foster parents, and review notes from social services. Tears rolled down her cheeks as she heard her life story told through the eyes of the executive class. She was a criminal and a scrounger, born and raised. Most hurtful of all was the defense lawyer's tone. He wasn't animated, or impassioned. He wasn't leaning over the rail with zeal, as he decried her character. No, it was worse than that. His tone was one of weary pity. Like she wasn't to blame for fraudulently seeking compensation; that anyone in her position would naturally try such a thing, because such people can't help it, and as such can't be trusted.

The defense recommended that she be cautioned for wasting court time, and undertake community service to broaden her résumé. The man sat down with heavy eyelids and arched brows, implying a chummy sympathy with the judges, like the hearing was just a formality.

Kelsey's lawyer was having none of it.

"Thank you for that patent infringement of my client's rights. So far, you've illegally referenced an expunged juvenile record - for which, I might add, no charges were ever brought – as well as cataloguing the failures of our childcare and education services to protect a vulnerable minor. Furthermore, you've made insinuations bordering on the defamatory. We will be seeking additional damages in light of this.

"Moving on to the small matter of the collapsed mine shaft. Your honors, in my documentation you will see the emergency evacuation protocol for the mine has been plagiarized from another jurisdiction. No adjustments have been made for the increased seismic risks of the local geology. More worryingly, if you turn to appendix item two, you will see the staff training log book is years out of date."

Kelsey sat back in her chair and watched as the defense's faces fell. Maybe she was going to enjoy today after all.

The hearing continued for several hours before each side made their closing remarks. The automaton judges conferred silently, with mechanical whirring and tilts of the head. Rising to their feet, the defense judge and the prosecution judge glided out from behind their desks and converged in the middle of the courtroom.

Between the two opposing sides and the judges' panel was a metal font with a domed glass lid, revealing an inner labyrinth of cogs and levers. Tall and slim, it was about the height of Kelsey's shoulders. Each automaton fed a granite-gray card into a slit on one side of the machine. The cards had neatly drawn black symbols on them, like those in the atrium.

Etching a verdict onto a final card, the central judge held it out for the clerk to collect. The man scurried forwards and took it from the automaton with a bow. He approached the metal font and fed it into the central slot.

The machine retracted all three cards at once. Levers and cogs cranked inside, and the gray cards sped through the complex system. The whirring subsided and three panels popped up inside the glass-covered dome. Each was red.

Kelsey's lawyer gripped her elbow excitedly. The verdict was unanimous: the mining company was guilty. Bowing to each other, the defense and prosecution judges glided back to their seats behind the panel. Rising to its feet, the central judge passed a gray card with glistening red ink to the clerk, who fed it into the machine. Two reams of white paper tumbled out of the sides. Kelsey's lawyer stepped forwards keenly and tore their strip off, while the defense's lawyer retrieved his with decidedly less enthusiasm.

Her lawyer returned and slapped the paper before Kelsey with a triumphant smile. Kelsey's head spun as she stared at the figure on the page. For the first time in her life, she felt free.

CHAPTER THIRTEEN

Michael had barely slept in the past two weeks. He'd tried every book in the public library, searching the archives for ways to decipher the sequela's purpose.

The history teachers at school knew nothing of the devices, and showing sketches had only aroused suspicion. He dared not show the actual piece to anyone for fear of reprisal. If they learned that he had one, there would be questions, maybe even to a Ministry inquiry. The truth would come out; that he broke the sacred rules and changed his letter. He had to find a way to save his grandfather, to reverse the punishment he was receiving for Michael's actions.

It was with trepidation that Michael approached Amal's house. He had seen the cracks deepening in his grandfather's mind with each day that passed. His mother was either in denial, or too busy with work, to notice.

The last time he had visited, four days ago, his grandfather had been in the garden, planting fully grown carrots in the flower beds. When Michael had suggested that they might be better off back in the fridge, his grandfather brushed the whole thing off with his usual charisma, covering his tracks by declaring it a horticultural experiment to try and get sweeter produce. This was followed by a lengthy explanation of the hormonal ripening process of root vegetables.

That was part of the problem. Amal was so articulate it was hard telling his sincerity from his bravado. What scared Michael the most was the sense that Amal himself no longer knew.

Michael had stayed so late in the library the past few nights that he'd run out of time to visit his grandfather in person. When he had eventually dropped by, all the lights were either off, or just the bedroom lamp was on, precluding any meaningful visit. It was thus with guilt that Michael appeared at his grandfather's house, as soon as his latest truancy detention had finished.

He'd dumped his school bag at home, refueled, and caught the tram to his grandfather's, keen to maximize their time together.

As he approached the house, a sense of unease stole across him. The front door was open, as was the garden gate. There was shouting coming from inside. He hurried into the gloomy house.

"Grandpa?" he called.

Michael followed the shouting into the living room, where the TV was blaring out an old western. Switching it off, he called out again. He scoured both floors, but his grandfather was nowhere to be seen.

Michael raced out of the house, calling for help. He banged on the neighbor's door until a man answered with a toddler on his hip.

"Hey, have you seen my grandfather? He lives next door," he panted.

The man called through to his husband, who joined them.

"Sure, I saw him early this morning, he said he was off to visit his daughter. Did he not show up?"

A sickness stole across Michael.

"No, and he's left the front door open. I don't think he's well," stammered Michael.

"His car's still here, so either he's on foot, or he's gone somewhere by tram. I'll call the police, and we'll ring your mom, too, then we'll start searching."

The father and daughter set off to warn other neighbors, while Michael and the man's husband took to the roads.

Dusk was in its final stages. Street lights studded the pink and blue sky like constellations as Michael circled a district several miles away. He had decided to split from Amal's neighbor, so they could cover more ground between them. After hours of going door to door, street by street, they had exhausted the immediate search radius, and needed to spread out further.

Michael's mother and their own neighbors were combing the gardens and woods by their house, which had freed Michael to use his mom's car.

He drummed the steering wheel, waiting for the signal to change. Clutching the sequela in his hand, he ran his thumb over the ridges, pleading with the device to return his grandfather safely. It had been fourteen hours since he was last seen, and, given his age, the police feared the worst. Michael had knocked on hundreds of doors, and covered miles of the city, crawling its suburbs, scouring the gardens and alleys for any trace.

Catching his own gaunt reflection in the rearview mirror, despair stole over him. Finally, he understood. The glass token was a debt; the Ministry's way of forcing him to atone for his actions, by threatening someone close to him until he submitted. He knew what he had to do.

Michael hit the gas. His car shot across the tar like a bullet, cutting through the narrowest of gaps between the oncoming traffic. He shuddered and gripped the wheel tighter, pressing the pedal harder to the floor.

He screamed as he rocketed towards the next interchange. The lights flicked through amber to red. He raced across the intersection. An oncoming car swerved violently to avoid him. Horns blared in his wake. He didn't look back. Racing on, he blasted through six more interchanges until he reached the open road. The speedometer was maxing out, quivering in the red zone.

As he sped towards the city boundary, a juggernaut barreled towards the interchange from the perpendicular freeway. Tears streamed down Michael's cheeks as he charged towards it.

The oncoming truck was less than a hundred meters away. Michael locked his arms firmly against the steering wheel. The whole car trembled. The juggernaut's foghorn was growing to a deafening blast. Closing his eyes, he thought of his grandfather.

Michael's eyed flicked open. The truck's horn was disappearing behind him. His car was rocketing through the open highway, unimpeded. He was alive. Dazed, Michael jerked his foot off the gas and let the car roll to a stop as the sun vanished below the horizon. The dark road ahead was deserted.

Michael pulled onto the dusty embankment and stumbled out of the car. Vomiting, he slumped against the sizzling hood.

Opening his palm, he stared at the sequela. He'd gripped it so tightly the symbols had imprinted on his skin. Michael's head lolled back, exhausted. He stared at the starry sky, longing for an answer. Was *this* his punishment? To live through the nightmare forever?

He wiped his mouth clean, climbed back inside the vehicle, and made an about-turn for home. As he retraced his route, his heart sank. He'd left a trail of destruction in his wake. Skid marks were scorched into the road at every intersection he'd cut through. He slowed and stared in horror at three cars crumpled into each other. The fire department were cutting one driver out of their seat, while another was being loaded into an ambulance wearing a neck brace.

He pulled onto a side street, avoiding the officer's gaze as police diverted traffic. A lump formed in Michael's throat as he watched the mayhem in his mirror. He never meant for this to happen. *He* was the one who was meant to pay.

Michael parked up some distance from the house, distraught that he was returning without Amal. As he approached his house, gathering himself, he saw a police car parked outside.

His heart froze. They were here to take him away; to punish him for the traffic accidents. But if they took him in now, he would never find his grandfather, or uncover the truth about the sequela. Pulling up his hood, he paced away.

"Michael?" came a cry from behind.

His mother waved at him from the front yard, beside two cops. "Michael, hey!"

Tearing himself away, he ran. Behind him, police doors slammed shut, and the engine started. Michael ran faster, his arms pumping, but the car was bearing down. The siren flicked on. They were closing in.

In an instant, the police car raced by. Michael slowed to a breathless halt and watched, perplexed, as the cops vanished into the traffic ahead. He rolled onto his back, wheezing, until the ringing in his ears subsided.

His relief evaporated as he realized what the police car meant. They weren't there to arrest him; they were there to tell his mother they were ending the search. Cold fear swept across him as he hurried back to the house.

"Mom, I'm so sorry. I can't believe he's gone and it's all my fault," said Michael, bursting through the door.

"What are you talking about? We found him!" said Val, with tears in her eyes.

Michael stepped into the living room and his mouth fell open. His grandfather sat on the sofa with a blanket over his shoulders, and a cup of tea nestled between his bandaged hands. He looked tired and vacant, but by some miracle he was still with them.

"Granddad, are you OK?" said Michael, approaching.

Amal didn't reply.

"The police found your grandfather by the highway. He'd been walking for hours. It's incredible he wasn't hurt."

"Granddad, oh my god," said Michael, falling to his knees.

He placed his hands on Amal's knees, but the old man looked through him. Michael recoiled in horror, recognizing that marble gaze.

"No, no, tell me this isn't happening - not to Granddad, not him," said Michael.

He'd heard rumors of the affliction, but it hadn't been seen in generations.

"What did we do to deserve this?" uttered Val.

She stole herself away, sobbing. Amal raised his head, and a frown flickered across his brow as the crying registered somewhere in his malfunctioning brain.

"I'm so sorry, Granddad, I'm so sorry," wept Michael, as he wrapped himself around the old man's legs, with his head on his lap.

Michael waited for the household to be asleep, then crept downstairs, realizing his mistake. For as long as the sequela was in his possession, his family was at risk - and he was safe. The whole purpose of the device, he surmised, was to keep him alive against all else, so he could suffer the consequences of his actions. It was a Ministry trick; a curse from the automaton. He had to destroy it.

Slipping on his shoes, he glanced at the census. Amal's ID card was nestled in the visitor slot, near Michael's.

He hesitated. It was illegal to be out in public without your ID card. But if his mom woke in the night and saw that he'd gone, there'd be hell to pay. Leaving it behind, he slipped out.

Gripping the sequela tightly in his hand, he marched towards the tram line. The nearest night route was a mile away. Michael skulked in the shadows beside a newsstand that was closed for the night. Waiting until the street was deserted, he approached the tramline. Kneeling down, he wedged the sequela inside the tracks, then darted back to the shadows and waited.

It was half an hour before the tram came. Michael was so tired he'd fallen asleep on the sidewalk. He woke with a jolt as the tram shuddered by. He watched the rolling box of light disappear, then ran to inspect the damage.

The sequela was fully intact. Picking it up, he examined the unblemished slab, shaking his head in disbelief. There *had* to be a way to destroy it.

His eyes wandered to the bridge. He hurried to the middle and regarded the pitch-black waters of the estuary. With one final look at the sequela and its shimmering symbols, he hurled it into the waves below.

The sequela was the penance he'd been given, but he refused to let his grandfather pay. Now it was just a matter of waiting for the Ministry to respond. Surely now they had no choice but to take back from Michael what he'd stolen from them?

The alarm clock blared 6 a.m. The morning was crisp, and a fine layer of mist hovered above their vibrant green lawn. Michael rushed to the mailbox outside but his mother was already there, closing it back up. She was wearing her clothes from the day before. Her bloodshot eyes widened as she saw him.

"What are you doing up?" she asked, astonished.

"Right back at you," said Michael.

"Your granddad. I thought maybe today would be his... I wanted to make sure I didn't waste it," she said, her voice cracking.

"Same," lied Michael, rubbing his bare arms.

The door across the road clicked open. The woman hesitated as she saw them, then hurried to her mailbox. Michael watched her shoulders fall before she disappeared back inside her house.

"Poor woman," said Val. "Come on, I'll make you pancakes."

Michael sat at the table, groggily shoveling pancakes into his mouth. Roused by the scent, his sister skipped downstairs to join the feast. A few minutes later, a familiar voice joined the fray.

"Morning all," said Amal. "I thought I smelled pancakes. Excellent. What brings you all here?"

"Dad, this isn't your house... You stayed at ours last night," said Val, gently.

Amal's mouth twitched, but he covered his bemusement with confidence.

"I know that, I'm just winding you up. I'm taking these pups for the road," he said, loading a plate with pancakes.

"There's no hurry, Granddad. Maybe you should stay a while longer?" suggested Michael.

"Have you tried sleeping in that guest bed, lad? No thank you, not with my back," he chuckled, helping himself to a liberal slather of syrup.

"Take your sister into the front room, would you, Michael?" said Val.

"Take me? I'm twelve, not six! *God*," fumed Sophia, storming off.

"You can put the TV on if you want," called Val.

"Who's this fine fellow, then?" said Amal, offering Michael a handshake.

Michael's mother bit her lip and busied herself in a cupboard, hiding her tears.

"I'm your grandson," choked Michael.

CHAPTER FOURTEEN

Anxiety fluttered through Kelsey as she approached her old home. The site of the rusted, warped gatepost made her queasy. Her feet rocked as she walked between cracked paving slabs and dirt-filled rectangles to the door.

In the two years she'd been there, the doorbell had never worked, so she knocked three times then leaped back. Her foster mother had a habit of opening the door and stepping through it in one fight-ready motion. Being a woman of some size, this often meant a swift ejection for whoever was calling.

The raging bull failed to materialize, so Kelsey knocked again, calling out as she rooted around for the spare key. It wasn't in the usual spot under the mat.

Beside the mat were three unopened milk bottles, warming in the midday sun. Weird. She moved them to the shady side of the porch.

Kelsey headed around the side of the house, past the broken basement windows, to the open back door.

The kitchen stank of empty beer cans and rotting cat

food. The couple weren't allowed to keep pets anymore, but her stepfather insisted on leaving out open tins to lure neighbors' pets. He would then lavish them with attention until his partner chased both him and the cats away. So, no pets. Unless you count roaches and rodents.

Kelsey picked her way through empty pizza boxes and soiled clothing, calling out as she went. The last thing she wanted was to startle two sleeping giants, especially if they were sleeping off hangovers.

Their bedroom was deserted. The duvet was so stained it almost looked like leopard print. Cheap trinkets and sugary snacks sat in overflowing grocery bags at the foot of the bed. Sunlight filtered through the violet curtains, which had such a low thread count they acted more like mood lights.

The living room was deserted, too. Kelsey checked the census on the wall and it confirmed they were both out. She heaved a sigh of relief. Looking closer, someone had replaced her name plaque with a guest space. Much as she hated this place, it hurt to be erased from it so quickly.

Nervously, she entered her old room. Her sleeping bag lay sprawled across the dirty mattress she'd inherited. Her posters were still on the wall, and her school books piled up in the corner. Stooping down, she stuffed her clothes, makeup, and other items into bags she'd brought. It didn't take long to gather everything she owned into three modest sacks. Surveying her room for the last time, she felt a sadness at the life she'd tolerated for so long.

As Kelsey stepped into the corridor, the front door banged open. Stacey, her rotund former foster mother, barged in. Her partner, Tony, was hobbling behind her, eclipsed from view.

"Dammit Tony, quit whining about the liquor store!"

"He humiliated me!"

"You had no money, jackass. What was he supposed to do, give it away?"

"Damned right. I forgot my wallet is all - he knows I'm good for it."

"Oh, he knows alright. He knows *exactly* what you're good for."

Stacey stopped in her tracks, locking eyes with Kelsey.

"Where in hell's name are you going with all that?"

"I'm moving out. I came to get the rest of my stuff."

"No, kid. You're already moved out. And that stuff ain't yours no more. It's mine."

A cry rang out from Tony's side of the hall.

"Shut that thing up already!" yelled Stacey.

She stormed off to the couch and grabbed a soda, revealing Tony's twig-like figure by the entrance.

Kelsey's mouth dropped. In her ex-foster father's arms were two swaddled babies. The cries of the first were rapidly spreading to its sibling.

"Now look what you've done!" moaned Tony.

Between his fingertips were two crumpled white envelopes.

"What *I've* done?" yelled Stacey. "It wasn't *my* name on those letters, but here *you* are, in *my* house, bringing me nothing but problems again."

Kelsey propped her bags against the wall and approached Tony, extending her arms.

"May I?"

His suspicion faded to relief as he foisted one of the crying babies onto Kelsey. She took the infant in her arms and rocked it, cooing.

"See? Gentle, like this," she whispered.

Tony watched with bewilderment, then copied her

bobbing motion. To his astonishment, both babies settled down.

"Where will they sleep?" asked Kelsey.

The man looked anxiously to Stacey, who rolled her eyes.

"Don't look at me, they're your problem," she snorted.

Tony led Kelsey through to the kitchen, carrying his baby like he had a sack of dynamite strapped to his chest.

"Would you?" he said, tipping the second baby into her other arm.

Kelsey accepted the infant, having little say in the matter, while he rummaged in the cupboards beneath the sink.

"I guess this'll do as a start," he mumbled.

He pulled out two old cats' travel crates and lay them on the floor.

"Are you kidding me?" said Kelsey, disgusted.

"It's only temporary. They're soft, look."

"How has this happened? You had all of yesterday to prepare - and don't say you didn't have money. I know they give you money when this happens," snapped Kelsey.

"I didn't ask for this, OK? I'm still getting my head around it. We tried, but we didn't have time to, you know, buy the things."

"Oh, but you had time for all this?" said Kelsey, gesturing to the beer cans strewed around them.

She passed him each baby in turn, and he tenderly lowered them into the cat crates. Kelsey then showed him how to make sure their swaddling was tight enough.

"They kinda look like me, don't ya think?" beamed Tony.

"Sure. I'm gonna go now. Get it together, you hear me?"

Tony rubbed his arm. "It's tricky, you know?"

"Save it. When I come back here tomorrow, these children will have cribs, or I'm calling the police."

Kelsey grabbed her bags from the corridor and left the house, trying to shut out the sound of a fresh beer can being opened.

Kelsey left the thrift shop looking like an altogether more mature woman. Discarding all of her old clothes in a part-exchange for swanky business-woman attire had felt particularly cathartic.

She was done with that life, those people, and those patterns of behavior. It was time to stand on her own two feet. Thanks to a broken system, her childhood had existed only on paper, and eighteen years later it had expired in silence. She wasn't letting that happen again.

Kelsey checked her hair and makeup in the washroom, surprising herself with her new guise. Gone were the Cleopatra eyes and scraped back hair. She combed it into a smart-looking side parting and let the locks hang above her shoulders. Wearing the suit her lawyer had provided, with a pastel green blouse from the thrift shop, she felt the part.

She re-rehearsed all the advice that woman had given her about posture, tone, and signaling. It had served her well in the hearing, and might serve her well here.

The receptionist was on the phone, but gave Kelsey a polite holding smile as she finished the conversation. Kelsey felt herself stand taller; this wasn't the reaction people used to give her.

"Are you here for the interview, ma'am?"

"Er, yes, yes I am," said Kelsey, opportunistically.

"Ah, thank goodness. They were worried you weren't coming. This way."

She led Kelsey through the chrome turnstile and down a series of corridors. The complex was a lot bigger than it looked from the outside. Kelsey glimpsed a packed lecture hall as they walked. Rows of students paid attention to a middle-aged woman wearing a jumper that looked like a sack, beside a projector showing schematics of what appeared to be boiler tanks.

"Take a seat in here, the panel will be through shortly. Do help yourself to water from the side," said the receptionist, taking her leave.

Kelsey crossed over to the crystal decanter and poured herself some mint-infused water. It was better than any she'd tasted before. She looked at the bottle in astonishment, necked her first glass, then poured another and inspected the meeting room.

Sepia photos of babies hung across the walls in mahogany frames. Some were asleep, some wide-eyed and inquisitive, others laughing. Her gaze lingered on the last photo: an overjoyed couple receiving their first child from the Ministry. She stared at it, unable to look away. The smiles on their faces looked so perfect, the creases around their eyes so genuine.

A secondary door opened and a man in a white lab coat beckoned her through.

"Doctor Santos, we're so pleased you could make it. Of course, there's no need for the usual formalities, your CV really speaks for itself. We thought we'd just cut to the practical demonstration, given our time constraints. This is my colleague, Professor Hestley; she heads up the research division here."

Before Kelsey could intervene, the woman was enthusiastically shaking her hand.

"Wonderful to meet you. Your paper on refined pluripotency was exceptional, we just had to get you in. I trust the voyage wasn't too challenging? I hear it can be rough at this time of year."

"No, uh, it was fine," said Kelsey.

Her eyes moved to the equipment in the center of the room. A thick clay bowl, wider than her arm span, sat on a wooden worktop. The bowl had two rims, spaced three inches apart.

The inner bowl was suspended on a cushion of black liquid. It held a lump of clay the size of Kelsey's torso.

The interview room featured a glass wall overlooking a factory floor, where the identical set up was replicated dozens of times. Those clay bowls were suspended on large, cast-iron tripods. Some were rotating above a flame: others were being dunked in splash pools. Automatons and human technicians attended to them side by side, adding fluids, and checking the readings on vast boilers and ventilation pipes that stood behind each clay bowl, rising three stories high.

"Please," said the woman, gesturing to the machine beside Kelsey.

The machine started with an elevated desk chair, like those at a dentist. Nervously, Kelsey climbed in. Before her were two sets of gloves, connected to long levers protruding from the worktop.

Kelsey slid her hands inside. To her surprise, metal discs lined the gloves, mirroring the articulations of her joints. She flexed her hands, jolting in shock as the ceiling above her moved. Two brass-plated mechanical arms, each the size of her entire body, swung down from the roof and hovered above the clay. On one arm was a scalpel; on the other a spinning buffer.

"The pedals are beneath your feet," urged the man.

"Maybe her lab has a different set up?" whispered the woman.

Kelsey reached her foot out and tapped the pedal. The arms descended towards the clay with a pneumatic hiss. She fluttered, trying to reset her grip, but it amounted to a spasm.

The scalpel sank into the clay, while the buffer struck it like a hammer striking a raw egg. The clay crust ruptured, and a viscous pink-brown amalgam seeped out.

Kelsey's foot jerked off the pedal as the haptic feedback startled her. The spinning buffer struck the bowl with a clang. A cupful of black liquid sloshed up, splattering the clay.

"What are you doing!" cried the woman, hitting an emergency release button on the wall.

A bell rang out in their chamber, and the machine jolted back from the table. Kelsey leaped down from the stool in fright, as the mechanical arms retracted into the ceiling.

"That was insanely dangerous, explain yourself!"

Two automatons glided into the room. One set about siphoning the black fluid away from the clay, while the other tried to stem the seepage of pink-brown liquid. Kelsey glanced at the glass wall beside her. The human technicians dotted across the floor were staring on with concern.

"I think there's been a misunderstanding," said Kelsey.

The professors' anger was palpable. They paced the interview room, wringing their hands in deliberation, while Kelsey sat in shame.

"We can't just let her leave, she's seen the assembly line; that's way above civilian clearance," hissed the man.

"How much do you know?" snapped the woman.

"I know this is where the Ministry handles fertility and child placements. But that's all I know, really. I came here to try and make a difference," said Kelsey, blushing.

"Oh, you've done that alright," fumed the man. "If the Ministry hears of this, all our necks will be on the line!"

"What scientific qualifications do you have?" asked the woman.

"Technically, none..." began Kelsey.

The woman groaned in despair.

"But I'm smart! And hard working. I've just... not had a good start in life. I'm trying to change that. Give me a chance," implored Kelsey.

"Like we have a choice. We need to do damage control, fast," growled the man.

He stormed off, slamming the door behind him. Moments later he appeared on the factory floor, taking charge of the clean-up operation.

"Here's the deal," said the woman. "You will keep your mouth shut. Tell anyone what you've seen and you will be prosecuted. If you promise *never* to do anything so reckless again, I'll take you on as a porter. But you'll need to get scientifically qualified fast. If our department's audited and you're on the books as you are, then the whole thing's blown."

"How do I do that? I got kicked out of school."

"Of course you did..." said the woman, rolling her eyes.

"Hey, it wasn't my fault!" protested Kelsey. "Sorry. I mean... I *did* want to finish my studies."

"Good. Then get yourself to night school. But take note: you'll need a referee, and it sure as hell can't be me."

The lights in the law offices were going out in quick succession. The firm was only small, so shutting up shop was a brief exercise for whoever was working late that night.

Kelsey climbed off the tram and hurried across the street. Her former lawyer stepped out, locking the office behind her.

"Wait, Ms Hadley!"

"Kelsey? Now isn't a good time, I'm running late."

"It'll only take a second - I need a reference for night school."

She handed over the form she'd collected. Val rummaged for her glasses, then tilted the form to capture the street light.

"This is not a simple request. The course requires me to act as a guarantor. If you fail to attend, or fail to meet the pass mark, there are consequences for me - both financially and reputationally."

Kelsey blushed. She hadn't bothered reading the form.

"That's crazy, why would they punish referees?" she protested.

"Because night school is an opportunity, and a limited resource. If they give a place to you, then someone else will miss out. This system ensures that the limited places only go to people who are serious about their studies."

"If this is about my trial, I'm sorry I was rude to you. I was in a bad place-"

"I'm not after an apology. All I'm asking is if you know what you're taking on here?"

Kelsey fidgeted with the hem of her blazer. Suddenly, the entire outfit felt ill-fitting.

"I won't fail you," she said, earnestly.

"It says you want to study biochemistry?"

"I've got a temporary job at the Ministry of Fertility, but I need qualifications to stay."

Val raised her eyebrows.

"Vacancies there are competitive. Congratulations. But I ask again, are you sure this is what you want? Night school is not like regular school. You can't bunk off if you don't like the teacher, or skip classes if you don't feel like it. And when you do get there, you'll be tired. Studying after a full day's work is exhausting, particularly when you're learning a new job at the same time. You'll need to take a professional attitude to how you eat and sleep."

Kelsey snickered, then realized Val was serious.

"Oh, er, when you say 'professional sleep'...?"

"I mean build your life around a routine that facilitates your goals. Don't let anything get in the way. This is an opportunity to shape your future, but you'll be working twice as hard as everyone around you while you do it. You must plan everything. Meals, travel, having fresh work clothes ready for each day. Expect your weekends to be life admin, homework, and sleep for the foreseeable future. Days will feel long, and you'll need your friends for emotional support."

Kelsey cast her eyes downward. The only true friend she'd ever known was standing before her.

"Kelsey, I have to ask again, is this really what you want?"

"When my parents abandoned me, there was supposed

to be a safety net; a system to catch me. But I've been bounced between families, institutions, the streets, and back. I've been through four schools and two cities. I've been called the loner, the weirdo, the smelly kid, because my clothes were different and the people looking after me didn't even know how to look after themselves. I was good at school, but even the teachers didn't think I belonged there. Today I went back to my last foster home, to get my things. My foster dad now has twins. Those two newborns are depending on that failure of a man for their entire future. They haven't got a chance. I can't stand by and watch what happened to me repeat itself across other generations. I'm joining the Ministry so I can change the system from within."

Kelsey dabbed away a tear from the corner of her eye, while Val took a long, searching look at her.

"There are many broken systems inside the Ministry. When you've fixed fertility, maybe you can fix the rest."

Val signed the form then hastened away towards a cab, wiping her cheek as she went.

CHAPTER FIFTEEN

V al swiped into the census and composed herself, before entering the living room with a breezy smile.

Amal sat in the armchair, staring vacantly at the wall. Sophia was curled up by his feet, doing her homework. Michael was in the kitchen, finalizing dinner.

"Sorry I'm late, everyone. How are we all today?"

"Mom!"

Sophia leaped up, giving her mother a tight embrace.

"Check it out," she continued, proudly showing a hydraulic design project she'd been sketching for school.

"Wowee, you can tell me all about this over dinner."

"It's going cold," called Michael, plating up.

Sophia skipped off, while Val knelt before her father.

"Hey Dad, how are you doing today?"

Confusion flickered across the old man's face. His lips quivered, and he uttered a faint moan with each rattling breath.

"Mom, come on," called Michael, irritated.

Val closed her eyes, clasping her father's hands, trying not to cry. "Come on, Dad, let's eat."

She led him through to the kitchen, where he gravitated towards his usual seat.

Michael was scrolling through their vertical herb garden, snipping off generous portions. Satisfied with his harvest, he released the brake. The troughs rotated back to their sun-optimized positions, while water filtered down from the uppermost plant beds to those below.

"What's this?" asked Amal.

"Madras. You're favorite, as requested," said Michael.

"I don't like spicy food," said Amal, shoving the plate away.

"Here, Dad, yogurt will soften the taste," said Val, adding a dollop.

Amal threw his bowl off the table and slapped his hands against his thighs.

"Stop calling me that!"

"Calling you... Dad?" said Val, aghast.

She reached down to clear up the mess, but Michael stayed her hand.

"Sophie, why don't you tell mum about your cool project?" said Michael.

His sister piped up eagerly, while Michael cleaned the mess and made his grandfather peanut butter on toast.

Amal crunched in silence for the rest of the meal, then left for bed.

"You're a good grandson to him," said Val, later.

She looked exhausted. Michael fought back a lump in his throat, knowing it was so far from the truth. He was the worst thing ever to happen to the poor man.

Two weeks had passed since Amal had moved in with them, and his condition was worsening. Rare moments of charm and lucidity had dwindled to almost nothing.

Michael bunked off class to spend time with him, hoping to glimpse one of those precious windows. Val had written to the school, assuring them Michael would study from home - something he was failing at dismally.

Not that he was being idle. He was pouring over library books, studying the history of Amal's illness, searching for treatments. There had been many experiments, but no cures.

His mother was supposed to be on the evening shift, but she was absent; running late at work again, no doubt.

Michael had spent the entire day trying last-ditch therapies from old medical books, to no avail. Left behind in Amal's shell was a scared, volatile stranger, baffled by the intruders around him. Michael couldn't bare it for a second longer.

Heartbroken, and at his wit's end, he put the ailing man to sleep. With Sophia under orders to comfort Amal if he woke, Michael bolted into the night.

Anger and despair drove him to the Ministry square. He had no leverage, no plan, but he had to try. In the chilly evening air, he stared at the up-lit dome. The steps seemed higher than before, the marble grayer.

A family huddled at the base, clutching banners and confetti, anxiously awaiting their child's return. Michael brushed past them and took to the steps.

"Happy birthday!" called one.

Ignoring them, he marched onwards. His legs felt leaden as he reached the green metal archway. There was a price to pay for his actions, and it was time to settle it.

The clerk didn't recognize him, gazing with the same weary condescension as last time.

"Your letter?"

"I don't have one," said Michael. "I'm here because I need to make a change."

The clerk's nostrils flared. "No changes. You must leave at once!"

"Please, I made a mistake."

"Security!"

Michael grabbed the man's lapels imploringly.

"Sir, I'm begging you, my grandfather's disappearing and it's my fault. I *have* to put it right."

Tugging himself free, the clerk leaped back and thumped a panic button. An alarm sounded as gold bars emerged from ceiling and floor, closing like jaws. From behind his fortress, the clerk watched as two automatons sped towards the intruder.

Michael darted towards the elevator, but the door was sealed. He stared around the atrium searching for clues; the answers *had* to be in this building.

His opportunity vanished as the automatons closed in. They raised their arms, ready to strike. With a cry, Michael fled through the archway, back the way he'd come. The machines hurtled after him, onto the stone veranda.

Michael ran down the marble steps, seizing the opportunity to gain ground on his more cumbersome pursuers. But as he neared the bottom he tripped, tumbling downwards. He ploughed into the solid square as a crumpled mess.

From the top of the steps, the two automatons glared at him. Michael moaned and flopped onto his back, spread-eagled. Satisfied they had neutralized him, the machines drifted back into the building. A bemused eighteen-year-old squeezed past them to rejoined his family, giving Michael a wide berth.

Alone and battered, Michael lay groaning on the tiles.

"Are you OK?" asked a stranger, leaning over him.

Squinting up at her, Michael recognized the face. It was the girl who shared his eighteenth birthday - the one who had sworn at him on the steps a few weeks back. Since then, the rag-tag teenage rebel girl had transformed into a professional woman. She looked even hotter for it.

Michael blushed at his own dire appearance. His entire body ached, and his head throbbed. Swiveling round, he propped himself against the bottom step.

"Seems like a crummy way to celebrate your birthday?" she said, helping him into place.

"It's not my birthday," he groaned.

"Oh. Then what were you doing up there?"

"Trying to lift a curse."

Kelsey laughed, then stopped short, realizing he was serious.

"You believe in magic?" she said, trying to sound non-judgmental, and failing.

"Look, if you can't help me, leave me alone," snapped Michael.

"Suit yourself. You're bleeding, by the way."

Kelsey turned and paced across the square without looking back. Michael cursed his rashness as he watched her go. He touched his bottom lip - his fingers came away stained in crimson. He'd never bled before, and the sight of it made him queasy.

A door opened somewhere behind him. He craned his aching neck, spotting a hatch built into the flat side of the sweeping steps. It was so discreet, it blended with the stone almost seamlessly.

A middle-aged man exited, closing the door behind him. Michael regarded him intently. There were three reasons for which humans were permitted to enter the Ministry. Two of those were common to all: adulthood and death. The third was the domain of a select and secretive few: research. This man was one of the few humans allowed to enter the Ministry multiple times. He was a scholar of mortality.

Michael hobbled over to intercept the man. The scholar wore a knee-length gray trench coat, which hugged his skinny frame and blended with the marble of the building. Tucked under his arm was a cracked, brown briefcase. He walked with a rigidity consistent with attitude rather than ailment.

"Excuse me," hailed Michael.

The scholar looked at Michael's blood-stained visage and quickened his pace.

"Hey, I said wait up - please!"

The scholar was making a beeline for the University pyramid opposite. Michael lunged for the man, catching his arm.

"Unhand me!" cried the scholar.

"How do I undo the curse?" begged Michael.

"What 'curse'? Are you simple? There are no such things," yelped the scholar, wriggling.

"I know what they're doing, and I need it to stop," pleaded Michael, pointing at the Ministry building. "They're punishing me, and I can't go on. I need to make it right."

"You need professional help."

"I need *answers*!" cried Michael.

He snatched the briefcase from the man's arm. The scholar seized the other end with a yelp, and the pair tussled over the cracked leather box. The scholar's defense was surprisingly spirited, but Michael prevailed. With a triumphant cry, he wrenched it free. The briefcase flew through the air, spewing its contents across the stone slabs.

"You fool!" cried the scholar.

He scarpered after the fragments in a panic. Michael picked up a piece by his foot. It was a shimmering maple leaf, infused with auburn and bronze.

"No, you mustn't touch it!"

It was too late. The leaf crumbled in Michael's hands.

"Don't move another muscle, you festering imbecile!"

The scholar pulled on a pair of white gloves from his coat and chased after the precious cargo. Michael watched in dismay as more of the leaves disintegrated in the wind. The scholar ferried armfuls back to his briefcase, but many slipped along the way. As the last stragglers turned to dust, the man gave up.

"Do you have any idea what you've done?" fumed the scholar.

He slammed his briefcase shut, turned on his heel, and marched straight back towards the Ministry.

"Please," implored Michael, "I have to save my grandfather."

"Such unconscionable waste! The impudence, the audacity, the callous indifference of an ignorant mind!"

The scholar stormed towards the invisible doorway. Drawing a long and complex key from around his neck, he inserted it into what looked like a weather pockmark. The door sprang open and the scholar leaped inside. Michael glimpsed a turnstile behind him, and an automaton stationed beyond.

"If I ever see you again, I'll report you!" snapped the scholar.

The door slammed shut in Michael's face. He traipsed back to where he'd accosted the scholar. Kneeling down, he rubbed his fingers in the auburn leaf dust. It was an ultra-fine sand, softer than any other.

He slammed his palm against the stone tiles in anger. It made no sense. He was trying to put it right, and they weren't letting him. They preferred to make an innocent man suffer.

Michael dragged himself to a bench at the side of the square and glared at the Ministry building. There was something he was missing. Maybe curse wasn't the right word. Contract. He'd violated the contract, and his grandfather was paying the price. He waited, praying the scholar would return so he could make a more balanced enquiry.

Two hours later, Michael was shivering with cold. Footsteps approached as Kelsey strode by.

"Hey, sorry I was rude earlier," called Michael.

She stopped at stared at him.

"You're still here? Wait, is this where you live? Are you a tramp?"

"Don't say 'tramp'."

"Why not?"

"It's not right taking a dump on someone's self-esteem when they're already on the ropes. People are people; some are lucky, some aren't, doesn't mean you should treat them any different."

"Huh. I agree," said Kelsey, taking a few steps closer.

"For the record, I have a home, and a family, and I know I'm lucky for that, but somehow I've ruined it all," said Michael, bursting into tears.

"Oh boy, uh, there, there," said Kelsey, taking a seat and awkwardly patting his shoulders.

"Sorry, sorry, it's been a tough few weeks," sniffed Michael.

"Ha, tell me about it," snorted Kelsey.

"You're a lot nicer than you first seemed," said Michael, accepting her offer of a tissue.

"What? I was super nice earlier, I tried helping you."

"Before that. We have the same birthday. I was entering as you were leaving. You swore at me."

"Did I? Sorry. I was in a crappy mood that day. Birthdays aren't my strong suit. Especially not that one."

"You don't remember me at all?" he asked, deflated.

"I'd remember you now," she said, grinning. "What happened?"

"I asked for a refund," he said, gesturing at the Ministry.

"For what? You're still alive, aren't you? Every day's a gift. You should be grateful, that's what I've decided," she said, smiling.

"Oh god. You're one of them," he groaned.

"So what if I am?"

"Transformative eighteenth birthdays are *so* cliché."

"Says the guy having a total existential crisis weeks later."

"In my defense, adulthood is not what they crack it up to be."

"It beats childhood. I'm certainly glad to be out the other side, at least. There's an open road ahead, and for once, I'm at the wheel."

Michael nodded.

"Not digging the driving metaphor? I've got one about gardening if that helps?" mused Kelsey.

Michael chuckled.

"Huh. You have a nice smile - in a wonky, 'I fell down a stone staircase' kind of way," she added.

She gave him a playful elbow.

"Ouch! Still sore," said Michael. "Where were you going at this time of night, dressed like that?"

"Dressed like what?" snapped Kelsey.

"A boss. You look like you could run the Ministry."

Kelsey couldn't help but grin. Michael glimpsed someone deeply earnest behind her cool visage. Not that he minded the visage. He was a fan of the visage.

"I've started night school. I'm training as a biochemist alongside a practical placement," she said. "On that note, I should go. I've got an early start this weekend if I'm gonna get through my assignments, and I've got flashcards to do on the ride home. Good luck with the curse."

Kelsey gave him a smile, then set off across the square.

"Hey, wait up. Which tram are you getting? Maybe I can walk you there?"

"Sure. So long as you're down with revision." She pulled a stack of cards from her satchel. "Test me on the blue ones, I suck at those."

Michael flicked through the cards. Her handwriting was immaculate, and her words captivating - even if the terminology was like another language.

The tram station arrived too soon. Michael lingered, longing to extend the quiz. The next service was five minutes away, so he doubled-down.

Kelsey hooted as he acted out the bullet point prompts like a game of charades. He was midway through an ambitious contortion when her laughter faltered.

"Hey, is that man OK?"

Michael followed her gaze. A shadowy figure was walking along the grassy roadside, swaying. They lifted a leg over the railing and struggled onto the edge of the river embankment.

The man's coat was familiar. His shuffle, too. The crop of white hair.

"Granddad?" cried Michael.

Before either of them could move, Amal disappeared from sight. A splash resonated in the darkness.

"Granddad!" he yelled, rushing to the embankment.

Michael's body ached as he ran; his muscles were bruised and slow. Kelsey ditched her satchel and dashed towards the railing, deftly vaulting it. She shed her outer layers and jumped into the water.

"Call an ambulance!" cried Michael, flagging down some passers-by.

The current was sweeping Kelsey and Amal downstream. Michael hurried along the embankment, clutching the railing, trying to keep pace. His grandfather's clothes were wet and heavy. As the old man thrashed around, his head dropped beneath the surface. Kelsey powered towards him and grabbed his collar, hauling him up. Gripping his chin, she pulled him flat.

"The ladder, grab the ladder!" called Michael.

He pointed urgently to a set of metal rungs fast approaching from downstream. If they didn't act now, the current would sweep them past it.

Kelsey kicked hard and seized the ladder, but the current was still dragging them away. Her arms stretched to breaking point as she clung on, trying to keep Amal's airways above the water.

Michael and the strangers scrambled down to the riverbank. Heaving the old man out, they lay him flat to cough up lungfuls of water. Shivering, Kelsey climbed the ladder, gladly accepting a stranger's coat. People on the street above directed the ambulance towards them.

"Granddad, can you hear me? Talk to me," begged Michael, clutching Amal's shoulders.

"He needs air. Let him breathe," insisted a stranger.

Michael watched with terror as his grandfather spluttered and retched, before slumping onto his back, wheezing. Two strangers wrestled the old man's sodden jacket and shirt away and wrapped him in a sweater.

An ambulance pulled up at the roadside, accompanied by a fire truck. The fire crew scrambled down the embankment with a stretcher and extended their crane overhead to winch Amal up to street level. The strangers scrambled back to safety themselves, while fire crew chaperoned the shivering Kelsey and shock-riddled Michael after them.

"Will he be OK?" stammered Michael.

Amal's stretcher disappeared inside the ambulance and the crew closed the doors. Michael gave a bewildered statement to the firefighters, while waiting anxiously for the doors to reopen.

"You can see him now," said a paramedic, several minutes later.

Michael climbed inside and grabbed his grandfather's hand.

"Fine day for a spot of swimming, hey, Michael my boy?" chuckled Amal.

Michael's face spread into an automatic grin, as he caught his grandfather's infectious smile, before bursting into tears. He clung to the old man's frame, crinkling the silver heat blanket in the embrace.

"What happened?" sobbed Michael.

"I wish I could tell you. The workings of my mind are as much a mystery to me as they are to you, dear boy."

The paramedic checked Amal's lungs with a stethoscope once more, then gave him the all-clear.

"Good news. Your lungs are clear, and you're not at risk of hypothermia anymore. Right now, you need rest. Going forwards, consider a chaperone. Would you prefer to recuperate at home, or be monitored overnight for safety?"

"Best avoid the hospital. Otherwise my daughter might find out," winked Amal.

"I think she might twig when you get dropped off in an ambulance, Granddad," said Michael.

"Damn. Well then, we'd better get working on a cover story," he chuckled.

Kelsey approached the rear of the ambulance. She had dry clothes on, and an emergency heat blanket folded over her arm.

"Hey Michael, I'm glad he's OK. I'm gonna head off now."

Michael blushed, wondering how obvious it was he'd forgotten all about her.

"Oh my god, how can I even thank you?" he gushed, leaping from the ambulance.

"Do you have a hair dryer?"

"Not with me..."

"Ah, then don't worry. We'll call it even."

She gave him a wave and returned her blanket to the fire truck.

"Wait!" said Michael. "There's gotta be something I can do to repay you. Can I take you out to dinner?"

Kelsey laughed.

"You wanna repay me? I could use a study buddy, and you were handy with those flashcards. Meet me at the library tomorrow at twelve?"

"It's a date," gasped Michael. "Well, a study date.

Unless...? Nope, study it is. Study is great. Not that a date-date wouldn't be great. Ha, that rhymes. Oh god, kill me."

Kelsey laughed at him. She leaned forwards and gave him a kiss on the cheek, then set off for the tram stop.

"Time to go, sir, if you're riding with us," called the paramedic.

Michael hopped into the back of the ambulance and took Amal's hand once again, smiling at him with pure love and relief. His grandfather looked back at him with a soft smile.

"Hello young man. Have we met?"

CHAPTER SIXTEEN

E mpty milk bottles decorated the doorstep. Kelsey could hear a baby crying from inside the house. She knocked loudly, then stepped back.

Tony answered in his typical uniform of boxers, bathrobe, and sandals. In one arm, he clutched the crying infant. He had a gauze strip and stitches across his forehead.

"Yeah?"

He took another second to process Kelsey's new appearance.

"Kelsey? What the... You look-"

"Choose your next words carefully, Tony."

"Please, uh, come in," he said, stepping back.

She followed him in, leaving the front door open. Stacey was a volatile woman, after all, plus the house stank. A large garbage sack lay propped against the wall. It wasn't in a trash can, or tied up, but it was overflowing with diapers.

"Ugh, what the hell, Tony?" said Kelsey, covering her nose.

"I've been meaning to take that out, I just haven't had a minute," he said, trying to placate the wailing child.

Kelsey grabbed the bag, tied the top, and carried it outside at arm's length. Marching to the rear of the house, she shoved it into the trash chute. The compactor whirred and crushed the diapers into a cube, then swallowed them down the pipeline. Kelsey re-entered through the back door, into the kitchen.

The other child was awake, lying in a vomit-stained pink onesie. Gurgling quietly, it regarded Kelsey with curiosity. She tried to smile, but her blood was boiling. The infant was still in the cat cage.

"Last time I was here, I made myself very clear," she growled.

"Yeah, you said you'd be back to get them cribs," yelled Tony, over the wailing child.

"No, I said I'd call the cops if you *didn't* get them cribs."

"Alright then, it was a mix-up."

"So, when you realized it was a mix up, why didn't you *do* something? One of you could've bought a crib from the thrift store, I've seen them there. And don't say you were busy, I know the two of you don't have jobs," snapped Kelsey.

"Lay off, will you? I've got my hands full here."

Kelsey surveyed the kitchen. The number of beer cans had grown, attracting flies to the after-party.

"You disgust me, Tony, both of you. Where the hell even is Stacey?"

"On vacation, she'll be at least a month," said Tony, lowering the infant into the spare cat cage.

"What? Where did she even get the money?"

"I mean she's in prison, dumb-dumb. Jeez, you put on a suit and it's like you never grew up here."

"You're right, Tony. I didn't grow up here. I stagnated

here. I trod water. I limped through those miserable years to the finish line. But unlike you, when I made it into the outside world, I made a choice to grow up *fast*. Grab a trash bag."

"Why?"

"You're gonna clean this mess up. These kids are *not* having the childhood you gave me, and god knows who else before me. You've got twenty minutes, or so help me god."

With that, Kelsey marched from the house, ignoring Tony's protests. She stormed down the street, meeting the neighbors' glares with defiance, as their tracksuits and tank tops jarred against her attire. The thrift shop was shutting up for the day when she arrived.

"Just a second, sir," said Kelsey.

"We're closed, ma'am, come back tomorrow," said the owner, not looking up.

"Please, it'll be quick. I need a double crib, and any baby clothes you have."

The man caught sight of her suit.

"Is this some kinda sting? I pay my taxes, honest to god. Most of them, anyway. I'll make it right, I swear."

"It's nothing like that, I'm not from the Ministry. Well, I am, but not that department. Look, I just need some baby stuff then I'll be out of your hair. I'll give you a ten percent tip if you stay open for me."

"I don't got no double crib, but I got couple of singles oughta do it. Ya'll can check out the baby clothes while I get them."

The man opened up and shuffled off into the cavernous stock room; an overflowing Aladdin's cave of unwanted crap. Kelsey filed down the aisle, past the "fur" coats and the row of identical toasters, to the baby section. She grabbed the best clothes, plus several outfits in the sizes up, then returned to the counter.

The owner returned with a battered-looking vintage cot and a modest steel equivalent. The former had the charm of wood, but the latter was sturdier, and had wheels.

Kelsey paid the owner, tipping him as agreed, then hurried from the shop. She ignored the neighbors' stares as she rattled the steel cot along the sidewalk with a wooden cot balanced on top.

Upon reaching the house, Tony's face bore a rare expression. Joy was reserved for beer alone, but this was something better: surprise. For a man so jaded by life, being pleasantly surprised was a phenomenon as rare as Hailey's comet. Ditching a half-filled sack of trash, he hurried to the door to help unload the cribs.

"How did you get these?" he marveled.

"Well, Tony, first I did this crazy thing called getting a job. Then I used my legs to walk ten minutes to the store, where I used the money from my job to buy these basic items for your children. It's not rocket science."

They carried the cribs into Kelsey's old bedroom, which was a disheveled mixture of her old bedding, a handful of old outfits, and a box of clean diapers.

Gathering the stray clothes into a pile, she ordered Tony to exchange them at the thrift store for blankets and toys. His mouth hung open, entranced by her new manner.

Kelsey's wristwatch chimed six-thirty.

"Oh crap, I'm gonna be late for class. I'll be back, and when I come, I expect to see your kids sleeping in these cribs, wearing clean clothes, and being nurtured. Have you read the starter guide?"

"Reading's not my strong point," said Tony, with an apologetic curtsy.

"Why didn't you ask for a large print or audio version? You know they have those - they tell you at the clinic. Ugh, I can't do all of this for you. Just make it happen. Get the recording, listen to it, and do what it says. No one's expecting you to be dad of the year overnight. They're just hoping you can be more than some guy in a bathrobe drinking beer while his newborns vegetate."

He looked at her, puzzled.

"While they do nothing," she clarified.

From the kitchen, the twins whimpered. Kelsey checked her watch.

"Dammit, I have to go. Get it together before I'm back."

"Look, Kelsey, I know you think I'm a waste of space, but I wanna do right by these kids, I do," said Tony, following her to the door.

"Good. Then prove it," said Kelsey, eyeballing him.

"I will. I swear."

The twins' whimpers turned into wails. Tony gazed at Kelsey with his awestruck mouth hanging open. After a moment, he leaned in closer.

Kelsey recoiled in disgust. "Jeez Tony, you're a piece of work."

She stormed out of the house with contempt, marching with dignity until she was out of sight, then sprinting for the tram.

———

Panting and sweating, Kelsey filed across to her desk and unpacked. Thanks to her sprints at either end, she'd only missed nine minutes.

Kelsey stared at the chalkboard, trying to catch up. She was smart, but the classes moved at a pace.

At the interval, a peer reluctantly helped her catch up. Kelsey spent the second hour recontextualizing the first, while trying to absorb fresh information on top of it.

When the three-hour class finally ended, to her immense embarrassment, the professor kept Kelsey behind.

"Are you serious about your studies, Ms Bailey?"

"Yes, I'm so sorry I was-"

"Sorry doesn't cut it here. We offer these classes on a limited basis. Your presence here deprives another of this opportunity."

"But I was helping-"

"Further lateness will result in a disciplinary, and we may withdraw your place. A letter will be sent to your referee, informing them of tonight's infringement. I suggest they pay the penalty swiftly; it doubles after a time."

Kelsey approached Val's law office with a handwritten letter. It was well after business hours, but she wanted her letter to arrive first. A groveling apology and explanation might mitigate whatever damage the Ministry was planning to inflict on her referee in the coming days.

To her surprise, a lone desk was illuminated inside the office. Val was sat between stacks of paperwork, twirling something silver in her hands.

As Kelsey knocked, Val nearly jumped out of her skin. Apologizing, Kelsey leaned closer to the glass, showing her face and waving.

Val snapped the locket shut, stowed it away, then buzzed Kelsey in.

"It's late, is everything OK?"

"I had to deliver this letter. Are you alright? You look upset," said Kelsey.

Val laughed once, exhaustedly rubbing her bloodshot eyes.

"Just overworked. What's so important that you'd deliver it by hand at this hour?"

"I got a disciplinary at night school and they said it will impact you. I came to make it right."

Val's nostrils flared. "I told you night school isn't like regular school. You can't take liberties with your punctuality anymore. Come on, Kelsey, this is basic stuff."

"It wasn't my fault! I was trying to help my old family. The Ministry has given my foster dad twins of his own, and he'll ruin their lives unless someone intervenes. He had them living in empty cat cages, in that filthy house. I had to help. He's the worst, but the kids deserve better. It took longer than planned, that's all. I was only nine minutes late, and I caught up on the stuff covered, but the professor's out to get me now."

"Kelsey, I appreciate where you're coming from is hard, but you need to draw boundaries. Everyone at night school is fighting personal fires, but they have to leave it all at the door. It's tough, which is why they only take students with a referee's endorsement. The professor's pissed because you failed to do what your classmates all managed."

"I'm so sorry, Val. The professor said you would be penalized because of me. Please let me pay the fine."

"It's not the money I'm worried about, it's the procedural toll. They'll put a strike against my name. I won't be able to sponsor further students until you graduate. It's those other youngsters you should apologize to. FYI, if you fail the course, they'll revoke my referee status permanently, so don't let this happen again. Now go get some rest. You look more haggard than me."

Kelsey fought back the tears as she made for home. She kicked a trash can, furious at herself, and the world, for trapping her like this. Boarding the night tram, she opened her text books and started her homework.

CHAPTER SEVENTEEN

The five-minute warning had elapsed long ago, but they'd been too busy kissing to pay any attention. As the library's overhead lights shut off, Michael and Kelsey scooped up their textbooks and scurried down to the lobby, calling out to the night warden to not lock them in.

He waited with the door open, and an expression of polite disapproval. Being the last people out most nights, they had developed a degree of familiarity with the warden, who, thankfully, was a patient man. They wished him well, before ambling towards the tram stop.

Kelsey stroked Michael's arm as they walked hand-in-hand down the cobbled street. Michael had grown to love that path, with its bumpy surfaces, ancient brick, and quaint gas lamps. Not to mention the girl he walked it with.

Normally the pair abstained from make-out sessions while studying. Or at least, Kelsey abstained and Michael respected the rules. His grades had certainly improved since they'd gotten together.

"I appreciate how patient you've been with me," she said, giving him a squeeze.

"Isn't this how all couples date? Libraries and no-touching rules on a Friday night?" chuckled Michael.

"I'm finding this first semester tough, and I know it's making me a buzzkill. Believe me, in another world you and I would be drinking wine on a beach, but right now I've gotta stick to the plan."

"It's a solid plan. Who's gonna make the world a better place if not you?"

She rested her head on his shoulder.

"Who's looking after your grandfather tonight?"

"Uh, it's Mum's turn. Why?"

"There's a mid-semester break next week. Which means tomorrow's homework can wait."

"Are you telling me Kelsey the library-creature has a free weekend?"

She nodded, pulling him into a passionate kiss. They caressed each other sensuously, then broke away with an oxytocin-fueled gasp of satisfaction.

"So how about it?" she said, running her hands through his hair.

"How about what?"

"Coming back to my place tonight?"

Michael's eyes lit up like it was Christmas. His utter inability to play it cool made Kelsey adore him even more, as she laughed in his face. He nibbled her lip, and the pair stumbled towards the tram stop, drunk with love. He was so content, so wrapped up in his affection for her, that he didn't notice the tall, metallic figure gliding through the shadows behind them.

Kelsey's apartment was immaculate. Michael kicked off his shoes as instructed and swiped into the guest space on her census. The place smelled brand new and gleamed like a show home.

"Man, I need a Ministry job," he chuckled.

"Pff, I could never afford this place on my intern salary. This is the consolation prize for getting trapped in a mine and having my bones broken. It's a sweet deal, I'd recommend it to anyone willing to asphyxiate in darkness two miles underground."

Michael looked at her, puzzled.

"Have I not told you about that? That'll be a good story for breakfast."

She pulled out a bottle of red wine from the cupboard, and two elegant glasses.

"It's beautiful in here. So... composed. It's very you," said Michael.

Kelsey sidled back to him and placed her hands on his chest.

"Well aren't you just saying all the right things? I'm glad you approve, you're the first person to see it," she said, giving him a kiss.

"I'm honored," he replied.

"You're horny, and on your best behavior," she laughed, pressing against him.

"You got me there," grinned Michael, as they fell onto the sofa.

———

Michael awoke with a jolt and checked the bedside clock. It was 5:55 a.m. He extricated himself from Kelsey's sleeping embrace and crept to the kitchen-lounge area, pulling on his clothes.

He hunted for her house keys. They weren't anywhere obvious. He glanced at the clock on the wall. 5:56 a.m. He frantically patted down the jackets hanging in the hallway. 5:57 a.m. Cursing under his breath, he scoured the kitchen, searching every drawer. 5:58 a.m. He crept back into the bedroom and rummaged through her purse. 5.59 a.m.

"Come on, come on..." he muttered, rushing to the bathroom. As he rifled through the cabinet, a bottle of mouthwash fell, smashing on the floor. Kelsey called out, startled.

"Michael? What's going on?"

She opened the door to find him standing in a pool of aqua blue and glassy shards, searching the cupboard like nothing had happened.

"What the hell are you doing?"

Her wristwatch chimed 6 a.m.

"Where's your mailbox key?" he snapped.

His eyes were wired, his tone panicked. Kelsey frowned, perplexed, and reached for her purse. To her dismay, it was lying on the floor, among the other contents of her drawer.

"Did you go through my stuff?" she snapped.

"There's no time – the key!"

She opened a secret compartment and handed it over, bewildered.

"Michael, what's going on?"

He sprinted for the door, leaving blue footprints in his wake. Hastening down the central staircase, he raced to the building's stack of mailboxes. With trembling fingers, he found Kelsey's and wrenched it open.

"Are you gonna tell me what this is about?" demanded Kelsey, catching up.

Michael staggered back from the mailbox and slumped against the opposite wall, staring at the empty hatch.

"Hey, I'm talking to you."

She slammed the box shut and pocketed the key. Michael's eyes refocused on her face.

"I had to check, you know?"

"No, Michael, I don't. Would you care to explain?"

"If my letter had come. Or yours. I was worried. I'm always worried. I had to know, and now I do, so we can go back to bed, and it's fine. Today is fine."

"Hold up. You're telling me you do this every day? Are you insane?"

"Is it insane to value each day?" snapped Michael.

He looked tired, gaunt. How had she never noticed those bags under his eyes?

"You're getting up at the crack of dawn to check if you're gonna die. I wouldn't call that normal behavior, Michael."

"Aren't you relieved?" he said, panting.

"No! I'm disturbed that my boyfriend has some weird obsession with death!"

"What I'm doing makes perfect sense. Maybe you don't value your life as much as I value mine!"

Kelsey blinked, taken aback.

"I beg your pardon? I don't value my life? I work thirteen hours a day, six days a week, balancing a demanding job and intensive studies, because I want to *make* something of my life. I'm not the one drifting through school without a plan."

"It's easy for you to say, you don't know what I'm dealing with," said Michael.

"*Nothing* has been easy for me. Don't you for a second think you're the only one with baggage. If there's stuff you wanna work through, we can do that, but you have to talk."

"Talk? To who? You? The person who's buried in her book every time we hang out? Who's too busy to go to the movies, or get a milkshake, or just be normal? Maybe think about what you're offering before you take the high road."

The pair glared at each other, equally incensed.

"I think this was a mistake," said Kelsey, pointing between the two of them.

"I think so too," snapped Michael.

"You should go."

"Fine."

He pushed open the lobby door and glared at her, with tears forming in his eyes. She stared back at him with cold revulsion and folded arms as he left.

Drying his cheeks, Michael got off the tram. He tried his best to recite the anger in his mind, but all he felt was shame. It was around 6:40 a.m and his street was deserted; all his neighbors were tucked up enjoying a Saturday morning lie-in.

Apart from Amal. As Michael approached his family home, he could see his grandfather propped up in front of the television. Michael looked from the old man to the mailbox. With trepidation, he opened the hatch, revealing a bundle of letters. Seizing them, he rifled through with trembling hands.

Sighing with relief, he slumped against the post, clutching the pile of bills and holiday postcards from distant relatives. He padded inside, taking a seat beside his granddad. Amal pointed to the band of marauding cowboys on screen with a cheeky glint.

"They're about to get spanked by the locals," he chuckled, before seeing Michael's face. "Michael, what's wrong? You look like hell."

"You know who I am?" said Michael, astonished.

"I like to think I know you pretty well," smiled Amal. "What's eating you at six in the morning? Ah, I know that puppy-dog face. You've had a lover's quarrel. Bad luck, we've all been there."

"Have you? Mom always said you and grandma were the perfect couple."

"Perfection takes work. Take these movies for instance; your grandmother hated Westerns. I could only watch them when she was out, which meant taping them. For her part, she was obsessed with model railways, and stuffed our garage to breaking point with the damned contraptions. She would slave over them whenever she had a spare moment, which was rare, given that we were lumped with four children. Did I say lumped? I meant... lumped. Yup, right the first time," he chuckled.

"When you and grandma fell out, how did you fix it?"

"The same way you fix anything. Figure out what the actual problem is, then talk it through until you find a solution together. The most important thing you can ever do is admit when you're wrong. If you're unable to do that, it means you're either lying to your partner, or worse, lying to yourself, and neither of those paths lead to good places. Are you seeing this girl seriously, or is it just a bad date?"

"We're a couple. Or we were, at least. I screwed it all up," said Michael.

"I've had my share of screw ups. Try me - I'll let you know where yours fits on the scale."

A horse whinnied on screen as the sole surviving cowboy fled the ambush. Michael contemplated, unsure where to begin.

"I'm scared of dying," he blurted, finally.

Amal chuckled, then realized he was serious.

"Oh. OK. Er, why?"

"Same reason as anyone; I don't want to lose what I have."

"Are you seeing the irony, kid?"

"But I had to check the mail to know if I was going to-"

"Die?"

"Yeah."

"And?"

"No. Not today, anyway."

"OK, so that's a bonus. But what would you have done if your letter *had* been there?"

This dumbfounded Michael. In all his fear of discovering a letter, he'd never thought about what he might do if it actually came.

"I don't know..."

"Wrong."

The old man sighed, flicking off the TV.

"The correct answer is: say your goodbyes, be grateful to those you love, and accept your time with dignity. It's the only course of action."

"Maybe," said Michael, staring at the carpet.

"OK, it's time," said Amal. "I told your mother you needed to know a long time ago, but she was terrified you'd become just like your father. Clearly redacting the past hasn't worked; you're growing more like him every day. But that doesn't mean you need to make his mistakes."

"What are you talking about?"

His grandfather took a deep breath and looked Michael in the eye.

"When you were born, your father changed. He was a kind-hearted, loving man, and he always meant the best. But once he had you, his worldview shifted.

"It was subtle at first, because he could hide it. Whether he was in denial, or ashamed, I don't know, but it didn't last.

"Within a few years he was a shadow of himself. He was anxious, sleep-deprived, and on edge the whole time. He dreaded the evenings, because they meant morning was approaching. He checked the mail every day at the crack of dawn, robbing himself of sleep. Once he knew his fate for the day, he would loosen up, only to tighten with each hour that passed. To catch him in a jovial mood, it was breakfast or nothing.

"Things worsened when your sister arrived. He suddenly had even more to lose, and he became intensely protective of the pair of you. One day, not too long after her birth, his letter came. And he made the worst choice of his life."

Michael stared at the old man, open-mouthed. All these years, both his grandfather and his mother had buried the truth from him.

"What did he do?" whispered Michael.

"He hid it."

Michael looked at him, perplexed.

"*Hid* his death letter? What even happened?"

"For one, it meant none of us knew his time was up. We all carried on as normal, thinking life was dandy. But he started acting even more neurotically than normal. He'd take you to school, then hang around outside the gates all day, barely putting your sister down even to walk. He'd drop by your mom's office unannounced, pretending he was visiting a client nearby, but he'd quit his job already, and was just trying to eke out precious time with her."

"Can people do that? Ignore their letters?" asked Michael.

His eyes were wide, his tone earnest, two facts that did not escape his grandfather's attention.

"In all my years, he is the only person I've known who was fool enough to try. And I know he regretted it. As with all things, Michael, there is a price to pay. The Ministry work to keep life and death in balance, and your father broke the equilibrium. He only had himself to blame for what happened. For... For..."

Michael stared at Amal anxiously.

"For what? Granddad?"

The old man's eyes had glossed over. His face softened, his shoulders dropped, and he stared through his grandson's chest. Michael grabbed Amal's arms and rubbed them, trying to rouse him.

"Granddad? Please, I need to know what happened to Father. *Please*," begged Michael.

But Amal was gone. Only faint, nonsensical mutterings about pancakes escaped his whispering lips. Michael leaned into the old man's shoulder and wept.

As he did so, the locks on the front door clicked open. Michael looked up, bewildered – no one was missing from the census when he'd arrived.

A tall shadow approached the threshold. Michael's mouth dropped open as an automaton glided into the living room; the same one that had chased him before, with the unmistakable mottled blue stains across half its bronze face. It froze, extending a silent arm towards Michael and his grandfather. Michael leaped to his feet, wielding a cushion.

The automaton continued to point. Michael followed the machine's eyes to his dribbling grandfather.

"No, please, don't take him, I beg you," moaned Michael.

The automaton shook its head. With its other hand, it opened a compartment on its torso and withdrew a small rectangular strip of something glass-like. It presented the piece for Michael to examine. It was a sequela. The symbols matched those he'd seen before.

"Is this the same one?" he asked, nervously.

The automaton gave a mechanical nod. Placing the glass between its finger and thumb, it snapped the top half open.

Inside was a super-thin sheet of something translucent, bearing his grandfather's symbols. The automaton glided closer to the old man.

Michael made a desperate lunge at the machine, but it blocked him with a single arm. Pinning Michael aside, the automaton held the strip beneath Amal's nose.

The old man sniffed. Something flickered across his face. His mouth opened, and he stuck out his tongue. The automaton placed the gelatinous wafer onto it and Amal swallowed.

The color returned to his cheeks at once, and he sat up straight in his chair. Staring the automaton dead in the eye, Amal said, simply, "Thank you."

With a nod, the machine released Michael, who crawled away gasping.

"Michael?"

"It's me, Granddad," he cried, scurrying to Amal's lap.

"I can see that, my boy. I'm asking what's wrong?"

"Are you... cured?"

"Maybe. Do I look like a block of ham?"

The return of his grandfather's terrible sense of humor answered Michael's question - at least for the time being.

"I'm aware of my predicament, if that's what you mean, dear boy. What's with the machine?"

"I don't know. It put something in your mouth, then you came back. I think it's on our side."

"'Our side'? My boy, who do you think's against us?"

"Fate?"

"Fate is neither for nor against us, Michael. It's beside us, and around us, like the air we breathe. Don't fight it. Let it flow through your hair like a summer breeze and enjoy the riches it brings. Do you like that? I read it on a fortune cookie once. Delicious stir fry, if I recall."

"Granddad, do you remember what we were talking about before the automaton revived you?"

"I do now," he muttered.

"You said my father made a mistake with his letter?"

Amal's expression turned to deepest sorrow.

"You said Father hid it. What happened then?" urged Michael.

Amal eyed his grandson and the automaton.

"As our metal friend here will attest, non-compliance comes at a price. Often, it is not the perpetrator who pays the price, but those around them. Your father kept his letter hidden for five days.

"Eventually, a mob appeared at the house. Five of them were clutching black letters, distraught. They kicked the door down, and seized your father. Your mother didn't know what was happening. She called the police who, at the time, included her old man.

"I arrived with a dispatch team and knew what we were dealing with right away. It wasn't something anyone in our precinct had experienced first-hand, just something they taught us at the academy which we had dismissed as folklore.

"But there it was, happening right before my eyes. The mob smashed the windows, destroyed the furniture, and seized your father. He was beat up pretty bad by the time we got there.

"My colleague and I dispersed the crowd, but there was no denying their letters. I confronted your father and he broke down. He admitted to burying his letter in the back yard.

"I retrieved it and told him to say his goodbyes. You were away at the time at a friend's house, and your sister is too young to remember what happened, but I know your mother carries it around with her every day. I see glimpses of it in her eyes. The sadness, the anger, the shame. I don't know that she's ever been able to forgive him."

"What were the black letters? I've never heard of them," said Michael.

"When a child is assigned, the parent, or parents, receive a white letter bearing its name. Most families don't realize the Ministry can take those letters back.

"For every day that a living adult resists their own death letter, a black letter is dispatched. Accordingly, an expectant family loses their unborn child.

"It took five days for the grieving families to track your father down and attempt to drag him to the Ministry themselves.

"As it was, I took him in a police car. His deadline was long gone and every minute risked another child's life. In the end, he barely had time to say goodbye to your mother or sister.

"When it was over, I returned to your mother. She was hysterical, overcome by guilt and the shame of his actions.

Relocating was the only way to shake the stigma that it brought. We moved to this city that same week, and started over."

"Why did he do it?" breathed Michael.

"You tell me, kiddo," said Amal, with a sad smile.

As the front door clicked open, three robed automatons glided into the room. Michael shrank to the floor in fear. Amal stayed perfectly still, his lips parted, his eyes tracking the machines' movements.

The front automaton seized the rogue unit by the neck and raised it from the ground. Whirring, mechanical noises rang out, but the machine offered no resistance.

The other automatons seized its arms. With a crunch, they tore them off, before ripping its legs from their sockets. The central automaton plucked the victim's head from its torso and dropped it among the rest of its body parts.

With extreme efficiency, the three shredded its remains, tearing each component apart. The lead automaton ripped open its breast plating, revealing a core of cogs and levers. At the center was a glowing red and amber hunk of stone five inches wide. As they wrenched it from the machine's torso, the light behind its marble eyes flickered out.

The three assassins rose to their feet and stared at Amal. The old man met each machine's gaze with a defiant dignity until one by one they glided from the room. As soon as the last machine was gone he exhaled with relief and slumped back into his seat.

Michael sprang to the curtain and watched the automatons disappear down the street, his heart in his throat.

"Help me clear this up before Mom sees it," he urged. "I don't want to be explaining this to her."

"You mean you know why this happened?" said Amal, faintly.

"Granddad, I messed up, OK? I messed up real bad. On my eighteenth birthday. I chose a letter, then I changed it."

"How? That's impossible."

"The automaton glitched. I think it hinted that my first choice was a bad one, fatal maybe. So I took it back. Then we struggled, and the machine broke. So I put a different letter in my locker, and burned the others, then ran. And ever since that happened, you've..."

"Suffered?" said Amal, wistfully.

Michael nodded.

"I've tried so many times to fix it, I swear. I've been to the Ministry, but they wouldn't listen. I tried giving myself up in your pl-"

He trailed off, ashamed. Amal looked at him, aghast.

"Michael, your life is a precious thing. To throw it away on my account would be madness. I'm an old fart. My letter's long overdue. Precipitating yours to stave off mine is delusional. Think of the harm it would do your mother."

"But I have to put it right," protested Michael.

"Controlling events won't change your death, but it will ruin your life. You're not immune from injury, there are innumerable ways you could inflict lasting pain upon yourself. Wake up, kid. Promise me you'll stop this madness, or you'll end up like this thing."

As Amal gestured to the mutilated machine, a shuffling rumbled upstairs. Someone was awake. Michael hurried to the cupboard and retrieved a large suitcase. He and Amal threw the pieces inside, before Michael dragged it upstairs as quietly as he could. He hid the mass under his bed, then hastily changed and showered.

When he returned downstairs, it was to the sound of

laughter. Amal was making pancakes, and his mother and sister were enjoying flowing conversation of a sort they'd not shared in weeks.

"Michael, take a seat. Look who's on amazing form today," beamed Val.

"He can't stop - there's somewhere else he needs to be, isn't that right, kid?" said Amal, with a knowing smile.

CHAPTER EIGHTEEN

The buzzer rang twice, but Kelsey ignored it, pulling the duvet tight around her. Her pillows were stained with mascara, and her cheeks puffy from crying. Abandoned text books littered her bed; failed attempts at distraction.

The buzzer rang continuously this time, forcing Kelsey to react. She stormed over to the intercom.

"What?"

"It's Michael, can we talk?"

"Go to hell," she snapped, slamming the receiver down.

Buzz.

"What part of go to hell don't you get?"

"I made a terrible mistake and I'm so sorry, please let me explain," begged Michael.

"I'll tell you what you can do: collect your crap and get the hell out of my life."

She buzzed him in and waited. Michael scaled the steps three at a time, arriving in a flash.

"Please hear me out," he panted. "You're the most

amazing person I've ever met, and that's part of why I acted so crazy."

Kelsey folded her arms, unimpressed. "You're a time-waster, and a mess. What was I thinking, dating a guy who thinks he's cursed?"

"*Thought* he was cursed," corrected Michael, with a nervous smile.

Kelsey did not smile.

"Please, can I come in and explain? If you don't like what I have to say, I'll leave right away."

Kelsey glared at him, then took a seat in her armchair. Sighing with relief, Michael aimed for the sofa, but Kelsey's arched eyebrow checked his presumption. Instead, he hovered like he was delivering a pitch.

"OK, here goes. The day I met you, I made a dreadful mistake. I switched my letter at the Ministry, and it's haunted me ever since. First, they came for me, then they made my granddad ill. I tried atoning, but they threw me out.

"That's when you found me in the square; appearing as this amazing, captivating soul, unshackled by the tripwires of my mind. You were inspiring, ambitious, and beautiful, and you transformed my outlook.

"Because of you, I felt free for the first time in months. Plus, you saved my granddad from drowning, which was super badass. Our library sessions since then have been the best weeks of my life.

"This morning, I realized how deeply I care about you, and I freaked out. I realized this amazing new person in my life could be taken away from me, and it drove me to make the same crazy mistakes as my father did before his death.

"I don't want to be like him, I want to be here, in the moment, with you."

Michael stared, earnestly, still catching his breath. Kelsey's expression remained as hard as a rock.

"You don't have a dad?"

"Not anymore. But as I told the kids at school, what I lack in the dad department, I make up for with a doubly-awesome mom."

"How did that work out for you?"

"Yeah, they bullied me pretty bad, so I stopped saying it."

Kelsey snorted. "Been there. Fine. You get one more shot. You still have to make it up to me, though."

The phone rang and Kelsey picked up.

"Tony? How did you get this number? What do you- For real? Ugh, fine. I'm coming over."

She hung up and fixed Michael with a trying stare. "How about that, it's your chance to make amends. We're about to visit my old life."

Michael tightly gripped his backpack as he followed Kelsey to her old street. The locals were leaning out on their porches, smoking, drinking, and arguing. There were no flower beds or manicured hedgerows. The trees had carvings and bouts of graffiti on them, and dog mess punctuated the sidewalk. It was a far cry from any neighborhood he'd visited.

Kelsey knocked on the grimy door, and Tony answered in a flash. He looked like a new man. Still an odd man, but a newer version of himself. He'd tamed his unruly hair into a slick ponytail. It accentuated the bald patches on either side of his forehead, but gave his chin some unexpected definition. He was wearing a set of suit pants, a shirt, and a tie, all of which were too big for his skinny frame, but an upgrade on his previous wardrobe. Tony looked flustered and relieved to see her.

"Thank you for coming, you're a hero, an angel, a- Who's this guy?"

"This is Michael."

"Sup. I'm Tony. I raised her," said the man, beating his chest.

"No, you didn't. How long's this gonna be?" said Kelsey, pushing past him.

"Three hours, maybe? The place is across town, and I gotta do some kinda test. The kids are in bed, asleep. Wish me luck!"

He hurried down the path, giving them a grateful wave.

"Welcome to the spa," said Kelsey.

Michael followed her into the gloomy household, breathing through his mouth. They peeled into the kids' room. The twins were asleep in their adjacent cots, tucked in under thrift shop blankets.

"Are they your siblings?" whispered Michael.

"Not in the conventional sense. If foster kids count as siblings, then I guess I've got around thirty," shrugged Kelsey.

"You were fostered?"

"Nine times in fourteen years. Plus some luxury stays in the Ministry's Childcare Patronage Centre."

"What's that?"

"The orphanage. They give it a fancy name so the kids there don't feel stigmatized. Instead we feel really, really normal," said Kelsey, tilting her head and gnashing her teeth.

They both chuckled.

"Did you ever know your biological parents?" he asked, tentatively.

"Only vaguely. I was four when I got put into care."

"What happened to them? If you don't mind me asking."

"They're meth heads. Social services intervened when I never enrolled at pre-school. I got moved to this city, and I've not seen them since."

An infant cried and Kelsey plucked it from the wooden cot, soothing it against her chest. Feeling left out, the other child kicked up merry hell.

"Can you get that one?" asked Kelsey.

Michael leaned into the metal cot and lifted out the tiny infant, wincing as he copped a whiff of its diaper.

"I think this one's ready for changing," he said, with watering eyes.

He lay the kid back on the cot and stepped back like it was a landmine.

"Down there," said Kelsey, pointing to the diaper box.

Michael fished out a fresh one and looked to the infant with dread.

"Uh, how does this work?"

"If the kid has less poop on them at the end, that's usually a sign of success," said Kelsey.

Holding his breath, Michael did the deed and hushed the kid back to sleep.

Kelsey's baby was not so easily placated. Cooing, bouncing, rocking; nothing seemed to work.

"I think it's hungry," she said, over the kid's cries.

Michael followed her directions to the kitchen and heated some bottled milk on the stove, testing its temperature with his pinkie.

"Feels about right. I always thought that Home Ed class was a joke, but who knew it'd come in handy?"

"I don't recall that class. Guess I was in isolation, or suspended again," snorted Kelsey.

Michael looked at his diligent study mate with surprise.

"I'm a good student. Just a terrible pupil," she explained.

They moved to the sofa while the infant drank. Michael could feel individual springs through the stained fabric. The child slurped, burped, and vomited its way through until the bottle was empty.

"Are you ready to sleep again?" said Kelsey in an infant voice.

The kid cooed back merrily, smiling at her.

"Apparently not," she laughed.

"What now?" asked Michael, perplexed.

"Pass me that manual," said Kelsey.

Michael picked up a scuffed pamphlet from the counter. It bore a Ministry emblem, and five babies of various ethnicities. *The First Year: A Parental Guide.* He handed it to Kelsey, who propped it open with one hand and skimmed the index.

"Here we go: Chapter 4: Attunement."

She read out the instructions and shared the diagrams with Michael, who gazed in bewilderment.

"I've always wondered why my work runs neonatal workshops when we already give parents these manuals, but now I get it: this thing is like a book of riddles. Thank god I've seen this one being taught. Bring that box over, would you?" said Kelsey.

Michael retrieved the box from the counter. It bore the same Ministry of Fertility logo as the pamphlet.

"Look for two small discs and a coil," instructed Kelsey.

Michael assembled the items as per the diagram. He placed one electrode on either side of the baby's temples, then magnetically clipped the wire between them, arcing over its hairline. An alligator clip linked the wire to a small copper box.

"You need to add the crank, then turn it to generate the magnetic field," said Kelsey.

The box was stiff, cramping Michael's hand within minutes.

"Do you want to swap?"

"No, I'm good," said Michael, wincing.

He switched to his other hand and continued charging the device. An indicator panel turned from black to cloudy green.

"I think it's ready," panted Michael.

"OK, you hold the baby and I'll show you how it's done," said Kelsey.

Kelsey passed the baby across, taking care not to ping the cables off in the maneuver. She pressed a button on the crank and pulled the arm out so it was perpendicular to the box. As it clicked into place, golden streaks shot across the green portal.

The baby's eyes widened. Leaning in close, Kelsey chatted to the child, while tracing her hands along the length of its limbs. She then manipulated each limb, extending and retracting them in distinct combinations, applying pressure to key joints.

The bronze box shutdown with a gentle buzz.

"Is it broken?" said Michael.

"Nope, that just means the session's over. Developmental stimulation is carefully metered. Some parents used to be overzealous, and their kids turned out like spaghetti. So the Ministry put capacitors on the boxes. It won't let us charge it until tomorrow now," said Kelsey.

"What about the other kid?" asked Michael.

"Good point, the Ministry issues a kit for each child. Check the crate?"

"Aha!" cheered Michael.

He wound the crank while Kelsey played with the dosed baby.

"How often are parents supposed to do this stuff?" said Michael.

"Hmm. Eighteen weekly exercises, fifty-two weeks a year, I'm gonna say: a lot."

"Do people really do *all* of them?"

"Some do."

"And if they don't?"

"Their kids will take longer to catch up. Some never will."

Wiped out and starving, Michael lingered in the shabby front yard while Kelsey did a handover. Tony was mouthing off at his job rejection. Kelsey was livid, because he'd stopped at a bar on his way back, landing them with the twins for an extra four hours.

"Sober up, and start being a father," she hissed.

"Don't take that tone with me, I gave you a home!" slurred Tony.

"You gave me nothing! You think a mattress on the floor is giving someone a childhood?"

"At least you had a mattress. S'more than I got growing up," he slurred.

"Oh, OK, so as long as your life was worse than mine, you're beyond reproach?"

"You think you're some big shot now, just cos you got fancy clothes and a big job? Think you're better than us, with your *words*?" slurred Tony.

"I *know* I'm better than you, because I don't give up and get drunk at every hurdle."

"Hey guys, shall we just cool it a moment?" suggested Michael.

"Screw off, kid," spat Tony.

"Show some grace, he just spent his entire Saturday looking after *your* kids," snapped Kelsey.

"It's fine, honestly," soothed Michael. "We're all just tired. Tony, bad luck on the job. For what it's worth, you looked pro in that outfit, so hang in there. It might just be a case of refining your interview technique."

"The hell is 'interview technique'?" scowled Tony.

"It's how people get jobs these days – we got sessions at school. There are adult drop-ins at the library though, and they're child-friendly."

"I'm not dragging my sorry ass across town again just to have some Ministry type laugh at me," said Tony.

"People are already laughing at you. Sober up, get a job, and you can change that," snapped Kelsey. "We're outta here."

Draining the milkshake, Michael leaned back with a satisfied sigh. Three courses of greasy diner food later and the young lovers were glowing.

"We would make great parents," mused Michael.

"Are you kidding me?" laughed Kelsey.

"Why not? We crushed it today."

"You're aware it's still Saturday, right? Same day where you woke up, acted crazy, basically dumped me, then begged me to take you back?"

"Yeah. And now we're ready to have kids," chuckled Michael.

"You're the worst," said Kelsey, grinning into her 'shake.

"I'm kinda serious though. Today made me realize I wanna be a father someday. And I wanna raise those kids with someone I love."

Kelsey stared at him, open mouthed. "Are you for real?"

"Completely. I love you dearly."

"Oh my god. I *knew* you were a virgin," she groaned.

"That's got nothing to do with it," blushed Michael.

"I'm pretty sure it's influencing your decisions right now."

"No more than normal. You're not my first girlfriend, Kelsey. But you're the first person I've ever loved."

"Eugh. Gross and lame. Eugh, eugh, eugh, have the rest of my 'shake and shut up already."

"If I tell you I'd gladly marry you, can I have the rest of your fries too?" he grinned.

"Unbelievable," laughed Kelsey, sliding them over. "Though I'm not marrying you. You'll be dead by thirty if you keep eating like this."

Michael chuckled, tucking into his second shake. When it came time to pay the bill, he insisted on paying as contrition for their fraught morning. Kelsey, however, was insistent she pay because the childcare took so much longer than expected. They halved it, then strolled back together, arm in arm.

"If you want to come back to my place tonight, I'd be fine with that," said Kelsey, pretending to roll her eyes.

"I had plans, but I guess I could move them around," joked Michael.

With a kiss, they headed for the tram.

"Rise and shine, mister," said Kelsey, giving Michael a prod.

He groaned and blinked one eye open. Sunlight was pouring in through the window, giving her an aura of splendor.

"I've not checked the mail yet, so feel free to run downstairs and confirm that neither of us will croak today," said Kelsey.

"Nah, I'm good," said Michael, stretching.

He sat up and rubbed his eyes, then thought about what he'd just said. To his astonishment, he really was fine with it.

"Just as well - that was a test. Congratulations, your reward is making us both breakfast while I wash my hair. I've made you coffee to sweeten the deal," she said.

Planting a kiss on his cheek, she hopped into the shower. Michael yawned his way through chopping a bunch of vegetables, then fried them up with some fake bacon. He set the table, poured some orange juice, and tuned into a smooth jazz station. When Kelsey returned, she was pleased with the effort, if not the music.

After a romantic morning, they went shopping to get Kelsey more smart clothes for work. Michael was useless for fashion advice, but he relished trying on flamboyant outfits to make her laugh, until the attendant kicked him out.

With a tender kiss, Kelsey called time at the bar on their date mid-afternoon.

"It's called life admin, I have to do it or my whole

routine falls apart," she explained. "My mentor taught me the concept. I'd love you to meet her someday. See you at the library tomorrow."

Michael strutted home like he was walking on clouds attached to springboards. Short of wearing a t-shirt saying "I got laid," he was doing a stellar job of advertising his recent shift in fortunes. Not that he knew it. He was too absorbed in dreams of Kelsey to show any self-awareness.

The bubble of joy around Michael popped abruptly as he reached his house. His sister was sitting on the doorstep, sobbing.

"Sis? What's up?" said Michael, hurrying closer.

"Granddad's gone," she croaked.

"Gone? What do you mean?"

"His letter came this morning. He tried waiting for you, but you never came, and his mind was failing. By the afternoon, he was so confused he couldn't even hold the envelope. Mum took him just now."

Michael raced for the tram. His mind tumbled as he counted each agonizing stop down to the Ministry.

As he ran to the marble square, a solitary figure greeted him; his mother descending the steps, alone. Seeing her son, she broke into a watery smile, opening her arms to embrace him. Michael stepped back, appalled.

"How *could* you?"

"Michael, I know you're upset, I am too. But he's at peace now. It's for the best."

"You took him there, you didn't even try!" he protested.

"He had an appointment Michael. You can't miss your

appointment. Have you learned nothing from your father?" she said, tearfully.

"I wanted more time," said Michael. "I needed to see him, to tell him..."

"You had plenty of time, but you chose to spend it elsewhere. That's on you," she said, glaring.

With tears streaming down his face, Michael turned and ran until he could hear nothing but the sound of his own thumping heart and the wind in his ears.

CHAPTER NINETEEN

Kelsey was glad to be at work. Michael was doing her head in, moping about the place, pining for his grandfather. She did her best to sympathize, but she didn't get it. She'd never had real parents, let alone grandparents. Grief seemed indulgent. If there was one thing living with Tony had led her to conclude, it was that life could either be what you made it, or what you let it make of you. She had limited time for the latter attitude in others.

She punched into the office and headed to the fertility ward to collect that day's assignments. Each day, the list was transmitted from the central Ministry building at the square to the print room at the fertility center. They learned of each child assignment at the same time as its parents. The center was constantly pressurized, rushing to fulfil each day's unique commissions.

Kelsey tore off the list and skimmed through the names. She always wondered how many families received their letters with joy rather than despair.

As she left the print room, Kelsey slowed. There was

shouting from the management office. She pressed her ear to the wall.

"And I told *you* we need more people supervising the extractions!" yelled Professor Hestley.

An unknown male voice burbled a response which Kelsey's boss rebutted.

"How do you expect me to run this facility when you won't properly equip us? My team reported the fault multiple times, and you stonewalled us. Your negligence has caused this nightmare!"

Kelsey sprang back as the door burst open. A smartly-dressed man stormed off clutching a Ministry briefcase. Kelsey peered into the office, where her boss was leaning over the desk with her head hung low in despair.

"Is everything OK, professor? Anything I can do?"

"Unless you can go back in time and re-synthesize last night's batch, no," she groaned.

"What's wrong with it?"

Hestley laughed bitterly, beckoning Kelsey in.

"Close the door. Is that today's list of parents? Poor devils. They're in for a rough time," said Hestley.

On the desk was a report detailing cerebrium levels in the synth tank. Kelsey's heart sank as she saw the quantities.

"These children will need serious support."

"Is the toxicity above the Heuer threshold?" asked Kelsey, rifling through the report.

Hestley's eyebrows rose, impressed. "No, it's just shy, which is perhaps worse. They're not severe enough to merit termination, yet the entire family's lives will be changed forever. Sometimes I despair of our system."

Kelsey gazed across the factory floor. The Ministry official was touring the floor, consulting workers, and arguing over equipment.

"We should tell the families."

"They can't know this was our fault – it would cause untold damage to the trust people place in our institution," said Hestley.

"Blame aside, they deserve to know what they're facing."

"Delivering such news is rough. Some parents will be distraught, others angry."

"And it's our job to help them."

Clutching the list of names to her chest, Kelsey made for the lobby, ready to meet the first family.

———

She lay out the pamphlets with a deep breath, hoping family number five would be more understanding.

"I know what that is," said the mother, shaking her head in disbelief. Tears welled in her eyes.

The husband looked nonplussed as he examined the brochure. *Supporting your child through learning and developmental difficulties.*

"What's this got to do with us?" asked the father.

"There were some complications during your child's gestation period. They're likely to require support in reaching normal developmental milestones. As they progress, we'll get more of a sense of their personal cognitive and physical potential, and the Ministry will try to provide equipment and guidance accordingly," said Kelsey.

"Our kid's a freak?" said the father.

"Absolutely not," said Kelsey, aghast. "They might experience the world differently to their peers, but this pamphlet shows that, with the right support and guidance, they can grow up to enjoy lives as fulfilling and meaningful as anyone else."

"A *pamphlet*? That's it? That's our support?" cried the mother.

"We'll be referring you to a pediatrician for bi-annual check-ups, but the day-to-day care will be your responsibility," said Kelsey.

"This isn't fair. We didn't ask for this, and we don't deserve it. You can't expect us to just go along with it," said the mother.

"I'm so sorry, I appreciate this is difficult news-"

"Do you? Have you ever been told you've got a disabled kid coming?" snapped the father.

"We're leaving," sobbed the woman.

"Please, madam, sir, you can't leave, your child is waiting on you."

The couple stormed out of the counselling room. Kelsey hastened after them, pamphlets in hand.

"How the hell do we get out of this place?" cried the woman.

Panicking, the couple charged further into the maze of corridors.

"You can't go back there, it's restricted! Security!" cried Kelsey, breaking into a run.

Two automatons sped past her, seizing the couple as they reached for the antenatal unit.

"Get the hell off us!" cried the man, struggling.

The ward doors swung open. An automaton wheeled a trolley out, accompanied by a matron. On the front of the trolley a name was printed in large Ministry typeface. *Edmund Ailsbury.*

"That's my son!" gasped the woman.

The trolley stopped abruptly, and the automatons

released the two parents. Quivering, they peered into the crib.

A tiny infant lay swaddled in a hospital blanket. Protruding from the bottom were a pair of prosthetic metal legs. The child's eyelids were sunken, caving into the sockets where its eyes should have grown.

"Is it...?" stammered the father.

"Your child is blind, I'm sorry. There is an excellent school for blind children in the city, though. Perhaps, when you're ready, we could arrange a visit for you?"

"Do the kids there have no legs too?" choked the mother.

The matron hesitated, looking to Kelsey for support.

"Uh, they accommodate a wide variety of needs, ensuring every child feels included," said Kelsey.

The father lowered his hands into the crib and picked up the tiny infant. Its legs clinked as he lifted, and the baby gurgled, anxiously. The man whispered soothing words as the child whimpered, bringing it close to his chest. He moved the blanket away from its face and stroked its cheeks.

The child's arm wriggled free of its swaddling. As the father reached to tuck it back in, a tiny hand wrapped around his forefinger. The child gurgled and settled down into a sleep. The man looked to his wife, tearfully.

"This is our son," he said, softly.

The woman shook her head, regarding the child with dread. Her face crumpled as she welled up with tears. "I can't do it. I'm sorry... so sorry."

She pushed past the trolley and disappeared down the corridor.

An automaton followed, to ensure she found the exit. The other returned to duty elsewhere; with the child in its father's arms, the center's duty of care was complete.

"She'll come around, she just needs time," croaked the father.

Looking down affectionately at his child, he rocked it gently in his arms. "Do you still have that pamphlet?"

Kelsey knocked on her boss's office door.

"Enter."

The woman was pouring over graphs and technical reports from the fertility factory floor. Through the glass wall behind her, technicians had isolated half of the tanks and were undertaking a deep clean.

"I don't get it," said Kelsey.

"Get what?"

"Why are we giving children to parents that don't want them? Some of them aren't capable of being caregivers. Earlier, I had to release a baby to a couple who were high," fumed Kelsey.

"Then you should report them and let social services investigate," said Hestley, continuing her paperwork.

"They don't always do that so well," snapped Kelsey.

"Is there a problem here, Kelsey?" said her boss, removing her glasses.

"What we're doing is wrong. If people aren't capable of raising their kids, or don't even want them, why are we delivering them? There are people out there longing for children of their own. Meanwhile, other lives are being ruined by unwanted arrivals. I don't get it."

Hestley leaned back in her chair. "Look around," she said, gesturing to the factory floor. "What do you see?"

"The production line," shrugged Kelsey.

"That line has operated continuously for three hundred

years. It goes back to the first days of the city. It's been upgraded and modernized along the way, but the core alchemy hasn't faltered."

"And?"

"It's our job to keep it running. It's *not* our job to decide who gets to have children. We bring babies into the world, we unite them with their parents, and from there on out it's the parents' choices that matter."

"But don't you see? We're part of the problem. We're setting some children on a path they may never recover from. Some parents are disasters waiting to happen," urged Kelsey.

"The Ministry sets the start line, the parents choose the path, the child walks it to adulthood. We make children, not decisions. If you don't like working here, we have plenty of people clamoring for your position. But it would be a shame to throw away all that hard work at night school."

"I want to be part of the solution, not the problem," said Kelsey, sourly.

"You already are. Preparing parents to receive their child is a vital part of what we do. It shapes their mindset at a critical time, and you do it well."

A segment of pipe gushed crimson sludge onto the factory floor behind them, as workers lowered it on a winch. They scrambled to shut off the stopcock, and clear everyone away from the corrosive substance.

"I don't want parents to face those conversations ever again. I want to fix the alchemy."

"Finish your studies and maybe you'll be capable."

"Surely there's someone we can talk to at the Ministry? To stop children being born to unsuitable parents?"

"Define 'suitable'," scoffed Hestley.

"I don't know, stable income, educated, loving?"

"How do you measure those things?"

"Aptitude tests, tax data, desire,"

"And get an ever-shrinking feedback loop of family types? What about those who would make wonderful parents but lack money on paper? Or those who grow into the role? Or those who are smart and wealthy enough to game the system, then neglect their children? By restricting access, you're making children a commodity. Such a system creates problems of its own."

"So how's it run now? Random chance? A lottery behind closed doors at the Ministry?" protested Kelsey.

"As with much of the Ministry, that's not for us to know. Was there anything else?"

Kelsey was about to argue further, but held her tongue, reading Hestley's glare. "No, professor. I'm on personal leave this afternoon – family funeral."

"I'm sorry for your loss. See you tomorrow," said Hestley, returning to her paperwork.

The neighborhood was certainly well-to-do. The lawns were vibrant green, the fences painted, and the cars had all their hubcaps. Kelsey tucked in her shirt, checked her hair in the window, and knocked.

The door swung open. The two women stared at each other, taken aback.

"Kelsey? I didn't realize we had an appointment today. Sorry, it's not a good time, I'm taking some personal leave," said Val.

At the same time, Kelsey offered her own immediate apologies, "Gosh, I'm so sorry to bother you Mrs Hadley, I must have got the wrong address, I was looking for my boyfriend's house."

Michael appeared in the hallway and waved, glumly.

"Ah, there you are. Thanks for coming, babe. You've not missed much. Granddad's still dead. No one else is here yet."

Michael paused, registering the awkward silence between the two women.

"Wait, have you two not met yet? Ah crap, er, Mom, Kelsey, Kelsey, Mom."

"Actually, Michael, we know each other quite well," said his mother, dazedly.

"You do? How?"

Kelsey's heart leaped into her mouth as she braced herself for a reputational mauling. Michael's mother hadn't met her at her best. Indeed, her best had been in the weeks *after* Val's interventions.

"She was one of my most impressive clients. I've been humbly mentoring her ever since, but really she doesn't need me at all, she's got it all figured out now. Apart from her choice in boys. I hope you like waiting, Kelsey, cos this one is *always* late."

Val stepped away with a smile, leaving them to it. Kelsey blushed in amazement.

"She likes you," muttered Michael, like he was commenting on the weather.

"She's a maybe on you," said Kelsey, elbowing him playfully.

Two hours later, the house was brimming with guests. Kelsey circulated with tea and coffee, providing liquid comfort to mourners from across generations. Michael was trapped in conversation with the boatload of visitors from out of town. He pretended to laugh at their anecdotes, but Kelsey could see through the façade. Pulling him aside, she swept him up in a bear hug.

"You're doing great," she whispered.

She planted a kiss on his cheek, then hurried to the kitchen where Val was calling for her help with a sandwich delivery.

The guests assembled in the back garden, forming a horseshoe. Val clinked her glass and stepped onto a kitchen chair, using it as a makeshift podium.

"Thank you all for being here today, to celebrate the life and passing of my father, Amal. He was a wonderful man, a loving grandfather, and a constant source of joy in our lives."

She welled up, taking a moment to regain her composure, among a ripple of well-meaning applause.

A lump formed in Kelsey's throat as she stared around Michael's circle of friends and family. She slipped away to the bathroom as tears formed in her eyes. Anger, frustration, hurt, all tumbled out as she mourned the childhood she'd never had, the relationships she'd been denied, the love she'd lost. She stood over the sink and stifled her sobs.

A knock at the bathroom door interrupted her tears.

"Just a minute," she called, drying her face.

"Kelsey?"

She opened the door to find Michael standing there. He looked numb.

"Were you crying?"

"It's nothing. Just an emotional day. Are you OK?" she said.

"I need the bathroom."

They do-si-doed past each other. Kelsey stole a precious second to compose herself in the corridor, then put on her best hospitality smile as an elderly visitor rounded the corner, looking for her coat.

The wake lasted several more hours before people cleared off. Kelsey stacked up mugs and plates as Michael and his family waved off the last of the guests in the pink dusk light.

The phone rattled in its hook. Sophia, the only one with energy left, called shotgun and answered. She held the piece to her ear and frowned.

"Listen," she said, holding it out for the others to hear.

It was a prerecorded message, playing on a loop.

"This is a Ministry reminder. You have not yet checked your mail for today."

Michael's face fell. He grabbed his keys and dashed to the front lawn. Wrenching the mailbox open, he grabbed the pile of letters inside.

He tossed the restaurant flyers and local news aside and fixed his disbelieving eyes on the last item in his hands. A single white envelope with his name printed on the front in Ministry writing.

He slumped to the floor and sat cross-legged on the path, staring at the letter in his hands. Kelsey watched with a dawning sense of horror.

"What is it?" asked Sophia, skipping out.

She saw the white letter and squealed with delight.

"We're getting a *baby?* Mom, come see! We're getting a baby!" she cried.

Val hastened to the door and stared at her son in astonishment. She looked from him to Kelsey, and her lips tightened.

"I think the three of us should talk," she said, curtly.

"Actually, I'm good. I've got to get to school, I can still catch the rest of tonight's class if I run. Thanks for having me over," said Kelsey, grabbing her things.

Michael stared in bewilderment as she rushed past him, disappearing down the street.

His eyes returned to the unmistakable letter before him. *Michael Hadley*. There was no mistaking the Ministry of Fertility emblem beside it, he'd seen it enough times on Kelsey's uniform. Besides, white envelopes were only ever used for this purpose. There was no escaping it; in twenty-four hours' time, he would be a father.

CHAPTER TWENTY

Kelsey paced into her night class and took the empty desk at the back.

"Kelsey, I thought you were on compassionate leave?" said the professor.

"Life goes on."

Frowning, the professor returned to the chalkboard. Kelsey inferred the page number from her neighbor and set about catching up.

But try as she may, she couldn't focus. The professor's words were a drone, her textbook a blur. Welling up and cursing under her breath, she fled the class.

Sobbing, she hurried through the streets until she was well clear of the school. Kicking a balustrade in anger, she realized where she was.

Her flight had taken her to the very bridge from which Michael's grandfather had fallen weeks ago. As she stared at the flowing black water, she fantasized about jumping off and letting the current sweep her into oblivion. She had tried *so* hard to get her life on track, making up for lost time. For the briefest of moments, she'd started believing she could have it all; an education, a career, a loving partner. But that was about to change.

Screaming with rage, she hurled her textbooks into the river, then sank to the ground, weeping. Kelsey had always vowed to be better than her parents; to be there as a mother. But this child was coming so early. She'd barely experienced adulthood, let alone made up for her lost youth, yet now fate was forcing her to choose. Her child's future, or her own.

CHAPTER TWENTY-ONE

Michael's mother sat him down, looking him square in the eye.

"Parenthood blindsides many people. How do you think your father and I felt when you came along? We were going to move to the coast and train as surf instructors for a year. Yeah, that's right. Because we were young too, once. The beach never happened, but you know what did? The best family I could have ever wished for. This isn't the end of the world, Michael, it's a new beginning."

"That's the cheesiest thing you've ever said," grunted Michael.

Val rolled her eyes and slid a plate of cookies towards him. A rare move from the Queen of Green. These were desperate times.

"I'm not hungry."

"Eat, else you'll be no good to anybody and we need to get planning."

"I'm not ready for this," quavered Michael.

"Tough."

"They can't expect me to do this alone?"

"That's not their business. They're giving you the gift of a child and it's up to you how you use it."

She loaded four cookies into a napkin and placed them in Michael's hand, then fetched her keys.

"The hypermarket should be open if we're quick. Come on, or you'll wake up tomorrow wishing you'd done this before you had a screaming child in your hands."

The room still smelled of his grandfather. Michael and Val shoved his empty bed against the wall and placed the crib into the center.

Mercifully, Val had insisted they get the pre-assembled model. She'd also told him what else to buy and paid for all of it.

Michael's head was spinning as he cleared wardrobe space for baby onesies, cardigans, hats, mittens, socks, vests, shoes, flannels, diapers, sensitive bath soaps, and a sling. Not to mention the cleaning mat, sanitizing wipes, bath thermometer, talcum powder, and baby monitor. Or the car seat and pram downstairs.

After much rearranging of furniture, Michael and his mother surveyed the new nursery.

"If we'd checked the mail earlier, we could have painted the room. I hope your baby likes elephant gray," she said, patting Michael on the back. "Now, are you ready for a crash course in diaper changing?"

"Actually, I'm up to speed on that one," said Michael, hazily.

"Oh really? Man of hidden talents. Here's a deal, I'll put the kettle on while you set up the baby monitor."

Through her forced brightness and pragmatism, Michael knew she was exhausted, reeling from Amal's loss. He'd never felt more grateful for his mother's support and love.

Not that he said it aloud. He was still too shocked to make sense to anyone outside his head.

Val scooted downstairs while Michael unpacked the monitor.

"Is it a boy or a girl?" asked Sophia, lingering in the doorway.

"I don't know yet, I'll find out tomorrow," said Michael.

"They might be neither," she mused, swinging from the handle.

"That's true."

"Why did Kelsey leave?" asked Sophia.

She used a rising intonation of such unconvincing innocence that Michael almost chucked the stack of flannels at her.

"Mind your own business."

"Does this mean you won't be going to university?"

This time he threw the flannels. Sophia scarpered, vowing to tell Mom, while Michael slammed the door. Nausea took hold as his future dissolved before him. Dreams of engineering vanished into the wardrobe of soothers and onesies.

As the night swept on, Michael sat in his bedroom, contemplating the new world awaiting him. He longed to hear the doorbell ring; to find Kelsey there, begging him to take her back and raise the child with him. But as dawn broke, he realized she wasn't coming. He was alone in this.

CHAPTER TWENTY-TWO

"Switch me to another duty," begged Kelsey.

"After yesterday's little outburst, you're in no position to be making demands. Do your job, or find a new one," snapped her boss.

Hestley slammed the door in her face. Kelsey slumped against the wall, clutching the day's list of inbound parents. There was nowhere to hide.

She straightened her shirt, then approached the lobby, agonizing over how professional to act.

"Mr. Hadley?" she called.

Michael gave her a filthy look. "So it's like that, huh?"

"I'm sorry, I didn't know how to... Where's your mom? I thought she'd be with you?"

"Mom's got work."

"So it's just you?"

"I don't know, Kelsey, is it just me?"

Blushing, she pretended to consult her checklist. "Uh, this way, you're ward three."

She led him through the labyrinth of corridors to the

antenatal unit, parking him in the seats outside. "If you wait here for a second, I'll be back with your child."

Hurrying into the ward, she navigated her way to the designated child in bed F11. As she reached the infant, her heart skipped a beat. The child was rasping; its bedsheets splattered in red. A metallic band clung to the poor child's midriff, dovetailing with stitches and bloodied gauze.

Kelsey glanced at the neighboring crib where a baby slept without complaint. Her heart pounded. The unit was deserted, save for automatons administering milk in the adjacent wards. Reaching into bed F11, she scooped the sickly infant up and switched it with the neighboring child.

She disposed of the bloodied sheets, then wrapped the healthy child in a blanket and carried her out.

"She's all yours," said Kelsey.

Michael stared at the tiny infant before him, sleeping so delicately. His heart melted as he cradled her, marveling at her warmth, the sweetness of her scent, the fragility of her body.

"Hush now, I've got you," he whispered.

A lump formed in Kelsey's throat and her eyes glistened as guilt rose within.

"Good luck, Michael," she uttered, disappearing into the ward.

Kelsey lingered by the doorway to the factory floor. As an automaton glided through, she took her chance and slipped into the restricted area. It was an hour past closing time, and the human floor staff were gone. Automatons operated the equipment by night, and Kelsey was determined to find out where things were going wrong.

She ducked behind a cooling tank as two machines drifted by. Undetected, she crept after them, staying hidden behind tanks and piping.

The automatons stopped before an aged wooden sculpture. It was four feet high and shaped like a human, with androgynous anatomy. The figure's head was bowed, and its arms hung by its sides. It stood on a circular platform carpeted by greenery. The wet moss covered much of the figure's lower half and was growing upwards across the cracked torso and arms. A narrow moat of water and lush flora surrounded the sculpture's feet.

Standing either side of the figure, the machines waited. Ripples radiated outward from the base of the statue. Kelsey gasped as the sculpture's head twisted round to meet the gaze of the nearest automaton. Its arm creaked as it raised its left palm out flat, facing up. The automaton extended a metallic arm and made contact.

Opening a hatch in the sculpture's hand, the machine turned to its partner. The second automaton passed a die-sized cube to the first. It bore a complex surface of groves, which the lead automaton slotted into the wooden palm.

The sculpture re-centered its head. Creaking, its ribcage opened up and outwards like wings unfolding. Water gushed from its body until all that remained in the dripping, damp cavity was enamel piping.

Two thick pipes rose from the sculpture's legs, converging in the torso like an upturned tuning fork.

A shadow passed up from the left leg pipe into the central block. As the top segment swung open like a doorway, the automaton reached into the dripping cavern and pulled out a dark capsule.

Twisting the top off, it removed a thin slab of glass from the middle, which it passed to its colleague. With the empty capsule replaced, and the pipe sealed, the wooden ribcage creaked shut.

The automaton retrieved the cubic key, and the sculpture lowered its arm, dipping its head.

The machines left the mossy pool and glided to a large metal cage. Using its fingers, the lead automaton split the glass slab like a pistachio shell. It teased out a shimmering strip covered in symbols. Kelsey recognized the strip's colors from the cerebrium she'd excavated in the mine.

The lead automaton placed the strip onto a golden grill hanging from a chain. Its colleague added droplets of serum, causing the hues of amber and gold to drain from the mineral strip into a collection pot below.

With the gelatinous strip rendered translucent, the assistant disposed of it, along with the cracked slab, while the lead automaton attended to the filtrate.

Carrying the pot, it glided over to a vat too tall for Kelsey to observe. She hastily scaled the maintenance ladder, relying on the factory's extraction fans to mask the noise of her steps.

The vat was full of yellow, milky water. In the center was an island of wet, gray sand, onto which the automaton poured the golden solution.

As its colleague returned, the pair lifted paddles from the rack and took up positions on opposite sides of the vat. Gliding in sync, they stirred half a rotation in one direction, then three quarters the opposite way. Kelsey had never seen automatons move like this. Their bodies loosened, swaying, as they augmented each paddle stroke with full body convulsions. The effect was a mesmerizing fusion of martial art, ritual, and dance.

As their movements became more complex, the mixture

thickened into a paste. The stirring turned to folding, then kneading, and sculpting. Repeatedly, they molded the paste into symbol-like shapes, then back into nothing. Kelsey realized they were making the same nine symbols in succession; creating and destroying them in ever quicker cycles until the clay was rising and falling like a virtuoso ballerina.

Their movements halted. The machines bowed to each other, then glided around the vat. They caressed the clay with their paddles, smoothing it into a perfect pebble.

Something clattered from the neighboring dock. Kelsey crept along the walkway to investigate.

Below her, two automatons were tending to a broad, shallow clay pot, like the one she'd seen in her interview weeks before, only this one had a lid.

The clay dish was suspended above a roaring flame. Boiling brown liquid oozed down one side of the pot, escaping the trembling lid. Using a chain pulley, the automatons raised the pot off the flame, shunted it along a rail, and lowered it onto the mesh floor.

They prized the lid off with a lever and stood back as steam billowed up, forcing Kelsey to recoil. Broiling fluid spilled over the pot's sides and into the underfloor gullies.

As the steam cleared, Kelsey's eyes focused on the inside of the pot. Her jaw dropped. Inside was a half-formed infant, curled in a ball, forged from blistering gray clay. Only the legs and lower arms were intact. The clay child's upper half had ruptured and was dissolving in the brown amniotic solution.

Lowering an overhead pipe, the automatons released a torrent of cold water onto the sizzling clay.

As the billowing steam cleared, Kelsey watched in

horror as the automatons scraped out the remains of the half-formed child. One flooded the clay dish with cleansing agents, while the other dumped the clay corpse in a refuse cart.

It wheeled the remains to a pit, locked the cart into position, and punched a control button. With flashing orange bulbs and a ringing bell, two trapdoors opened. Smoke belched from the smoldering pit, clearing to reveal a churning inferno.

Below, a mechanical grinder tore through blistered clay and boiling paste. With the crank of a lever, the cart tipped up, flinging the child's remains into the hellhole.

A metal hand seized Kelsey's shoulder. She yelped in fright as an automaton snatched her from the ground and glided along the platform at speed.

"I won't run, just put me down!" implored Kelsey, as they descended the elevator.

The machine obliged, but kept a firm hand on her shoulder as they stepped onto the factory floor. Kelsey gulped as it marched her to her boss's office, rapping its metal knuckles against the door.

"Enter," came Hestley's clipped reply.

Her face soured as the machine thrust Kelsey in.

"Infiltrating a restricted area? Did you learn nothing from your interview? You'd better have an excellent explanation or I'm calling the police."

"I'm sorry, boss, I was only trying to understand!"

"Understand what?"

"Why birth abnormalities are increasing. It's devastating so many families, and you're expecting me to deliver these kids to them with no way of explaining what went wrong, or preventing it again."

"What if nothing went wrong?"

"What do you mean? I just saw-"

"What do you think our purpose is here, Kelsey?"

"Making life."

Hestley shook her head. "We neither create lives, nor take them away. Such responsibilities lie with the Ministry alone. *We* fulfil orders. Every commission is unique, bringing with it infinite possibilities."

"Possibilities like defects?"

"There are no 'defects'. The Ministry encodes every child most deliberately."

"Then explain that hellish fire pit," fumed Kelsey.

"Occasionally, errors arise during the bake, which result in termination. These are deeply regrettable, and an inherent risk of what we do."

"So we *do* make mistakes?"

"None that leave these doors. If human error causes irreparable damage during a bake, the infant is terminated, and the guilt is ours to bear."

"I don't understand. How can you say we only release successful bakes, when we have patently unhealthy children awaiting collection?"

"Every child on the neonatal ward is exactly as the Ministry intended them."

"But intentional defects bring untold suffering to both family and child! Why would they-"

"It is not our place to challenge the Ministry's wisdom, or the principles of our covenant, Kelsey. There is a reason that area is restricted; we only allow access once workers are qualified and emotionally equipped to understand what they're seeing. However, you've circumvented the protocol designed to protect you, and in doing so, have created a fork in the road. What you witnessed cannot be unseen. Where once you may have left this place, your freedom is now forever bound to it. The Ministry cannot allow this knowledge to corrupt the masses. If you leave, knowing what you know, they will ruin you. Stay, and you can achieve the transcendental. Are you a slave to your misguided principles, or are you ready to uphold the sacred?

CHAPTER TWENTY-THREE

Michael woke with a start. It was 4 a.m., and the baby was bawling. Again.

"Michael!" yelled Sophia, thumping the wall from her bedroom.

"On it," he groaned.

Groggily, he hurried through the darkness, stubbing his toe on route to Amal's old room. Even the slightest baby gurgle still caused him concern. Yesterday he'd found her chomping a sock and nearly had a heart attack. The Ministry guarantees that she'll live to be eighteen, but what condition she arrives in is down to Michael.

He scooped his daughter up. "Shhh, shhh, Daddy's here," he whispered, rocking her.

Olive was defiant; proudly utilizing her full vocal range. Michael's sister yelled again, forcing him to retreat downstairs.

Pressing Olive to his shoulder, he bounced her up and down, while one-handedly retrieving formula from the fridge. He warmed it on the stove, then took a seat on the armchair as she fed. Olive had his grandfather's spirit; food had been the only thing that ever shut him up.

Twenty minutes later, she was placated and back in her crib. Michael collapsed face-down onto his mattress, exhausted. When he woke again it was 9 a.m. His mother was at work, and his sister at school. In a delirious haze, he poured orange juice onto his cereal, and propped his text book open on the kitchen table. The words blurred as he tried forcing his sleep-deprived mind to mechanical physics. Slapping his cheeks to stay awake, he started to get into the flow.

Olive cried from upstairs. She was up for good now. Which meant changing time. Then bath time. Then washing the bed sheets. And the blankets and clothes from yesterday's dribble and sick. Then feeding time again, because apparently it was always feeding time. Then it was time for the Ministry-mandated sensory stimulation exercises.

"Let's see if Daddy can figure out today's puzzle," he said, smiling exhaustedly at his child.

He affixed the magnetic cranial stimulation kit to her scalp without incident - both of them had become used to that part of the routine, with the help of a distracting song Michael had composed. It helped him remember the steps required to set up the damned thing, and seemed to keep her entertained as she joined in with merry gurgling.

He consulted the Ministry of Fertility's bewildering instructions.

"Successively tap each of your child's joints. Follow these with mirrored movements on your own body. Now lightly manipulate your child's hands to touch their own joints in the same order. Repeat this full-body scan eight times. Conclude with a soft-tissue massage using the exercises on page two."

Michael groaned, looking at the clock. Where had the morning gone?

"OK kiddo, here we go," he said, with forced brightness.

By the end, Olive needed changing again. Then he had to dry the clothes that had been washed earlier. And wash his clothes, which now had fresh streaks of baby sick across them. Then feeding time. Then auditory stimulation exercises from the manual.

The slamming of the front door woke Michael abruptly. He sat up, mopping the dribble from his mouth. He'd fallen asleep on his textbooks again.

"Here are your next assignments," said Sophia.

His sister dumped a sack of books and print-outs on the kitchen table, then marched upstairs.

"Oh, and your dumb friends are here to see you," she yelled.

Michael checked Olive was secure in the Moses basket, then answered the door. Three of his school friends were lingering on the front lawn.

"There he is, dad of the year!" called one.

"Good to see you, buddy," said another, grabbing him in a bear hug. "Woah, you smell funky."

"Yeah, babies have that effect," sighed Michael, raking his chaotic hair into place.

"Can we see her?" asked the third friend.

"You'll have to be quiet; she's sleeping."

The three guys followed him into the house, pretending they hadn't heard his request to take their shoes off.

"Dude, she's super cute," whispered the first.

"What's this thing?" said the second, picking up the cranial stimulation kit.

"That's for her attunement," said Michael, snatching it off him.

"Her what?"

"Do you guys pay any attention in school?" said Michael.

"Not really," laughed the third.

As they caught up on school life, Michael felt a rush of energy; anecdotes of his old teachers and playground rivals brought laughter and joy. But as the conversation wore on, bitterness set in. His friends' care-free, cavalier attitudes infuriated him.

Olive stirred, and Michael seized his opportunity to turf out the trio. Hiding behind childcare excuses, he waved them off, assuring them he'd try to make soccer on Friday.

Flouting the roster, Sophia refused to cook dinner, arguing that she had too much sleep to catch up on. Michael's evening study slot thus became cooking the family meal.

Val got home late and exhausted while Michael cleared up. The pair were too tired to catch up in any meaningful way beyond superficial pleasantries. She ate in silence as he tried to cram some last-minute study. Within a few minutes, Val had crawled to bed. Michael followed suit not long after, as the lines on his textbook swirled.

His daughter had other plans. Namely, a sleep-bleep test; seeing how quickly she could wake up again, raising merry hell before Michael rushed in to soothe her back to sleep. Val attended the fourth instance, but the fifth awakening was back on him.

No matter what he did this time, Olive refused to settle. Donning the harness, he wrapped his daughter up and took her out into the cool night air.

As he shuffled beneath the flickering glow of their

street's gas lamps, he glimpsed metallic figures working ahead. Sheltering behind a tree, he watched on.

Two automatons were lowering a square enamel pipe into a trench, which led from the roadside to a new property on the corner.

As one covered the new pipe with soil, the other approached the property's front lawn with a tall sheet of metal. Raising its arms high, it drove the metal into the ground, hammering on the top until it was half-buried. It repeated the action with a second hunk of metal, also about the width of Michael's shoulders.

The second automaton joined. Gripping one embedded sheet each, steam gushed between their fingers as the metal glowed red hot.

They wrenched the sheets from the smoldering ground. Somehow the bases had fused together, forming a V-shape, and enabling them to extract a two-meter slice of earth. In its place they installed a rectangular pipe and soldered a mailbox on top.

They seeded the bare soil, then loaded the construction materials into a truck and departed. Michael traced the new home's trench to the distant, up-lit dome of the Ministry.

He looked from the Ministry to the infant sleeping in his arms and fear swept across him. He knew minors didn't get letters. But parents did. And he could attest to the impact that had on a child.

Hurrying home, he laid his sleeping daughter to rest in her crib, then set his alarm for 5:55 a.m. Tomorrow could be his last day, and he couldn't bear the thought of letting it slip like he had with Amal, or getting it so wrong like his own father had. To protect her from death, his or otherwise, he had to know what was coming.

CHAPTER TWENTY-FOUR

Three weeks had passed since Olive's birth. With finals imminent, Michael urgently needed to study, but he was a haggard wreck. His dreams of university were becoming so distant, he wanted to skip finals altogether. With Olive wreaking havoc on Val and Sophia's lives, he knew he needed to get a place of his own ASAP, which meant getting a job, not pursuing further study.

But Val was adamant that he graduate high school first, insisting she use her annual leave to babysit Olive during the exams.

Michael leaned over the cot, reading his revision flashcards in a cooing baby voice. Olive gurgled back, happily filling a diaper as he spoke.

Sophia burst in from school, distraught; a girl she liked had spurned her in the canteen. Michael gave her a hug, then encouraged her to talk it out while he changed Olive. He did his utmost to pretend her myopic concerns mattered, offering supportive "mmm-hmms" throughout the tirade. Alas, after several minutes his weary mind slipped into torpor. Next thing he knew, his sister was storming off, decrying his callousness.

He took Olive down to the kitchen, placing the Moses basket on the counter as he prepared dinner while reciting physics equations.

The doorbell rang. Michael scooped up Olive and went to answer.

Kelsey stood before him. She looked professional, beautiful, and embarrassed. Michael's heart leaped upon seeing her, but his face hardened as the hurt of her abandonment came rushing back.

"Can I come in?"

"I'm kinda busy," he said, tilting Olive forwards.

"I'm sorry I screwed up. It was awful, and I totally understand if you don't want to give me another chance, but-"

"OK great, so I guess we're done here?"

"Wait, please! I panicked, alright? My entire life I've been ignored, forgotten, bounced between families and houses. I promised myself when it came time for me to have a kid, in the distant, distant future, I'd do it right; I would be there."

"You've nailed it so far."

"I know I failed you both, but you gotta know, I never wanted it this way. I've been fighting the odds since I was a kid. Finally, just as I've managed to drag myself out of the gutter, get a proper education, a career, a loving relationship, it's all thrown into the air. I couldn't handle it."

"Sounds tough. At least our relationship is one less thing you need to worry about now."

"Don't you get it? This sorta thing is precisely why I avoided a relationship! Your priorities get changed, and next thing you know, you've got no qualifications, no job, and I've become a useless meth head like my folks."

"*That's* what happened to your parents? Why didn't you tell me?"

"Because I'm ashamed! You're from this normal family, with money, and a car, and I'm from the state, from the street, from nowhere. The truth would have scared you away."

"Yet in the end, it wasn't me who got scared off."

"Not because I didn't love you! I was afraid, is all. I couldn't sacrifice my future for a baby. Not yet."

"Sensible call. It's been the nail in the coffin for mine."

"But I don't want it to be all-or-nothing. We should be able to have both, surely, even if some things take longer? I'm reducing my hours at work so I can take Olive for half the week during your finals."

"Very noble. Quick question: how will a small family afford to live off one person's junior part-time wages?"

"I thought maybe your mom could help us out, cover your half of things if you're living at mine?"

Michael shook his head. "If only. I know we look comfortable from the outside, but Mom's treading water. She only told me this after Granddad's death, but we owe compensation to a lot of other families after my father's... Never mind, it's not important."

"Hey, I told you my parents were addicts and that I was homeless, you could at least be straight with me. You once told me you don't have a father anymore, but you never explained why?"

Michael closed the door behind him and whispered so his sister wouldn't hear.

"My dad tried to outrun his death letter. Five newborns were terminated because of him. Mom has to compensate each family until the kids' eighteenth anniversaries. Now you know why she works so late. Granddad did a lot of the after-school childcare while we were growing up. If he had died at the same time as Grandma, I don't know what would have happened to us."

"That's awful, I'm so sorry."

Michael watched as realization spread across her face. "It's all making sense now, hey? Why I was crazy about checking the mail?"

Kelsey nodded, blushing. "I don't know any good way to say this, so I'll just say it. I want you in my life, and I want this baby to have two parents. I want to do this with you, Michael."

Michael nodded without smiling. For weeks he'd dreamed of this moment; Kelsey begging him to take her back. Yet it felt cold. The romance they'd shared was from another life.

"It wouldn't be like before," warned Michael. "Us, I mean. Our lives. It would be hard for a long time. I mean *really* hard."

"I know, and I'm committing to the long-haul."

"After my finals, you'll have to go back to full-time work. It's the only way we'll be able to afford to live," said Michael.

"I know. I'll have night school too, so we won't see each other much. But we could meet during my lunchbreaks? The canteen's child-friendly," she smiled, nervously.

The sound of a saucepan lid hitting the floor echoed from the kitchen as a pot boiled over.

"Crap - dinner. If you're serious about this, you can start proving it from now. Here, take Olive while I finish cooking. Her soother's upstairs if she needs it," he said, hurrying inside.

Kelsey's heart melted as she stared at the beautiful, wriggling baby in her arms. She imagined the myriad of paths her life could have taken, and tears formed in her eyes as she clung proudly to the one she was choosing. The one with her wonderful, precious daughter, Olive.

But in the back of her head, a dark truth grated, growing louder by the second. This wasn't the child they were supposed to have.

CHAPTER TWENTY-FIVE

EIGHTEEN YEARS LATER

Michael couldn't sleep. Even on the higher dose, the meds couldn't stop his whirring brain. He slipped out of bed, careful not to wake Kelsey, and crept downstairs to the basement.

Two decades' worth of marital detritus greeted him. He waded through the junk until he found a dusty suitcase. It was heavier than he remembered. The case jangled loudly as he lay it flat, flicking the latches open.

Pieces of metal glistened like a treasure trove. He lifted out the severed arm, enamel breast plates, reams of cogs and levers. Realizing the scale of the task, he hastily set down several dustsheets, before methodically laying out the components.

He surveyed the debris with a heavy heart. Even if he could figure out how to reassemble it all, there was no guarantee it would work again. Besides, would its reactivation somehow summon the Ministry to his doorstep again? That very fear had kept him from attempting the repair it before now. But things had changed. Olive was no longer a child, and that meant there was a much greater risk at play.

The clock chimed for 6 a.m. Michael rushed upstairs, out to the mailbox. Closing his eyes with dread, he gathered all his strength and wrenched the flap open. Today was critical. With trembling hands, he rifled through the stack of letters.

Sinking to his knees, he dropped the pile and wept with relief. Damp grass soaked through his sweatpants as he rocked.

Four doors down, a neighbor's mailbox slammed shut. The man disappeared before Michael could see his face.

Wiping away his tears and brushing the grass from his knees, Michael headed inside. To his surprise, his eldest daughter was up.

"Olive?"

She paced about the kitchen with a frenetic energy, flitting between tasks.

"Are you OK?" asked Michael.

"Excited," she gasped.

"There's no mail," said Michael, waving the stack of bills triumphantly.

"There is mail, you're holding it."

"You know what I mean, none that matters."

"Dad, no one cares about the mail except you. God, you're not gonna go all weird on me, are you, now that I'm eighteen? Have you taken your meds?"

Michael's face hardened.

"That's not for you to ask," he snapped.

"What? I want you to be chill and enjoy today, rather than go all loopy again," she shrugged.

"Hey, watch your tone missy!"

"It's not 'missy' anymore, it's ma'am."

"Are you kidding me? It's been ma'am for like ten minutes, you wanna pull that kinda power play already? At least wait til lunch!"

"I'm a woman now, Dad. Get used to it."

Olive stomped off upstairs. Michael mentally cursed whichever Ministry official had decreed that eighteen-year-olds *weren't* children.

He hurried down to the basement and cleared the fragmented automaton back into the suitcase. Now was not the time. He hid it, padlocked. The broken parts were calling to him, but he had to lay low. Like Olive said, he couldn't go all loopy on her, not today.

Mid-morning sun bathed the Ministry square. Rays glinted across the gilded inscription around the dome.

REGULATING LIFE TO LIBERATE LIVES

Michael swallowed nervously as he glared at the all-too familiar words, writ large across the imposing building.

Kelsey and Olive looked stunning in their finest attire and elaborately styled hair. Michael had tried his best, but having distinctly fewer follicles to arrange, he reaped less spectacular results.

Damien and Leon, their two boys, joked around with their second cousins, who were visiting for the occasion, while Olive nervously practiced the creed under her breath.

"Why are your fingers covered in oil?" chided Kelsey.

"Oh, I checked the car tires earlier, didn't want to risk us being late," lied Michael.

Wiping his hands on a handkerchief, he hastily erased the evidence of his automaton tinkering in the basement. If the others found the broken machine, they'd freak, and there were certain questions he wasn't ready to answer.

Val arrived, bestowing a hug upon her granddaughter with the air of an elder stateswoman. Hot on her heels was Michael's sister, Sophia, and her wife, Nina. Despite the occluded weather, Nina was wearing sunglasses, and her cheeks looked puffy.

"Have you got a second?" asked Sophia, taking Kelsey aside.

"Always," smiled Kelsey.

"Congratulations on the promotion. Director, hey?"

"You heard? Thanks! That means a lot. When my predecessor announced her retirement, I was worried they might bring someone in from another city. I still can't believe they chose me; it feels like a dream come true."

Kelsey couldn't help but grin from ear to ear. Eighteen years of hard graft, while juggling a young family, night school, and the baggage of her own past. She'd climbed from being the most junior employee, to Director of Fertility.

She was glad to see the back of Hestley. The outgoing director had grown sour over the years as Kelsey's brilliance had shone through. Initially, Hestley had wielded the threat of reporting Kelsey to the authorities for 'spying' in the restricted area as an intern. Kelsey later learned from Val that this was saber rattling. Suppressing evidence is a felony, so Hestley would have been incriminating herself were she to report Kelsey so belatedly. Once Kelsey learned that, she stopped tolerating her boss's foul attitude, and they moved to protracted cold war; each holding a nuclear deterrent for the other.

When Hestley had first given her the 'with us or against

us' choice between complicity and prison all those years ago, she had framed it as a duty, almost like she was offering Kelsey a way up in the world. With hindsight, Kelsey could see she was just covering her tracks, making up for lax security and protecting her own record.

Kelsey swallowed as the bitterness of that moment resurfaced. She had just learned that the Ministry was routinely encoding deformities into newborns, offering no explanation or support to the families. Hestley had been right; it was a fork in the road. Against the odds, Kelsey held her tongue. She doubled down at night school, became indispensable at work, rose through the ranks, all with a single goal: challenge those insidious sacred principles, and change the system for good.

Finally, she was at the top, wielding the power to challenge the Ministry. She was psyching herself up for the battle ahead.

"Kelsey?"

She snapped out of her daydream and realized Sophia was staring expectantly at her.

"Sorry, what did you say?"

"I said... Uh... Given you're top dog now... Gosh, I can't believe I'm asking this so soon, it's really not... But we're desperate and... OK, I'll come right out with it: we need your help."

"With what?"

"Having a kid, obviously. Nina and I have been holding out for eight years and it's breaking our hearts, not to mention ruining our marriage."

Sophia paused, choking up. Kelsey placed a consoling hand on her arm.

"Please, there must be something you can do as director?"

Kelsey's youngest son, Leon, bounded over, interrupting with a photo request. Kelsey assured him she'd be over in a moment. Sophia faced away, hiding her tears.

"I'm so sorry Sophia, my center doesn't allocate the babies. It's the Ministry who commission births and stipulate the recipients."

"I don't get it, but you're the Ministry of Fertility!"

"We're builders, nothing more. The central Ministry are the architects. They tell us what to build and where it belongs, we make it happen. I know the system's unfair, and believe me, I wish I could help, but it's not in my gift right now."

Sophia composed herself, then gave Kelsey a hug.

"Congratulations again on today, you've raised a wonderful young woman," she said, choking up.

Sophia hastened back to her wife and the pair distanced themselves from the group, consoling each other in private.

Meanwhile, in the thick of the clan, Michael was fussing over Olive.

"Now remember, when they present you with your envelopes, don't touch any of them until you're certain. Once you touch one, that's it, you're committed," he said, smoothing the sides of her blazer.

"You've told me this like a gazillion times already," she scowled.

"And be respectful of the Ministry officials. That's of the utmost importance," he continued.

"Dad, I get it. I won't screw it up. Are you done?"

Olive's fidgeting fingertips betrayed her nerves, so Val came over to patch up the cracks.

"You'll do just fine honey, it's as easy as picking a sandwich from a deli. There's nothing to worry about."

Olive eyed up the Ministry building fearfully. A rich

chime reverberated from the mighty dome. With a gulp, and much fanfare from her sprawling family, she began the ascent.

Michael watched his daughter at the celebratory meal after. Relief had returned her confidence, and she led the table in jokes and laughter. He, however, was tense. Overnight, the world had become an infinitely more hostile place for his family. He glanced around the restaurant. Were the other diners staring? They definitely were. Michael glared at a couple nearby, his eyes narrowing.

"Relax, hun, you're acting weird again," whispered Kelsey.

Michael feigned a casual smile and shifted his gaze, as he'd become so adept at doing. Kelsey gave him a kiss on the cheek, then headed to the bathroom.

When she emerged from the cubicle, Sophia's wife was there, lingering at the sink.

"Hey, can I have a word?" said Nina, awkwardly.

"Nina, you must believe me, there's nothing I can do. I know it's tough but you have to hang in there."

"There must be something, please, I'm begging you. We've done all we can, yet our prayers go unanswered. It's like we're invisible to the Ministry, like our pain means nothing to them. I'm only coming to you because we're desperate. We're good people, you know that, all we want is a family of our own," she sobbed.

"And you both deserve it more than anyone, but you have to understand, I make babies, not parents."

"Can't you reassign one to us?"

"That's prohibited," said Kelsey, nervously.

"But I heard that sometimes babies get switched?"

"Where did you hear that?" snapped Kelsey, eyes blazing.

"Just... around. You know, you hear things."

"Well, I've never heard of that. Certainly not on my watch. We're done here."

"Please, Kelsey, all we want is a baby!"

"And I can't give you that, alright? I can't just make extras - the Ministry sends the genetic information to us for each child. God, why are we talking about this? It's classified! This conversation ends now," said Kelsey.

Kelsey reached for the door, but Nina grabbed her arm. "Please, Kelsey. This is ruining our lives."

Kelsey broke free, alarmed. "What you're asking is both illegal and immoral. I can't even imagine what the punishments would be. I'm sorry Nina, but my hands are tied."

———

Snuggled in bed, Kelsey and Michael reflected on the day.

"I can't believe our baby girl's an adult," said Michael.

"Mmm," said Kelsey, distracted.

Michael rolled onto his elbow. "You OK?"

"Something your sister said. Nina, too. They both want me to work miracles."

"I'm sorry. I shouldn't have suggested it."

"You *told* them to speak to me? Michael, what were you thinking?"

"I was thinking maybe my wife, the Director of Fertility, could help my sister and her wife have a baby."

"That's not how it works," groaned Kelsey.

"They're two of the most caring people in this city, surely they deserve-"

"Why do people suddenly think I control this? Our department has *never* been involved with assignments! How many times do I have to say it?"

Michael pondered for a moment, then lowered his voice. "Could you bump them up the waiting list?"

"There *is* no waiting list! There are recipients, and that's it; who gets what is decided before the letters go out. What you're asking is impossible, not to mention unfair. Drop it," snapped Kelsey.

She flicked her lamp off, huffing into the darkness. Dejected, Michael rolled over, glancing at his bedside clock. Seven hours until the morning mail. Seven hours to Olive's fate.

CHAPTER TWENTY-SIX

Ninety-six babies due in forty-eight hours. More than double the usual average. The Fertility Center was at maximum capacity and running behind. Necking a third midnight coffee, Kelsey rubbed her eyes and scanned the list of expectant parents, ensuring they hadn't missed any commissions.

Her eyes lingered on the penultimate family. The Broxleys were due to receive triplets the day after tomorrow. Kelsey grimaced, seeing their zip code. She'd been fostered in that area, and it was no place to raise a family. She paced the room, wringing her hands, as Nina and Sophia's tearful pleas rang in her ears.

Kelsey drew the blinds and stuffed a sheet of Ministry headed paper into her typewriter. She copied the Broxleys' birth commission form, changing only the parents' names. Splitting up the triplets wasn't an option – it would cause too much of a paper trail.

An automaton glided into the office. Kelsey froze, fingers hovering above the keyboard. The machine delivered a chemical report then paused, noting the Broxleys' open certificate.

"That will be all, thank you," she quavered.

The machine gave her a modest bow and glided away.

Snatching the forged document from her typewriter, she placed it among the authenticate commissions. She tucked the original birth certificate in her jacket pocket, knowing she would need to dispose of it away from prying eyes.

With her fingers trembling, she forged an announcement letter for the triplets, then hurried from the office.

Kelsey parked her car a few blocks away, then approached on foot. She counted down the sleeping households until she reached Sophia and Nina's home. An argument raged upstairs in the only illuminated room.

As Kelsey tried to listen in, a cacophony of barking erupted before her. She sprang back as the neighbor's dog snarled against the fence. Kelsey thrust her forged letter in the couple's mailbox and beat a hasty retreat.

The midnight streets were quiet, and she was home within twenty minutes. Michael was pacing the living room in his pajamas, apparently rearranging the books on the shelf.

"Michael. Go back to bed," she yawned, stepping through the door.

"Ditto that," he said, taking her jacket, chivalrously.

"Leave it," snapped Kelsey, snatching it back from him. "I'll meet you upstairs, I need a minute."

"Everything OK?" he asked.

"Work stuff. How come you're up so late?"

"Couldn't sleep. I was thinking about... you know... so I tried distracting myself with a bit of feng shui. Like what I've done with the place?"

He gestured to the shelves, which he had stripped of books and transformed into a photographic shrine to their children.

"Did you take your meds?"

"They were delicious. My compliments to the chef, whoever that is. Probably some faceless automaton, knowing the Ministry," he yawned, heading upstairs.

Kelsey waited until Michael was in the bathroom, then set about hiding the letter. She knew she ought to burn it, but she couldn't risk someone finding her in the kitchen mid-act, and the garden was equally risky, unless she wanted to make a show of it and stoke an entire bonfire as a rouse. No, it had to be quick and discreet. Somewhere she could light a flame. The basement!

Kelsey seldom ventured into the basement; it was very much Michael's personal cave, where he lived out his frustrated engineering dreams with half-complete model trains and matchstick bridges. She surveyed his messy empire, and wondered what might have become of his career if he hadn't borne the brunt of the childcare. He was a loving father, if over-protective, but he'd loosened up since the medication started. He was sleeping full nights again, which was a huge turning point for them.

Kelsey tried the desk drawers, searching for a lighter, but they were locked. A clatter upstairs. Someone was fetching a drink from the kitchen. She had to act fast - no time to burn it, she would have to hide the letter and come back later. Maybe that was for the best, anyway. Knowing the Ministry, burned letters probably release some sort of chemical that the automatons can sense. In fact, the more she thought about it, the more dangerous the idea of burning it seemed. This was not a situation she'd ever anticipated, and her only choice now was to adopt the least-bad option.

She approached the shelving and looked for the dustiest item there. It was an old chocolate box. She popped the lid open and peered inside. Her heart softened as she discovered the treasure trove of childhood postcards from Michael's grandparents.

Kelsey perched on Michael's shabby work seat, ignoring the chunks of foam that protruded through the torn fabric. She barely recognized the old man in the photograph; she'd only met Amal once when he was alive, when she'd fished him out of a river. Back then he'd looked so lost. Here he looked vibrant - she could see where Michael got his cheeky glint from.

The handwriting on the next card was familiar - it was from Michael's mother, wishing him good luck with his exams at elementary school, and another for his mid-grade exams. Kelsey stared at the words on the page and felt a sadness in the pit of her stomach, seeing the love and encouragement she'd never received as a child.

She thought of the consternation she'd gotten from her foster parents, the rows that would break out if she asked for text books, the fights she got into at school when other kids called her out for having smelly clothes, the derisive attitude towards education and the authorities that had prevailed in the households she'd passed through. If it wasn't for the mining accident, and Michael's mom agreeing to be her sponsor, maybe she'd never have climbed out of that rut.

Plucking the last item from the tin, she marveled at the inscription.

Michael Senior, loving father, beloved husband.

Below it was an order of service, detailing songs and readings, and the reception address.

Flipping the card over, Kelsey gasped as she saw Michael's father for the first time. There were no photos of him anywhere in the house, nor at Val's or Sophia's places.

The man was the spitting image of his son. Kelsey recognized that melancholic smile at once; the look of someone very much in love, and very much treading water. She stroked the photo and covered her mouth as tears formed across her eyes.

Shoving the cards back into the tin, Kelsey buried the stolen birth certificate deep among them. She stowed the tin away, ensuring it aligned with the shelves' dust marks.

Creeping back upstairs, Kelsey climbed into bed and took Michael in her arms.

"I'll always be here for you, no matter what. I hope you know that," she whispered.

He patted her hand, hazily.

"Me too, my love."

Kelsey woke in a cold sweat. It was 5 a.m. and a terrifying thought had struck her. Grabbing her jacket and keys, she bolted for the car.

She'd been so preoccupied with delivering the forged certificate, she'd forgotten about the original. In less than an hour, the Broxleys would receive their *authentic* baby letter from the Ministry. She had to intercept it, or the whole plan would be exposed.

Kelsey sped across town to her old foster district. Her

gleaming car jarred against the decrepit burned-out shells dotting the sidewalk.

She scoured the broken windows, fallen fences, and boarded doorways. The neighborhood was abandoned. The Ministry had removed the residents' mailboxes, leaving only the narrow posts protruding from wild ground.

Yet two parents were due to receive a child somewhere around here in a matter of hours. With the Broxleys' address etched in her mind, she counted down the houses, continuing until she reached the end of the street.

Her mouth fell as she reached a crossroads. A new estate stretched ahead for several blocks. The front gardens were manicured, and the homes beautifully renovated.

Kelsey slowed to a crawl, drinking in the pristine neighborhood until she reached the Broxleys' house. The gentle rays of dawn caressed the pastel window frames and velvety lawn.

Ditching the car, Kelsey hurried over, wincing as the gate squeaked open. Screwdriver in-hand, she crept toward the family mailbox.

In all her years, she'd never examined one in detail. There were no rivets to unscrew; it fused seamlessly with the enamel pipe rising from the grass.

Besides the keyhole, the only way in was the narrow hand-delivery slit between the hood and the front panel.

Forcing the screwdriver into the slit, she levered down. It held firm, so Kelsey threw her full body weight against the handle.

The screwdriver slipped out, slamming Kelsey to the ground and grazing her knuckles on the way.

Cradling her bleeding hand, she fished for a handkerchief in her pocket. She wiped down the mailbox, then tied it around her knuckles as a bandage. With no alternative, she plucked out a hair clip and turned her attention to the lock.

Engine noises pricked her ears as a cleaning cart approached. The automaton in charge was driving the suction van close to the curb, while two humans paced ahead, sweeping leaves and litter off the sidewalk into its path.

Kelsey scrambled away from the approaching workers, pressing herself flush against the side of the house.

Her screwdriver lay abandoned on the lawn, glinting in the morning sun. Kelsey held her breath as the workers approached. Neither batted an eyelid at the splatters of blood on the grass beside it.

In the room above Kelsey's hiding place, an alarm clock rang. A light flicked on, and a pair of sleepy voices muttered to each other.

Cursing, Kelsey darted for her screwdriver. She snatched it off the ground, wiped the last of the blood splatters up as best she could, and smoothed the chipped paintwork on the mailbox with her thumb. At a glance, it looked normal, but on the slightest closer inspection, the scratch marks told a different story altogether.

Kelsey hurried through the open gate and sprinted to her car. She sped home, making it across town in just fifteen minutes.

On arrival, she checked their own mailbox which was mercifully empty, then slipped back into bed beside Michael. His feet were cold and damp, but she didn't have the bandwidth to ponder why. Her head was already spinning. She had broken the law, and failed to cover her tracks. Consequences were coming, and she knew it.

CHAPTER TWENTY-SEVEN

Michael thrust lunch bags into his boys' hands and hurried them out as the school bus tooted by. Kelsey rushed out in the opposite direction, blowing Michael a kiss as she dashed for work.

He and Kelsey had decided he should only be in the office three-and-a-half days a week while the kids were still at school, to make sure someone was at home when they got in each day. He also did all the cleaning and laundry, meaning they could keep the household running without needing paid help.

Michael poured himself another coffee as the laundry churned. Ever since Olive's eighteenth birthday, his compulsive mail-checking had returned.

Kelsey had been so tired from work the past few nights that she hadn't noticed him sneaking out at the crack of dawn to check. He wondered how long he could get away with it before it triggered another colossal row.

Clapping his hands, he pushed that to the back of his mind and headed to the basement for his favorite part of the week.

He took an old jam jar that was sitting atop his toolbox and rootled through the decoy bundle of electrical wires until he found a key.

He pulled out a folding photo frame, and set it on the desk. Smiling at the portraits of his father and grandfather, he set about his work. Unlocking the desk drawers, he laid out a mound of paperwork.

"Where did we get to?" he muttered.

It had taken years to amass these resources, and curtailing his research to one modest day a week took all of his will power. That and a generous helping of medication designed to curb his "obsessive qualities". If by "curb" the doctor meant "learn to hide better", then Michael considered the medication a resounding success.

He spread out the materials and flexed his fingers, feeling the familiar rush of excitement. He *knew* he was on to something, but he had to work fast; any day now the Ministry could silence him for good.

The paperwork was a rich portfolio of evidence. Cuttings from old newspaper obituaries, fragments of old Ministry handbooks, funeral notes, and hand-written notes from the handful of interviews he'd conducted in secret.

The one thing they all had in common? Deaths. *Undocumented* deaths. Michael still had so many questions to answer. How did these people die? Why did they rebel against the system? Why is there no public record of their passing? Whatever the outcome, he was going to blow this whole thing wide open.

Michael consulted his watch; the next interview was due to start in a few minutes' time. He was to call a contact he'd been pursuing for weeks. A man whose wife had vanished after her death letter, only to reappear six days later, begging him to hide her.

Michael had found an old newspaper cutting which referenced the woman's death, and noted that the date differed to that of another report, which had prompted him to dig deeper. It was a sensitive area, and the widowed man had terminated Michael's first three calls. None of this was helped by the fact that the woman died thirty years ago, and the widower's hearing was failing. But, finally, he seemed open to talking.

Michael had requested a face-to-face meet, but the elderly man remained skittish, so Michael settled for a phone call for now.

As he reached for the receiver, ready to dial the man, the phone rang. Michael froze, blinking. He wasn't expecting an inbound call. Maybe the man had misunderstood?

"Mr. Carter?" said Michael.

"It's your sister," said Sophia, panting.

"Is everything OK? You sound a bit off."

"Michael, the most amazing thing has happened. We're having a baby!" she cried.

Michael cheered with joy, and for a minute the pair tumbled over each other with excitement, questions, and exclamations.

"Woah, woah, slow down, you're telling me Nina doesn't know?" said Michael.

"She left for work before I checked the mail, and now she's in surgery all day. It's going to be the most wonderful surprise when she gets home tonight! I can't believe it, this is a dream come true. But I need your help. I've got to get the house ready for our baby. Work's given me the day off to prepare, and it's your day off too, right?"

Michael stared at his desk of investigative materials, and the photos of the dead father figures in his life.

"Er, not exactly my day off, but... Of course, I'll be right over," he sighed.

CHAPTER TWENTY-EIGHT

Ministry birth commissions were at their seasonal peak, pushing the fertility center to its limits. Kelsey's assistant tapped on the door and leaned into her office.

"Your family's here to see you, ma'am. They're in reception."

Kelsey did a double-take.

"My family?"

Her own kids had no business being there, and she shuddered at the thought of former foster parents showing up. Her mouth dried as she realized what time it was.

She paced through to the neonatal delivery unit, where Sophia and Nina were tearfully clutching their three babies between them.

"Triplets!" proclaimed Sophia, joyously.

"We had no idea," gushed Nina.

The pair were grinning from ear to ear with watery smiles.

"They're perfect. Thank you, and your whole team, for making our dreams come true," said Sophia.

"We do our best," smiled Kelsey.

"Do you want to hold her?" asked Nina, offering up one of the children in her arms.

Kelsey took the infant and basked in a moment of pure joy, with the two delighted new mothers. As she looked down at the child, a sense of guilt nagged at her; a sadness she couldn't quite articulate.

"I should be getting back to work," she said, handing the child back to Nina.

"Oh, of course. We just wanted to see you, and say thanks. You've saved our lives, I can't begin to tell you," gushed Sophia.

"No thanks needed, just doing my job. I'll catch you guys at the ceremony on Saturday," said Kelsey.

She paced away from the women.

"Director, can I borrow you for a moment?" called a receptionist.

Kelsey diverted her path for the main lobby and approached the front desk.

A couple were standing nearby, being restrained by a security automaton. The adults were in their late thirties, slightly overweight, and red in the face. The man clutched a letter in his hand and was glaring at the staff.

"This family say they have an appointment today, but there's no record of them on the system," said the receptionist.

Kelsey's mouth dried.

"May I see their letter?" said Kelsey, extending a hand. *Melanie and Kevin Broxley.*

The heading was followed by the names of their triplets, today's date, and that very collection time.

"We got this in the mail yesterday. How can we not be on the list?" protested the man.

"Please, we've been waiting for children for years," implored the woman.

Kelsey stared at the letter, trying to control the tremor in her hand. She made a show of consulting the day's roster, which she knew didn't contain their names, having compiled it herself that morning.

"I'm afraid there must have been some sort of mistake, you're not on here," she said, returning the clipboard to the clerk.

"There must be something you can do? We can't just leave. We've prepared the house, we've told all our family," stammered the woman.

"We *want* this," begged the man.

"I'm sorry, this facility doesn't do assignations, we merely fulfil the commissions we receive. The Ministry handles all letters. It's possible there was an error on their side? Or maybe this was a hoax?"

"A hoax?" said the woman, her eyes widening.

"It happens, from time to time. Like I said, we have no record of you at our end, so I'm afraid we can't help. I wish you all the best with your endeavors, but I must be getting to a meeting now," said Kelsey.

"Please help us! The Ministry won't listen - we tried asking before, when we were desperate for kids. Now this happens and it's too much. You must have some contact with them; you work for them, right? Take the letter - maybe you can show it to them?" begged the man.

Kelsey looked at them both, and took in the despair and hope in their pitiful eyes.

"I'll see what I can do," she said, tucking the letter inside her jacket pocket, and turning on her heel.

Kelsey closed the door to her office and hurried to the window. She drew the blinds then slumped into her chair, dizzy with guilt.

In the gloom, she stared at the Broxleys' authentic letter and her eyes fell on the Ministry emblem.

Her heart skipped a beat. She pulled her drawer open and checked the headed paper she'd used two days prior - the crests were different. It was subtle, but it was there. She had to find her forged version and modify it before anyone noticed.

There was a knock at the door. She stuffed the letter into her jacket and dried her eyes.

"Director, I've got the files you just requested," said her assistant. "Are you OK?"

"I'm fine, pass them here, thanks," sniffed Kelsey.

She rifled through, looking for the birth certificate she'd forged for Sophia and Nina's triplets, but it was gone.

"Where's this morning's cohort?"

"Oh, they've been sent to the archives already, ma'am, for Ministry processing. This is tomorrow's batch. Is there a problem?"

"No, that's fine, thank you," said Kelsey.

Kelsey stared at the folder with a hollow pit in her stomach. This wasn't good.

Kelsey waited until her colleagues had left for the day, then hurried to the elevator, descending two levels below ground. She made her way through the long, echoing corridors, past the vast stock rooms where they kept the wealth of chemicals required for the clay solutions, and past the equipment rooms, where automatons were carrying out nightly maintenance of the factory's kiln components.

She reached the archive room, but it was locked. Being classified as a central Ministry jurisdiction, humans were prohibited inside; it was for automatons only.

As she peered through the window, an automaton glided towards the door. Kelsey leaped back and hid around the corner as it glided away, trailing her original path. Kelsey darted through the closing door, into the archive room.

As the door slammed shut, the overhead lights flicked out. Kelsey froze, waiting for her eyes to adjust. A soft glow diffused through frosted glass bricks in the floor above.

Kelsey marveled at the room. It was far deeper than she expected. Thick enamel pipes stretched from the ground upwards. She could only guess at what they supplied. Are these what fed genetic material to the wooden sculpture?

Stacks of filing cabinets lined the room on both sides. In the center was a segment of fence; two thick timber bars blocking the path. Kelsey stepped closer. The rear side had metal buffers affixed. Above them shone a red signal light.

Extending away from the buffers were train tracks leading to a metal shutter on the far wall. The vast archive room appeared to connect to a gated tunnel.

A clang sounded as shadowy figures glided across the basement overhead. Kelsey felt a shiver of scrutiny and hastily refocused; she had to find the Broxleys' file before it was shipped to the central archives forever.

She searched the cabinets, soon finding yesterday's date. But the folders inside were blank; no names, and no certificates. Instead, the cabinets contained graphs she'd never seen before.

Some listed elements, others detailed the ingredients in

each tank, and heat-humidity ratios of the kilns. The cabinets opposite held the same data for a date nine months prior.

Kelsey marched to the far end of the chamber and dug out the oldest records she could find. They went back decades, revealing lists of elements she didn't recognize. She seized a file that predated her own birth and compared the ingredients with those from the current set up.

The results shocked her. As far back as the records went, the Ministry had been experimenting with birthing procedures. They were using the two factories to run split tests on the alchemy of the fertility center. And the evidence was hidden in the vaults of a chamber accessible to automatons only.

Somewhere in the corridor, a door slammed. A shadow moved across the windowed door. Kelsey stuffed the files back and dived behind a row of cabinets.

The archive room door buzzed open and the overhead lights flickered to life. An automaton glided into the row behind her. Kelsey felt the cabinet rumble against her as the drawer opened.

A klaxon sounded from the far end of the room, and an orange light flashed overhead. A great rattling shook the chamber. Kelsey peered out to find the automaton facing the train tracks expectantly.

The shutter lifted, revealing a dark tunnel beyond. A distant light was growing brighter, and with it the clattering of metal. A cart slammed on its brakes as it burst into the room, screeching to a halt just shy of the buffer. The compact engine on the front let out a cloud of steam, which vanished into the vents overhead.

The cart was brimming with rectangular strips of glass, each embossed with symbols colored in the precious sunburst colors of cerebrium. The automaton fed the individual strips onto a vertical belt, which conveyed them through a ceiling hatch to the level above.

With the cart emptied, the automaton cranked a lever, rotating the end segment of track 180 degrees. A green light shone above the tunnel.

Steam billowed from the driverless engine, and it chugged its way back into the darkness, while the shutters closed behind it.

The automaton glided back towards the exit and held its palm to the wall. Kelsey, realizing this was her only way out, hurtled after the machine and through the closing door, landing as quietly as she could in the corridor. She held her breath painfully until the machine had disappeared.

Gasping, she hastened to the elevator and back to the human levels. She had failed to swap the Broxleys' letters. But she had learned a disturbing truth. They were experiments. Each and every one of them.

Her mind turned to her children. Was Olive from Factory A? Was that why the baby she'd switched her with was ill? Because it was from Factory B? Or was it the opposite way around? Was Factory B making things better?

Her head spun. All this time, she'd worked to improve the lives of children. What if this whole facility was making them worse? What if she was facilitating something unspeakable?

CHAPTER TWENTY-NINE

"I'm sorry about the other day, Alfie, a family thing came up, you know how it is," said Michael, the next morning.

Against all the odds, he'd got the old blighter back on the line, despite missing their long-awaited phone meeting.

"You were going to tell me about your uncle. I understand there was a complication around his death?" Michael gripped his pen, poised to capture the old's man's testimony. "Hello?"

The line went dead. Michael slammed his receiver down in frustration. Why were these people so hard to contact?

The basement door swung open and Olive descended the staircase. Michael leaped from his chair and swept the paperwork from his desk.

"What have I told you about knocking!" he cried, shielding the pile behind his back.

"What's with the papers?" said Olive, peering down from her vantage point.

"Private!"

"Ugh. Weird. By the way, Mom says hurry up."

Michael tidied his papers away, locking the drawers. By the time he was upstairs, the others were waiting in the car.

"I still don't get why we've got to spend our whole Saturday at some baby thing," protested Olive, as Kelsey drove them onwards.

"Hey, I'll have you know when your mother and I were your age we were hosting our own 'baby thing'," said Michael. "Who was that for again? Oh yes, *you*. As a teenager, your auntie Sophia had to put up with you crying every night for two whole months. The least you can do now is repay the favor by eating free cake and meeting your new cousins."

"We won't be there the whole day, sweetie, relax," added Kelsey. "We're going to show our support, then we'll leave them to it, give them space."

"What are you talking about? They love having people round," said Michael.

"Maybe some people don't love *being* round," snapped Kelsey.

"Yeah!" agreed Leon, their youngest.

"Don't you start," groaned Michael.

"Speak for yourselves. I love free cake," shrugged Damien.

"That's my boy," said Michael, reaching backwards to low-five his docile middle child.

As they crossed Sophia's front yard, the neighbor's dog went nuts with excitement, startling the life out of Kelsey.

"That damned animal," growled Kelsey.

"Jeez, Mom, it's just a dog, chill out will you?" snapped Olive.

Nina rushed out to greet them on the porch.

"Thank you *so* much for coming," she gushed "Come on in, there's plenty of cake!"

"Roger that," said Damien, piling in enthusiastically. Olive and Leon followed closely behind.

"Sorry about the dog – new neighbors, new nightmare. Please, after you," beamed Nina.

"How did you already know about the dog?" muttered Michael, following Kelsey inside.

"Oh, er, I saw it from the car when we were looking for a spot."

"But we came from the opposite direction?" frowned Michael.

"Leave it, will you? I can't do this right now," snapped Kelsey.

Michael backed away with his hands raised, and followed after his kids in search of cake.

Thirty minutes later and Kelsey was seated on the sofa, in a fog of her own thoughts, nursing an untouched slice of something.

"You gonna eat that, Mom?" probed Damien.

To his astonishment, she handed it over, then stood resolutely. With a deep breath, she approached a crib, where one of the babies was sleeping. The sleeping child was strapped in by a harness, while the mechanical crib rocked it gently.

"Isn't it amazing? We just *had* to get one. They sleep like little angels when they're in one of these nests. It was crazy expensive, but totally worth it for the peace and quiet," said Sophia, sidling up.

She had one of the other triplets in her arms.

"Say hello to your auntie," she cooed, waving the baby's hand at Kelsey.

Kelsey forced a smile and waved back.

"This one's been sleeping in a Moses basket. When Michael helped me with the baby prep we thought we were only getting one child, you see. Then we turned up at your facility and we got three! It's incredible! I could've sworn the Ministry normally puts the number of kids on the letter though, right?"

Panic swept over Kelsey. Her mind flashed to the start of the week, when she'd been crawling around Sophia's garden in the darkness, feeding a forged envelope into their mailbox.

"Kelsey?" said Sophia, bringing her back down to earth. "They normally print the numbers, right?"

"Uh, yeah, normally. Weird, huh," muttered Kelsey.

"Don't tell me they're gonna take two of them back," laughed Sophia, digging Kelsey in the ribs.

"No, that won't be happening. Excuse me, I'm not feeling so good," said Kelsey.

She hurried out of the party and onto the front lawn, where she vomited against the mailbox. Michael caught up with her.

"Woah, honey, are you OK?" he said, placing a hand on her back.

"I'm fine."

"You don't look too great, maybe I should drive you back?" he suggested.

"Michael, just leave me alone. I got this," she said, wiping her mouth.

"Got what? You wanna tell me what's going on? You've been acting really weird this whole week."

"You wanna tell me what you're doing in that basement of yours? Don't think I don't know about your locked drawers."

Michael's face sagged, taken aback.

"That's what I thought. You keep your secrets, and I'll keep mine, how about that? I'll get a cab home - don't follow me right away, I need some space from your family. I'll see you back at the house."

Michael watched perplexed as his wife straightened up and marched away. This wasn't the Kelsey he knew; something was seriously wrong.

CHAPTER THIRTY

For so long, a chip had rested on Kelsey's shoulder. Her former director, Hestley, had given her an ultimatum: to fall in line or face prison for her bold incursions into classified business. Kelsey had chosen to partake in a broken system, with a vow to herself to make it better from within. By rising up, she could challenge the status quo, she had reasoned. Yet, eighteen years on, the system felt more broken than ever. She was the director, and all she had achieved in that time was a sticking plaster. As she surveyed the excited crowd before her, guilt swirled in her stomach. If only they knew the truth. The experiments. The secrecy. On her watch. And she was powerless to stop it.

She blinked hard, trying to bring herself out of her guilt and despair, into the present moment.

The crowd bustled through the gleaming new building. Children and adults with metal limbs and permanent electrodes on their scalps played with the center's toys and giggled together, supervised by a new clutch of automatons wearing soothing pastel uniforms over their shiny exteriors.

Exhausted family carers seized the precious time to enjoy the free coffee and snacks, and adult conversation with their peers. Photographers mingled in the crowd, catching candid shots of the attendees, while reporters interviewed the delighted families.

Kelsey straightened her lapels, then stepped up on a chair and clinked a flute of orange juice.

"Ladies, gentlemen, NBs, thank you all for being here today. It is my honor and privilege to formally open the first disability resource center in our city. Neonates, adults, and their support network are all welcome here. This space allows those with individual needs to be supported in their development from day one, and for their families to connect with others along the way. Thank you for your support, and here's to no child being left behind," said Kelsey.

She raised her glass proudly, to enthusiastic applause from the hundred or so attendees. Photographers buzzed around her while reporters jostled to get their questions answered. Kelsey fielded a barrage of inquiries into the cost of the new building, the disability rates among the center's newborns, and the long-term goals for the center. This was followed by in-depth interviews with each newspaper and radio network.

After two hours, Kelsey was exhausted. She left her colleagues to close the event, and headed out into the forecourt.

"Director?" came a call from behind.

A besuited woman hurried towards her. She had a long, red ponytail and clutched a notepad.

"No more interviews today, thank you," said Kelsey, marching onwards.

"I'm not a journalist. I'm Detective Clarkenwell. We are unburdened."

"May we use it well. How can I help you, detective?" said Kelsey, taken aback.

"There's been a report of malpractice in your department. Birth defects, children going to the wrong parents. Does that ring any bells?"

Kelsey swallowed, hard.

"No, it does not. We follow best practice at this institute. If there was malpractice, I would know."

"Mind if I drop by the office, take a look at the records?"

"Of course. I trust you have a warrant?"

The detective's face soured.

"It's being processed."

"Excellent. Make an appointment with my staff once the warrant's in place. Perhaps I'll see you in a week or so," said Kelsey.

"I'll have it first thing tomorrow," said the detective, coldly.

Kelsey paced away towards the fertility center, feeling the detective's eyes lingering on the back of her head. She hurried through the lobby and weaved through to her office, checking over her shoulder several times as she went.

Kelsey hit the elevator button and waited for the doors to close, then collapsed against the side, gasping for breath. The doors chimed open and an automaton stood in the threshold. Kelsey stepped past it awkwardly. The machine's head rotated, keeping its gaze fixed on her, as its body glided into the elevator.

Kelsey hurried through the corridor, past the mechanical and chemical rooms, to the archives beyond.

She peered through the door window, to the tunnel at the far end. The orange light was flashing, and the klaxon sounding. The hatch opened, and a steam cart puffed into the room. An automaton appeared from the sidelines, carrying a bronze filing cabinet, which it deposited directly on board. It rotated the cart, then dispatched it again. The whole operation took less than a minute. With the exchange over, the automaton glided from the room.

Kelsey slipped inside as it left, hastening to the area the machine had been lurking. It had been tending to the opposite row to her explorations the day before.

Hidden in the shadows was a line of tattered bronze cabinets, distinct from the others. Kelsey pulled the nearest drawer open and rifled through. There it was; the date she'd been searching for.

She grabbed the folder and placed it flat, then flicked through until she found the birth certificate she'd forged for Sophia and Nina's triplets. Now she knew what to look for, it was easy to spot. She snatched the record and tucked it into her jacket, then lay in wait by the door. It took an hour for another automaton to come by and give her an out.

Hurrying through the lobby, she bid farewell to the night porter, then set off for the only place she could think to go.

Kelsey entered the tattoo parlor. The tiny shop looked like a lantern strapped to the corner of a derelict neighborhood, where two in three street lamps were defunct.

The bearded, bare-armed tattoo operative was a human billboard for his own trade. Barely a patch of skin was untouched by some swirling emblem. His customer was a shaven-headed man of similar age, receiving a curious pod of dolphins to the top of his neck.

The buzzing tattoo pen shuddered to a halt as she entered. Both men glared at Kelsey.

"Is Carl in?" asked Kelsey.

"You a cop?" replied the tattooist, warily.

Kelsey lifted the base of her shirt to reveal a set of wings tattooed on the left side of her abdomen.

"Old customer," she said.

The tattooist jerked his head backward. Kelsey followed the steer though a beaded curtain, along a corridor stacked with laundry machines, past an empty room with large floor cushions and opium pipes, until she reached a door.

She glanced back at her lengthy escape route, then knocked.

A man opened the door with improbable haste. He had more piercings than a pin cushion, at least as many tattoos as his colleague out front, and a pink feather boa draped around his shoulders.

"Who are you?" he snapped.

"You don't recognize me, Carl? I've not aged *that* badly," winked Kelsey, flirtatiously.

"Kelsey?" he gasped. "You look... like a fed."

"Relax, I'm not here to bust you. That is, assuming you're willing to help out an old friend? I need a favor."

Carl's eyes flicked to the distant storefront.

"Dammit. Come in," he muttered.

His cupboard-sized office made the storefront look like a stadium. Shelves clung to every inch of wall, from floor to ceiling, stuffed with contraband from passports, to money, to powder.

"Still plying the old trade huh?" she said, eyeing up the stock. "I thought you'd have learned after my parents."

Carl shifted uncomfortably.

"What do you want?"

Kelsey pulled Sophia and Nina's letter from her jacket.

"I need a central Ministry emblem on this document."

Carl inspected the paper.

"You know these people?" he said, curiously.

"Never mind that. Can you do it or not?"

"How much?" he said, attempting to recline, and immediately hitting a shelf.

"Put it this way. If you *don't* do this, I'll tell the cops all about your little powder party back here, and the things I saw when you hired me as your "intern". If I recall, the pay never materialized for that role, did it? Some would call that fraud, Carl."

The man scowled. With much muttering, he retrieved a forgery kit.

"Wait on the sofas. I'll be thirty minutes," he snapped.

Kelsey took a seat in the hazy shisha room. The thick smoke scratched at her eyes and scorched her lungs until she could bear it no longer. She staggered out into the night air, spluttering, to recover against a broken street lamp.

Carl marched out to find her sometime later.

"I said the *sofas*," he snapped. "Since when do we do transactions in the street? Wait, is this a sting?"

"If this was a set up, I wouldn't have breathed your crappy air for twenty minutes. Gimme that!"

She snatched the letters and examined the forgery of the forgery. The new emblem was spot on.

"Nice work. This makes us about a thousandth of one percent even for you ruining my parents' lives forever," said Kelsey, tucking the paperwork away.

"Naw, girl, we're even. You're in deep too, got the feds breathing down your neck, I can tell. Which means you won't be snitching on me anytime soon."

He grabbed her coat and pulled her close, boring into her pupils with bloodshot eyes. His breath stank of stale cigarettes and powder.

"Don't ever threaten me again. Understood?"

Kelsey broke free and stepped back, heart racing. The days when she would have shrugged such intimidation off were long gone. She had a family of her own now. Violence meant something.

Carl spat by her feet, then stormed back toward the parlor.

"And don't ever come back!"

CHAPTER THIRTY-ONE

Michael signed for a parcel, stowed it beneath the reception desk, then let his eyes glaze once more as workers swiped into the building without bothering to greet him.

He had barely slept, waiting for Kelsey to come home. He pondered her absence last night. When she had finally rung the house at 7 a.m. it was only to say she'd been held up in the office after the night porter allegedly locked her in a store room.

Michael twirled a pen in his spare hand. It didn't stack up. Either she was having an affair, or her work obsession was spiraling. He didn't know which was worse.

He fielded some calls, signed guests in, and waited for the morning rush to subside. As 9:30 a.m. came around, he surreptitiously lifted a notebook from his satchel. He turned to the page with the folded corner, and scrolled down the list of crossed out names.

~~Ellen Mundie - parent disappeared~~
~~Beth Keller - arrested~~
~~Jonathan Hardwick - abductor?~~

~~Chrissie Coles - neighbor still alive~~

He reached the next name on the list.

Owen Drakes - ghost?

Michael dialed the first of several numbers he'd found for the mysterious man. It rang out, so he tried the second, only to be met by a young woman's voice. Wrong number.

Visitors and colleagues interrupted his inquiries, forcing him to terminate calls and hide his notebook each time until he was free from scrutiny. Michael worked his way through the numbers until finally, on the fifth attempt, an old man answered.

"Mr. Drakes? Don't hang up! Please, just hear me out," urged Michael.

Silence.

"I just want to talk. I think we have something in common. I'm not going to report you, but I need to understand what happened to your parents."

All Michael could hear was the man's heavy breathing. After a moment, there came a clipped reply.

"Public library. Top tower. Eleven o'clock."

The line went dead.

Michael checked the clock. The library was way across town, he'd have to leave immediately. He hurried to the bathroom and doused his face and armpits with water, then knocked on his boss's door, assuming a croaky voice.

"Hal, I'm coming down with a fever, I think I oughta take a sick day."

His boss leaped up, alarmed, waving Michael away hastily, ordering him to take as long as he needs.

Michael glanced at the model of the latest bridge on which the firm was working. A beautiful suspension design, the sort he'd dreamed of building as a teenager.

"Maybe when I'm back we could talk about my-"

"Get gone, Michael!" cried his boss, pulling out a disinfectant spray.

Michael checked the clock as he hurried toward the library entrance. It was 10:50 a.m.

"Excuse me, where's the staircase to the tower please?" he asked the front desk.

"Oh goodness me, sir, there are more than three hundred steps. Trust me, you'll wanna take the elevator up, and use the steps on the way down."

"Right, thanks," said Michael, pressing ahead.

"Oh, but sir, you'll need to buy a ticket!" called the receptionist.

Michael doubled back, exasperated.

"There's a tour just about to leave, you'll make it if we hurry."

Michael handed over his ID card hastily and the woman punched it into the system.

"Done. Have a pleasant trip, sir. The view of the Ministry dome is particularly special. I recommend the-"

Michael snatched his ticket and ran to the tour group, joining the tail end just as they crammed into an elevator.

The metal cage ratcheted upwards for several minutes until they reached the tower's viewing level.

"This way, folks. Behold our beautiful city," said the guide, ushering them onto the platform.

A mesh fence surrounded the panoramic platform, keeping the tourists safe from the 150-feet drop. As they spilled out of the elevator, Michael searched his group for the old man. It was 10.59 a.m. and he was nowhere to be seen.

Michael's eyes tracked upwards to the shaft rising above the viewing platform. *Authorized personnel only.* Michael glanced around, then ducked under the cordon and hurried up the twisting metal staircase towards the radio mast.

There was no protective mesh encompassing this platform, just a rusty old railing. Michael peered over the side as the frigid wind buffeted him. A fall from here would mean paralysis for life, at the least.

Gripping the central mast as tightly as he could, Michael shuffled around the rickety old deck until he came face to face with an old man.

"You're late."

"Barely," panted Michael. "Did we really have to meet up here?"

"I've always hated heights," said the old man. "It seemed a worthy challenge."

"Your parents-" began Michael.

The old man reached into his pocket and pulled out a locket. He held it open for Michael to see. A man and woman were pictured, arm in arm on their wedding day.

"They were real people," said the old man.

"Why is there no official public record of them? I looked everywhere. They're named in an old news article, but that's it. The report said they disappeared, leaving you behind?"

"They've been expunged," said the old man. "It's their final punishment."

"Punishment for what?" asked Michael, edging closer.

It was hard to hear the man above the howling wind.

"They made a decision that's not allowed in our society. They chose to reject the options they were given, and carve out their own path in life."

"You mean they committed suicide?" said Michael. "Are you sure they didn't both get their letters?"

"Mom did, Dad didn't. Neither wanted to be without the other, so they rebelled. Mom never reported to the Ministry. Instead, they let the ocean take them both. Their bodies were never found. They left a note for me, explaining what they'd done. Imagine reading that aged ten.

"Naturally, I went to the police. The coastguard mounted a search but came back empty-handed, so it was all hushed up. I never saw the note again. The police came to my house and took away all photos of my parents. They removed them from the records, they even changed my name. Of course, as soon as I became an adult, I changed it back. To this day, I wonder if that's the reason I was never granted children."

Michael realized the section of railing behind the old man was missing. The old man shuffled backwards.

"Owen, talk to me," said Michael, edging towards him with outstretched hands.

"Now you know their truth. Soon you will know mine, too, as I vanish in their wake."

"Owen, don't do this," begged Michael. "Think of the consequences!"

"I've lived with the consequences my whole life," said the old man.

"You won't make it to the other side. You'll vanish forever, like your parents. It can't be what they wanted for you," Michael implored.

"That's the whole point. It's not about what they wanted for me. It's about what we each want for ourselves. 'Regulating life to liberate lives.' I'm done playing their game. And I sense, Michael, that you are too? After all, if you believed the words of the creed, you wouldn't be here. The only question now, Michael, is: are you ready?"

"For what?"

"*True* freedom," smiled the old man.

He leaned back and plunged from sight. Michael screamed, reaching out in vain. He crawled forwards and peered over the edge. The man's body was in ruins; smashed across a car way below.

Passers-by recoiled in horror, while staff rushed to the bloody scene like an ant colony in turmoil. Michael's horror turned to panic as the growing crowd below looked upward, pointing. Staggering to his feet, he fled the scene.

CHAPTER THIRTY-TWO

K elsey necked her fourth coffee of the day and massaged her temples. The lines on the chart before her were blurring into one.

"Excuse me, ma'am," called her assistant, "There's someone here to see you, she says she's-"

"Got an appointment," interrupted Detective Clarkenwell.

"Trouble getting the warrant, detective? What happened to 'first thing'?" said Kelsey.

"It is first thing. I work nights. Wait, did I not make that clear? My apologies. I hope you've not been anxiously waiting all day for my arrival," said the detective.

"This facility has run in continuous operation for more than three hundred years. I can assure you, we don't wait anxiously for anyone," snapped Kelsey.

"Quite the pad you've got here," said the detective.

She took a seat in Kelsey's chair, putting her feet up on the desk.

"What a view," she continued, surveying the factory floor.

"Our practices are not for your eyes," said Kelsey, drawing the blinds.

"Oh, but they are," replied Clarkenwell.

The detective tossed a letter across Kelsey's desk. Kelsey read the warrant, which granted the police twenty-four-hour access to the entire site.

Clarkenwell eyed up Kelsey's crumpled shirt.

"Wearing yesterday's clothes are we?"

"Our, uh, laundry machine is broken, it's being fixed today," muttered Kelsey.

"Mmm," nodded Clarkenwell, with a sage smile. "Well, while you're fixing your laundry, perhaps someone could show me your archive room? There are some documents I need to inspect. I do love getting right down into the nitty-gritty. But that's just me. I'm a sucker for detail."

Kelsey was damned if Clarkenwell visited the archives unsupervised. She presented the inspection warrant to an archival automaton. The tail end of the document had a series of fine holes punched in a pattern too precise for a human hand to replicate.

The machine inserted the document into a cavity at the side of its torso, where it checked the security code.

Satisfied, the automaton returned the warrant and led the pair to the archive room.

Clarkenwell whistled as they entered the chamber, immediately noting the echo.

"Holy crap, is that a tunnel? Where does that even lead?"

She looked excitedly from the automaton to Kelsey, neither of whom reacted.

"No idea. This area's off limits to non-automatons," said Kelsey.

"So, this is the first time you've been down here?"

"Yes," said Kelsey, trying to sound relaxed.

"You like it?"

"It's... unexpected."

"Yo, can you take us to the birth certificates that are awaiting shipment please?" said Clarkenwell.

Kelsey glanced at the bronze cabinets, then kicked herself. Had Clarkenwell seen her look? She waited for the automaton to lead the way.

"You sure it's your first time here?" asked the detective, raising an eyebrow.

"I think I'd remember a place like this. It's got a rail road for Pete's sake," scoffed Kelsey.

The automaton wheeled around and gestured to the bronze cabinets. Clarkenwell stepped forwards, keenly.

"Mind if I do the honors?" she said, pulling open the first drawer.

She tugged out a folder and examined the files inside.

"Hot dog, now *this* is the good stuff. I'm gonna be a while, director, maybe you can go get some fresh clothes or something? I'd hate for you to look disheveled on my account."

"Happy to stay," said Kelsey, stiffly.

"Suit yourself. I hope you like watching people read," chuckled the detective.

The taunt echoed in Kelsey's head as Clarkenwell spent the next three hours painstakingly combing through birth certificates.

She slammed the last bronze drawer shut with a triumphant clang.

"I'm gonna take a bunch of these, is that cool?"

"We don't allow files to leave the premises," said Kelsey, thinking on her feet.

"Photocopies will be fine," smiled Clarkenwell. "Perhaps our metal friend here could oblige?"

Clarkenwell passed her selected folders to the automaton.

"While we're waiting, director, I would like to ask you a few more questions. Unless... goodness," said Clarkenwell, checking her watch. "This must be late for you. Surely you've got a home to be getting back to?"

Kelsey pursed her lips.

"Is that one of your questions?"

"Asking as a friend," said Clarkenwell, with a sarcastic wide-eyed smile.

"You get three questions, then we're done here."

"Ooh, is this a game now? I love games. Alright, let's start with: has this facility ever had problems fulfilling Ministry birthing commissions?"

"A certain percentage of our bakes fail. We've reduced that number significantly over the past few years," said Kelsey.

"How about paperwork. Ever encountered irregularities? Babies getting delivered to the wrong families?"

Kelsey's heart rate quickened.

"No."

"Hmm. How about the people you've worked with; would you say you trust them?"

"I've never had reason to doubt them."

"Dang, I'm out of questions. I had some really good ones lined up. Can we play again?"

The automaton returned, handing a stack of

photocopies to Clarkenwell, before placing the originals back in their cabinets.

"Will that be all, detective?" asked Kelsey, through gritted teeth.

"That's all for today, thank you, director, but I'd love to play again tomorrow. I'm sure we'll have even more to discuss once I've poured through these lovely copies some more. Come by the station tomorrow, say, 4 p.m?"

"Am I under arrest?" said Kelsey, alarmed.

"Not at all, director. That's the last route we want to go down, especially for someone of your stature and public profile. It would be quite the scandal, and no one wants that. Your attendance at this stage is entirely voluntary. You would merely be assisting us with our inquiries."

Kelsey forced a cold smile.

"I look forward to it. See you tomorrow, detective."

CHAPTER THIRTY-THREE

Two days had passed since the man jumped from the library tower. There had been no mention of the incident in the papers, despite the number of eye witnesses. Owen Drakes's name was conspicuously absent from the obituaries list, too. Michael had tried calling the registrar's office, but they insisted they had no record of Mr. Drakes ever having lived. So Michael called the land registry, then the sanitation department, then all the dentists in town, desperately trying to find some trace of the old man.

It was like his entire existence had vanished from the city's records overnight.

Disembarking the tram, Michael approached the hospital and surveyed the directory. Intensive care seemed most likely for a man who'd fallen twenty storeys, so Michael set off.

He hung back as the elevator emptied around him, watching the ward receptionist check other guests upon entry. Michael approached, smiling politely at the man behind the counter.

"Good afternoon, I'm here to visit my grandfather," said Michael.

"Certainly, sir, what's his name?"

"Owen Drakes," said Michael.

The clerk frowned, rifling through a list of patients.

"No one by that name, sir, are you sure he's on this ward?"

"I think so, he had a bad fall. Like, really bad," said Michael.

A glimmer of suspicion flashed across the clerk's face.

"Uh, let me inquire further, sir, perhaps I can track him down for you?"

The clerk picked up the phone and dialed a short internal number.

"Hello, three one six? I've got a gentleman here making inquiries about a recent fall victim. He says he's looking for his grandfather. No, no record of the name. Could you send someone? Thank you."

The clerk hung up and gave Michael the warmest smile imaginable.

"If you just take a seat on the waiting bench there, sir, one of my colleagues will be with you shortly."

"Oh, er, which colleague?" said Michael, uneasily.

"Just take a seat, sir, it's no problem," said the clerk, a little flustered.

Michael glanced around. The other ward staff were looking at him warily.

"I think I must have made a mistake; he must be at a different hospital. Thanks," blurted Michael.

The clerk called after him, urging him to stay. Michael bolted for the elevator, then realized what a foolish move that would be. As the doors chimed open, he darted into the stairwell and pressed himself flush against the wall.

Peering through the window space, he watched a security automaton glide out of the elevator towards the intensive care unit.

Michael hurried down to the main concourse and entered the gift shop. He bought a bouquet of flowers and penned a hasty 'get well soon' card at the checkout. With his cover embellished, he set up camp in the corner of the food court, waiting.

After thirty minutes, the clerk from the intensive care unit entered the food court with a colleague. As the pair joined the line for hot food, Michael took his chance and returned to the stairs.

He deliberately overshot by a level and entered a random psychiatric ward. There, he made inquiries about his fictitious grandfather, using a thin cover story about a hip replacement. The clerk redirected him to the prosthetics wing, as expected.

Michael lingered, extending his gratitude until the timing was perfect. As he made to leave, he deliberately tripped, bumping into a psychiatric patient being transferred.

This in turn caused the patient and their carer to collide with another resident. A row quickly erupted, triggering a tidal wave of discord across the ward.

The ruckus snowballed as other patients and staff became embroiled. As the clerk dialed security for urgent assistance, Michael slipped away.

With security occupied upstairs, he approached the intensive care ward once again. The clerk from before was still away on lunch. Michael peered through the window and scanned the list of names on the board, selecting one that sounded old.

"Hello, I'm here to visit Mr. Eckstein," said Michael, hoping the gifts would assuage any further questions.

"Certainly, sir, you'll just need to sign in right here," said the new clerk, sliding over a clipboard.

Michael hastily scribbled a false name, then put "nephew" under the relation field. He slid the form back, and set off towards the random unit slowly.

He peered into each room as he went, observing patients in various states of trauma and respiratory support. He spotted Mr. Eckstein, a surprisingly youthful man, asleep, with layers of bandaging around a severe leg burn.

Michael glanced back; the clerk was busy with paperwork. He hurried down the corridor until he reached an unmarked room. On the patient name sign it merely read: *Ministry Aware.*

A life support machine whirred beside the bed, while yards of cable extended from the man's nose and wrists into various intravenous drips. The patient himself was in a full-body cast, and under so many layers of bandage Michael could barely recognize him. As Michael slipped inside, the only clue as to the identity of the human beneath the reams of plaster was the pile of bloodied clothes in the corner.

Michael lay the flowers and card on the side table and stared at the unconscious old man. The notes at the end of the bed said he was in a coma, but would likely have catastrophic brain damage should he regain consciousness at all. Paralysis was also expected.

This wasn't what he'd chosen.

Michael approached the breathing machine by the old man's head and watched the pump wheeze up and down through its glass tube. Kneeling down, he unplugged the machine. It let out the last of its air with a depressurizing hiss.

As the old man's lungs gurgled, the heart monitor flatlined. Michael hastily turned the machine off, silencing the alarm, then made a beeline for the exit.

"Just a short visit today, sir?" asked the clerk.

"Uh, yes, thank you," said Michael.

"Just a sec - you need to sign out, please."

A nurse was approaching the old man's room. Michael hastily signed out the wrong name, then flung the clipboard back and sped into the corridor.

Cries of 'call a code!' echoed behind him.

Michael mashed the elevator button as the commotion escalated. The doors chimed open, and the previous clerk stepped out with a colleague.

Michael dipped his head and brushed by, hitting the *down* button. As the doors slid shut, the original clerk recognized his face.

"Stop that man!"

The two terrified civilians in the lift gave Michael a wide berth as the elevator descended. All of a sudden, it ground to a halt in-between levels. He forced the doors apart and peered into the upper level. A security automaton was gliding towards them from the far end.

Stooping down, Michael decided to take his chances on the level below. He swiveled out underneath the mid-way ceiling and dropped.

Barging medics aside, he raced down the adjacent staircase to the food court. By now, it was teeming with people. He fought his way across, nearing the main atrium, but security staff were sealing off the exits.

Michael darted sideways through a porters' door. He stumbled into a long service corridor, full of stock for the hospital's eateries.

"No civilians back here!" cried a porter.

Michael leaped over a stack of crates and burst through the fire exit, sprinting for the tram stop as the hospital pre-alarm rang out.

"Do you know why I've called you in?" said Michael's boss, sternly.

Michael shook his head, wondering if it was something to do with the two-hour lunch break he just took.

His eyes fell on a brown box on his boss's desk.

"Recognize these?" yelled the man.

He slammed a wad of papers down before Michael. It was a breakdown of all the building's phone calls from the last twelve months. Several rows were highlighted, increasing in frequency towards the present month.

"Explain," fumed the boss.

"It looks like a phone log," shrugged Michael.

"Drop the attitude. Right now, I'm deciding whether to simply fire you, or to press charges with it."

Michael sat up, nervously.

"I don't understand. What's going on?" he said, unconvincingly.

"Oh, please. Every time you're in my office you drop engineering suggestions about bridge design and structural load bearing, yet now you're pretending you can't fathom a simple list of phone numbers? I don't buy it for a second; you know exactly what this is. We've been through this list with a fine-tooth comb and cross-referenced it with the city directory. None of these numbers are clients, or even prospective clients. They're private citizens - many of them dead! All of these calls were made from *your* desk, during *your* shifts. Take this number, for instance. You called this person nine times in two days! What the hell's going on? Is this some kind of corporate espionage?"

"I don't know what to say," mumbled Michael.

"You'd better think of something, or I'm calling the police," he said, snatching up the phone.

"OK I admit it! It was me!" blurted Michael.

His heart raced as his mind frantically tried to plot a course through the danger. If his boss called the police now, there would be all kinds of questions, including where he'd been that morning. If they traced him to the hospital, and what he did to the old man, unsanctioned phone calls would be the least of his worries.

"I'm so sorry, I'll pay back the costs. Please don't have me arrested, think of my kids!" begged Michael.

Glaring at him, the boss threw the receiver down with disgust.

"I don't know what's going on with you, Michael, but you can take it somewhere else. Get the hell out of my building."

CHAPTER THIRTY-FOUR

Kelsey sat down in the police interview room with a shudder. Her mind crashed back to her arrest eighteen years prior. She couldn't believe she was back there with the same lawyer beside her. The only difference being that this time, her lawyer didn't know the full truth of the matter.

"Good afternoon Ms Bailey, thank you for coming to interview with us today. For the purposes of the audio record, may I reiterate that you are here in a voluntary capacity, and that we appreciate your cooperation. Present with Ms Kelsey Bailey is myself, Detective Jane Clarkenwell, Sergeant Damon La Rue, and Ms Bailey's attorney, Ms Valentina Hadley."

Val's presence was a great comfort to Kelsey. Michael's mother had saved her bacon all those years ago, and Kelsey was confident she could do it again.

"Are you comfortable, Ms Bailey? Have you been to a police interview before?"

"That's an irrelevant question," interjected Val.

The detective nodded with a smile, then flicked through Kelsey's file, raising her eyebrows ostentatiously as she turned the pages.

"You had quite the upbringing," said Clarkenwell.

"You're straying from irrelevant to unprofessional, Detective. I suggest you dispense with my client's personal history and cut to why you've brought us here today," said Val.

"We strive for the highest professional standards here, ma'am, I can assure you. Something I'm sure your client can relate to."

Kelsey's heart fluttered. Clarkenwell was fishing, trying to provoke her. Did that file have evidence against her? Could they prove what she had done?

"Tell me, Ms Bailey, how does a former recipient of the foster system come to be director of the city's fertility center?"

"Hard work, tenacity, and a great deal of personal sacrifice," said Kelsey.

"Mmm. Quite," mused the detective.

"We've had reports of malpractice at your center, Ms Bailey. Namely, the misallocation of children," said the sergeant.

"Is that a question?" said Val.

"Has Ms Bailey ever witnessed malpractice at the facility? If so, what steps were taken to report or remedy this?" asked the sergeant.

Val looked at Kelsey, expectantly.

"Uh, I have no such recollections. In my experience, the center has largely been a force for good," said Kelsey.

"Largely? But not entirely?"

"Elements of the child-allocation system are flawed."

"Interesting. Do you think such views might drive a person to undermine the system?"

Kelsey swallowed.

"Don't answer that," muttered Val.

"Ms Bailey?" continued Clarkenwell, tapping Kelsey's file. "If you have something to share, I suggest you do so now."

Kelsey's could feel her brow moistening.

"Are you accusing my client of something specific, Detective, or just fishing for clues?" said Val.

"I'm just doing my job, ma'am, as are you, as is Ms Bailey. To that end, I would love to know more about these 'flaws' she perceives in the system. What kind of things are we talking about?"

"Birthing practices are confidential," said Kelsey.

"You seem nervous, Ms Bailey?"

"I'm fine," said Kelsey.

"Perhaps you can talk in general terms about your grievances with the system?"

"To what end, Detective? Either you have a case against my client, or you don't. We're not here to help you build one."

"I'm merely asking questions, ma'am. If your client has nothing to hide, there's no harm in answering. Ms Bailey, your grievances?"

The memory of switching the triplets flashed across her mind again. Kelsey shook her head, gathering her thoughts.

"Uh, in my opinion, our birthing system is imbued with injustice. Initially, I petitioned the Ministry for change, but my predecessor was hostile to the idea. I have accepted the limitations of my position, and chosen to focus on helping families downstream in the pipeline," said Kelsey.

"Sounds to me like you still want change, though. If you *could* change the system, would you?"

"Enough with the leading questions," interjected Val.

"It's legitimate," shrugged Clarkenwell.

"You're constructing a false narrative around my client and trying to get her to incriminate herself, which is ludicrous given that you've still not explained why we're here. My client is a dedicated professional, committed to the care of all children commissioned and distributed through her facility."

"OK, let me put it another way, then. Given your clear frustrations with the system, Ms Bailey, and your predecessor's attitudes towards reform, have you ever been tempted to go against protocol?"

"You don't have to answer that," urged Val.

"No, I'm sick of this," snapped Kelsey. "I resent the implication that wanting to improve a system would make me some kind of criminal. There is a multitude of improvements that could be made to the Ministry's systems, and if you've been on the receiving end of them as much as I have, maybe you'd understand that. I *care* about the impacts of my work. Maybe if your facility did the same, the city would be a better place. Tell me, Detective, are you people still throwing minors in Infinity chambers?"

Clarkenwell's mouth soured. Her sergeant's eyes widened.

"Where did you hear about that?" he flapped. "That's a very serious allegation. If you wish to register a formal complaint, we can absolutely-"

"*Me.* You people did it to *me*, eighteen years ago. I've worked day and night to make something of my life after institutions like yours failed me time and again, and my reward is to be harassed at work and judged by two hypocrites like you? We're done here."

Kelsey stood up in disgust, mastering all the pious rage she could muster, and hoping to high heavens that it was as convincing a performance as it felt.

"Ms Bailey, please sit back down," said Clarkenwell.

"Are you formally charging my client? If not, she is at liberty to leave," said Val.

"I'm sure your client will want to hear the outcome of our investigation into the archival materials. Her name came up."

Clarkenwell slid a folder across the table.

"This may come as a shock, Ms Bailey. I'm sorry you had to find out this way."

Kelsey stared at the documents before her. On the left was the birth certificate of a child she didn't recognize. On the right was her own daughter's name.

"What is the meaning of this?" said Val.

"Eighteen years ago, under your predecessor's watch, there was an irregularity. Multiple irregularities, in fact. It appears yours was one of the families affected."

"What are you saying?"

"I understand you are Ms Bailey's mother in law, which makes her children your grandchildren, yes? The child on the left is your actual grandchild. But, for reasons unknown, she was reassigned to another family. The child on the right is in fact another family's child, which you've been raising, through no fault of your own," said the detective.

A knot tightened in Kelsey's stomach. Val's shoulders slumped as she read the birth certificate of the unknown child.

"You mean... *this* is my grandchild?" she said, her voice cracking.

Kelsey stared at the table in silence.

"I appreciate this must be a shock to both of you. We're seeking to bring justice to the matter. Ms Bailey, would you be prepared to testify against your former director?" said the sergeant.

"What happens to my daughter now?" asked Kelsey, faintly.

"Er, which one? The child you've raised or your *actual-*"

"Olive *is* my actual daughter," fumed Kelsey. "I've tended to her night and day since she was a baby. Don't you *dare* tell me she's not my daughter."

"Er, of course, ma'am, it's a sensitive situation-" began the sergeant.

"You haven't answered her question," snapped Val. "What happens now?"

"Oh, er, well, given that both individuals are now legally of adult age, there is no further action to be taken. The matter of parentage is somewhat moot," said the sergeant.

"*Moot?* You're calling our family's lineage *moot?*" said Val.

"Can I contact him? The boy on the left, I mean. My... my son," said Kelsey.

"Technically, he's your partner's son. Being a spouse, you're only parent by proxy, but-"

Clarkenwell elbowed the sergeant, halting his clumsy rambling.

"I understand why you'd want to make contact with your son, but I'm afraid that won't be possible," said Clarkenwell.

The detective leaned forward to retrieve the

photocopied birth certificate, but Kelsey snatched it up, clutching it to her chest.

"You're telling me I have a son, and now you're telling me I can't see him? Why the hell not?" fumed Kelsey.

"Because, ma'am, your son died on his eighteenth birthday."

CHAPTER THIRTY-FIVE

Kelsey paced towards the parking lot alone. Val opted to take the tram, needing space to digest the evening's bombshell.

As Kelsey rummaged for her keys, a police car pulled up before the station. Two officers ushered out a woman from the backseat, whose figure Kelsey recognized immediately.

The cuffed woman hung her head as they led her inside. A pang of guilt stabbed at Kelsey; Professor Hestley, her former director, was about to take the fall for Kelsey's crime.

But as the woman trudged to the station, something peculiar struck Kelsey. Hestley's body sagged like she was resigned to her fate; like she'd known this was always coming. She put up no fight, showed no defiance; she was ready to atone. But for what?

"Ms Bailey!" came a call from behind.

A red-headed ponytail bounded towards her.

"One more thing," said Clarkenwell. "We came across another anomaly last week. Something more recent. It's from the past two years in fact, since you became director."

"Why didn't you ask me in the interview?" said Kelsey.

"Perhaps you're not the only one frustrated by their department's processes," shrugged Clarkenwell. "When I was going through your archives, I found the strangest thing. It bore a striking resemblance to a case that came into the station not long ago. See, this couple came in. They were awfully upset, really distraught. They said someone had stolen their children. All three of them, no less. See, this couple were expecting triplets. Yet, when they went to collect them from your facility, with what they assert was the correct paperwork, they were turned away. The date stuck in my mind. You know me, Ms Bailey, I love those little details, so I couldn't help but notice, as I was going through your facility's archives, that a set of triplets were indeed born that day. And this is the darndest thing, Ms Bailey. You'll never guess who they were delivered to?"

"Who?"

"Why, your sister-in-law, of course. How about that? It seems a heck of a coincidence, doesn't it? A set of triplets getting delivered to your sister-in-law on the *same* day as another couple claiming they were denied their own triplets."

"Fraudulent child collection attempts are not unheard of," said Kelsey.

"Sure, but this couple – something about them seemed so... *real*. Like they'd been truly wounded, you know?"

"Did this couple have any evidence to back up their claim?"

The detective stepped closer. Kelsey could smell her perfume as she leaned in, lowering her voice, with a sultry smile.

"That's the rub, isn't it, Ms Bailey. They said they gave

you their documentation. You wouldn't know anything about that now, would you?"

Kelsey swallowed hard.

"If I had received documents, they would be in the archives."

"Mmm. I thought you might say that."

"Are you... are they... accusing me?" said Kelsey.

"Of what?"

"I don't know, the whole insinuation's ludicrous!"

Clarkenwell stepped back and sucked in the cool evening air. She stuffed her hands in her pockets and gazed up at the stars, while Kelsey tried to control the trembling in her legs.

"They're not pressing charges against you, Ms Bailey. Their evidence is circumstantial at best."

"Good."

"But they're an interesting couple, those two. They've both got previous convictions for fraud."

Kelsey's mouth twitched. She couldn't believe her luck.

"There you go, then," she gushed, relieved.

"That's certainly the view most people in my department have taken. But me? I'm a curious soul. I can't help but think: it must have taken something major for two convicted felons to seek out police help."

"I wouldn't presume to know," said Kelsey.

Clarkenwell held her gaze for a long moment, then cracked a polite smile.

"Drive safely, Ms Bailey."

CHAPTER THIRTY-SIX

Michael leaned through into the hallway, while doing up his tie. Kelsey was tugging on her shoes in a hurry.

"Don't work too late tonight, my love," he said, softly.

"Are you my boss now?" snapped Kelsey.

"I'm worried about you, that's all."

"I'm fine."

"You know what I mean."

"I said I'm fine. Stop overthinking things. Get the boys to school, and get yourself to work, OK?"

Michael's face fell, wounded. Kelsey rolled her eyes and paced over to him. She gave him a quick peck on the cheek, squeezed his hand, then marched to the car where Olive was waiting.

Michael followed her to the doorstep. The cold stone sapped warmth from his feet.

"Have you heard from my mom lately? She's not returning my calls," called Michael.

Kelsey pretended not to hear as she climbed into the car.

"Have a great first day, sweetie, you'll be great!" called Michael.

His daughter gave him a sarcastic thumbs up, then pointed to her usher's uniform and pretended to vomit. She was clearly enthralled by her new holiday job.

Michael waved them off, then nipped back into the hallway. He slipped on his shoes and grabbed a blazer, then called to his sons, who were feasting at the breakfast table.

"Damien? Leon? Don't be late for school. And make sure there's some bread left for the rest of us, you pair of locusts!"

He grabbed his satchel and set off toward the tram stop.

As he neared the interchange, he slipped off the sidewalk and took up position on a nearby park bench, camouflaged by bushes.

Michael watched the morning commuters; mini lines of suits and bowler hats, spaced at regular intervals, aided by the painted tiles beneath them.

Trams came and went, skimming off the constant stream of commuters. After twenty minutes, his two sons appeared in their school uniforms, dashing for a carriage, piling on just in time.

Michael waited until they were well out of sight, then left his hiding place and retraced his steps.

As he neared his front yard, the neighbor opposite stepped out, raising an eyebrow at Michael's premature return.

"Forgot my sandwiches," called Michael, in a strained jokey tone.

Michael hastened inside, waving them goodbye, then slammed the door, cursing. He pulled off his tie, dumped his satchel, and headed down to the basement.

He settled into his torn-fabric seat, unlocked the desk drawers, and spread his research across the table.

Over the years, the list of case studies he'd compiled had grown dramatically. Naturally, his efforts had accelerated now that he was jobless. With more time on his hands, he'd traced four new cases in the last few weeks alone. Old newspaper clippings, visits to the registry office, and cold calls, all hinted at unregistered deaths, and a scandal brewing beneath it all.

Owen Drakes, the man he'd met on the library tower, had vanished from the registry without a trace, despite being a living, breathing human just weeks ago. There wasn't so much as a fake name in his place; he'd been almost completely scrubbed.

Almost.

Through his research at the registry, Michael had discovered a recurring Ministry code. The letters E.F. followed by a four-digit number and a date appeared in death records, but only in very specific instances.

Michael stumbled across the first recorded instance when investigating Owen's story – initially tracing his missing parents' records, then tracing his own. The code had appeared in the registry books the day Michael euthanized Owen in hospital. As far as the public record was concerned, that discrete string of letters and numbers was the only hint that Owen had ever existed.

This discovery prompted Michael to backtrack. He realized that the number in Owen's code was the next in a sequence. It followed on from the last "E.F." which he tracked down to a separate record dated four years prior.

Following Owen's passing, Michael had hastily made a list of all of the E.F. entries, and dates, then cross-referenced them against the newspaper archives for those days. It had been painstaking work, and he was on first name terms with the staff at the facility now, after repeated visits. That was until last week, when he arrived to find his access had been revoked. The staff were unable to explain why, but their demeanor had changed dramatically.

Michael had packed up hastily and left before they could seize his notebook. Now working from the privacy of his basement, he was drilling into the list of mysterious, anonymous deaths.

He was determined to discover the people behind the codes, but it was like hitting a brick wall.

Michael had learned early on it was necessary to fish for details before revealing the true purpose of his call. Sometimes he pretended to be conducting a consumer survey. Anything but the truth. On the few occasions he'd led with "I'm investigating some unusual deaths," the person on the other end would hang up before even confirming their name.

So it was with great tenacity and patience that Michael had compiled this list of eighteen suspected "E.F.s", or Extraordinary Fatalities, as he'd decided to call them.

Contacting the E.F.s' surviving relatives, however, added to the complexity. Many had moved or died since their loved ones' disappearances.

Michael spun the rotary dial and listened as the line rang.

"Hello?" came the crackled response.

"Good morning, is that Mrs. Jenson?"

The line went dead. That happened sometimes when the surviving relative had changed their surname, following the death. Michael scrawled a date in the margin, to remind himself to look into her new surname and try again in a few days' time.

He dialed the next number on the list.

"Hi there, is that Mr. Alison?" said Michael.

"Speaking," came a clipped reply.

"I'm calling from the law firm Plimpton and May. We've received some documents from your late wife's estate, and believe you should be the beneficiary."

There was a pause. Michael waited with bated breath for the man's reply.

"Like, money?"

"Well, we would need to go through some standard vetting procedures before I can disclose the full details, Mr. Alison, just to check your credentials. I'm sure you understand."

"What kind of details?"

"According to my records, your wife Eleanor died on October 18 two years ago. Is that correct?"

"It is."

There was a new tone in his voice. Somewhere between pain and hope.

"Please can you confirm the manner of death?" asked Michael.

"She got her letter like anyone else," snapped the man.

Michael allowed a silence to linger as the man stewed.

"Sorry, sir, that's not what it says here," said Michael.

"She drowned," conceded the man, heavily.

"I'm sorry to hear that. You'll excuse the impudence of the next question, but we have to be sure, is all. Was the drowning accidental or...?"

"Or what?" snapped the man.

Michael allowed the silence to grow once again.

"Thank you for your time, sir, have a pleasant day," said Michael.

"Wait, what about the money?" said the man.

"I'm afraid you didn't clear security. We can only distribute funds with verified individuals," said Michael.

"Alright! She drowned but... she didn't get a letter. She did it herself. She chose to end it. Are you happy now? You made me say it."

"I'm sorry for your loss, Mr. Alison. I appreciate this must be a difficult conversation to have, but were you able to deposit your wife's body at the Ministry, after she'd died?"

"No. They took it from me. No idea where it went, but it wasn't to the Ministry, that's for sure. When they pulled her from the water they..."

The man welled up for a moment, then regathered himself.

"...they put her in an unmarked police van. Or at least I'm guessing it was police. It was automatons that handled her. The vehicle drove in the opposite direction to the Ministry and hospital. It's the last I saw of her."

"So you have no idea where they took her body?" asked Michael.

"Maybe they were driving to the mountains. That's all I can guess," said the man.

"Noted. Thank you, Mr. Alison, we appreciate your time. We need to do some confirmatory paperwork this end, then we'll be back in touch shortly."

Michael hung up and surveyed his spread of newspaper clippings. Lifting a sepia photograph printed on yellowing paper, he examined the image carefully.

Woman pulled from lake after being found by runners. Husband distraught as...

He punched the air, and set up his typewriter. He had her.

Michael tucked his report into a folder and stowed it securely in his satchel. If he hurried, he could catch the last mailing slot.

He was banking on there being no line at the copy house; he needed several photocopies so he could approach all the news outlets, while keeping the original for himself.

As he marched down the street, a Ministry capsule twirled into life.

The capsule was about three feet taller and wider than Michael. Such portals were stationed on every street corner in the city; tall, bulbous tubes protruding from the ground. Some were made of translucent enamel, while others had been embellished to complement the color schemes of adjacent businesses. The capsule on Michael's street had been painted by a former resident, so he had been told, with permission from the Ministry. It bore a painting of an automaton holding a child's hand, against an ocean sunset. Michael had grown used to it, so never paid it much notice. But on this occasion, it caught his eye. For the first time in all his years living there, it was in operation.

The capsule door rotated open, revealing an automaton and a woman. The woman had a red ponytail and seemed delighted to see Michael. She gave him a cheerful wave, while chewing on a slice of pizza.

"Mr. Hadley? It seems we caught you at a good time. Heading out, are you?"

"Er, yes, to the post office. Sorry, who are you?" inquired Michael.

"Detective Jane Clarkenwell. I was hoping we might ask you a few questions?"

"Ah, I really am in a hurry. It'll be closing soon," said Michael.

"Anything important?" she said, nodding to his bag.

"No," said Michael, hastily.

"Good, then I'm sure you won't mind us imposing for a few minutes. Shall we step inside? Nothing worse than gossiping neighbors," said the detective.

Michael glanced across the way at his curtain-twitching neighbor opposite.

"This way," he sighed.

The woman and the automaton followed Michael home. The machine ceased gliding only to step over the doorstep, before continuing into the living room. It parked itself in the corner with a fixed, inscrutable stare.

Michael regarded it nervously. Was this one of the machines that had barged into his previous home, tearing its fellow automaton limb from limb?

"Don't worry about my colleague, she's here for formality, that's all," said the detective.

Clarkenwell breezed in and made herself at home on the couch. She gave a nod to the family photo hanging on the wall.

"Lovely family," she mumbled, shoveling more pizza into her mouth.

"Thanks," said Michael, eyeing up the cream sofa anxiously.

"How's the laundry machine?"

"What?"

"Heard a rumor it was broken."

"Er, it's fine," said Michael, perplexed.

"Figures," nodded the detective. "Forgive the crumbs. Didn't expect you to be leaving at this time of day. Thought I had time for lunch but then you checked out on the census, so we had to hot foot it into one of the pods. Any idea why we're here, Mr. Hadley?"

Nursing the satchel bag, Michael shook his head.

"There was an incident at the library last week. You wouldn't know anything about that, would you?"

"An incident?" said Michael, conjuring his best innocent face.

"Come now, Mr. Hadley, let's not be coy. Your ID card places you at the scene. You bought a ticket for the rooftop tour, 11 a.m.. Am I jogging your memory?"

"Ah, yes, come to think of it, I was there, and there was a slight... incident. An old man fell from the roof," said Michael.

"How do you know it was an old man?" said the detective.

"Uh, it looked like he had white hair as he fell, and his voice sounded male," said Michael.

The detective made a note, then peered up from her pad.

"How interesting. You're the first person to say the person made a noise as they fell. Tell me, where were you standing at the time?"

"I was overlooking the east side of the city. The library parking lot," said Michael, truthfully.

"Any idea how someone was able to fall when there are safety nets all around the platform?"

"I guess he fell from higher up. There's another level by the radio mast, right?" said Michael.

The detective made a note.

"Some people reported seeing a second person on that level, shortly after the victim fell," said the detective.

"Why are you calling him a victim?" said Michael.

"I beg your pardon?"

"The old man. Maybe he wasn't pushed, maybe he jumped?"

"What makes you think that?" said the detective.

"Odd place to try to murder somebody, isn't it?" said Michael.

"Who said anything about murder?"

"He fell from one of the tallest buildings in the city. If someone pushed him, they would presumably be trying to kill him, wouldn't they?"

"The Ministry decides whether people live or die, not people like you and I. If the individual received their letter that morning, then it is plausible they acted irrationally. But no letter was issued, Mr. Hadley, which means this must have been an attack."

"Or a protest?"

Clarkenwell's brow soared. "Protest? At what?"

Michael shrugged. "You'd have to ask him that."

The detective eyed him up for a moment.

"That will be difficult. He's dead."

"From the fall?"

"What do you think?"

Michael held his tongue, as the detective let him stew. After a moment, she continued.

"I see two possibilities. The man was murdered, and has been robbed of his ascension. Or, the man sought to end his life, and forgo his ascension. In either scenario, a third party is required, either to push, or to follow the act through," said the detective.

"Follow it through?"

"We found a further transaction on your account at the hospital gift shop. You bought flowers. Who you were visiting?" said the detective.

"They were for my wife," said Michael.

"I wasn't aware she was ill?" said the detective.

"She's not, I just wanted to get her flowers."

"From a hospital?"

"It was the nearest shop."

"To what?"

"My lunchtime walk."

"I see. From your job at... Ah yes, you were let go, weren't you? I believe it was the same day as your shopping trip?" said the detective.

"I was fired. So what?" said Michael.

"The timing doesn't seem odd to you?" said the detective.

"What's odd to me is that a man falling from the library roof hasn't been in any of the papers."

"You've been looking?"

"I read them daily, I've seen no mention. Someone falls from the city's tallest tower and dies, and not a single paper writes it up? To me that's more suspicious than the death itself. It smacks of a cover up," shrugged Michael.

"And who would be covering it up?"

"The Ministry. They don't want people to know the truth. That they're not the only arbiters of death," said Michael, boldly.

Finishing her last crust, Clarkenwell wiped her fingers clean on a napkin.

"An interesting theory. Wanna hear mine? Someone pushed the old man off the tower. Then when that didn't kill him, they went to the hospital to finish the job. His life support machines were turned off. Ripped clean outta the wall. Fairly amateur, if you ask me."

"Maybe whoever it was, was just respecting the old man's wishes," said Michael, his eyes blazing.

The detective smiled ever so slightly.

"There's a term for that. It's called assisted suicide."

The automaton twitched sharply. The detective raised a hand as if soothing it.

"It carries a life sentence. Thirty years in an infinity chamber," the detective continued.

"Only one problem," said Michael, his heart racing. "For there to have been a crime, there needs to be a victim. And the Ministry's already expunged the old man's entire life. How would the court case play out? An anonymous body, with no records in the registry office, no mention of his death in the paper, no record of his stay at the hospital? It's like he never existed. Last time I checked, you can't murder someone who doesn't exist."

The detective's lips pursed.

"You're quite right, Mr. Hadley. In the scenario you describe, it would be quite impractical for the Ministry to press legal charges. But you of all people should know, there will be other consequences."

The front door opened and Olive spilled in from work, immediately kicking off her shoes and stepping into the living room. She recoiled in shock at the sight of the automaton and detective.

"What's going on?" she asked, alarmed.

"Your father's been assisting us with an inquiry. He's be most enlightening," said Clarkenwell, rising to her feet.

"Give us a moment sweetie, they're just leaving," said Michael, stony-faced.

Olive backed out of the room warily and retreated upstairs. The automaton glided into the corridor, following her, then stopped. Its head rotated towards the basement door. Michael's heart rate rocketed as it edged towards the handle.

"We're done here, get out of my house," he blurted, standing abruptly.

"Gladly. By the way, I strongly advise you to reconsider mailing whatever it is you're about to mail. I'd hate for your situation to get more complicated than it already is," said Clarkenwell, rising to her feet. "Oh, and for what it's worth, Mr. Hadley, I'm sorry about your daughter. That must have been difficult news to receive."

Michael looked at her blankly.

"You don't know? I'll leave you to talk with your wife. You two have some catching up to do."

"You know my wife?" said Michael, taken aback.

The detective whistled to the automaton, which was frozen with its palm placed flat against the basement door.

"Let's go," she called. "I'll see you round, Mr. Hadley."

Clarkenwell left, trailed by the automaton. Closing the door, Michael sank against the wall, hyperventilating.

The detective's words echoed in his head. *I'm sorry about your daughter.* What did she mean? And how did she know his wife?

Kelsey was hiding something from him, it was the only explanation. She'd been acting so strangely lately, turning up at weird hours in the night, being evasive in person. And now the police are talking about their daughter?

Michael hurried upstairs and ransacked his bedroom, searching Kelsey's things for clues. Panting, and empty-handed, he stepped into the corridor, wondering where the hell his wife might hide something she wanted to keep secret.

Olive was in the hallway, on her way to the shower.

"Why were the police here, Dad?"

"Nothing to worry about, sweetie, they just wanted to know if Daddy had witnessed something. They're gone now," he smiled.

Olive frowned, then continued on her way. Michael waited until the shower was running, then hastily searched her bedroom too.

No drugs, nothing that looked stolen, no plane tickets. He racked his brains, trying to think what Kelsey was hiding from him.

A jolt came to him out of the blue. *You've got your father's eyes.* It had felt weird when she'd said it, but Michael had been too distracted to challenge her on it. At the time, he'd accepted her explanation - that Val had been showing her photos of his father. But that was impossible, she'd destroyed them all out of shame. There was only one copy remaining, and it was kept secret.

Michael's stomach churned as he realized where Kelsey must have gone. He rushed to the basement and seized the dusty chocolate tin. Tipping the contents onto his desk, he shoved his grandfather's letters and family photos aside until he came across the outlier. There it was. And beside it, a new, crisply folded piece of Ministry paper.

Michael's hands trembled as he picked it out from the pile. What had Kelsey done? What did it have to do with Olive?

As he unfolded the paper, a familiar voice greeted him from the top of the stairs.

"We need to talk," said Kelsey.

CHAPTER THIRTY-SEVEN

"What the hell is this?" cried Michael.

The folded birth certificate was clutched in his hand, the dusty chocolate tin in the other.

"Shh, keep it down," hissed Kelsey.

"Who the hell are the Broxleys?"

"I said keep it down!"

Kelsey closed the basement door and crept down to join him. With great effort, and an angry tremble in his voice, Michael brought his voice down to a simmer.

"Kelsey, I need you to be straight with me right now: why is there a birth certificate hidden in our basement that bears the names of our niece and nephews, and *some random family's surname?*"

Kelsey slumped onto the bottom step, clutching her head in her hands.

"I was trying to do the right thing. They were in pain, and they begged me."

"Who?"

"Sophia and Nina. They asked me to use my position at the center to get them children."

"And you obviously told them that's illegal, right? Kelsey, tell me you told them that."

Kelsey shook her head, bitterly.

"But think of how happy they are now, Michael. Don't they deserve that?"

"Are you crazy? What if the Ministry finds out? What if it takes them away, or worse? Oh god, this is why the police know you, isn't it?" cried Michael.

Kelsey's jaw slackened.

"The police?"

"Some detective was round here earlier. Red hair. Said she knows you. Is this why?"

"It's... dealt with."

"What does *that* mean?"

"The kids aren't gonna be taken away. I was careful, alright? I covered my tracks, and the Ministry got what they wanted. It's a win-win."

"Oh really? Then why are you *hiding* this?"

"I don't deserve to be on trial here! Not from you. *You* should be thanking me. Think about how happy your sister is now - Nina too. They were miserable before, fighting all the time. I fixed that, OK? Me. I took a huge risk for your family because I love them, and I want them to be happy, and now some other family doesn't have kids because of me, and I have to live with that," said Kelsey, welling up.

"Wait," said Michael, as a dread dawned on him. "This doesn't make sense. The detective said you knew something about *our* daughter. There's something you're not telling me."

Kelsey's face paled as she looked at her husband. He shook his head, sensing what was coming.

"You didn't..."

"I didn't steal her, if that's what you're asking," sniffed Kelsey.

"So what, then?"

"You were eighteen, Michael, I was just trying to help. Out of nowhere, you'd been landed with a baby you didn't ask for. It broke our relationship; it ruined your dreams of college. I couldn't bear the thought of you having to struggle any harder. The baby you were assigned... it wasn't a life you deserved," said Kelsey.

"What do you mean?"

"The child assigned to you was baked with... complications. I wanted to protect you, so I... I switched them," she sniffed.

"You *switched* them?" fumed Michael.

"I didn't deprive anyone! All I did was spare you a hard life, alright? I know what that's like, Michael. I know what it means to have your youth stolen, and to struggle every single day just to get by. I didn't want that for you, I wanted you to be happy."

"You... you gave my child to some other family," stammered Michael.

"And gave you *our daughter*!" protested Kelsey.

"I need to see my child. My real child. The one you made me abandon," choked Michael.

"Wait, it's not as easy as that, it's complicated," begged Kelsey.

She tried blocking his way, but Michael brushed past her.

"If you managed it eighteen years ago, I can manage it now."

"Michael, please," she begged, tears streaming down her face. "The boy is dead."

CHAPTER THIRTY-EIGHT

M ichael pulled up at the memorial park. The gates were locked, and the park keeper's chimney was smoking.

He drove along the wooded perimeter until he was out of view of the house, then approached the iron fence. The sturdy black rails were spear-tipped.

Michael climbed onto the hood of his car, then took hold of the rails, just below the sharpened tips. Hooking a leg onto the top beam, he launched himself over.

He traded his dignity for a soft landing, allowing a hedge to break his fall. With leaves and twigs in his hair, he set off in search of his son's plot.

A crimson sunset bathed the memorial park. It was a beautiful space, with lakes, fountains, and birds. Michael wondered why his mother had never invested in such a thing for his late grandfather or dad.

A meandering path took him to the allocated plot, where he knelt on the damp grass. There, a statuette rested on a modest plinth.

The bronze metalwork depicted a diminutive figure in a

wheelchair. Strapped to the back of the chair was an oxygen tank, with tubes reaching over the boy's shoulders into his nostrils. A blanket covered his bony knees, and a withered arm rested across his lap.

By contrast, his other arm was outstretched, triumphantly. In his hand, he was proudly clutching a Frisbee. A huge smile adorned the boy's face. His eyes were carved so as to capture the sunlight, giving them a warm twinkle.

Beneath the statuette was an inscription:

The bravest boy we could have wished for. He lived every one of his eighteen years to the full.

Michael reached out a hand and rested it on the statuette. He covered his mouth as he wept, overwhelmed by guilt for the son he'd never known, and pain for the parents who had lost the boy they loved.

Sitting on the grass, he stared at the figurine until he could barely see it in the darkness. Shivering, he climbed to his feet and made his way to the fence.

Of the many hedges and trees encompassing the park, it took some searching to find a branch low enough and strong enough to give him the boost he needed to overcome the railing.

He fell to the ground with a heavy thud. Groaning, and nursing his ankle, he limped back to the car.

Michael hobbled down the basement steps. Seizing the empty chocolate tin, he doused it with engine oil.

"What are you doing?" cried Kelsey, hurrying down after him.

Michael lit a match and tossed it into the tin, which erupted in flames.

"Michael!" yelled Kelsey.

He pulled out the note Kelsey had given him. It was the handwritten address of his son's memorial lot. He scrunched it up and tossed it into the fire.

Michael watched, silently, as the edges of the paper curled and charred, fragmenting and rising out of the flames. A delicate halo of ash fell like powder around the blazing tin.

With the note gone, Michael reached into his pocket once again. Kelsey's mouth hung open as she realized what he was holding. The document that could see her jailed for life.

Michael stared at the Broxley family's birth certificate for a long moment, then tossed it into the fire.

Kelsey descended the steps, as the desk began to smolder. Michael's eyes remained glued to the burning tin, indifferent to mounting smoke. Grabbing a plank from the junk pile, Kelsey placed it over the tin, smothering the flames.

Delicately, she took Michael's hands in hers.

"I'm so sorry I hid it all. There was no way to tell you... I was only trying to protect our family," she croaked.

Michael continued staring at the smoldering tin.

"If you want to protect our family, you need to be part of it," he said, distantly.

"What do you mean?"

"Stop running from us. Stop trying to fix every other family in this city. Be with the one you created," said Michael.

Kelsey nodded, tearfully.

"Thank you for not going to the police," she said.

"What you did for Sophia was a kindness. Turning you in would only have brought pain, and there's been enough of that tonight," said Michael.

"We can start again," said Kelsey, stroking his arm.

"You're sure the detective's done with you?" said Michael.

"You just burned the only evidence. We're clear."

"Good," said Michael, nodding distantly. "I don't know if I can ever forgive what you did; taking my son from me. But I'm grateful we have a daughter, and I'm grateful she has a mother. So there's that."

"I... I understand," said Kelsey. "I hope with time, we can heal. At least we don't have to worry about the police anymore."

"At least there'll be no link between you and the Broxleys, if the detective calls again," said Michael.

"Why would she come back?" said Kelsey.

Michael tapped his fingertips together, staring at the floor.

"Hey, Michael, answer the question. Why would the detective come back? More to the point, you've not even told me why she was here in the first place?"

Michael thought for a moment, then swallowed.

"Because I killed a man."

CHAPTER THIRTY-NINE

Kelsey groaned as the morning sun blasted her eyelids through the naked window. She rolled over and dragged herself into the shower. Her wet feet slopped across the tiles to the suitcase holding her last clean outfit. Curtains, bathmat, laundry detergent. She recited them in her head as she approached the refrigerator, cursing its emptiness.

She donned her jumpsuit and headed for the tram stop. It took a few minutes to track down; she was still getting her bearings around the rental. Having notified her staff that she was taking a personal day, she clutched her backpack and headed to an old district she'd not visited in some time.

The rusty iron gatepost felt oddly reassuring to her fingertips. She knocked on the door and stepped back.

"Kelsey?" said a gray-stubbled man in a delivery uniform.

"Tony?" she replied, astonished. "You're wearing clothes."

"How comes you didn't ring the bell?"

"That thing *works* now? No way."

She gave it a push, and marveled at the tacky tune that played out.

"Who is it?" came a familiar yell from the living room.

Kelsey peered around the doorway. Her old foster mother was sitting on the sofa, as rotund as ever. Age had taken the fight out of her. Blotches of melanin stained her sagging skin, and a Zimmer frame was parked in front of her seat.

"It's Kelsey," yelled Tony, from beside Kelsey's head. "She's a little deaf now," he added, in a bad whisper.

Kelsey nodded, nursing her ear.

"Hey kids, get out here, come see your big sister," yelled Tony.

One of the twins bounded out of the room eagerly, with a huge grin across her face.

"Hey sis!" yelled the first, tackling her with a bear hug.

"Woah, steady there Taylor, let her settle in before you go knocking her over," said Tony.

"Good to see you, Taylor," smiled Kelsey.

Although the house still stank of beer, Taylor's hair at least smelled of strawberries, even if it was in a putrid, chemical kind of way.

The second of the late-teenage twins slouched out from the bedroom with a surly expression, hands firmly in his pockets. He stumbled over a pair of shoes as he approached, then swore, cursing loudly at whoever left them there, until Taylor pointed out they were his shoes.

Kelsey wished she had been able to spend more time doing the coordination exercises with the kids when they were babies. Tony had tried his best, but it left them both wanting.

"Great to see you, li'l bro," said Kelsey, beckoning Seth over for a hug.

He gave her a cursory back pat and broke away to skulk in the corridor. He definitely took after his mother in temperament.

"Did you bring the thing?" said Tony, anxiously.

"What thing?" said Taylor, excitedly.

"Kelsey's brought a piece of kit that'll make you smart," said Tony.

Kelsey cringed at his appallingly undiplomatic phrasing, but Taylor didn't seem at all bothered.

"Cool!" said Taylor. "Hey doofus, I'm gonna be smart," she added, pretending to karate kick her brother.

Seth scowled and shuffled down to the kitchen, where he cracked open a beer.

"Do you need this?" asked Tony.

He handed Kelsey a multi-stained, tattered child-rearing manual; the original booklet he'd been given when the twins had been delivered some eighteen years ago.

Kelsey flicked through it with uneasy nostalgia. It was a miracle anyone had ever raised a kid off such a baffling set of instructions. The workload was utterly impractical. She consoled herself that the revised guidelines she'd introduced were making a practical difference by being actually intelligible to parents.

"No, that's OK, but thank you. I was hoping to speak to both of the twins, just to make sure they understand the procedure. It would be good if you and Stacey hear it too," said Kelsey.

Tony rounded up the twins and cajoled them into position on the couches, ready for Kelsey to present. She unloaded her backpack. In one hand, she held up a brass bowl with a cord attached to it. In the other, a small glass jar containing a pill.

"This is a neuro stimulator, and this is a neuro plasticizer," she said, raising each hand in turn.

The room looked at her blankly.

"Together they form a new experimental remedial treatment being piloted by my department, under license from the Ministry.

"I would like to give you both the opportunity to be among the first to receive it. It will help alleviate deficiencies in cognitive processing abilities, including gross and fine motor skills, auditory signal processing, and comprehension.

"It will require a twelve-month commitment to corrective therapy, followed by an intensive two-year reeducation program to consolidate the new neural networks in your brain.

"While there is a bursary available, it is slightly less than you would make were you earning during that period," said Kelsey.

"The hell is this bitch babbling on about?" yelled Stacey.

"She's trying to make the kids smart," said Tony.

"I'm already smart, I don't need no fancy crap," slurred Seth.

"Yeah you do, you're as dumb as me, jackass!" cheered Taylor.

Seth leaned over to thump his twin on the arm, but Tony intervened.

"Hey, cut it out, your big sister's trying to do a good thing here. It's an opportunity. Ask her what you need to know."

Taylor puzzled for a moment, then piped up. "How does it work?"

"The medication kinda turns your brain to putty, and

the therapy helps us to reform it so it's better connected," said Kelsey.

"So I'm gonna have a mushy brain?" said Taylor, warily.

"It will feel weird, and probably quite disorienting while the treatment's going on, which is why the first year would be residential, to ensure you're always in safe hands," said Kelsey.

"What if it goes wrong?" said Seth.

"It's a risk. A small one, but it's there. Worst case scenario, long-term cognitive impairment. Potentially an indefinite reversion to childhood, which would result in long-term dependency. But that's highly unlikely. We've modeled this extensively using our existing child techniques, and the chance of success is more than ninety percent. But really, the most important thing here is whether or not this is something you want. It's a big commitment, and-"

"I'm down!" said Taylor, excitedly.

Kelsey smiled, softly. "That's wonderful, Taylor, but you don't have to decide right now. I'm going to leave some brochures here for you all to read, and I'll come back in a week to see where you're at. If you have any questions in the meantime, you can always come by my office."

Kelsey passed the sample items around the room, and listened to Taylor's story about a new boy at her supermarket who stacks the aisle two down from her.

Her wristwatch chimed.

"Eek, I've got to fly. Take care everyone, think about what I said, and read the brochures together, please," said Kelsey.

Gathering her things, she made a hasty exit. Seth paced after her across the broken paving slabs.

"Wait up. This brain thing. Is there another way?" he asked.

Kelsey paused and looked at him. She could see his mother's hostile face lurking in his scowl, but also his father's earnestness.

"There is, but it would take around twelve years, and there's no guarantee it would work as effectively."

"What's it called?"

"Going back to school," said Kelsey.

Kelsey rocked up at the family house an hour later, feeling flustered. Damien and Leon were helping to load up the car with Olive's things.

"Sorry I'm late everyone, I'm here now," she puffed.

"Wow, Mom's actually around to help, that's a first," snarked Damien.

"She can't be worse than Dad, he's done *nothing* all day," piped up Leon.

Kelsey grabbed the top box from the stack Damien was carrying, as he wobbled under the weight, passing it to the empty-handed Leon.

"What can I do?" she said, with forced brightness.

"Get Dad out of the basement," said Olive, heading back inside.

Kelsey groaned and headed downstairs. Michael was hunched over his desk, scribbling frantically.

"What are you doing?" said Kelsey.

"She can't go. I've found strong evidence that the water at the university is unsafe. Look at these reports – do you see the bromine levels?"

Kelsey took the paper and glanced over it.

"Where did you even find this?" she asked, turning the copied pages.

"The water company has a public records library," said Michael.

"This report's over sixty years old, Michael," said Kelsey, slapping it back down.

"So?"

"So what's this really about?"

Michael turned away, bashfully. His shoulders twitched, and he tried to stifle a sob. Kelsey placed a consoling hand on his shoulder.

"I don't want her to go. She won't be safe."

"Of course she will, you're just being your usual paranoid self," said Kelsey.

"Don't touch me, I don't deserve your sympathy. I've put our family in danger," said Michael.

"If this is about the old man at the library, you have *got* to move past that. If the feds were going to charge you, they would've done it by now," said Kelsey.

"That's exactly my point. They haven't come for me, which means they'll be going for someone close to me. It's how they work," said Michael.

"Nonsense."

"They covered up a man's death, even though it was witnessed by dozens of people. They can do anything they want," said Michael.

"But why would the feds bother with us?"

"The feds don't care. It's that detective who cares. She's got it in for our family, like a vendetta. She threatened us, you know? When they couldn't press charges, she said there would still be 'consequences'. I think she means our children," said Michael, welling up.

A knot tightened in Kelsey's stomach. The detective

didn't strike her as the type to make idle threats - or to take losing lightly. She stared at Michael with revulsion.

"You're telling me our daughter's in danger because of what you did?" said Kelsey.

Gone was the reassuring, weary tone, from years of soothing Michael's anxiety and checking his meds. This was a credible threat he had brought on their house, and the anger in her voice was palpable.

"Fix it. I don't care how, Michael, just make it go away, OK?"

Olive called from upstairs, hurrying them.

"Coming sweetie," Kelsey replied. She turned back to Michael and leaned into his ear. "Not a word of this to the kids. Get your act together and let's go."

The porters were smartly dressed in waistcoats and ties. Michael followed Kelsey and Olive through the red-brick archway into the stone cabin, where a wizened woman with a dragonfly brooch greeted them.

"Olive Hadley?" she said, scrolling down the list of newbies. "Ah yes, here you go. Ooh, it looks like someone's changed your room. You'll be in the newly refurbished G4 in the main courtyard."

The porter slapped a key on the desk and Olive signed it out. The trio took a campus map and proceeded into the main courtyard, dragging a large wooden cart laden with Olive's possessions.

The scale of the campus astonished Michael. He'd been past the complex so many times, but he'd never appreciated how many buildings, private gardens, and courts were packed into its hallowed walls.

Automatons with bowler hats glided through the stone courtyards as they navigated their way past the great fountain and the old alchemy labs to Olive's residence block.

Across the lawn, a stooped figure traversed the cloisters. Michael peered closer, recognizing the face. He had aged somewhat in nearly two decades, but the man's features were unmistakable; it was the scholar he'd accosted outside the Ministry all those years ago.

He was clutching a briefcase close to his chest. Michael wondered if it contained the fragile leaves that he'd glimpsed last time.

As if sensing his gaze, the man looked outward. He locked eyes with Michael and stopped in his tracks. His mouth fell open as he recognized him instantly.

Michael hastily pressed on after the others, praying they hadn't noticed the silent interaction. He dragged the wooden cart faster, hurrying Olive and Kelsey onwards until they were well into the next courtyard.

He glanced backwards over his shoulder. There was no sign of the old scholar; perhaps he was busy reporting them.

"Michael, this way," called Kelsey, as she and Olive marched across to the far side.

Ivy swept across the front of the ancient brickwork, licking at timber frames and leaded windows.

They parked the cart by the base of a twisting, wooden staircase, then carried up the first load of Olive's belongings.

Stepping into her new room, Olive squealed with excitement. The carpet was faded, with bleached patches where stains had been rubbed out. Dust swirled in the sunlight streaming through the old, latticed windows. A tatty-looking armchair occupied one corner. Opposite was a single bed, and adjacent to that, a small refrigerator.

"It's perfect!" cried Olive.

She ran and jumped onto the bed, which creaked loudly. Kelsey and Michael dumped their heavy loads and looked around with curiosity.

Michael ran his finger over the window sill, noting the thick coating of dust. The paintwork was chipped around the edges, and one of the diamond-shaped window panes had been recently replaced.

He moved to the chest of drawers. There were mug rings and scuff marks imprinted on the wood, alongside two faint, crimson stains. Michael's eyes moved to the bleached carpet, and a chill swept over him.

"Are you sure you're happy in this room? Maybe we should see if you can be moved," he said, uneasily.

"Are you kidding me? This place is awesome! Look at the view, I can see the lawn, I've got that old cedar tree surrounded by stone archways, it's like a palace!"

Kelsey beamed with pride, stroking the shabby old fabric. There was definitely a romantic quality to the centuries-old place.

"We should move her," whispered Michael.

"Are you mad? We've only just got here," said Kelsey.

"I think something bad happened in this room," said Michael.

"So what if it did?" said Kelsey.

"What if they switched her to this room when they saw she was with me?"

"What are you talking about?"

"Think about it. It's how they punished me all those years ago - through my grandfather. What if they do it again? They're going to get to me through Olive. She's not safe here," hissed Michael.

"What happened to Amal was nothing to do with the

Ministry punishing you, Michael. It was probably baked into him as an embryo. Congenital defects were common in his generation, and some manifested late in life."

"You can't be sure. God, we should never have let her come here," hissed Michael.

"So what, we should just keep her cooped up at home wrapped in cotton wool for her whole adult life? Get a grip. And, for the record, if anyone has put her at risk, it's you, when you took it upon yourself to push someone off a god-damned roof," snarled Kelsey.

"That's *not* what happened, I told you already! It's rich you throwing that back in my face after what you did. Do you really want to have that conversation?"

"What conversation?" interjected Olive, sidling over.

"Nothing, sweetie," said Kelsey, glaring at Michael.

"Can you two please stop arguing just for today?" begged Olive.

"Of course, sorry. I think we need to buy you some essentials, shall we find the campus store?" said Kelsey, sweeping her daughter up in a side hug.

"I'll stay here," said Michael.

"OK, but Dad, don't go through my stuff again. I know you did the other day and it was not cool," said Olive.

Michael's mouth hung open, embarrassed, as his daughter and his estranged wife departed.

He peered from the window and watched them disappear across the courtyard, then scoured the room for security weaknesses, concealed entrances, anything he could conceive of.

His eyes fell on the room key which Olive had left on the dresser. Seizing it, he hastened downstairs, only to run into a new family arriving, laden with bags.

"Hey, nice to meet you," said the mother, waggling her

fingers beneath several heavy straps. "Are you on moving day duty too?"

"Uh, yes, my daughter's just moved in upstairs. Do you want a quick hand?" he said, trying his best to appear normal.

"Oh, would you mind? Thanks ever so much, there's more on the cart," said the mother.

She stepped away to reveal a cart brimming with an absurd number of possessions.

"I didn't realize all three of you were moving in," he muttered, grabbing a stack of boxes.

Michael carried two loads to their flat then extricated himself from the offers of tea and cake which, somehow, they'd already managed to extract from the travelling circus.

He hurried through the courtyards out into town.

"I need a copy of this," he said.

He slapped the key down on the locksmith's counter and glanced at his watch. It had taken him twenty minutes to walk there. If he wasn't back soon, Olive and Kelsey would get suspicious. The locksmith eyed it up and looked at Michael.

"ID card?" he said.

Michael hesitated. "Do I pay in advance?"

"It's a Ministry lock. Anyone who requests a key copy has to submit their ID. Ministry system does a quick check, then on we go. Prevents fraud."

"Er, what if I forgot my ID pass?" said Michael.

"Not carrying your ID is a felony."

"Of course, yes. Er, let me just double-check," said Michael, patting himself down.

"This *is* your key, sir?" said the locksmith, frowning.

"Uh, it would appear I'm unable to pay. I'll just take my key and come back another time," said Michael.

The locksmith snatched the key away.

"Sorry, sir, but I'm obliged to keep any keys which fail an ownership test. I'm required to return them to the Ministry. If it is indeed yours, they will see that it's returned to you in short order."

Michael's face paled. "No, no, I can't go back without it."

"It's not my decision, sir."

Michael dived onto the counter, grabbing the locksmith's arm.

"Are you insane? Get off me! Security!"

The man groped for the security button by the cashier, but Michael had his other hand pinned. Michael prized the key from his fingertips, then leaped from the counter.

The locksmith lunged at the button, triggering an alarm. Michael fled the store as heads turned. He weaved his way through the winding old side streets before slowing to a brisk walk.

Catching his breath, he melded into the stream of parents and freshers flowing toward the university entrance.

He gave a confident wave to the wizened porter, who somehow remembered his face from earlier, and slipped through into the main courtyard.

When he reached Olive's apartment, it was deserted. There was a ruckus from the door opposite. He heard Kelsey's voice, and Olive's laugh. He took a second to compose himself, then knocked and stepped in.

"Ah, the traveler returns!" declared the other mother. "Kelsey, your husband was an angel earlier and helped us lug all of Tarquin's things up these creaky old stairs."

"What a jolly good egg he is," said Kelsey, in a mock posh accent, making Olive snort with laughter again.

Her laughter stopped when she saw Michael's sweaty

brow and bedraggled hair, and she cringed all the way into her armchair.

"Where did you go, *dearest*?" said Kelsey.

Dearest?

Michael read the script immediately. Clearly, they were playing happy families today. Make a good first impression with *Tarquin* and the Yuppies.

"Uh, I was looking for you, *my love*. We should probably be leaving," said Michael.

"We're all having a nice time. I don't see a burning urgency," said Kelsey, curtly.

"No, well you wouldn't," snapped Michael.

"Maybe you should go, Dad, you look tired," said Olive.

She leaped up and hastily led him to the door.

"You don't have to stay here," whispered Michael.

"Dad, I *want* to be here. Quit worrying for two minutes, will you? I'm fine. I'll catch you soon."

"Wait, I've got your-"

Olive cut him off with a kiss on the cheek, then closed the door in his face.

―――――

More than twelve hours later, Michael hurried across the stone paving to his daughter's block, shivering. His breath misted in the air. He was freezing, having waited over an hour for the night porter to step away from the front desk. With no torrent of new arrivals to hide among, stealth had been the only option. It had taken longer than planned, but he'd finally made it back inside the university campus.

The hairs on his neck tingled in the pale rays of dawn. He had to be quick. He crossed the deserted courtyard to Olive's stairwell. By the entrance was a series of enamel pipes. He zeroed in on his daughter's name, and plucked her room key from his pocket.

He stuffed the key in her mailbox and turned.

It wouldn't open.

Michael checked the giant clock face on the front of the banquet hall. 5:59 a.m. The mailboxes were always sealed in the minutes before 6 a.m., presumably to allow the vacuum mechanism to work.

He danced from side to side, rubbing his arms as he waited for the clock to chime.

A shining glint caught his eye, moving through the cloisters. An automaton glided into the courtyard. Cursing, Michael ducked down behind the mailbox.

Vapor from his hot breath billowed upwards like a smoke signal. The machine's head rotated with a series of mechanical clicks as it focused on Michael's position.

The machine glided towards him. It was slower than usual on the uneven paving stones, but its caterpillar tracks were sturdy, and still made it faster than a human.

As Michael searched wildly for an escape route, the courtyard clock chimed six. Leaping up, he thrust the key into the lock once again, begging for mercy.

The machine was closing in fast. Its cold eyes were locked on Michael's shivering figure.

He turned the key with a cry. The archaic hatch fell open with a clang, revealing a barren, empty chamber.

Michael slumped backwards as relief crashed over him. In the same moment, the automaton's powerful arms raised him from the ground, snapping him out of his trance.

Michael cried out in protest, kicking and squirming as he dangled by the scruff of his neck, rasping for air.

He clawed at its impassive face, begging for release, but the machine was deaf to his words and unmoved by the contortions of pain across his face. Its grip was firm and precise, applying no direct pressure to Michael's body, merely clutching his collar, and letting gravity strangle him under his own bodyweight.

"He- help- m- me!" rasped Michael. "O- O- *Olive!*"

He kicked out, striking the mailboxes beside him with a clang. Michael kicked again, harder, and louder, with every last bit of strength in his body.

His eyesight failed.

His legs fell limp.

A window burst open.

A woman screamed.

Michael blacked out.

Sometime later, Michael came to. He was on a bed, and something was covering his mouth. He fumbled around, groggily, until his hand made sense of the oxygen mask strapped over his face.

He tugged it off and sat up, taking in his surroundings. It was somewhere between an infirmary and a police cell. On the wall was a university emblem, and a photo of some academic he didn't recognize.

A thin, scratchy blanket covered his legs. He drew it tight around his shivering body, then reached for the mug of hot tea by his bedside, seeking to revive his fuzzy brain further.

No sooner had he taken a sip than he spat it out, spraying tea everywhere as he scrambled back, terrified.

The same automaton that had accosted him in the courtyard now stood guard in the corner of the room, staring at him.

The mug shattered across the floor as he recoiled. Almost instantly, the cell door flung open and Olive rushed in.

"Dad! Are you OK? They wouldn't let me in while you were unconscious – they said you needed to recover."

"Get that thing away from me!"

"Relax, Dad, it's not going to hurt you. Just drink the- Ugh. Right. Now I need to find you more meds. Great."

"What was in the tea?" said Michael, baffled.

"Nothing. Just... your usual stuff, alright?"

"You know about that?"

"Uh, duh. Before Mom moved out, she showed me where you kept it. So I could check you were taking it like you should. I'm guessing you skipped yesterday's dose, huh?"

"That's none of your... Why am I here? What even *is* this room?"

"It's a holding cell. Normally for drunk students, but apparently today it's for my doofus dad, who won't take his meds," scowled Olive.

"The machine... it tried to kill me," whispered Michael.

"No, Dad, it didn't. It restrained you because you were trespassing. It thought you were a threat to the students."

"Why would I hurt a student?"

"I'm not saying you would, Dad. But maybe you could start by telling me what the hell you were doing in the first place?"

Michael shook his head despondently.

"You wouldn't understand."

"Don't dismiss me, I'm not a kid anymore! I've put up with this kinda stuff from you for years. It's not cute anymore, it's not quirky or 'under control'. You're behaving like a genuinely crazy person."

"Look at these marks and tell me I'm making it up!" protested Michael, showing the raw skin around his neck.

"I'm not denying you got kinda strangled, I'm asking what the hell you were doing trying to break into my mail at the crack of dawn," she snapped.

"I was trying to protect you," said Michael.

"From what? Making friends like a normal fresher? Uh, *mission accomplished.*"

"From the Ministry."

"That doesn't make any sense."

"They're using you to get to me. To punish me."

"For what?"

"Mistakes I've made."

"You're punishing yourself, Dad. You've been doing it for years, and it's making you miserable," she said.

"If you knew what I knew-" began Michael.

"I know enough. I know about your little research project, for one. All those weird deaths you've been obsessing over. Yeah, that's right - I broke into your conspiracy factory in the basement. Took me weeks to find the key to the desk. And what did I find? A full-on *crazy person's* drawer. But I thought, hey, I can see past this, he's still a good dad, so what if he's got a hobby that's absolutely insane? I'll bring it up later. Then you and Mom decided to divorce, or go on a break, or whatever the hell it is you two are doing, and suddenly you were too fragile to confront about anything. Maybe I should've said something sooner. In a way, it was all leading to something like this."

"How can you say that? If you truly saw my research, you'd know what's at stake! Our world, our deaths, the Ministry is *lying* to us," begged Michael.

"Listen to yourself, Dad! You've got a problem. And no

wonder it's gotten worse with the amount of free time you have these days."

"What do you mean?"

"I know you don't have a job. Were you planning on telling us ever, or were you just gonna wait until we got evicted? Who do you think paid the last two bills? It wasn't Mom, that's for sure, because she's moved out, assuming you had it covered. I'm not there to cover for you this month, Dad, so you're gonna have to get it together pretty quick."

"Yes... Yes I'll fix the money, of course... But I need to get my report published first. You understand that, don't you? People need to know the truth. But... I can't publish it... they've already threatened you once," wept Michael.

"Who?"

"The Ministry!"

"We're back to this again?"

"All I want is for you to be safe and happy."

"Right now, the biggest threat to my well-being is you, Dad. Until you can admit you've got a problem, we're done here. I need you to leave me alone for a long while. If anything like this happens again, it will be *me* going to the police, not just the university."

"Olive," pleaded Michael.

But she was gone. He slumped his head against the table and groaned in despair. From the opposite side of the room, the door opened again. A familiar voice greeted him.

"Kids, hey?"

Michael dragged his head from the table and groaned as a familiar red ponytail and trench coat entered.

Clarkenwell took a seat opposite him, chomping merrily on an almond croissant, shedding pastry flakes across her half-tucked shirt.

"Do they have other cops in this city or is it just you?" groaned Michael.

"I could say the same about criminals."

"I'm not a criminal, I'm..."

"Misunderstood? No doubt. I was just about to finish my shift for the day, when we got the call. I heard your name and I couldn't resist. I guess part of me was curious as to what you'd screwed up this time. Trespass?"

The door opened again and Michael sat up, astonished. Val entered, looking impeccably dressed for the hour. Clarkenwell doffed an imaginary cap to Michael's mother, before taking another generous bite of croissant.

"Some retirement you're having, Ms Hadley. Your family like to keep you busy, don't they?"

Stony-faced, Val took a seat at the foot of Michael's bed and stared coldly at the detective.

"Are you planning on arresting my client?"

"Well, let's see now, he was caught trespassing, while trying to infiltrate another citizen's mail, and now he's lying to police by trying to claim he's not a criminal. I make that three charges to get us started, so, yeah, probably gonna be arresting him," shrugged Clarkenwell.

"From my understanding, the only witness was the campus automaton, and machines can't be called upon to testify as sole witnesses. Meaning you don't have a case," said Val.

"Ah, but there *is* a human witness, isn't there? Your client's daughter."

"You expect her to testify against her own father?"

"She doesn't have a choice. She will be called as a witness, and she will be obliged to tell the truth."

"She will exercise her right to silence."

"We'll see. Sometimes family can surprise you," smiled the detective.

"Are you arresting my client or not?"

"No. But only because it's late and I don't wanna go back to the station. I'll release your client under caution for now. We'll be in touch should the university decide to seek prosecution."

Val rose silently and marched to the door where the automaton stood sentry. She glared at the machine defiantly until it opened the door. Michael scarpered after her, not daring to look at the machine directly.

"See you soon!" called Clarkenwell.

Michael had to double-step to keep pace with his mother. She stayed half a pace ahead, striding in pointed silence until they were several blocks clear of the university.

"You seem determined to make the same mistakes as your father," she snapped.

"It's the opposite, Mom, I'm trying to avoid his mistakes. I want my family to be safe, that's all," choked Michael.

"They *are* safe. You're the one jeopardizing that. I trust you've learned the truth about Olive?"

Michael nodded.

"Then you should be keeping your head down, not pulling ridiculous stunts like this. No good can come of meddling with the Ministry's process, you should have learned that years ago!"

"Someone's got to challenge them," said Michael.

"What does that even mean?" she snapped.

"The system's rigged. People should be allowed to choose."

His mother's face fell. "Don't tell me you're one of them."

"One of who?"

"The deniers. The tin hats. The idiots who ignore the choice they're given, deny the choice they've made, and pursue their own insanity at the cost of everyone around them!"

Michael said nothing for a while, as he followed his marching mother to her car.

"How did you know to come for me?" he said, after a while.

"Your daughter told me what had happened. I figured you must be out of your mind trying something like that, so thought it best you have some sane legal representation."

"She doesn't want to see me again," said Michael.

"Can you blame her?"

"How do I keep her safe if I can't see her?"

Val said nothing as she climbed into the car. He reached for the passenger door, but she pulled away, leaving him alone in the street.

Michael's eyes moved to the Ministry dome on the horizon, which rose high above the surrounding buildings. If he was going to take on the system, he would have to go it alone. But he would not be silenced anymore. Drawing his coat tight around him, he set off for home at speed.

CHAPTER FORTY

Kelsey lowered the operating seat until it was flat like a dentist's chair. Taylor pawed at the periscope clumsily, trying to adjust it. Kelsey helped her nestle the viewing piece across her eyes like ski goggles. A thick hose was attached to the back of each lens, stretching up to the ceiling, to a control panel across the room.

"Is that comfortable?" asked Kelsey.

Taylor nodded. Her usual buoyancy was missing, now that the procedure was becoming a reality.

"It's not too late to change your mind, you know?" said Kelsey, stroking her half-sister's hand.

"I'm good. Let's do it," said Taylor, assertively.

Kelsey gave her assistant a nod, and she injected a solution into Taylor's arm.

"You might feel a bit woozy for the first few sessions, like you're swimming, but that's perfectly normal. Just focus on your breathing, or raise a hand and we can take a break anytime," said Kelsey.

Taylor gave her a thumbs up.

"I'm starting the ocular stimulus now, you should start to see things on your goggles," said Kelsey.

The automaton turned a lever on the control panel, which emitted a soft hum. Kelsey peered into the glowing box and slid the first of several vinyl filters over the projector.

Hovering a foot above the box was a funnel, which connected to the periscope.

"Tell me what you see," said Kelsey.

Taylor mumbled for a moment, chewing on her lip.

"Taylor?" said Kelsey.

Taylor gurgled, then began to choke. Kelsey leaped from her chair and rushed over to her sister.

"She's having a reaction to the meds, get the adrenaline, quick!"

Her assistant plunged a needle into Taylor's outer thigh. The automaton killed the ocular device, while Kelsey pulled the goggles off. Taylor's pupils had dilated to fill almost the entire width of her eyes.

"Another dose, hurry!"

The automaton glided to Kelsey's side, emitting a faint electrical crackle.

"No - her heart's beating, just wait, we need to see if her brain responds," urged Kelsey. "Come on, Taylor."

The teenager's pupils began to constrict, but they soon plateaued, leaving the blacks of her eyes ten percent larger than normal.

"Taylor, can you hear me?" implored Kelsey.

The teenager's mouth opened and closed silently like a fish out of water.

"Call an ambulance, we need to get her to the hospital."

Kelsey sat on the floor with her back to the office door. Her cheeks were puffy and tear-stained. Taylor's condition was stable, but it would be some days before they could fully assess the implications of the treatment.

The hour was late, and all staff had gone save for the automatons. Kelsey watched as they prepared the kilns for the evening bake. It was a quiet night - only five children had been commissioned.

She dragged herself from the building and walked a while until she found herself at the outreach center along the road. She slipped into the back and observed a night class. An audience of vulnerable adolescents were being taught the practical life skills they would need for independent living.

Tonight's class was all about cleaning. The children were having a great time messing around, spraying each other with the water-filled mock bottles, and throwing wet sponges around. The teacher patiently let them familiarize themselves with their new tools, before moving on to a role play exercise.

At the back of the hall, a half-dozen parents mingled politely, enjoying the free coffee and snacks, swapping stories of frustration and hilarity from their lives as carers.

A parent spotted Kelsey at the door and beckoned her inside.

"Director, how lovely to see you!"

Kelsey stepped in, awkwardly, not really in the mood for her public duties.

"We were just saying what a lifeline this new center has been. In fact, we've nominated you for a city award."

A lump formed in Kelsey's throat. How would they feel if they knew her experimental treatment had just landed Taylor in hospital?

"That's kind, but I'm sure there are others more deserving than me," replied Kelsey.

"Nonsense, you're a community hero. No one was championing families like ours until you took over. We owe you a debt."

Kelsey graciously bowed out, fighting back the tears of guilt. She sucked in the evening air and composed herself. Turning on her heel, she retraced her steps, making a beeline for the office. There had to be a reason Taylor's intervention went wrong. It was on her to fix it.

CHAPTER FORTY-ONE

Michael paced the block. Yet again, he couldn't sleep, such was his anxiety about Olive. She wasn't returning his calls, and had blocked the house number, so he was reliant on trying through phone boxes.

A door opened across the street. Michael paused in the shadows and watched. His ancient neighbor stepped out and looked around furtively, before climbing into his car.

Michael had seen the man do the exact same thing the night before. He wasn't dressed for any kind of work, and it was well past the hour of socialization. There was only one direction in which the man's car could be headed.

The Ministry.

Michael's brain whirred as he considered the unimaginable. Grabbing his car keys, he set off after the old man.

He hung back half a block or so, maintaining a discreet distance. Sure enough, the old man soon pulled over by the Ministry square.

He climbed out of his car and hobbled towards the vast, domed building. As he neared the front steps, he detoured to the side, approaching the invisible doorway Michael had first observed years back.

The old man glanced around to check the square was empty, then knocked on the door. A hatch opened at eye level, and he placed something through. The hatch closed. The old man bowed to the door, then hobbled back to his car.

Michael hid until the old man was gone, then climbed out of his car and approached the hatch. He patted his pockets for something of value, then settled on his wristwatch.

He knocked on the door and the hatch slid open. A sliver of light warmed his face. Michael could see no one operating the hatch, but there was a collection bowl affixed to it.

Michael deposited his wristwatch, then stepped back. The hatch closed. Michael bowed, and walked away. Was that it? Had he just stumbled across the secret of Ministry offerings?

A grating sound pricked his ears. He turned in time to see the hatch reopen and spit his watch onto the stones below. The offering bowl was immediately retracted, and the hatch slammed shut.

A security automaton glided out onto the raised platform at the top of the grand steps, clicking its head to scan the square below. Michael snatched up his wristwatch and hurried back to the car.

Driving home, Michael pondered what they wanted. They had accepted *something*, but he had no idea what. He hurried back to the old man's house and knocked frantically.

His aged neighbor shuffled to the door and opened it a fraction.

"Yes?" said the old man, peering at Michael from behind a security chain.

"What's your secret? The thing you just dropped off at the Ministry, what is it?" said Michael, desperately.

The old man's eyes widened fearfully. "Get off my property!" he rasped.

He tried to slam the door but Michael wedged his foot in the gap.

"Please, just tell me and I'll leave you in peace!"

"Go, or I'll call the police!" cried the man.

With his hands raised in surrender, Michael removed his foot. The old man slammed the door shut, swiftly turning the deadlocks.

Michael slouched home and sank onto the couch. The old man had more wrinkles than a cabbage, yet he was still going strong, while others like Michael's father died so much younger. The old man had to be cheating the system. Why the hell else would he be conducting a secretive ritual using a little-known invisible hatch under the cover of night? Michael had to discern the secret for his own family. But how?

It hit him like a bolt. He couldn't believe he'd been so stupid. He rushed down to the basement, rummaging through all his detritus until he reached a dusty old suitcase.

Hauling it out onto the floor, he flung the lid open, revealing the broken automaton inside. He lifted the first piece up to the light and marveled at it. This machine had sacrificed itself to help his family once before. If he could repair it somehow, maybe it would help them again.

Michael worked through the night, fueled by coffee and despair at the impending 6 a.m. deadline that could see his family snatched from him. In his time at the engineering firm, before he'd become sidetracked by his morbid private investigations, he'd used the quiet hours to swot up on his mechanical skills, with the hope of one day being able to leverage an apprenticeship.

That ship had sailed, but at least his knowledge was being put to use now, as he assembled cogs and levers, and rewired the internal mechanisms, which seemed to be powered by some sort of gas exchange.

The eyes needed polishing. Both were intact, though one was cracked. He traced his hand wistfully over the beautiful blue stain that infused the machine's cranium and upper vertebrae.

Michael fitted the last of the external plating, a jigsaw of enamel and metal, then rotated the chair to face him.

He marveled at the figure before him. On tenterhooks, he inserted the final piece; the machine's heart, if you could use such a term.

It was a pyramid-shaped piece of cerebrium, around the size of Michael's thumbnail. It bore the same sunburst colors as the stains on the gas exchange outlets. He pressed it into place, then activated the four valves below it.

The vacuum tanks hissed, re-pressurizing. Michael closed the automaton's chest plates and stepped back, fearfully.

With a metallic clinking, the machine rose to its feet. Its head rotated, surveying the room, then stopped abruptly two-thirds of the way around.

Something was jamming in its neck. Michael blushed,

knowing he hadn't quite been able to straighten out all the damaged parts.

The machine tried several more times then reversed course, rotating its head the long way to reach the other side.

It then rotated its wrists, tested its arm motion in all planes, before taking a precarious step forward.

Michael shuffled back further. The machine turned its head to focus on him, then rotated its body to catch up. It glided towards him until it was just inches from his face.

Michael raised a trembling hand. Furtively, he patted the automaton's chest. The machine released a jet of steam. Michael leaned back sharply, ducking the plume of hot air, while the automaton hastily tightened a valve around its neck.

As the air cleared, the machine's hand flew upwards. Michael cowered, anticipating a heavy blow. After a moment, he peered out between his fingers. The machine patted him gently on the chest, then glided backwards.

"I... I need your help," Michael stammered. "My daughter's in danger. From the Ministry. They want to use her to punish me. There's an old man across the street, a neighbor, and I think he's figured out a way to protect his family. There's some sort of offering the Ministry accepts. Can you show me what it is?"

The machine stared at him blankly. Michael was about to explain again when the doorbell interrupted. He hurried upstairs, sealing the basement behind him.

"Kelsey? What on earth are you doing here at this hour?"

He examined Kelsey's face further and realized she wasn't there to fight. She bore an expression he'd not seen on her before. Genuine fear.

Standing on the path behind her was a young woman he

didn't recognize. She looked to be around the same age as Olive, but she had the innocent, vacant expression of a child, and was wearing a hospital gown.

"What's going on?" said Michael, warily.

Kelsey looked him in the eye. "I need a favor."

CHAPTER FORTY-TWO

Taylor sat on the couch, seemingly unaware of her surroundings. Stirred by the noise of new arrivals, Leon trundled down the stairs. Upon seeing his mother, he squealed with joy, launching himself at her with a sweeping hug. Kelsey's heart ached as her youngest son's arms wrapped around her.

"Mom, you're back!" he cheered. Then he saw Taylor. "Who's she? Why's she dressed weird?"

"This is Taylor, she's my half-sister, which I guess makes her your half-aunt. She's recovering from an accident, so she's gonna stay here with you and your dad for a bit, until she's ready to go back to her own home."

"Are you gonna stay too?" asked Leon, optimistically.

"I can't right now, sweetie," said Kelsey.

"Why not?" he pressed, crestfallen.

Kelsey glanced at Michael.

"It's complicated."

"Remind me why she can't stay with her own family?" said Michael.

"Because they're the worst. I think Stacey's exact words

were, 'She's your mess to clean up now'. She's over eighteen, so technically they don't have to house her anymore."

"What about Tony? I thought he was a half-decent father these days?"

"Tony does what Stacey orders. Look, I don't want to talk about their hideous relationship right now, I just need you to help me with this. *Please*. The hospital won't take her back, they say she's stable so there's nothing more they can do, and I can't keep her at my apartment while I'm at work, because she's just not safe on her own. Please, Michael. I know things are rough between us right now, but if you still love me at all, I really need your help."

Michael sighed, wearily.

"Of course. She can stay as long as she needs."

There was a clatter from the basement.

"What was that?" said Kelsey.

"Nothing," replied Michael, hastily.

Heavy thuds emanated from the hallway. Kelsey peered at the basement door with alarm. Michael darted past her, blocking it off with unconvincing nonchalance.

"You should probably head off," said Michael.

"Michael, tell me what's going on," demanded Kelsey.

There was a bang at the door. Then another. The impacts shook Michael's body as he tried to enforce his blockade. He gripped the door handle tightly, but it twisted against him. The door creaked open. Michael's feet burned as he was pushed back across the carpet. With a hissing plume of steam, the automaton stepped into the hallway and fixed its stony eyes on Kelsey.

Her mouth fell open.

"What the hell is this thing doing in our house?" she exclaimed.

"Don't freak out," urged Michael.

"You're hiding a Ministry automaton in the *basement!*"

As the steam cleared, Kelsey faltered.

"I know this machine," she stammered.

"What?"

"I've seen it before – years ago. Before I met you. It worked at the city nursing home. I was hiding there and it found me."

"Did it report you?"

"No... It brought me food. Or at least, I think that's what it was doing. It might have been intended for the resident whose room I was squatting in."

"This is incredible, you're saying this machine has already helped us both!" beamed Michael.

"Maybe. But there was something else about it. The manager there wanted to get rid of it, but I can't remember why..."

Kelsey's eyes widened as the memory came flooding back; the panic in the care home, the elderly woman going into cardiac arrest, the manager's despair.

She stepped backwards, fearfully. Her voice was suddenly dry.

"This machine isn't what you think," she croaked.

"What are you talking about?"

"It killed an old lady."

"You saw that? Why didn't you report it?"

"I didn't see it directly, but this machine was the last thing to go into the old woman's room."

"How many years ago was this? Maybe you're confusing it with another? There are lots of automatons..."

"Impossible – have you *ever* seen another machine that looks like this?"

Michael glanced at the mottled blue stains across the automaton's face and shook his head.

"What if it's a suspect or something?" continued Kelsey. "There could be a bounty on its head!"

"Don't be ridiculous. Besides, the Ministry have had eighteen years to find it. No one's kicked our door down in that time."

"This thing's been in our home all that time? Are you *insane?*"

"It was broken, I kept it in a suitcase," said Michael, sheepishly.

"I want it gone. Right now. What it did to that woman…"

"But you never actually saw it do anything! You said it yourself, the woman was elderly. Maybe it was just her time?"

"She didn't have a letter, Michael, you know what happens to souls that die without their letter! That's why I remember it so clearly. I've not seen this machine since the manager got rid of it that same day; I think she suspected it too. I don't want it in our house, Michael, it's dangerous!"

"Wait, please Kelsey, give it a chance. I used to think it was sinister but I was wrong, OK? I've *seen* it do good with my own eyes."

"In which case it would be a stolen Ministry artifact you've kept hostage for two decades!" fumed Kelsey. "It could roll out of the house and report us to the police at any moment!"

"Not this one. It's different, Kelsey, I swear. It's on our side – I don't think it follows the Ministry's rules. That's why they tore it apart. It brought me something that healed Granddad; a token of sorts. At first, I didn't know what to do. I thought it was cursed."

"Wait, *that* was the curse? Some 'token' was the great

hocus pocus you were tormenting yourself over all those years ago?" cried Kelsey.

"Not exactly, but the point is, I threw the token away, and Granddad kept getting worse. This same machine kept tracking me down, and finally it administered a strip of medicine to Granddad directly. It was like nothing I've seen before. It *healed* him, Kelsey, he remembered who he was again."

Kelsey's jaw slackened. She looked from Michael to the blue-stained machine and back. Surely her husband wasn't referring to what she was thinking of...

"Describe the token it gave your granddad – the 'strip of medicine'," said Kelsey.

"It was weird," mused Michael. "It came in a thin glass slab with symbols embossed on the edges. It looked transparent, but then under the light it glimmered like a slick of oil. This automaton cracked it open and took out a liquidy-wafer-thing which it placed on Granddad's tongue. It was super weird, like it was tailor made or something, because the symbols on the glass matched those on Granddad's tattoo."

Kelsey leaned against the wall, processing.

"I've seen those 'slabs'," she said, faintly. "We use them at work. They're part of the bake. I always thought it was just the serum that was used, I never knew there was any residual liquid in the vessels. The slabs go back to the Ministry..."

"...who control people's health," completed Michael.

Kelsey stared at him, with a deep sense of foreboding. Most worrying of all, her paranoid, skittish, sleep-deprived husband was starting to make sense.

"I could use a coffee. You?" said Michael.

Kelsey nodded and they moved through to the kitchen. The automaton lingered in the hallway.

"Does it just stay there?" said Kelsey, as the coffee brewed.

"I don't know what it can or can't do yet. This is its first day back in operation in almost twenty years. I did my best putting it back together, but I'm pretty sure it's not supposed to leak steam every ten minutes."

Kelsey's unease was growing. The thought of keeping another Ministry secret so close to home filled her with dread.

"You need to return it, Michael," said Kelsey, wringing her hands.

"Are you crazy? This thing can help us protect Olive."

"From what? Her father's paranoias? Michael, this isn't right, it could get us into a lot of trouble. It's stolen Ministry property and we're already on their list."

"List for what?"

"All kinds of things! We've both been investigated by the police. We've both done things we regret. We need to keep our heads down, now more than ever."

"Now? Why now? Kelsey, what's happened? Has this got something to do with Taylor?"

Michael's eyes darted to the couch, but the teenager was missing.

"Wait, where's she gone?"

Kelsey spun around, also clocking Taylor's empty seat. She leaped to her feet, calling Taylor's name.

From the hallway, a loud thudding resonated. Michael and Kelsey hurried towards the sound. The automaton leaped over the threshold and sped across the garden path. Kelsey's eyes widened as she saw Taylor standing in the middle of the road, clutching the sides of her gown, looking distressed. A horn blared. Brakes screeched. With a surge of speed, the automaton powered forwards and dived for Taylor.

Both she and it vanished from sight as the blaring truck swept past with a screech. Kelsey called out in horror. She ran forwards. On the far side of the road were two bodies, wrapped like lovers spooning. Neither was moving. She fell to her knees, placing a hand on Taylor's cheek.

The teenager's eyes flickered open, sleepily. She became aware of the machine wrapped around her, and its large, shielding hand cradling her skull from the ground. Startled, she struggled against it, moaning. Kelsey soothed her, as tears of guilt and relief flooded her eyes.

The truck driver was angrily pacing towards them from a hundred feet down the road.

"What the hell are you people playing at!" he cried.

Michael intervened hastily.

"I'm so sorry, mister, our daughter's not well and she got out of the house. Sorry if we gave you a fright. She's alright, no harm done."

"Yeah, only thanks to that machine. Where were you people?" fumed the man.

"We'll take it from here, thank you for stopping," said Michael, curtly.

The man's eyes softened when he saw Taylor's vulnerable figure, crying in Kelsey's arms. He muttered something semi-conciliatory and returned to his truck.

The automaton climbed to its feet and carried out a systems check for damage. It was a little scuffed, but otherwise all parts remained in working order. Michael gave a forced, friendly wave to his curtain-twitching neighbors, and ushered the group back inside.

They returned Taylor to the couch, got her a drink and

blanket, then put on a children's TV show, which seemed to soothe her. The automaton sat beside her, appearing to watch the show too. Michael and Kelsey retreated to the kitchen, and resumed their coffee making.

"I can't be responsible for her, not if she's going to be like that," whispered Michael.

"Please, it's only a couple of weeks," urged Kelsey.

"Why can't you keep her with you?"

"I told you! I'm not allowed guests at my rental place, and if the Ministry finds out what happened to her, they'll fire me for sure. I have to keep her off grid, until she's better."

"Why? Did *you* do this to her?"

"It was an experimental procedure, alright? It was supposed to help her, but it didn't work as expected. She's regressed much more than I anticipated and it's too soon to tell if it's permanent or temporary."

"I'm calling Tony. Her family have to take some responsibility for this, too."

"No! We can't push them – they might report me for malpractice. I have to see if she gets better first. I *can* make her better, I swear, I hope, but I need time. Please, Michael, I'm begging you to help me here."

Michael rubbed his itchy, bloodshot eyes.

"I need something in return," he said.

"Name it."

"I want my wife back."

Kelsey's shoulders dropped.

"It's not that simple, Michael."

"Why not? I miss you!"

"You killed a man," she hissed.

The automaton's head clicked around from the couch and fixed eyes on Michael.

"No, Kelsey, I *saved* a man from a situation he could no longer bear. I respected his freedom. After everything you've been through, I thought you of all people would understand."

"After everything I've been through, I *value* my life, Michael, and those of everyone around me. I want to make their lives better, not shorter," she hissed.

"Me too! That's why I rebuilt the machine!" urged Michael.

"This is exactly the sort of behavior that drove me out, Michael. You're obsessed with trying to game the system. You can't beat life! You will only make yourself miserable trying."

"That is so hypocritical coming from you," snapped Michael.

"No, it's not! I cheated twice and I regret it deeply, you know that. What I did, switching the babies, had consequences I never imagined. I realize now that the only way forward is to make the system work for you. If you try to beat it, you'll lose every time."

"This is what you call 'making it work'? Hiding your lobotomized half-sister here?"

"It's temporary."

"How about us, are we temporary?"

"Please, Michael, I can't do this right now. You kept things from me. I miss the man I used to know - when our children were growing up. You had yourself under control, you were taking your meds, living your life, not just desperately trying to fend off the inevitable," said Kelsey.

"That's what I've been trying to tell you all! There's *nothing* inevitable about our death letters! I know that now. There's a way to bargain with the Ministry."

Michael's eye glimmered as he pictured his ancient

neighbor making the offering at the Ministry under the cover of darkness.

Kelsey's eyes fell to the stack of envelopes on the table.

"What are these? Are you behind on your bills?"

Michael tried to snatch the letters away from her, but she was too quick.

"Michael, there are multiples from each utility. Since when are you in financial difficulty? I've been subbing you for the kids' expenses. What's going on?"

"It's nothing, I've got it under control," said Michael.

"You're still working, right?" said Kelsey, warily.

Michael pretended not to hear, and busied himself in the cupboard.

"Oh my god. Since when?"

"Only a few weeks," said Michael.

"You mean you were fired before I even moved out, and you didn't think to tell me?"

"Really? You wanna play the secrets card? Last time I checked, I didn't lie to you about our daughter's birth," snapped Michael.

"I was trying to protect you! I've apologized a hundred times, what more can I do?"

"Stop judging me for trying to protect her now, then! You brought her into my life, I'm trying to keep her alive. You need to respect that."

Kelsey's wristwatch chimed.

"I need to be at work. You should try it sometime, it'll help with the bills," said Kelsey, hurrying to the couch.

"And I'll just look after your sister for free then, will I?" called Michael.

Kelsey knelt before Taylor, and reassured her she'd be back soon. The girl didn't take her eyes from the screen. Kelsey kissed her forehead, then hurried for the door.

"There should be some of Olive's spare clothes upstairs, I'm sure she won't mind. Can you mention it if you see her before I do?"

Michael glanced at the floor and felt his cheeks burn.

"That's unlikely..."

Kelsey stared at him with dread.

"Oh god, Michael, what did you do?"

"I'm banned from campus," he mumbled.

"Perfect. Just perfect. And you wonder why we're separating," said Kelsey.

She stormed from the house, leaving Michael alone in the hall, wondering what the hell he was going to say when Damien woke up and saw the new tenants.

CHAPTER FORTY-THREE

The boys had never seen an automaton like this. Leon, the youngest, found its battered visage entertaining, and took delight in prodding its bumpy armor. The machine sat, idly, putting up no resistance to the curious child. Its eyes remained locked on the TV screen, beside Taylor.

Damien, by contrast, was unnerved. He was older, and knew from school that the automatons belonged to the Ministry. Michael could sense his unease, but instead of the barrage of questions he'd anticipated, his eldest son was subdued, choosing to eat breakfast in the kitchen, away from the machine and the woman in the hospital gown.

Michael took Damien to the side, as the boys prepared to leave for school

"Don't tell anyone about our guests, OK?" he whispered.

Damien nodded, looking at the floor.

"They won't be here for that long, they just need to a rest a little, but it's best if no one else knows. We don't want to overwhelm them with lots of visitors."

Michael glanced over at his youngest son, who had abandoned his shoelaces in favor of watching the TV beside his new human-sized teddy bear, Taylor.

"Your little brother might be tempted to tell people about the automaton, or Taylor. If anyone asks, just tell them he has a vivid imagination, OK? Can I count on you, Damien?"

His son nodded, then slouched out of the door. Michael snatched Leon away from the TV, tied his laces, and ushered him out after his brother.

With a sigh of relief, he waved them off, then closed the door and headed for more coffee. With a jolt, he remembered Taylor, quickly doubled back and deadlocked the front door, then checked in on the guests.

Taylor was absently chomping on a bowl of cereal, with her eyes still glued to the screen. The automaton sat patiently beside her.

"If you need me, I'll be downstairs," said Michael.

The machine rotated its head with a steady clicking and stared at Michael, then turned back to the TV.

Michael descended to his basement desk. How much could he trust his boys? They were only children. They weren't to know what was at stake. Too many loose words could lead to a house call from social services, or the police. Harboring a mysterious woman in a hospital gown? A Ministry automaton mysteriously battered? Such ramblings would raise suspicion.

There was only one thing for it. He had to go on the offensive, get the upper hand against the Ministry. It was time to expose the truth, and release his evidence to the world.

Unlocking the desk drawers, Michael stared at the contents in disbelief. A rising wave of panic took hold as he pawed his hands through the empty spaces. He cried out in despair, frantically searching the surrounding cupboards and shelves until he found a discarded folder, where the sole copy of his report had lived. In it was a brief handwritten note from Olive.

Dad, I did this to protect you from yourself. Please get help.

Michael broke down in tears. It wasn't just the report that was gone, it was his notes, newspaper clippings, leads; every piece of evidence he'd painstakingly amassed. Months of work destroyed.

With a cry of anger, he threw the empty drawers across the room, shattering them against the concrete. Michael curled on the floor, weeping.

Enraged, and desperate, Michael dragged himself out of the basement. He had to get answers, and that meant confronting the machine.

A strange sound greeted his ears; someone was cooing and giggling. The TV was off, and Taylor sat cross-legged facing the automaton. It was kneeling down playing a clapping game with her, where they tried to mimic each other's moves, making the sequences more complex each time.

Taylor squealed with delight each time the automaton caught her out. She rolled onto her side laughing, then sat back up and held out her own hands, improvising her own pattern in reply.

The automaton paused, rotating its metal neck to gaze at Michael, before resuming the game. Tentatively, Michael took a seat beside them on the carpet.

"Can I play?"

Taylor giggled, immediately setting a haphazard rhythm for Michael to imitate. The game seemed to involve listening, then copying, then doing a sort of duet, where your partner is fractionally ahead of you, and you need to try and keep up with their claps. If they can get three moves ahead of you, they score a point.

Michael found Taylor's laughter infectious, but it couldn't alleviate the lead weight in his chest. As he continued playing with Taylor, he spoke indirectly to the machine.

"I need your help. I have to protect my daughter. She just turned eighteen, meaning she's at risk. I know there's a way to stop them sending her letter, but I don't know how. The Ministry wants some kind of payment. Can you show me what it is?"

The machine stared at him, silently.

"Please, this is the whole reason I put you back together," urged Michael.

The machine rotated its head back towards Taylor, then resumed the game, much to her delight. Michael watched, despondently, then dragged himself upstairs, exhaustedly. He threw some of Olive's clothes down into the hall and yelled to the automaton to help Taylor to change, then crawled into bed.

The doorbell roused Michael several hours later. He stumbled downstairs to find his sister at the door. She looked desperate.

"Sophia? What's going on? It's a weekday, why are you-"

"You weren't answering the phone. I tried your office but they said you don't work there anymore? None of that matters, you need to come right now - it's Mom. Her letter's come."

Michael's head spun. He hastily locked the house up and rushed to his sister's car.

They sped to the Ministry square. Val had instructed Sophia to bring Michael straight there, assuming she could find him in time.

As they reached the square, a smartly-dressed woman could be seen walking towards the mighty stone steps. They ditched the car and sprinted after her.

"Mom, wait!" begged Michael.

Val turned, giving him a pleasantly-surprised smile.

"Aww, my child. I'm so glad I got to see you one last time," she said, taking him in her arms.

"Mom, this morning, what happened, I'm so sorry," sobbed Michael.

"Shh, it's in the past. You have a life ahead of you. Use it well, stop wasting it on things you can't control. My path is at an end, but yours is at a fork. I beg you now, make the right decisions."

She released him, and took her daughter in her arms, whispering words of love and comfort into her ear.

With a final embrace, she turned, and set foot on the steps. This time, her foot was on the finality side of the staircase, where the white marble was infused with sunset pink.

The death entrance was at the opposite end of the grand Ministry to the birth side. Michael glanced across the steps to the families on the sunrise side. As they cheered their eighteen-year-old on, he loathed them with every fiber of his being, trembling with fury as his mother ascended in parallel.

"Don't go, Mom, there's another way, I can save you!" Michael blurted.

Val froze. She turned sharply and hastened back towards him, with a look of deep concern. Clasping his hands earnestly, she looked deep into his eyes.

"My child, I implore you: *learn* from your father's mistakes, do not repeat them. I am happy with the life I have lived. Do not tarnish this moment for me. I have one death, and I want it to be on my terms. Your father chose a path of shame. I am choosing the path of dignity."

"But it doesn't have to end like this!" protested Michael.

Sophia gently pulled his hands off of Val's, and wrapped Michael in a side hug. Val smiled at her daughter gratefully, then climbed the steps.

She walked purposefully, and steadily, reaching the top within a minute. Smoothing her clothes out, she approached the door of death. With a proud smile, she presented her letter to the clerk, and stepped inside.

CHAPTER FORTY-FOUR

Michael woke with a start. He'd fallen asleep at the kitchen table. Someone had placed a blanket over his shoulders, but the rest of the house was silent. He peered groggily through to the living room, which was empty. Someone must have put Taylor to sleep in Olive's room.

His brain started to recollect the evening. He'd had some sort of panic attack at the Ministry; everything was a blur. He vaguely recalled being brought back to the house, with Sophia doing a care handover to Kelsey, who had tended to him and broken the news to their boys when they got back from school. Suddenly, the addition of their half-sister and an automaton provided a welcome distraction in the grieving household.

Midnight rain lashed down against the blackness of the kitchen window. Michael stirred and made himself a cup of tea. As the kettle boiled, he collapsed to the floor, weeping, as he remembered his mother was gone forever.

A tapping at the front door interrupted his grief. Michael stirred and dragged himself onto all fours. The tapping repeated. He climbed to his feet and cleaned his face with a tissue, then approached the darkened hallway. He flicked on the porch lantern and pulled the door open.

Standing before him was the automaton, dripping wet.

"Where have you been?" asked Michael.

The automaton's hands were cupped together. It held them out for Michael to see. Sheltered in its hands was a tiny flower, the likes of which Michael had never seen before. It had transparent leaves, which glistened with color when struck by the porch light.

"Why are you bringing me this?"

Across the street, the neighbor's door opened. Michael watched as the old man hobbled out into the rain, shuffling along his water-logged path, clutching his rain jacket tightly. In his left arm he was shielding a small package from the rain, while fumbling for his car keys. The old man drove away, leaving Michael staring at the automaton's cupped hands once again.

"You mean... This is the offering I need?" he gasped.

The automaton nodded.

Michael grabbed his keys and plunged out into the rain. Reaching his car, he froze, realizing the automaton wasn't following him.

"Come on, we need to hurry!" he hissed.

The machine didn't budge. Michael hurried back to it, frustrated.

"Are you coming or what?"

The machine delicately transferred the flower into Michael's hands.

"I have to do this alone?"

The machine nodded. With no time to argue, Michael hurried to the car and set off for the Ministry.

He spied on the old man's ritual, then waited for him to

leave, before checking the square was deserted and delving into the rain.

Michael knocked on the secret doorway and the hatch slid open. He delicately tipped the flower into the collection bowl then peered closer, trying to see who was operating the corridor.

The hatch slid shut abruptly. Michael waited anxiously as the rain soaked through to his skin. A minute passed and there was no rejection of the gift. Tentatively, with much checking over his shoulder, Michael crossed the square, back to his car.

As he placed his wet hands on the wheel, he felt a cocktail of emotions. Relief that his family would be safe come morning, and bitter regret that the offering hadn't arrived just one day sooner. Eighteen years he'd kept that broken machine hidden in the basement like a sack of trash. As he crossed the sodden streets, the cold truth gnawed at him: if he'd acted sooner, his mother would still be alive.

CHAPTER FORTY-FIVE

TWELVE MONTHS LATER

K elsey unscrewed the vial and inserted a pipette. Squeezing droplets into the beaker, she watched with trepidation.

Nothing happened.

Sighing with relief, she leaned back, clasping her hands with delight. She held the flask up to the light and marveled. A prism of color danced across the room as the liquid swirled.

A shadow glided past the doorway. Kelsey hid the beaker behind her back and froze, with her eyes fixed on the door handle. After a moment, the shadow glided away. She exhaled a steadying breath and returned to her solution.

Kelsey's face fell. An earthy orange pigment was spreading through the mixture.

"No, no, no!" she moaned.

She set the beaker down, backing away with her hands clasped behind her head, imploring it to revert to its previous state. But the reaction was complete. The solution was a murky, swirling mess.

Cursing, Kelsey thumped the wall in frustration. She drew a long, controlled breath, then returned to her journal and entered the outcome of the experiment, along with the precise quantities of each chemical she'd used.

Wearily, Kelsey returned the ingredients to their respective shelves. She'd realized early on in her operations that it was substantially quicker, and more discreet, to do the experiments in the store room itself, rather than trying to smuggle everything up and down from the lab each night. So long as she didn't blow herself up, it was just about tenable.

She cast her eyes down the long list of attempts. She'd felt certain it was going to work that time, but mixture three hundred and seventy-nine simply wasn't to be.

Kelsey slapped her notebook shut and returned to her office, where she stowed it away securely, before heading home for the night.

It was already 10 p.m. The kids might still be up, if she was quick. Although she'd promised to stop calling after nine, after a complaint from Leon's teacher that it was disturbing his sleep. How the teacher had found out about the late-night calls, Kelsey didn't want to think about. She was doing her best to straddle three worlds, as she juggled her family, her work, and her desperate attempts to find a treatment for Taylor.

Kelsey flopped down on the couch of her rental apartment and poured herself a large glass of alcohol-free wine. She was determined not to repeat the same miserable mistakes of her foster parents. Though she was damned if she wasn't getting herself some sort of liquid stress-buster, even if it was just a placebo.

Aside from the sofa bed, the apartment was bare, trapped in a perpetual state of temporary dwelling. Maybe it was because she'd spent her youth moving from pillar to post that she didn't believe it was worth setting down roots; or maybe it was because, deep down, all she wanted to do was move back home. But just as she thought she was ready to forgive him, Michael had crossed a line.

She closed her eyes and remembered the times they'd spent together when they were first dating, back when his mom - rest her soul - had won her the settlement money from the mining accident. It felt a lifetime ago. For a brief few weeks, their lives had felt uncomplicated. Which was saying something, given that she'd been doing daily night school on top of her day job.

To his credit, Michael had stuck by her, hanging in there through the arduous study sessions, knowing they had something special. And she'd stuck by him when his first baby letter came, albeit with a slight blip. She could forgive herself that, given what she'd been through. The important thing was that they came good for each other, and raised three beautiful children into the wonderful young people they were today. So how on earth did such a loving marriage become collateral along the way?

She winced. The fake wine tasted bitter tonight. Kelsey tipped it into the sink, then leaned against the stainless steel rim, peering out across the city.

The red beacons atop the hospital's chimneys glowed steadily through the dark. She thought of Michael, and felt a pang of heartache, missing him terribly.

But, as she pictured him arriving for work, her yearning turned to anger. She'd done everything in her power to help him, and she'd been fool enough to think it was working.

Until, of course, he did something she could never understand, and, most likely, could never forgive.

CHAPTER FORTY-SIX

Michael pushed the trolley along the ward, stopping by the next bedside. He leaned down and retrieved the sloshing bedpan, stacking it on top of the others.

Wheeling a trolley with one arm was something of a fine art that he'd perfected over the past three months.

From time to time, it did cause him cramp, owing to the uneven weight distribution. Such a twinge struck his shoulder, so he employed his go-to remedy using the nearest doorway.

Leaning into the edge of the frame, he pressed his body weight against the top of his right arm, gasping as his architectural masseuse relieved much of the tension.

Standing up straight, he rolled both shoulders back a few times to recalibrate. As if feeling neglected, the stump where his left arm used to be tingled with invisible pinpricks. Michael scratched it good and proper, then resumed his bedpan collection duties.

As he trundled through the sleepy ward, he took care not to clatter the pans; he didn't want to disturb the sleeping patients. Not that it was always easy to see in the dim night lighting. The writing, that was. The bedpans were easy enough to find, but what Michael was really interested in was the patients' charts.

The advantage of having one arm was that his superiors assumed his laggardly pace was down to his disability, when in reality it was because he was reading the footnotes of every bed he attended.

Michael would make a quick note in his diary of the patient's initials and diagnosis, or, if he was being watched, would memorize the details until he had a moment of privacy. His record was eight patients; that was the upper limit of his working memory before he had to fake a toilet break and write them all down.

Michael trundled through the ward, noting the two new arrivals with interest, as well as the one empty bed. His predictions from yesterday were well off; he'd been expecting a full house of survivors. He'd have to cross-reference the fatalities against the other cases he'd been monitoring.

His dataset was growing each night, and his accuracy was improving, albeit only at a general, macro level. He was still a long way from being able to predict specific cases.

As he finished that ward's bedpan round, he predicted there would be a six percent mortality rate by this time tomorrow, across those beds.

He washed his hand, relying mainly on the flowing water rather than a scrubbing action, then grabbed his coat. 2 a.m. meant it was Michael's mid-shift lunch break. He hopped into his car and headed home. It was a tight turnaround to get it all done within the hour, but his system was licked.

He turned the joystick that had replaced the steering

wheel in his modified car, and pulled up outside. The automaton greeted him at the door, holding out a delicate, translucent flower in its cupped hands. Michael collected it in his offering tin, and sped off for the Ministry.

Watching the minutes tick by, he cursed his luck as he was forced to wait for some late-night revelers to cross the square. With the coast finally clear, he hurried towards the secret door.

The hatch slid open, swallowing his offering as usual. In the twelve months that he'd been doing the nightly ritual - barring the weeks he was hospitalized - the flowers had never once been rejected. Nonetheless, Michael waited ten seconds each time to be sure, before heading back to the car.

Some hours later, he finished off his hospital shift and returned home in time for the 6 a.m. mail call. Knowing he'd delivered his daily offering gave him a new confidence when checking the mail each day.

Sure enough, the box was empty. Content with his ritual's success, he yawned and headed inside.

Taylor was up, as always, being an indefatigable early riser. She bounded over to give him a hug. It was like having a human-sized Labrador waiting at home.

Taylor's condition gave Michael mixed feelings: on the one hand, she was so often joyful, and her child-like playfulness brought levity to the household; on the other hand, he knew she wasn't supposed to be this way, and he suspected sometimes she sensed it too. Occasionally her mood would dip, and she would stare outside at the adults walking by, transfixed by their alien lives.

Today, however, she was on her usual energetic form, and seemed particularly keen to show him something. She tugged Michael by the sleeve until he followed her into the living room, where she proudly presented a stick painting she'd been working on.

Michael smiled, touched by her rose-tinted depiction of their family's existence. He felt a lump in his throat as he saw Kelsey painted beside him, holding his hand. Across from them, she'd painted her own parents, Tony and Stacey, arm in arm.

Kelsey had initially asked Michael to care for Taylor because her legal parents were refusing, following the accident. But their attitude had changed over time, and they had grown eager to see their daughter – Tony in particular.

This quickly became a source of serious tension. Kelsey prevaricated, trying to shield them from seeing Taylor, still clinging to the hope she might have a breakthrough in the remedial treatment. Underlying the guilt was a credible fear that Tony – or more likely Stacey – would report her to the Ministry, resulting in her being arrested, and her and Michael falling under a degree of police scrutiny they could never withstand.

Kelsey had managed to keep Taylor's parents at arm's length for six months before she finally acquiesced to their requests to see her.

The first visit did not go well. They knew Kelsey was shifting Heaven and Earth to try and find a cure, but she was also responsible for their daughter's diminished condition. Even Stacey was heartbroken. The couple reacted by effectively ex-communicating Kelsey.

So, it was with a heavy heart that Michael gazed upon Taylor's naïve drawing of one big, happy family.

"I love it," he said, with forced cheer. "Let's put it right on the fridge. You wanna help me make breakfast?"

Taylor clapped her hands enthusiastically and grabbed the flour from the cupboard. She giggled, slapping a palm to her forehead, then set about trying to scoop the entire load up with a teaspoon.

The automaton hovered beside her and offered a larger spoon, then demonstrated the improved technique. Michael thanked them both, and cracked on with the rest of the preparations.

He always enjoyed cooking pancakes. It wasn't exactly a kale smoothie, but it made him feel close to his late grandfather.

Michael and Taylor toasted each other with a grin, then shoveled the syrupy stacks into their mouths. Once they'd gorged their way through a plateful each, Michael placed the remainder into the oven to stay warm for the boys. Rubbing his itchy eyes, he took a seat on the couch, and beckoned Taylor to join him.

"What are we reading today?" he said, through a sleepy yawn.

She disappeared for a moment, then returned clutching a pirate story.

"Red Rum *again?*" laughed Michael.

Taylor grinned, nodding her head eagerly.

"Alright, but you'll have to do most of the reading this time."

He turned to the well-worn first page and placed his finger under the first word, encouraging Taylor to make the "T-H" sound of "the". She tried her best as they went through the text, but required prompts for every syllable. As yet, she was only capable of copying auditory cues after they'd been demonstrated.

After a few pages, she became restless. She started absent-mindedly probing the nub of Michael's amputated arm, while staring at the page. Michael knew better than to try and plough on.

"Great work. I think you deserve a break. Want to play a game with Toma?"

Toma was the nickname Michael had given the automaton, who tended to Taylor each day while Michael was asleep. The automaton had played a central role in improving her motor skills.

Damien and Leon bounded down for breakfast, lured by the smell of fresh pancakes. Yawning, Michael ruffled their heads as they ate, then bade them good days.

In the hallway, Toma waited for him with cupped hands. Michael smiled. Of all the bizarre daily rituals his family had fallen into, this was the most unexpected.

"Show me, I can't wait," he said.

Toma opened its hands and revealed an immaculately-folded paper crane. It nudged it forward to Michael, who received it gratefully.

Thanking the automaton, Michael retreated to bed. He closed his bedroom door and placed the crane on the dresser, beside the hundreds of other beautiful origami figurines Toma had made for him. With a smile, he flopped down onto the bed, knowing his family was safe for another day. Finally, he could sleep.

CHAPTER FORTY-SEVEN

Kelsey couldn't help but hold her breath. It took an hour to get to this stage each night, and the last stage was always the most critical. She squeezed the pipette load into the solution and watched anxiously as the two clear liquids swirled around one another in the flask.

She was behind on her schedule, having exhausted the facility's supply of several rare chemicals. There had been a week's delay before the stock had been replenished that very day.

She held up the flask, moving it past the light. A full spectrum of color flashed across the room, then vanished as the angle changed.

With apprehension, Kelsey set down the flask on the table and watched as the swirling liquid slowed to a barely perceptible eddy. No spontaneous diffusion of color, no change in consistency. For the first time in three hundred and eighty attempts, the solution was stable. She clapped her hands to her mouth in astonishment, stifling a gasp of joy.

Kelsey sealed the flask, stowed it in her lab coat pocket, and headed to her office, carefully avoiding the gliding automatons on route.

Closing her office door, she drew the blinds and approached the two cages by the wall. Each contained a lab rat. Both rats were lethargic and disoriented. One was trying to fathom the running wheel, but couldn't even get a foothold to begin with; it kept pawing at the base and slumping onto the straw beside it. The rat in the neighboring cage was being useless in a different way; compulsively brushing its back against the railing.

Kelsey rinsed out the rats' water dispensers, removing all trace of the neuro-plasticizer medicine she'd mixed in. It was the same drug she'd given Taylor over a year ago, and just as potent.

She cursed herself daily for causing the whole situation. Had she followed protocol and tested sufficiently on lab rats *before* putting Taylor in the firing line, none of this would be happening. But her eagerness to make a difference had cost them everything.

Kelsey mentally flipped a coin. Into one dispenser, she poured pure water. Into the other, she poured water infused with her new transparent solution; batch three hundred and eighty.

Using a soft stick, she coaxed each dozy rat towards their drip. The creatures' base instincts took over as soon as they were within close range of the liquid, and they sipped thirstily.

Kelsey sat at her desk and noted the time and respective dosages in her journal. She stared at the page with excitement. Could this be the batch? The miracle cure that would finally undo her greatest shame?

There was a metallic knock at the door.

"Come in," said Kelsey, quickly hiding her journal in a drawer.

An automaton glided in, then moved to the side. Behind it entered a familiar, and most unwelcome, shock of red hair.

"Director, burning the midnight oil again, I see?"

Kelsey's face soured. "How can I help you, Detective Clarkenwell?"

"It's the funniest thing, director, I was reflecting on some cold cases, and you just popped into my head. I thought I'd come and see how you were doing?"

"I'm working. If that will be all, my colleague here can see you out."

Clarkenwell sauntered around the office. With one hand casually in her pocket, she prodded and lifted Kelsey's various affects. Kelsey held her tongue as the detective examined her diploma, her community awards, her bookshelf, even her pot plants. It was clearly a mind game intended to rile her. It was working.

"Your half-siblings, right?" said the detective, holding up a photo of Taylor and Seth.

"Are you here to discuss my private life or my work, detective? I'm willing to discuss one, but not both."

Clarkenwell chuckled and put the photo back. "That's a good line. I should use it at home. Speaking of, how *is* your home life?"

"Private. How about yours?" snapped Kelsey.

"Get to see much of these two?" asked Clarkenwell, gesturing to the photo. "They're not your kids, are they, and yet, the adult girl's living at your family home. Taylor, right?"

Kelsey glared at the woman.

"I take it that's a yes to all that," continued the detective.

"How about your husband? I was sorry to hear about his... accident."

Kelsey stood up abruptly, her blood boiling. "Get the hell out of my office."

"Hey, we're on the same side here, director. We both work for the Ministry, so in a sense, this is my office too."

Clarkenwell meandered over to the nearest rat cage. She pressed her fingers through the mesh and made a chirping noise. The lethargic rat paid no attention, merely rolling onto its back as if drunk. The detective frowned.

"Unless you have a warrant to be here, I'm calling security, and will be filing a harassment report with your superiors," quivered Kelsey.

Clarkenwell rolled her eyes, as if Kelsey was ruining a perfectly pleasant gathering. She swaggered to the door.

"I guess I'll be going, then. Sure would hate to get a complaint at this time of year, my pay review's coming up. Oh, but there was one quick thing. The financial fraud team said they were notified of irregularities in your department's expenditure. Apparently, you've been burning through your rare chemicals at quite a rate this year. Any theories?"

"We have a research budget in this facility," said Kelsey, tersely.

"I thought you might say that. Yet, when my team looked through the accounts, there seemed to be no mention of new R&D activities that would cause such a gaping hole in your supplies."

"Perhaps your team is looking at an old report. I'll have my secretary wire you our latest records at his first convenience."

"How very kind, I look forward to it. You wouldn't believe some of the crazy theories my colleagues have been throwing around," laughed Clarkenwell. "Maybe I'll share them with you sometime. They keep talking about things like penalties for using experimental substances without a license. Dang, those sentences are *crazy* harsh. I read a couple of them and even I was like, 'who came up with this stuff', you know? It's draconian. Personally, I'm all for restorative justice. Nothing I like more than to see an offender rehabilitated. But, sadly, I don't make the rules, I just catch people breaking them. See you again soon, I'm sure, director."

Clarkenwell disappeared from sight, followed by an automaton. Kelsey thumped her desk in anger, cursing the woman's timing.

She crossed over to the rat cages and peered down at the two residents. One was still lumping around on its back, half-asleep. But its neighbor had changed dramatically. It had figured out the running wheel, and was a hive of activity.

Kelsey lifted a partition from both cages, and watched as the two rats reacted to the new doorway available to them. The one on the wheel immediately hopped off and scurried to the doorway. It sniffed the threshold, then stepped inside.

Both rats now had access to an individual maze connected to their respective cage. The sleepy rat continued lounging, so Kelsey gave it an encouraging nudge with the stick. It limped towards the doorway, then gazed listlessly into the passageway beyond.

Its energized comrade, by contrast, had blitzed its way through the maze, overcoming the dead ends and false turnings, and located the food reward on the far side.

Kelsey hurried to her journal excitedly and made a note beside her last entry.

The serum works!

She slammed the book shut, and grasped her knees in disbelief. Hope. There was finally hope for Taylor. But she had to act fast – Clarkenwell was circling, and could yet ruin everything. She had to perfect the serum before the detective shut her down.

CHAPTER FORTY-EIGHT

Michael glanced around the dimly lit corridor. The coast was clear. Whipping out his notepad, he scribbled down the new patients' maladies, and the fatality rates from the previous night.

So far, his prediction was holding up. The only problem was: he had no idea why. He was no closer to identifying a root cause behind the patterns of who lived and died.

The doctors did their best with all patients, but even they seemed none the wiser as to who would actually make it. None of their footnotes featured any sort of prognosis, just instructions for treatment. The only system Michael knew of that reliably staved off death was his own, secret offering system.

The door at the far end of the corridor swung open. Michael hid his notepad and gripped his trolley, ready to resume work, until he caught a better look at the newcomers. They looked to be in their late twenties. Both were furtive, and seemed concerned.

Michael shrunk into the shadows and watched as they

scurried into the ward beyond. Silently, Michael wheeled his trolley after them.

The couple stepped inside a single-occupancy room at the end of the ward. It had been empty last night, but clearly today there was a new guest, who had a couple of after-hours visitors.

The male visitor lingered in the threshold, with his hands rigidly shoved into his pockets and his shoulders hunched up by his ears.

The light from the open cubicle lingered like someone had left the refrigerator door open. It caught the tears on the young woman's face as she stepped inside, with her hands covering her mouth.

Ditching the trolley, Michael skulked closer, approaching a side window into the room and peering in.

The new patient was on life support. An iron lung wheezed beside them, among a forest of cables and drips.

The grief-stricken woman edged closer, while her accomplice hissed at her to be quick. She took a seat on the patient's bed and raised a hand to the unconscious woman's hair. The patient looked even older than Michael's ancient neighbor, with thin, wiry white hair and skin like old boots.

Thick bandages covered the woman's wrists and thighs. From the few patches of skin Michael could see, her complexion was a sea of yellow and blue, like she was a giant human bruise. She looked as close to death as anyone he'd ever seen in the hospital.

His eyes darted to the woman's medical chart, but her name was missing. In its place were simply the words: *Ministry Aware*. A chill swept over Michael as he realized what he was looking at.

The injured woman's eyes fluttered open. She blinked hazily at the visitor, and gave a small, pained tilt of the head.

Tears flowed freely from the younger woman as she leaned in and kissed the patient's forehead.

The older woman closed her eyes, and nodded once more.

The weeping visitor took a deep breath, then unplugged all of the life support equipment in the cubicle. The mechanical lung wheezed to a halt, and the old woman fell still beneath her defunct mask. With a final exhalation, her head rolled to the side.

As the grieving lady sobbed, the younger man hurried in, steering her away towards the exit.

Seeing Michael, the couple froze. Michael, equally shocked, made no movement, and simply stared back at them.

The young man took a cautious half-step forwards, then, sensing they would meet no resistance, took his partner's arm and fled past Michael to the exits beyond.

Michael watched the couple leave, then retraced his steps, returning to his bedpan collection in the neighboring rooms as if nothing had happened.

A security guard burst into the ward, dripping with sweat, and flanked by two automatons. One glided straight for the dead woman's cubicle, while the other secured the far exit. The man made a beeline for Michael.

"Have you seen two civilians up here? We had reports of intruders," panted the guard.

Michael nodded. "I saw two people leaving, but I figured they must be nurses or something. I didn't see them properly, they were gone pretty much instantly."

"Which way did they go?" urged the guard.

Michael pointed in the opposite direction to the couple's actual escape.

"Thanks. This way!" yelled the guard, racing off and radioing his colleagues.

A cardiac alarm sounded from the dead woman's room. The automaton must have reconnected her machines. The on-duty night medics hurried from the adjoining wards to answer the call, but Michael knew there was nothing that could be done. As his watch chimed 2 a.m., he slipped away from the futile resuscitation efforts, and headed home to collect that night's offering.

CHAPTER FORTY-NINE

Kelsey stared at the cage, speechless. It was less than twelve hours since she'd administered batch three hundred and eighty to the lab rat, and all trace of its initial miracle recovery had vanished.

Gone were the cognitive and sensory improvements. All that remained was a twitching rat, which had been experiencing seizures since she'd arrived, possibly even through the night. She sank into her desk chair, truly deflated. How could she possibly hope to fix Taylor, when her best efforts only made things worse?

She peered out onto the factory floor and stared glumly at the staff settling in to take over from the automatons' night bakes. As her mind drifted, Michael's words came back to her from all those months ago. He'd been so insistent that Toma, his fugitive automaton, had "cured" Amal's symptoms with a strip of gel.

That's when it hit her.

The day couldn't go quickly enough. With agonizing clock-watching, Kelsey saw it through, waiting until the last of her colleagues had gone home.

She had finally realized what was wrong with her batches. Her cure was missing a vital ingredient; one that couldn't be synthesized on site, but which came directly from the Ministry.

Kelsey thought back to the archive room, and the train delivering embossed glass slabs. The slab alone would be of no use; the vital ingredient was contained within them. Hypothetically, Toma could crack one open for her, but there was no way she could smuggle a raw slab out of the lab; the automatons guarded them more closely than anything else. Her only hope was to steal one during a bake.

Suppressing her nerves, she strode across the factory floor with the air of a diligent director carrying out a spontaneous night inspection.

The automatons paid her little notice; it had been many years since she was apprehended for spying on the bake process as a junior. As director, her authority now allowed her to observe bakes unchallenged by the machines.

She followed the automatons to the humanoid wooden sculpture, in its pool of crystal water. It unfolded a creaky, moss-covered hand, revealing a glass slab, which one of the machines retrieved.

They glided to the kiln, where they prepared the bake mixture from overhead chutes, stirring it into reddish-brown putty.

Kelsey watched eagerly as they cracked the glass slab along an invisible seam, and poured the glimmering liquid into the clay mold.

The lead automaton resealed the embossed glass slab and placed it onto a slow-moving vertical conveyor belt leading to the upper level.

As the machines sculpted the clay mix, Kelsey seized

her chance, snatching the glass slab off the rung before it was lifted out of reach.

Her landing caught the automatons' attention. Two sets of mechanical eyes locked on her position.

The nearest automaton dropped its paddle and extended a hand to the wall. Its metallic palm hovered above a large red kill switch that would abort the entire bake.

Kelsey froze. She stared at the half-formed lump of clay before her; the makings of a child due to be born at dawn.

The automaton extended its other hand towards her.

"Please, I really need this, it's for research, it's... to help someone," implored Kelsey.

The automaton inched closer towards the kill switch.

"Wait!" cried Kelsey.

She couldn't be responsible for an abortive bake, not after all she'd done to reduce them. Besides, there would be a Ministry inquiry, and she couldn't risk any more scrutiny right now, not with Clarkenwell already probing her off-book chemical usage.

With a defeated sigh, Kelsey placed the glass slab into the automaton's palm. The machine deposited it high on the conveyor belt, then stared at Kelsey until it had disappeared.

Kelsey hurried to her car, desperate to leave the facility as quickly as possible, and hoping above all that the automatons had no motive or mechanism to report her attempted theft to the Ministry.

As she drove, a pair of headlights caught her attention in the rearview mirror. Traffic was rare at this time of night, and she was taking the back streets.

As Kelsey turned the corner, the lights followed her.

She turned another, and they followed again. Someone was tailing her.

A red signal halted her in her tracks. As the other car pulled up close behind, Kelsey caught a flash of red hair behind the wheel. Her anger boiled over.

As the signal flicked to green, Kelsey hit the gas, speeding away, determined to burn off the detective.

She screeched round a corner, but the detective was close behind. Both drivers were accelerating rapidly, neither willing to blink in the face of the other.

Kelsey leaned hard into another bend, skidding into the oncoming lane. It was blind luck that it was empty, as she barreled down the damp street.

That woman had no right, she told herself. None of them had any *right* to control her this way. She was a *good* person. She deserved to be free. She wasn't about to give up on Taylor and go down without a fight, not yet.

If she could just get home, she'd be safe for at least the night. The detective wouldn't be able to question her there without a warrant.

Clarkenwell's driving confirmed as much. The detective seemed every bit as desperate as she was.

Kelsey's knuckles were white, and her heart was pounding as the engine screamed under the strain. Speeding towards the next intersection, she glanced at her rearview mirror.

The detective's car had vanished. She looked again. Still nothing. Something wasn't right. It wasn't like Clarkenwell to simply give up. She was up to something – maybe trying to cut her off.

Any second now, that red-haired tormentor would burst out of a side street, or skid into her mirror once again, Kelsey knew it. She could feel it. And she wasn't going to let her win.

Gripping the wheel tightly, Kelsey rocketed across the intersection. The speed needle was trembling in the red zone as the engine roared.

You. Don't. Own. Me.

That was the last thing Kelsey could remember thinking before the world went black, with a deafening crash of metal and glass.

CHAPTER FIFTY

M ichael cursed his luck. He'd been deployed to another department for the night, meaning he couldn't do his usual wards "research".

Consulting the printout, he unloaded the requested blood bags from cold storage onto his trolley, plus a handful of saline replacements.

Michael reluctantly wheeled the lot towards the operating theater. He couldn't get away with playing coy about his arm when he was covering emergency department shifts; people's quality of life actually depended on him moving quickly. He tended to keep this secret to himself, but, shocker, he was capable of working fast.

As Michael unloaded the bags in the operating room, a patient was wheeled in at speed. Frenzied doctors and nurses obscured the patient from view, while the lead doctor briefed the room.

"Female involved in a car crash, thirty-seven years-old, multiple traumas to the head, chest, and right leg. Suspected internal bleeding. ID card says Kelsey Bailey."

Michael's heart froze.

Denial rung in his ears. He forced his way close to the patient's bedside and peered through the medics' weaving arms.

Kelsey's beautiful face lay before him, unconscious on the stretcher. Only, for the first time since he'd fallen in love with her, she wasn't beautiful at all, she was damaged.

Terror rose up inside Michael as he called her name desperately. Pushing the nurses aside, he grabbed Kelsey's hand, shaking her, trying to rouse her, as panic filled his brain.

Medics bundled him out of the room, overruling his pleas, as they summoned a security automaton.

He pawed at the machine's chest plates feebly, sobbing, repeating Kelsey's name.

The machine deposited him in the waiting area, then glided back to the emergency room.

Michael rushed from the hospital and leaped into his car. He raced home, searching for Toma. The faithful automaton was nowhere to be seen. Michael tore through the house in a frenzy, searching for a flower the machine might have left behind.

"Dad? What's wrong?" said Leon, sleepily.

"Nothing, go to bed," croaked Michael.

"Dad?"

"I said go!"

Their usual 2 a.m. rendezvous came and went. Hours passed by and still there was no sign of Toma.

Weeping, Michael curled into a ball and rocked from side to side, delirious with worry.

"Micka sad?"

Michael's head jerked up, startled by Taylor's sudden appearance.

"Why Micka sad?"

"Uh... It's complicated," he sniffed.

Taylor screwed up her face, thinking, then grabbed Michael in a bear hug.

"I look after you, Micka," she cooed.

Taylor's innocence only made Michael's heartache worse. If she knew the pain coming their way...

A faint scratching sounded from the hallway. Michael recognized the pattern at once. Breaking Taylor's embrace, he rushed to the door, opening it to the missing automaton.

"It's almost 5 a.m! Where the hell have you been?" he yelled.

Toma's head was dipped. Michael didn't know it could even tilt like that. The machine's knees were grazed, and stained with grass and dirt.

Before Michael could interrogate it further, running footsteps interrupted.

"Tomeeeee!" squealed Taylor.

She barged past Michael clumsily, flinging herself around her beloved companion; the machine that spent every waking minute of each day with her.

The automaton placed a tender arm around her back. Michael had never seen the machines hug before.

"Play time!" Taylor cheered, jumping up and down.

"Not now, Taylor. I need to talk to Toma," said Michael.

"Patty cake?" grinned Taylor, ignoring Michael and swinging from Toma's arm.

Toma tapped its hands together in a pattern. To Michael's astonishment, Taylor understood.

"Yay! Yes, yes, I like," she cheered.

Taylor skipped into the lounge, where she tipped out some toy building blocks and began playing with earnest concentration.

Michael was stunned. Since when did automatons use sign language? Since when did Taylor understand it?

He shook the amazement from his mind. There was no time to dwell. He had to save Kelsey.

"Do you have the offering?" he hissed.

Toma unfurled a hand before Michael. In place of the usual translucent, shimmering flower, was a withered clutch of five black petals around a shriveled stalk.

"I don't understand, what's this? Where's the usual one?" stammered Michael.

The automaton shook its head.

"No, no, this can't be right. There's no way they'll accept this."

The machine shook its head again. Michael's despair boiled over into anger.

"You have to find one!" he yelled.

Toma's head twitched, as if looking upstairs to the sleeping boys. Michael flinched, lowering his voice, but continuing urgently.

"We're running out of time," he hissed. "Kelsey's in surgery and if we don't pay the tribute within the next hour, she could die!"

Toma let the black petals fall to the ground, and placed a hand on either side of Michael. The gesture was baffling. Was this supposed to be consoling him?

Toma settled into a firm grip, then lifted Michael out of its way, and glided into the living room.

"What the hell are you doing? *Help* me!" cried Michael, chasing after the machine. "Hey, are you listening to me?"

The automaton retrieved something from the bookshelf, placing it in Michael's palm; an origami figure of an automaton. Michael stared at it in bewilderment.

"We don't have time for this, Toma, Kelsey's dying!"

The automaton stared at him blankly. Michael thumped the machine's chest in despair.

"Did you hear me?" he yelled, pounding its metal plating.

"No! Tomee!" cried Taylor, aghast.

She leaped up, throwing herself around Toma in a fierce embrace, shielding the robot from Michael's blows.

"Taylor, get out the way, you don't understand what you're doing!" begged Michael.

"Tomee!" she insisted, clinging to its frame.

Michael staggered backwards, clutching his hair with despair. Toma was ignoring him completely, while Taylor was totally blocking him from getting anything meaningful out of the machine. They were Kelsey's only hope of survival, and they were squandering what precious time she had left.

Toma stroked Taylor's hair, soothing her into a quiet murmur, then gave a series of hand signals.

The child-woman's face erupted into a beaming grin and her moaning turned to laugher.

"Silly Micka," she giggled.

Toma delivered three more hand signals.

"OK!" chimed Taylor.

She planted a kiss on the machine's cheek, then turned to Michael.

"Silly Micka," she laughed again, before planting a kiss on his cheek too, then scarpering upstairs to her room.

The machine turned away from Michael and glided into the kitchen. Opening a drawer, it pulled out a screwdriver.

"What are you doing?"

Toma pointed the screwdriver at its chest, then sat down at the table.

"I don't understand?" said Michael.

The automaton repeated the gesture, then slid the tool across the table. Michael took a second to process what it was implying.

"No, there must be another way," he implored.

Toma gave a slow, mechanical shake of its head.

Michael picked up the screwdriver and tried to gather himself. His head was spinning. The entire family's future was in his hands. The boys were asleep, clueless that their mother had been in a car crash. Taylor was playing upstairs, blissfully unaware that her fragile world was about to be shattered forever.

The passing seconds echoed from the kitchen clock. Kelsey's only chance of survival was sitting before him, but Michael was paralyzed. What the machine was asking him to do was something Taylor would never forgive. Could he even forgive himself? After all it had done for his grandfather, now this?

Toma was special. It cared, nurtured, hugged. Did that mean it could also feel pain? Michael couldn't bear the thought. If he did this, he might save Kelsey tonight, but what about tomorrow? What if Olive needed him?

Indecision was paralyzing him. As if reading his mind, the machine seized Michael's hand. Gazing at him through its cracked stone eyes, it guided the tip of the screwdriver to its breast.

"I'll never forget you," whispered Michael.

Toma nodded once, then sat up tall, staring straight ahead, past Michael's shoulder.

With a trembling hand, and tears rolling down his cheeks, Michael prized open the automaton's breast plate.

He turned the four steam valves off in turn. Steam billowed from the machine's joints, which fell loose, dislocating from their sockets. Michael raised the screwdriver to Toma's sunburst mineral heart. Whispering a final goodbye, he prized the mineral out.

The glow drained from Toma's eyes, and its chin slumped to its chest.

Michael stared at the butchered machine, his lips quivering. The tiny stone heart was scorching hot, burning into the palm of his hand. He gripped it tightly, wincing through the pain, and ran for his car.

Michael screeched up by the Ministry and rushed across the square. The first rays of sun were warming the top of the dome. Michael had never tried to make an offering so late. He had no idea if they'd even answer his call.

He pounded the shutter until it slid open. The usual glow from the corridor beyond was gone; in its place was a distant red flame. A cold draft emanated from the hatch. Michael placed the tiny stone heart down in the collection bowl.

"Promise me you won't take her. I'm begging you!" he cried.

The hatch slammed shut in his face. Michael stepped back, staring at the doorway with bated breath. Ten seconds passed.

Nothing.

Michael turned and fled, racing to the hospital. He dashed through to the emergency department front desk.

"Michael? What's wrong?" said his colleague.

"My wife, Kelsey, she was in an accident," he panted. "Is she out of surgery yet?"

His colleague placed a consoling hand on his, then looked her up on the system.

"They've moved her to ICU room two."

Michael was gone in an instant, racing to intensive care. He sped past his supervisor.

"Oh, Michael, can you change the bedpans on ward C?"

Ignoring her, he sprinted to the isolation rooms, skidding across to room two. Gasping for breath, he peered through the window.

The adrenaline and energy drained from his body as he stared through the glass at Kelsey's damaged body. Tears swelled in his eyes as he stepped inside.

Kelsey Bailey, read the sign at the foot of her bed. Her ID was nestled in the census on the wall behind her, ready to direct her letter to the hospital mail room.

Kneeling by her side, Michael pressed her hand to his cheek, weeping. He glanced at the clock on the wall. In the next few minutes, he would know if he'd done enough. At the stroke of 6 a.m., he'd know if his wife was to live or die.

"I'm sorry I ever pushed you away," he whispered. "I'm here now, baby, I'm here, and I will do whatever it takes to make things right. Stay with us, please. I can't lose you again."

CHAPTER FIFTY-ONE

NINE MONTHS EARLIER

"Dad?" called Olive, knocking hard on the door.

Their first meaningful attempt at reconciliation and Michael had been a no-show at the coffee house.

Olive was so pissed off that she was tracking him down to give him a piece of her mind. This was no way to treat a daughter, especially after all he'd put her through at the start of the year, what with the separation, and the trespass. He was going to get an earful.

She knocked again, then tried the handle. The door opened without resistance.

Olive knew the family routine well enough to know the boys would be at school, and Toma and Taylor would be at the park. An open door could mean only one thing: her useless father was hiding out at home. Again.

Given that he'd been the one pressing to meet her for so long, failure to show up was definitely weird. But then, that was her father. Or at least, her father since she'd turned eighteen. Erratic, nervous, reclusive. And now, on top of that list: flaky.

She entered the house, calling his name again, scouring the downstairs. It was deserted. Sighing with frustration, she descended into the basement, willing to bet her entire savings that he was in his cave, researching some new crackpot theory.

But the basement was empty. Huh. Weird. Outside chance he was asleep? She moved to the upstairs bedrooms, but they were all empty too.

Her eyes moved to the last room in the house. The bathroom door was ajar. A faint dripping of water-on-water echoed from the tiled space.

"Dad...?"

With growing trepidation, she stepped inside.

Olive screamed.

Michael was slumped across the bath tub, covered in blood.

Olive fell to her knees and scooped his head out of the shallow water, desperately trying rouse him.

His blood seeped into her clothes.

Deathly pale, Michael murmured, faintly.

Olive rushed to the phone in his bedroom, hammering the dial. The operator answered immediately.

"I need an ambulance! My dad's been in an accident, he's lost a lot of blood, please hurry," she cried.

She slammed down the receiver, knowing they would trace the address, and rushed back to her father.

Beside him in the blood-filled tub was a half-empty bottle of gin and a wooden strip with deep bite marks in it. Michael's forearm was bumpy and blistered where an infection had overrun his skin.

At the top of his arm was a loosely-fastened band of fabric, soaked in blood. In his left hand was a saw.

A deep gash had torn through his upper right arm. The flesh had been hacked through to the bone.

Olive tried not to be sick. Leaning over the bath, she pulled the band of fabric as tight as she could. Michael wailed with pain as it pressed into his exposed nerve endings. Olive gagged as the severed flesh shifted beneath her fingers.

"Hello?" came a call from downstairs.

"Up here!" cried Olive.

She urgently dialed her mom while the paramedics whisked Michael's semi-conscious body into the ambulance. Olive climbed in with him and rode to the hospital.

"Why did you do this, Dad?" she wept.

Michael wheezed, pointing feebly at the infected skin. Olive shook her head in disbelief.

The ambulance came to a halt and the rear doors opened, revealing metallic hands waiting to haul Michael's stretcher out. Behind them stood a team of medics waiting to admit him to the emergency room.

As Olive climbed out, Kelsey spotted her and raced over, aghast at the blood stains across her clothes. She wrapped her daughter in a tight embrace as they watched Michael get stretchered out. Kelsey's knees buckled as she saw her husband's severed arm.

"What have you done?" she cried.

Michael could hear medics reading his medical report somewhere above his gurney.

"... Loss of blood, risk of heart failure and brain damage unless we operate immediately..."

"Michael, how could you do a thing like this? Answer

me!" wept Kelsey. "How could you do this to us? To your kids?"

"... May have to amputate..."

"I never meant to..." stammered Michael "The Ministry... did this to me..."

"Dad, I *found* you, I know you did this to yourself!" wept Olive.

"Yes... to save... myself... from them... from their infection!"

As the medics sponged away the blood, Kelsey and Olive saw the full extent of his rotting flesh.

"Why didn't you get treatment for this!" cried, Kelsey.

"Then they would have known I was sick... They would have sent my letter... I had to... Stay off-grid... Protect you all... It was the only way..." he whispered.

Kelsey shook her head in disbelief. "You *let* the infection spread!"

"I had remedies... but the books were wrong, the herbs didn't work..."

"... Infection's spread to his nerve stems..." murmured a medic.

Kelsey stared at her estranged husband in total disbelief at the pain he had chosen to endure; pain that had driven him to sever his own arm. She felt guilt that she hadn't been there to notice the signs, and she knew Olive would be feeling the same. Their absence had allowed his mental state to deteriorate in ways they had never imagined possible.

"You both believe me, right?" said Michael. "If the Ministry knew I was sick... My letter would have come..."

He was fading in and out of consciousness, as the medics worked frantically to stabilize the bleeding.

Olive tore herself away, unable to bear another moment of it. Kelsey stared at her mutilated partner, broken.

"How could you do this to us?" she whispered.

Michael stirred, beckoning her closer with a feeble finger twitch. She forced her way past the medical automatons to his side, pressing her ear to his lips.

"I'm sorry... so sorry my love... I didn't want to die."

CHAPTER FIFTY-TWO

THE PRESENT DAY

K elsey cracked open her swollen eyes, letting in a
slit of bright light. Her eyelids felt heavy, and
her vision was blurry.

Her head hurt. Everything hurt. As her brain slowly
came online, signals of pain flooded in from every part of
her body.

Gasping, she tried to sit up, but she couldn't move. She
strained her eyes, processing her unfamiliar surroundings.

A machine bleeped near her head, but she couldn't face
it; something hard was restricting her neck movements.

She gazed at the foot of her bed, squinting.

"Michael?"

Michael awoke with a start and rushed to Kelsey's side.

"You're awake," he gushed, welling up with relief.

He stroked her cheeks tenderly, barely touching them,
such was his fear of causing any pain to her fragile, damaged
body.

Kelsey rasped, unable to speak further. Michael grabbed

a beaker, punching a straw through into the water. Pressing a button on the wall, he raised the back of the bed slightly, then held the straw to Kelsey's mouth.

She sipped thirstily then spluttered, unleashing agonizing pain across her ribs. She tried to wipe her chin, but she couldn't lift either arm.

"Don't worry about moving right now, I've got you covered," soothed Michael.

"What happened?" said Kelsey.

"You were in a car accident."

The night before came back to her in flashes, as she remembered leaving the facility and being chased by a car. The driver... there was something about the driver... Red hair...

"The detective! Is... is she here?" stammered Kelsey.

"What? No, why would she be?"

Kelsey slumped, confused. Michael rubbed her hand gently.

"I was so worried I'd lost you. You're my partner, my soul mate. I never want to let you go ever again," choked Michael.

Kelsey looked at him, at his tender face, and his missing arm.

"I guess this makes us about even," she said, with a groan.

"I never stopped loving you," said Michael, weeping freely.

She felt his hand in hers, and rubbed her thumb across his knuckles.

"I always thought you were the dumb one. Hacking off your own arm to try and cheat death. Yet here I am, in hospital for trying to cheat life. Turns out we're both as dumb as each other."

"Perfectly suited, if you ask me. I'm so sorry we drifted. I'm sorry for everything," wept Michael.

"Me too. I love you, Michael. Always have, always will," said Kelsey, her eyes filling with tears.

"You should rest," he said, wiping tears from his cheeks.

"Can you call the kids? I don't want them to find out if my work calls or something."

"I doubt they'll be up at this time. But I'll try the porters at Olive's university - they should be able to wake her. Then she can look after Taylor."

"Can't Toma do that?" said Kelsey.

A lump formed in Michael's throat as he pictured Toma slumped and lifeless at the kitchen table. He had to warn Olive before Taylor found the robot's body and freaked out.

"Don't worry about it. I'll sort all that stuff out, you just rest. I'll be right back. I'm not leaving this place without you ever again," he said.

Kelsey smiled at her beloved, broken husband, and squeezed his hand. Michael leaned forwards and gave her a long, tender kiss on the forehead, then left the room.

Michael was glowing. After years of getting it all so wrong, he finally had another shot at making amends, and living his life with the woman he'd loved since the first days of his adulthood. What had happened was horrific, but she was alive, and that was all that mattered. Together, they could overcome anything.

Following some hasty phone calls, the university porters had roused Olive, who was now looking after Taylor and the boys. Basking in relief, with his errands completed, Michael returned to the ICU.

He backed into ICU room two carrying a tray of tea, coffee, juices, and smoothies. He wasn't sure whether Kelsey wanted any of them, but he wanted her to know she could have anything she wanted, anytime. He was there for her. For real, this time.

Michael opened the door with his back, so as not to spill any of the drinks. On the off-chance she was awake, he was ready to greet his wife with a "ta-daa".

His face fell.

"What's going on?" he said, confused.

Automatons surrounded Kelsey, removing all the medical equipment plugged into her body. Kelsey was sitting up, wincing as they pulled the IVs out.

She fixed Michael with a desperate, broken look. His eyes fell to her hand, and the slender item clutched in it. A faded yellow-brown envelope, with Kelsey's signature on the front.

Time stood still as Michael processed the situation. The automatons glided out of the room, taking Kelsey's redundant drips with them. Michael shook his head in disbelief, refocusing on Kelsey's face as if her hands were completely empty.

"I got your favorite - freshly squeezed OJ," he said, approaching the bed.

"Michael..."

"Or if you don't want that, there's hot tea."

"Honey..."

"I got brown sugar and white too, cos I know you like to mix them."

"Michael, stop. It's over."

Kelsey placed a hand on his cheek and stroked his face gently. Michael swallowed, shaking his head as tears flooded his eyes.

"It's OK, sweetie, it's my time," said Kelsey, her voice quavering.

"But I did the offering," stammered Michael.

"I'm sure you did everything you could, sweet man, but my fate was sealed when I picked this envelope nineteen-odd years ago."

She guided his hand to set the drinks aside, then placed her letter in its place.

"Feel it, Michael. That's what my decision feels like. It's not your fault, it's not anybody else's, it's just my reality. I was given three paths, and this is the one I chose."

"You deserve more," whispered Michael.

Kelsey looked at him softly. "I'm not sure that's true."

"I can't carry on without you. I know we've been distant, but I always thought, in the end, we would..."

He trailed off, sobbing. Kelsey soothed him, stroking his hair.

"This is the end, my sweet, and we did it. We're OK now, my love. Listen, we don't have long, my appointment is soon. The machines will be back for me in a minute or two, so I need you to promise me one thing before I go."

"Don't say these things!" begged Michael.

"This is happening, sweetheart, whether you or I like it or not. The only thing we can control here is how we part, and I want to see your beautiful smile one more time. Listen to me, honey. Look after the kids, I know you will. Be kind to Olive, she'll forgive you in time, she loves you deep down. And I..."

Kelsey faltered, composing herself.

"...I need to thank you.... For everything you've done for Taylor. I said I couldn't look after her because of work, and the risk of investigation. You cared for her every day, no questions asked. But the truth is, Michael, I couldn't face her. I couldn't bear to look at what I'd done to her."

Kelsey stared at the ceiling, forcing her tears away. She didn't want to waste another precious second on misery, but the guilt was overwhelming. She would never be able to fix what she'd done.

"I nearly did it, you know? I nearly had a cure. You're her only hope now, Michael. I need you to take my ID card and go to my office before my clearance is deactivated. In my top drawer there's a journal. The key's in my bag, here. You *must* protect that journal. The last solution I entered works, but the dose I tested was too strong. I need you to find a way of getting it perfected. I think it can reverse the damage I inflicted on Taylor, but if the dose is wrong it'll make her worse. Get the journal, Michael, then it's vital that you find the chemical store in the building. It's on basement level one. Get everything listed in the recipe, because you won't be able to get those substances anywhere else; they're controlled by the Ministry. *Don't get caught.* Can you do this for me, Michael?"

Michael stared at her, catching up with the tidal wave of information.

"But... There's no way I can get to the clinic and back before your appointment. You'll have to go..."

"Alone. I know," said Kelsey.

"I can't let you do that!"

"It's not your choice honey, it's mine. Fetch my ID card from the wall, would you?"

Michael retrieved it in a daze and handed it to Kelsey, who tenderly placed it in his breast pocket.

"Listen to me, Michael. I can live with dying alone. I'll be alone once I'm across the threshold, so a few final steps before that make no difference, right? What I *can't* handle is dying knowing all my efforts to save Taylor were wasted. Please, Michael, see my work through, make it count for something. Fix her – I was so close."

Two automatons entered the room and glided to either side of the bed. Kelsey retrieved her letter from Michael's limp hand, then pulled him close for a final kiss.

"Goodbye, sweet man. Now hurry, I beg you."

Michael watched the machines wheel her out of the room. His head spun as he stared at the empty space where her bed had been seconds before. Then he ran.

CHAPTER FIFTY-THREE

I t took Michael an hour to take all of Toma's remains to the basement. Only having one arm made the task difficult, but it was nothing compared the psychological mountain he faced.

Grief, shock, and denial halted him in his tracks at every turn. He snatched moments in the basement to weep, away from his children's concerned eyes.

Occasionally, Damien helped him carry smaller pieces of the dismantled automaton, depositing them in the dusty suitcase without question. Neither spoke; they weren't ready to discuss what had happened to Toma. Michael was numb, and Damien afraid, so the pair worked in silence.

Olive put on a brave face as she kept Taylor and Leon occupied in the living room. Michael had been avoiding her, not knowing where to begin. But, with Toma finally cleared away, he could hide no longer.

Temporarily placing Damien in charge, Olive stepped away from her care duties and cornered Michael in the kitchen.

"When are you going to tell us what's going on? When can we see Mom?" she whispered.

Michael stared at the floor, gripping the back of the kitchen chair until his knuckles turned white.

"Dad? You're scaring me."

"Is everyone in the living room?" croaked Michael.

"Yeah... What's going on? Is Mom OK?"

Beckoning her to follow, Michael made his way into the living room and surveyed what was left of his family.

The only thing more painful than seeing the fear in his children's eyes was the glimmer of hope behind it.

"There's no easy way to say this," said Michael. "Your mother's letter came this morning. It was delivered to the hospital. She won't be coming back."

The color drained from Damien's cheeks. Beside him, Leon looked puzzled, not really understanding. Olive stammered in denial, shaking her head.

"No... no... when you called, you said she was-"

"I was wrong."

Olive rushed out of the room, collapsing in the hallway, sobbing uncontrollably. With a cheerful expression, Taylor sidled out after her, wrapping her arms around her affectionately.

Michael looked at Damien and Leon, unsure what else to tell them.

"We'll be holding a wake here in two days' time," said Michael.

"What's a wake?" asked Leon, earnestly.

"It's like a goodbye. I'll need you boys to be strong. Can you do that for me?"

His boys nodded. Leon still looked puzzled, while Damien simply looked broken. Michael flicked the TV back on for them and drew a deep breath, bracing himself for the task ahead. Taking their address book from the shelf, he made his way to the phone, and began dialing.

CHAPTER FIFTY-FOUR

The wake passed in a blur of mournful relatives, friends, and strangers. Dozens of families arrived, tearfully pressing Michael's hand, gushing about the transformative impact Kelsey's outreach center had had on their lives. Seeing their earnestness, he felt a pang of guilt for ever criticizing his late wife's devotion to her work.

It was with exhaustion that Michael saw off the final guests late that evening, and retreated to the basement alone.

Do this for me – heal Taylor.

Kelsey's last words rang in Michael's ears. Opening her journal, he flicked through the immaculate reams of handwritten notes.

He skipped to the most recent entry; the last solution Kelsey had devised. Beneath the chemical ingredients were her observations:

Significant cognitive improvements observed, but subject suffered seizures. Try micro dosing.

Michael traced his hands over the writing. He could barely comprehend how, just three days ago, Kelsey had been alive, vivacious, determined; working on this cure at full tilt. Now, she was gone forever.

She'd traveled to her death alone, sacrificing companionship in her final moments to instead try and save Taylor; entrusting Michael with the urgent task of smuggling this secret cure away from the Ministry's tentacles.

But he'd failed her. Kelsey's ID card had gotten Michael into her office, and he'd managed to rescue her experimental journal while the automatons took her to the Ministry. But as he continued the mission, trying to access the chemical store room, Kelsey's card failed. The reader flagged it as 'deactivated', delivering an alarm tone. That's how he knew she was gone forever.

Of course, he'd had to flee, as soon as the card got swallowed. The penalties for using someone else's ID card were severe, and his family had enough on its plate without him getting arrested for fraud.

Alone and exhausted in his disheveled basement, Michael stared at the list of obscure chemical ingredients Kelsey had noted in her journal. He didn't recognize half the words on the page; substances like these didn't exist in the city's stores. As Kelsey had said, they were controlled by the Ministry. There was simply no way he could progress Taylor's cure without them.

He slammed the book shut in anger. The injustice of it all was more than he could bear. He'd done everything in his power to protect his family; making daily offerings, building his entire life around it, yet nothing had worked. Kelsey had been taken from all of them, Toma had been taken from Taylor, and the same opaque system arbitrating their deaths was thwarting him now; stopping him from realizing the cure Kelsey had been working on. As his arm stump throbbed, painfully, a sickening feeling grew in the pit of his stomach. He'd been allowed to survive, when she had been taken. This was his punishment.

All his life, he'd lived in fear of the system, suspecting the Ministry was, at its heart, an institution of cruelty. One by one they had taken from him the most precious people in the world. He had tried everything conceivable to placate the authorities, kowtowing to their supremacy.

No more.

It was time for revenge.

CHAPTER FIFTY-FIVE

Midnight. The hypermarket was practically deserted. The cashier regarded Michael warily as he unloaded the first jerricans onto the belt.

"Having car trouble, sir?" said the cashier.

"No, why?"

"Oh... no reason. Few folk been complaining of car troubles lately, is all."

The cashier tapped his assistance bell, illuminating a lantern above his till.

"What's that for?" asked Michael.

"I just need my supervisor to authorize the transaction. We have a limit on certain items."

The cashier hesitated, not scanning the second can. His smile faltered as his eyes darted around.

Snatching the jerricans from the belt, Michael threw them into the cart and ran for the exit.

"Hey, wait! Somebody stop him, he hasn't paid!" cried the cashier.

None of the shelf-stackers dared stop Michael and his

metal battering ram. His expertise at one-handed trolley steering was finally coming in useful, as he picked up formidable speed. He hurried to his car and threw the cans in the trunk, speeding away as the security guard puffed onto the lot with a tell-tale napkin under her chin.

Michael drove to three more supermarkets, repeating his purchase, but this time staving off suspicion by buying a smaller number of cans, and preemptively using the explanation of a friend's car having broken down nearby.

Still, even with the multi-store strategy, it wasn't going to be enough. At the final store, a brainwave struck. Michael bought a thin-tipped vacuum cleaner nozzle, some duct tape, and a couple of large trash cans, then drove to a gas station.

He was careful to choose a pay-at-pump station. Unobserved, he filled the new trash cans with fuel. Using the duct tape, he sealed the lids on top. Then, with great difficulty, and much cursing, he loaded them into the rear passenger seats. He wasn't sure which came off worse from his one-handed lifting technique: the car's paintwork or his hip, but it was a grim struggle to get them in.

Following a careful drive home, Michael set to work. He dragged the cargo onto his front lawn, beside the mailbox. He taped the thin-ended vacuum nozzle to the first jerrican, and poured the contents through the letter slit.

The dark liquid sloshed down the insides of the enamel piping, disappearing into the mail network below ground.

The quirky design of the mailboxes meant that a narrow nozzle was the only way to get anything in, and it severely limited his speed. It took a couple of minutes to empty each jerrican, which was tiring work for Michael's arm. Fleeting respite came only when he transferred the nozzle to each new canister.

Michael glanced around the empty neighborhood at regular intervals, keeping his eyes peeled for dog walkers or street cleaners; anyone who might discover his preparations.

With the last jerrican empty, he turned to the much larger, brimming trash cans. He dunked the empty can beneath the oily surface until it was full, then poured it into the mailbox.

The decanting took almost two hours, and required several breaks for immense arm cramp. With the last of the fuel finally transferred, Michael hid the empty equipment in his basement.

As dawn broke, he hurried upstairs to rouse the kids. They were groggy and confused, but heeded his urgency.

"No time to explain, it's nearly six and we have to act quickly. Grab a coat, put on your shoes, and get outside."

"Dad, what the hell's going on?" said Olive, concerned.

"You, Taylor and the boys, go stand on the sidewalk," cried Michael.

He rushed down to the basement, but Olive was close behind.

"I told you to stay outside!"

"Not unless you tell me what's going on."

Michael grabbed Kelsey's journal from the desk and thrust it before her.

"Take it. I don't deserve it anymore."

Olive stared at him, bewildered. She flicked through the pages while Michael rummaged around among his tools, winding a rag around a stick and dipping it in oil.

"This is Mom's handwriting. What is it, her log book?" frowned Olive.

Police sirens sounded outside.

"They're here, we don't have much time," said Michael, breathlessly.

He rushed upstairs, but Olive grabbed his hand as he reached the front door. Michael stared at his daughter, seeing the distress in her eyes. He snatched a deep breath and braced her for what was to come.

"Your mom spent the last year of her life trying to cure Taylor; to reverse the side effects of the experiment. Her last wish was for me to continue the work. But I was only able to salvage her journal; I couldn't get the chemicals we need for it to work. I failed her, Olive, just like I've failed you all, in so many other ways. This is my last hope. It's the only way I can truly protect you."

He broke free from her grip and hurried across the yard. Flashing blue lights were fast approaching. Kneeling down, Michael lit the tip of his oil-soaked rag stick.

"Dad, you're scaring me," said Olive.

"It'll be OK, sweetie. You'll all be safe now, I promise. I need you to go stand with the others," said Michael.

Four police cars and two fire engines screeched up before the house. Officers trained their guns on Michael, while fire crews banged on the neighbors' doors, urgently evacuating them.

Olive backed away from her father in horror, clutching the journal to her chest, then fled to the others.

The police swiftly erected a perimeter, forcing the other residents several hundred yards away. Frightened neighbors emerged in nightshirts and dressing gowns, seeing the blue lights and Michael's burning stick.

Next door, automatons had dismantled the neighbors' mailbox. They were feeding in a hosepipe to syphon out the dumped fuel.

A shock of red hair pushed its way to the front of the crowd, raising a megaphone.

"Mr. Hadley. This is Detective Clarkenwell. Step away from the mailbox."

Tears clung to Michael's eyes. There was only a small window of time to do the deed.

Only a handful of citizens knew how vulnerable the mail system was in the minutes before delivery, including his former boss. Fine vapors flooded the tunnels as the tubes became pressurized. It was something his previous firm had been tasked with fixing, but the redesign was years away from delivery. From his eavesdropping, he knew that a medium-sized explosion, precisely-timed, would be enough to overload the existing safety valves. By igniting the gasoline, he could trigger a chain reaction across the entire city's grid, destroying the network for good. Something Clarkenwell was all too aware of.

"Permission to shoot, ma'am?" called an officer.

"You wanna get us all blown up? Hold your fire!" hissed Clarkenwell.

The detective raised the megaphone once again.

"It doesn't have to be this way, Mr. Hadley. Let's talk."

"I think it's a bit late for that," laughed Michael, bitterly.

As the last of his neighbors were bundled away, he turned his attention to the crowd.

"The Ministry has robbed us for too long!" he cried. "They have taken our loved ones and controlled our lives. No more! Today, that ends once and for all! I will set you free!"

"Michael, don't do this," warned the detective.

Michael's face was set hard with grim determination. The other residents would be safe enough; he was to be the epicenter of the explosion. The blast would burn every inch of flesh on his body. It would mean a lifetime of agony. But it would liberate every other soul in the city.

Tears rolled down his cheeks as he pictured Kelsey.

"I'm sorry, my love," he whispered.

Clutching the burning stick, he approached the mailbox. As he walked, a cry sounded from across the street.

"Micka! Cuddle!"

Taylor had broken free from Olive's hand, and was running towards him with wide arms.

"No, Taylor, stay back!" cried Michael.

But Taylor had no way of understanding the danger. She burst into the garden, wrapping her arms around him with glee.

Michael staggered backwards, clutching the burning stick above his head.

"Get back!" he begged, shaking himself free.

"Taylor give cuddle, make Micka better!" she cooed.

"Taylor, you have to get away, you'll be burned, this is dangerous, you'll-"

He faltered. There was no way she could comprehend the pain she would endure. He had to get her away from the explosion.

Security automatons were closing in on both sides, and would soon be within striking distance. A voice came over the megaphone.

"Taylor, this is Detective Clarkenwell speaking. Micka's put a treat for you in the mailbox," she said, coldly.

Michael's heart froze in total disbelief. Clutching the burning stick, he had no free hand to restrain her with, and his words were lost amidst Taylor's cheers. She tore herself away, bounding to the mailbox with delight.

"Taylor, no!" he screamed.

Flames licked Michael's hand as the stick's fuel dwindled.

"Go to Olive!" he begged.

But Clarkenwell drowned him out, coaxing Taylor on with promises of a gift. The infantile woman probed the mailbox, giggling.

Automatons had scaled the fences on either side and were just yards away. Michael had seconds to act.

He had to light the mailbox now. Unless he launched himself forwards, the Ministry would win. Their legacy of lies would continue, unchallenged, for generations more, trapping millions in a system of secrecy, servitude, and pain. He couldn't let them get away with it. His sacrifice was the only way to set them all free.

The fire would cleanse him of his past failures, as he redeemed the lives to come. Fear coursed through his veins as he braced for the agony.

"Mickaaaa," gurgled Taylor, playfully.

Kelsey's face flashed across his mind as he gripped the flaming stick.

"I'm sorry, my love," he whispered. "I'm so sorry."

CHAPTER FIFTY-SIX

Michael dropped the burning stick and fell to his knees in surrender. Tears streamed down his cheeks as he watched Taylor clinging to the mailbox, thwarting his one and only chance to break the Ministry's stranglehold on them all.

Metal hands pinned him to the ground with brute force, winding him in the collision. A metallic knee pressed down on his spine as an automaton dragged his hand backwards, cuffing it to his belt strap.

Michael watched the splint burn on the grass beside him. A thick black boot landed by his cheek, snuffing it out for good.

Kneeling down, with a cold, satisfied expression, Clarkenwell read out his arrest rights.

Taylor stopped playing with the mailbox and wandered closer, sensing something was wrong. As she rushed to hug Michael, an automaton blocked her path.

"Micka!" she wailed.

"It'll be OK, Taylor, stay calm!"

Her face was wrought with fear as the automatons dragged him away.

"Micka, stay!" she cried.

"Be good for Olive," said Michael.

The machines bundled him into a police van. As the metal doors slammed shut, his terrified family vanished, and he was plunged into darkness.

―――

Some days later, Michael sat alone in the court's waiting room, his lawyer having stepped out to submit final paperwork on his behalf.

Olive entered, dressed in a formal suit, ready for the hearing. Her face was ashen; exhausted. Suddenly becoming the primary carer for two boys and a vulnerable adult was taking an immediate toll on the young college student.

"Olive, are you even allowed back here?"

"Your lawyer negotiated access. I'm technically here to give you legal counsel."

"How are you holding up?"

"How do you think?" she snapped.

Olive took a minute to compose herself, then sat before her father, looking like she'd aged a decade in the past three weeks.

"I spoke to your lawyer, and she's confident she can get you a reduced sentence if you plead guilty-"

"I *am* guilty."

"... On the grounds of diminished responsibility."

"What do you mean?"

"You weren't thinking straight. Mom died, and you

obviously you had some kind of breakdown. The court will be lenient, if you agree to extensive therapy."

"I didn't have a breakdown."

"Right, so you just decided to blow up the neighborhood on a whim? I'm not a legal expert, Dad, but I don't think that's gonna land too well."

"It wasn't a breakdown, and it wasn't a whim. It was the only logical course of action available to me after years of researching the deceit of those who rule over us."

Olive's lips tightened.

"This kind of paranoia is *exactly* what I'm talking about, Dad. When did you last take your meds?"

"That's irrelevant. The evidence I found is incontrovertible."

"I've seen your 'evidence' and it's crackpot stuff! We've been through this – you need *help*."

"So you're one of them now?"

"What?"

"The Ministry. You're one of them?"

"What are you talking about?"

"You're taking their side. Either you're against me for no reason, or you're one of them."

"Dad, I *am* your side, and I'm trying to help you. We *need* you to get better, and you can't do that in prison. The boys need you, Taylor needs you, I need you. I'm begging you, do as your lawyer says. Make the plea, agree to the therapy, and don't go to jail for no reason."

"So you'd rather I let them strap electrodes to my head and shock me into submission, than speak the truth?" snapped Michael.

"I want you to be *around!*" cried Olive. "Mom's gone. Don't you get it? We need you more than ever."

The door opened and Michael's lawyer stood in the threshold, clutching a stack of folders under her arm.

"It's time."

Michael stood alone in the dock. With the prosecution's closing remarks finished, the judge extended a mechanical hand towards him. The court clerk rose, articulating the automaton's order.

"The defendant will now enter their plea," declared the clerk.

Michael looked at the sparse gathering of supporters on his side of the room. Olive and Sophia were the only faces he knew, among the handful of reporters and law students following the case. Sophia gave him a watery thumbs up, while firmly clasping her niece's hand.

Turning his back on them, Michael faced the three blindfolded automatons. His lawyer slid the prepared statement onto his ledger with a solemn nod.

As Michael stared at the words she'd drafted for him, his blood boiled. It was perfectly crafted, and would no doubt win him a reduced sentence. But it simply wasn't true.

He shoved the paper aside and cleared his throat.

"The Ministry killed my wife, my mother, my grandfather, and my father. In time, it will kill every living soul in this room, without warning, or explanation, leaving nothing but pain and confusion in its wake.

"From birth, we are taught that our mortality is preordained. But I have seen behind the mask, I have uncovered the truth; secrets the Ministry has hidden from all of us. Lives lived outside its rules. I refuse to acknowledge the legitimacy of this system. The Ministry is murderous, and it must be stopped. In the name of its victims, the mortal souls held hostage in this very room, and citizens across this blinkered city, I plead guilty as charged. My only regret is that I did not succeed."

Gasps rippled through the court, while the photographers' cameras erupted into action. Michael's lawyer planted her forehead on the table in despair.

The two mechanical side judges glided from their seats to the brass cube in the center of the room, where they inserted their coded slips. The central judge rose to its feet and extended a metallic hand to the clerk, who relayed its verdict into the machine.

Three red flags immediately filled the glass domes. The decision was unanimous: Michael was guilty.

The brass cube printed out a slip, which the clerk tore off. The two side judges glided back to their places and stood either side of the third, ready for the sentencing. The central judge stood up tall, its legs locking straight with a chime. The clerk stepped into the center of the court and, reading from the slip, proclaimed the judges' conclusions.

"This court finds the defendant guilty of all charges. The sentence will be fifty years in an infinity chamber. No visitations. No parole. This court is hereby adjourned."

The three judges rotated on the spot and glided away to the chambers beyond. Michael glanced at his sister and his daughter one final time. Sophia was a picture of shock, while Olive wept into her shoulder. With the clinking of cuffs, the mechanical bailiffs dragged him away.

CHAPTER FIFTY-SEVEN

FIFTY YEARS LATER

Michael sat cross-legged on the pure white floor. His pupils were slits, permanently narrowed by the glare. Beside him was an empty metal tin and spoon, both licked clean.

The igloo-like cell was silent, save for the crinkling and shuffling of paper as he worked. Michael folded with precision, holding the edges still using his knees and toes to compensate for his missing arm.

He cursed as the paper slipped, cutting his finger. He stared at the brilliant, glistening red bead on his bony hand. It dropped onto the pristine floor, adding a defiant dash of color to the sterile infinity chamber.

The droplet vanished, returning the room to its barren state. The only permanent color in Michael's environment came from his grimy skin, and the food stains on his jumpsuit. As he sucked his finger, his lips brushed the band aids covering his other digits. War wounds from earlier in the week.

Red blemishes spread across the white paper as Michael resumed his work, creaking his stiff limbs around with difficulty. A hatch appeared in the floor beside him, swallowing the empty tin and spoon. He stared, transfixed; collection shafts were the only places where Michael ever saw shadows.

He shook himself out of the trance, chastising his frail mind. The tray was fading from view, so he had to finish up fast. Hastily completing the final folds, he tossed the beautiful origami flower into the shadow.

Remembering his cut, he leaned over the hatch and squeezed his fingertip, speckling the flower and tray with blood, before the floor sealed over.

He rocked back on his knees, placing his hand against his opposite shoulder, and breathing deeply into his diaphragm. With each exhalation, he uttered the names of his loved ones, starting with those needing his protection, through to those deserving his penance.

"*Sophia-Olive-Damien-Leon-Taylor-Kelsey-Mom-Pops-Father*," he gasped.

Sitting up straight, he tapped both shoulders in alternation, eight times, before repeating the whole flow. Rock back. Shoulder clasp. Breathe in. Vent names. Grounding taps. Again.

Michael rocked and chanted on repeat, getting progressively faster until the names blurred into a breathless chatter. As the minutes passed, his head grew lighter, until he slumped onto his side, panting.

His confidence in the offerings had grown over the years. For one thing, he had never requested the paper, it simply appeared early on in his sentence. He had fashioned it into a flower, and returned it, thinking of his family. Since then, the paper had kept coming without fail. Of the thousands of folded flowers he's presented, the Ministry had not rejected a single one.

Michael's attitude to the Ministry had softened over his years in solitude. He had tried fighting the system, and he had lost. The only way to live with true freedom, he realized, was to stop fighting the system, and to respect it.

The Ministry gave him paper because they wanted a dialogue with him. Not in words, but in gestures. Giving and receiving; true symbiosis. His paper orchids were offered as tokens of devotion. He submitted to the system in exchange for his family's prosperity. In return, he trusted that the Ministry was looking after his loved ones. Of course, he had no proof that this was the case; he hadn't seen another soul, human or mechanical, in decades.

Over time, Michael's guilt had been replaced by gratitude. Not a day passed in which he didn't think of Toma. Without that automaton's help, he'd have never discovered the real orchids, or been able to care for Taylor, or indeed briefly heal his grandfather. Yet, when the machine had forced him to sacrifice it, the Ministry had double-crossed him. They had accepted Toma's cerebrium heart, but taken Kelsey's life, too.

Only now, with all these years of reflection, had Michael come to see Toma's true intention. Perhaps the automaton had known Kelsey couldn't be saved, or that Michael couldn't progress while remaining dependent on its help. He suspected the automaton knew all along that this was where Michael's path would lead. If so, he owed the machine another debt of gratitude; it had guided him to a place where he and the Ministry were one. After struggling to achieve the impossible his whole life, he had finally accomplished it. From the infinity chamber, Michael could devote himself entirely to working with the Ministry, in a deep partnership, so that they both may keep his family safe.

"Toma... Yes..." muttered Michael, pensively.

If he ever saw the outside world again, rebuilding the beloved machine would be a top priority. With the right tools, maybe he could find a way to bring it back. After all, he'd managed it once before.

Wincing, and painfully stiff, he rose to his feet. With his hand extended forwards, he shuffled through the infinite whiteness. Four steps, five, six...

The invisible domed wall met his fingertips. Never letting go of it, Michael set about his daily laps, shuffling in an endless circle. When he tired of walking, he sat, vegetating, until he'd recovered the strength to continue.

An endless, circular walk. This was how he passed the day – not that night and day had any meaning in a chamber of perpetual light.

His hip struck something hard and smooth. Michael's eyes focused on the white toilet before him. It was the subtlest shade off its surroundings. Feeling his way down to the seat, he sat and defecated. Locating the sink, he washed his hands, face, and neck, and brushed his teeth. He was hoping to shave, but couldn't find the invisible-white bathroom cabinet in time. All too soon, the bathroom retracted back into the walls and floor.

The shadowless room rotated again. When it settled, Michael's foot was flush against something coarse and squidgy. With difficulty, he lowered himself onto the pure-white futon, laying side-long, and burying his face in his arm.

Michael awoke to the chamber rotating. The panoramic light made sleep a mammoth achievement in itself, and the Ministry was careful to never let him have much of it. Bleary-eyed and poorly rested, Michael clambered to his feet, knowing from bitter experience not to linger on retreating furniture. He performed a lap of the perimeter, searching for the bathroom. His foot stumbled across that day's answer; a near-invisible white bucket filled with water.

Shedding his baggy jumpsuit, he washed himself, relishing the sensation of the wet sponge against his wrinkled skin. They must have been particularly pleased with yesterday's orchid to be giving him warm water today.

As a buzzer sounded, the bucket rotated away. Michael tossed the sponge after it, then grabbed the towel and dried himself off, before throwing on a clean new jumpsuit.

Michael commenced his pacing of the room, shuffling around the exterior with his hand against the smooth wall.

"Kelsey-Mom-Granddad," he muttered, "Father-Sophia-Olive."

He paused to catch breath.

"Damien-Leon-Taylor," he murmured, shuffling onwards.

A scent interrupted his travels. Michael scarpered into the center of the cell, hungrily shoveling the tin of hot stew into his mouth. He deliberately spilled dribbles of gravy over his immaculate jumpsuit. Every day, Michael reveled in acts of culinary graffiti, knowing they would endure until his next outfit was supplied.

With the food devoured, he turned his attention to the blank sheet of paper that came with the meal tray. Completing the flower in better time than yesterday, he tossed it into the vanishing hatch.

"It's for my son, you understand?" he squawked.

His voice was grainy and peculiar; underused for so long. Rising to his feet with a satisfied sigh, Michael prepared to resume his circular pilgrimage. But before he could begin, a doorway appeared in the domed wall ahead.

Michael's jaw dropped as it slid open, revealing a shadow-filled corridor beyond. He shuffled closer, peering into the expanse. His eyesight was poor; ill adjusted to anything that wasn't gleaming white. In the doorway stood a figure Michael didn't recognize. A warden?

The young man beckoned Michael through into the corridor.

"This way, sir."

"What's happening?" said Michael.

"Your sentence is complete. You're being released."

CHAPTER FIFTY-EIGHT

The warden escorted Michael through a dank, concrete-lined corridor. Thick, sealed doors lined the walkway, each fitted with a viewing portal. An automaton was monitoring the other inmates. It slid one of the portals open, briefly flooding the corridor with light, before snapping it shut.

Michael blinked and mumbled, overwhelmed by the sensory stimulation. He walked like he was drunk, his brain no longer sure how to handle straight lines.

The warden deposited Michael in a dressing room, where his clothes were waiting. It was the same suit he'd worn to court. It took several minutes for him to change in the cramped cube, vaguely remembering how to use buttons and fasten a tie. The fabric hung looser than he remembered, and he had to slide the belt to its tightest notch.

Flecks of color shot across his vision like his brain was short-circuiting. Was it his imagination, or was the bulb overhead getting darker? Michael squinted at the plaque to his side.

Sensory Readjustment Cubicle 4.

Above it was a smooth, flat surface, diffusing from matt black to dark silver as a mirror formed before him.

Michael whimpered, seeing himself for the first time in decades. He pressed his gnarled fingers to his creased face in disbelief. Contours sank deep across his cheeks and brow. His eyes were yellow, and his hair had thinned to a few white wisps.

The warden escorted him through security, to the edge of the prison grounds. The building was like a giant golf ball; a pure white sphere covered in hexagonal dimples.

Michael had often wondered how many others were being held in the substructures within. He'd not seen or heard another inmate, or employee, in all his time there. He wanted to ask the warden many things, but couldn't remember how conversations began. So they walked in silence to the front gates, with the warden supporting Michael by the arm as he swayed.

Buzzing the turnstiles open, he ushered Michael through. Michael's face was wrought with concern; where was he to go?

Familiar with such panicked looks, the warden waved him on his way with a curt explanation: "Your family are collecting you."

With that, the door buzzed shut, and the light flicked red. The warden departed, leaving Michael blinking in the sun.

He peered around for his family, but they were nowhere to be seen. From the edge of the parking lot, a suited stranger waved at him.

"Michael, over here," she called.

The woman marched over to meet him, as he shuffled closer in bemusement. She threw her arms around him tightly. Michael gasped at the brush of another human's skin on his.

The stranger stepped back, framing him in her arms, smiling at him adoringly.

"Taylor?" said Michael, with disbelief.

She beamed at him. "I was worried you wouldn't recognize me!"

"But you're... Look at you," he stammered.

All trace of the floppy, clumsy, dependent kidult was gone; here was a competent, composed business woman. Behind her, the passenger door opened and a second woman climbed out. She also looked familiar.

Her face was hard-set, fierce, and angry. Those eyes, those cheeks, they brought impossible memories flooding back.

"Kelsey?" gasped Michael.

The woman shook her head, uttering a cold, bitter laugh.

"Sorry to disappoint you, Dad," said Olive.

Michael's head spun as he processed his mature daughter standing before him. The last time he saw her, she was a semester into college. Now she looked like she held tenure as a professor. Michael gazed from her to Taylor in astonishment.

"How is this possible?" he croaked.

"We've got some catching up to do, Dad. Fifty years' worth, to be precise."

Olive stared at him, unsmiling. There was a blazing resentment in her eyes. She shook her head, bit her lip, and briskly walked away to regain composure. She didn't want to vent all her frustration in one immediate tirade. There would be plenty of time for that.

"She'll be OK, she just needs time," whispered Taylor.

"Taylor, you're..."

"Better?"

Michael nodded, searching her face with amazement.

"I have Olive to thank for that. She perfected Kelsey's formula," smiled Taylor.

"How?" squawked Michael.

Years of disuse had rendered his voice strange and angular. The very act of conversation felt like a trance.

"No idea how she did it, you'll have to ask her yourself," grinned Taylor.

"Will she talk to me?" said Michael.

"I can still hear you, you know?" snapped Olive.

"Will you, then?" repeated Michael.

"I don't know, Dad, I guess it hangs on whether I can forgive you for pleading guilty when you didn't have to, and getting yourself shut away for basically our whole lives. Do you know what it's been like? We had to make to do without you *or* Mom. It didn't have to be that way, but you chose to make it like that. You missed my wedding, my children being born, their entire childhoods, *their* weddings, *their* kids growing up, you missed it all. When we drove here, I was almost excited to see you, but now I'm just angry. I don't recognize you at all, it's like I have no idea who you are. I'm not sure I ever did."

"Did any of them die?"

"What?"

"Your family. Your brothers' families."

"No. That's such a weird thing to-"

"Then it worked. It was all worth it," breathed Michael.

For the first time in fifty years, the tightness in his chest was gone. He closed his eyes and exhaled freely, feeling the wind running through his wispy hair. Fresh air, cut grass, a dusty road, bird song, the sun on his ashen skin, all these sensations bombarded his senses and he smiled, drinking them in.

"It was *worth* it?" fumed Olive, breaking his daydream. "You're seriously gonna stand there, with one god-damned arm, looking about a million years old, and tell me it was *worth* it?"

"The orchids worked. We made it through the penitence," said Michael.

"Unbelievable," said Olive, storming off to the car.

"She'll come around. *I'm* glad to have you back, Micka," grinned Taylor.

Offering her arm, she escorted him to the car.

"There are a lot of excited grandkids waiting to meet you."

An hour's drive later they were home. Michael's lip trembled as he shuffled out of the car, to a place he recognized instantly.

Olive hung back, having not said a word on the entire car ride home. She let Taylor assist Michael from the car to the house.

The picket fence had been replaced with hedgerow, and the large paving slabs replaced with ornate checkered tiles. But the house looked much the same, albeit now clad in a small forest of wisteria.

He and Kelsey had saved hard to afford this place. It held so many of their memories, good and bad.

Michael's eyes lingered on the enamel pipe protruding from the ground, and the mailbox atop it.

"Looks like we're both still standing," he muttered.

Taylor led him to the living room, which was rammed

with faces Michael didn't recognize.

"Everyone, there's someone you've all been waiting to meet. To four of us, he's "father", to many of you he'll be not just grandfather but *great*-grand father! This is Granddad Michael!" she declared.

The room fell silent. Michael blushed, casting his eyes around the unfamiliar people, who were eyeing him up like he'd landed from another planet.

"Granddad Michael!" cheered a man, toasting him.

His enthusiasm broke the ice, and triggered a ripple of toasts, which escalated into a full applause and whooping from all corners. From the grateful smile Taylor gave, Michael inferred that the instigator was her husband.

With the ice broken, the strangers' frowns turned to smiles of relief and warmth. Tiny infants threw themselves around Michael's leg with a giggle, nearly knocking him over, before their parents apologetically plucked them away.

Michael glimpsed a piece of scrunched paper in one of the child's hands. It looked almost floral. Before he could look in detail, Taylor was ushering him into a chair, where a piece of cake materialized in his hand.

Two elderly women pressed through the crowd of youngsters and stood before him. Michael frowned, piecing the faces together. His jaw dropped.

"Sophia? Nina?" he gasped.

"Don't you take that line with me, big brother, we look fantastic for our age. You're the one with a face like an accordion," grinned Sophia.

She leaned closer, hugging his head to her chest. As he squeezed her arm, gratefully, a bald man with glasses approached. Nina and Sophia slipped away, giving Michael space with the newcomer.

"Hey Dad," he said awkwardly.

"Damien?" said Michael, flabbergast.

"Minus the hair," he grinned.

Michael did a double-take. The aged bald man in front of him was the same tousle-haired lad he'd left behind fifty years ago. He'd missed an entire lifetime.

"Oh, and this is my partner, and our soon-to-be-adult daughter, Hope," said Damien.

A kindly-looking woman came forwards and bowed to Michael. Before her, sitting pertly in a wheelchair, was their daughter. Judging by the age gap, she must have been born when Damien and his wife were in their early forties, almost twenty years ago.

Their daughter's bony knees showed beneath a thin blanket. A withered hand rested across her lap. With her functioning arm, she reached forwards and gave Michael a warm handshake with the maturity of a young college student.

"It's so wonderful finally meeting you, Granddad Michael, I've heard so much about you!"

Hope's words were clipped, like she was out of breath, but her smiling eyes brimmed with energy.

Michael's mind flashed back to the memorial park, and the statuette of the son he'd never known. The similarity was uncanny.

He clasped his granddaughter's hand with warmth, and sorrow. Guilt welled inside him as he met her bright, engaging gaze. This was the child Kelsey had denied them, when she switched their unknown boy out for baby Olive. Decades later, the child was back, in a new guise, this time in his son's family. Was the Ministry punishing Damien's family for Kelsey's sins?

A timer chimed on the girl's wheelchair.

"Time for an injection. It was lovely meeting you, Granddad, see you again," she wheezed.

Damien wheeled her about and they headed off to find some space. Michael watched them go, confounded by guilt.

He didn't have long to dwell, for another set of grandchildren swiftly arrived, proudly paraded by a now-adult Leon, who was, by the looks of it, a fashion designer. His partner and their children must have all received children as young adults, because their entire mini-clan was conspicuous in the room by its avant-garde, finely-cut attire, and it spanned two additional generations; three sets of fashionista parents in their late twenties, and their assorted rabble of under-tens.

Michael's eyes lingered on Leon's wife's earrings. He couldn't quite make them out behind her flowing hair, but it almost looked like a set of gilded orchids. She blushed, following his gaze, and hastily combed her hair forwards, obscuring them from view. Leon cottoned-on, and the pair whisked their own grandchildren away muttering a mish-mash of excuses about getting food and drink.

Fresh relatives replaced them, with reunions and introductions coming thick and fast throughout the afternoon. Michael kept pinching himself, expecting the room to rotate and the colors and people to dissolve at any moment, returning him to the bleached white of his chamber. After fifty years in isolation, hallucinations had become his bread and butter. The only thing assuring him this occasion was real was the taste of *actual* bread and butter, as Taylor dutifully refilled his plate with fresh scones and hot tea.

Despite the regular sugar injections, by 4 p.m. Michael was exhausted. The tidal wave of social interaction had drained him. Still, he felt a strong sense of pride. The family had flourished because of him; because of his offerings, and the system he'd devised in prison.

But for all the reunions, there was one absent friend he wanted to check on. Michael excused himself for a bathroom break, reassuring Taylor that he could manage unaided.

Alone in the corridor, he shuffled to a familiar doorway. It was unlocked. Placing a mottled hand on the banister, he descended, step by aching step. The familiar musty smell of damp concrete and wood greeted him like an old embrace.

The basement had been cleared out substantially since he was last there. His eyes gravitated towards the small stack of original items, which had been carefully preserved on a shelf, and lovingly kept free of dust.

Michael's eyes moved past the charred chocolate tin to the suitcase where he had stashed Toma's mechanical body.

The case was much lighter than it should have been, and almost completely silent to move. With trepidation, he opened it up.

Michael gasped. Thousands of origami flowers filled the container. Some were pure white; others were speckled with blood. He shook his head in disbelief, as the scale of the betrayal sank in.

Grabbing the suitcase, Michael dragged it upstairs, spilling paper flowers as he went. He forced his way into the center of the living room, silencing the guests.

"What is the meaning of this?" he demanded.

"You tell me, Dad, you're the one who made them," shrugged Olive.

"I want to know why in hell's name they're *here*?"

"You can thank Taylor for that. I was gonna chuck them in the trash, but she insisted on keeping them safe until you were released. Glad to see you're being an ungrateful ass, as predicted."

"*I'm* ungrateful? I did this for *your* protection. For all of you!" cried Michael.

"Folding a bunch of flowers? Right..." scoffed Olive.

"I kept a covenant with the Ministry! They gave me the paper, I made the offering, and together we kept you all safe. It was simple until you went and ruined it!"

"Here we go," groaned Olive.

"You don't believe me? Why else would they give me the paper each day?"

"Er, maybe so you could *write to us*, you loon?"

"You people never wrote to me," snapped Michael.

"We weren't allowed to!"

"And Toma... What did you do with Toma's body? It was in the suitcase... We need it to... To protect..."

Concerned whispers echoed across the room as the extended family tried to fathom who Toma was, and why Michael thought there was a body in the basement.

"Somebody answer me!" he demanded, wild-eyed.

"The Ministry took it, OK?" fumed Olive. "It was the same detective that arrested you – she came to the house after you were sentenced. She had a warrant to search for the missing machine, and her team found it in the basement. *Your* basement."

"This is bad," stammered Michael, looking at the pile of undelivered offerings. "This is really bad. They won't like this at all. We have to move these quickly."

"What?"

"We have to deposit these right away, all of you are in danger!"

"I knew this gathering was a bad idea. You're clearly not ready for-"

"There's a secret hatch – a door – there's no time to explain. You'll see when we're there."

"No, Dad, we won't, because we're not coming," said Olive, folding her arms.

"What?" blinked Michael.

"We made a pact before your release, that once you were out, we wouldn't tolerate any of your unhealthy behaviors. It's not good for anyone, least of all you."

"But... but this is different! This is urgent!" protested Michael.

"Really? Or is it just another one of your weird, baseless superstitions? If your little origami project kept you going while you were in prison, that's terrific for you, but the rest of us were trying to get on with our lives, and do our best to deal with raising our own families, launching our careers, finishing school, and all the stuff you should have been there for."

"Every minute these offerings remain here puts us all in danger," urged Michael.

"Says the guy who just got out of prison for trying to blow up an entire neighborhood?"

Michael scooped up the spilled flowers, then zipped up the case. He dragged it to the front door, his estranged family watching in bemusement.

"Micka, let's talk about this," begged Taylor.

"Do you want me to die? Is that it? Do you want each other to die?" he cried.

"No, of course not. That's not what Olive was-"

"I did all this for a reason!" he grunted, struggling out into the yard.

"Where are you going?" said Taylor, concerned.

"To fix this! Before we face the consequences."

CHAPTER FIFTY-NINE

Michael staggered off the tram. Fighting his aching, brittle body, he dragged the suitcase across the square, ignoring onlookers' wary stares. Reaching the hidden stone doorway, he banged against the hatch urgently.

No answer.

Michael banged again, begging them to open up. His pleas turned to demands, then threats, as he grew increasingly desperate.

The hatch stayed shut.

"OK, OK, I'm sorry. Look, I'm leaving them here for you. Use them, remember my family," begged Michael.

Michael flung open the suitcase and tipped the orchids onto the floor.

"You see? I am your devoted servant!"

A gust of wind snatched Michael's offerings from the floor and scattered it across the square.

Michael cried out in horror, watching his family's security vanish before him. He launched himself after the tumbling pieces, but his aching frame couldn't keep up. He fell, landing hard on his knees. The stone showed no mercy against his frail, starved body. Whimpering with pain, Michael desperately scrabbled for the fragments of papers around him.

A polished boot landed by Michael's face, trapping a paper orchid underfoot. Beside it, a polished black cane.

With a grunt, the stranger knelt down and retrieved the offering. A wrinkled hand, with neatly-painted black nails, held the crumpled offering out towards him.

"We are unburdened," said the woman.

Straining against his decrepit neck, Michael gazed upon the stranger. Despite the years, he recognized her instantly.

The woman's face was wrinkled, and her eyebrows wiry. Her red hair had turned white, but her piercing stare hadn't faded one bit.

"You," sighed Michael.

"Yes, me," smiled the detective.

CHAPTER SIXTY

Clarkenwell led Michael to a bench, where they sat overlooking the Ministry's imposing dome. The *REGULATING LIFE TO LIBERATE LIVES* maxim glimmered in the uplighting.

Michael's eyes flitted to his abandoned suitcase, and the flapping paper orchids blowing in the breeze. His heart was in his mouth, willing the hatch to open. If those inside took just one of his offerings, it would be an indisputable sign.

"They won't," said the detective, reading his mind.

Michael bristled. He'd always hated her presumptuous manner.

"I thought I was done with you," he growled.

"On the contrary, I was rather hoping our paths would cross here. In fact, I was counting on it."

Clarkenwell offered Michael a stick of gum, which he declined with a scowl.

"You planned this?" he demanded.

"In a sense. I knew you were getting out today, and I figured this place would be high on your list. We're creatures of habit, after all," she said, winking.

"Is that it? You've come to gloat?" said Michael, bitterly.

"No, I did my share of that while you were banged up," grinned Clarkenwell, shoving her hands into the pockets of her dark trench coat. "I'm here to die."

She pulled out a tattered-looking envelope, with an elaborate, swirling signature scrawled across the front. Michael stared at it in amazement, feeling a peculiar pang of triumph.

"Mind dialing down your joy?" she grunted.

Michael blushed, forcing his features back under control.

"Sorry," he muttered.

"Pff, no you're not. I know your type and this is like hitting the jackpot. Enjoy your moment."

Clarkenwell rose to her feet as the clock struck 9 p.m.

"Wait, that's it?" said Michael.

"What were you expecting, a goodbye hug?"

Michael scowled. "Is no one here to see you off?"

"Do you see a crowd of tearful well-wishers?"

Michael shrugged.

"You're not the only one who screwed things up," said the detective.

"Before you go, detective, answer me this - how come I never met anyone else like me? You know, like... heretics?"

"Solitary confinement generally nips that possibility in the bud."

"Before prison, I mean. I spent so many years seeking answers, scouring the city's archives for others who wanted to defy the Ministry, but there's no trace. I know they expunge the records, but I still thought I would at least meet some people in twenty years of looking."

"Doubt is a rare thing in this city, Michael. Even if you were to stumble across another like-minded soul, it's unlikely you would ever cross paths again. The Ministry would make sure of it."

"With a death letter?"

"Not if it can be avoided. Too messy. These people are the ones who don't always come quietly. Instead, the Ministry prefers to 'course correct' such people's lives. Some might receive a child to keep them busy. Others might lose their jobs, or be implicated in a scandal to discredit them. The Ministry stays one step ahead. It protects the herd by ensuring cancerous individuals can't spread their ideology to others."

"And knowing all that, you still worked for them?"

"Like I said, you're not the only screw-up here."

Clarkenwell folded her gum into a wrapper, stuffed it in her pocket, then shuffled to the edge of the bench, preparing her walking cane.

"So long, Michael Hadley. Enjoy what's left of your unburdened life."

"Wait! What do I do now? They won't accept my offerings!" called Michael.

"I figured you'd be worried about that. Don't worry, I've left you a goodbye gift that'll take care of things."

"What do you mean?"

The detective huffed and slouched backwards against the slats.

"From the looks of your rather pitiful origami efforts, you're familiar with the Ministry's offering system."

"You know about it?" said Michael.

"I was a detective, Mr. Hadley. There are a lot of things I know that others don't – including the reason they only accept a particular flower."

"Because it's... special? It's hard to find... which *proves* your loyalty, your devotion!"

"You really think the Ministry's into them for their aesthetic qualities? And there you had me thinking you were an intelligent man, Mr. Hadley."

"So... it's something about the plant... a property? Something they... extract?" pondered Michael.

"Bingo."

"But what about loyalty?"

"Prison really did a number on you, hey? I miss the old Michael. What happened to the one-armed rebel willing to take down the system just to expose the 'truth'?"

Michael glared at her, and Clarkenwell chuckled.

"OK, don't answer that. My point is, you're assuming your relationship with the Ministry is based on mutual respect, a sort of unspoken love. In reality, it's transactional. Each side gives and takes. You have to learn the Ministry's language, then you can have a dialogue. Right now, you're just shouting at a stone wall – literally."

"And the plants... that's their language?"

"The plants embody the oldest and only language our city knows: utility."

"But they'll see I was trying, with the origami, they'll know my intentions were true, so that... that surely that counts for something?"

"To you and I intentions are everything. To the Ministry, what are they but unfulfilled promises?"

"How do I speak their language? Please, detective, I'm just trying to protect my family. If you understand intentions, surely you understand that. It's all I've ever wanted. It's all Kelsey really wanted, too, in her way."

"I understand, Mr. Hadley, better than you can imagine. Which is why, from tonight, you won't have to worry about lackluster 'intentions' anymore. You'll be able to fulfil your promises to the Ministry."

"I don't understand..."

"The flowers - I thought it was time you had the real thing."

"What? You know where I can find one?"

"It's already yours. When you go home, you'll find it bedded beside your mailbox."

"Bedded? Impossible - Toma and I tried that. It never worked. You can't plant them, or graft the stems or anything. When you pick the flower, the whole plant dies, right down to the roots. Toma showed me once - that's why they're so rare. You only get them in the wild, only those deserving can find them. If it was as simple as just *planting* one, everyone would have one!"

"There was a time everyone did," shrugged Clarkenwell. "According to legend, at least."

Michael's eyes widened. After all his efforts, the detective had known more than him all along.

"Why don't more people know about this?" he stammered.

"It would appear our ancestors chose to forget. A necessary sacrifice to facilitate the constructive delusions we endure at the hands of our beloved Ministry."

"But these plants give immortality! Why would our ancestors ever sacrifice that? Your legend's a lie. It has to be."

"Believe what you want, Michael. I'm merely offering you a way out of your current predicament."

"If what you're saying is true - that all citizens used to have these plants - then how come they all just vanished?"

"They were relocated."

"Where?"

Clarkenwell raised a surprised eyebrow at Michael's naivety.

"The Ministry *took* them?"

"Received might be a more accurate description. According to the legend, our ancestors volunteered them gladly."

"Idiots!" spat Michael.

"Perhaps. One family regretted their decision, however, and stole their plant back from the Ministry building in its earliest days. Of course, there were repercussions. They were forced into hiding, and became nomadic. The lineage is impossible to trace, but centuries later here we are, passing that same plant on. I can name the person who gave it to me, and in turn, you shall be able to do the same. Use it wisely, Michael."

"Will it protect my whole family?"

"Only those who live where it's planted."

"So... to protect everyone, they'd all have to move into the same place?"

"Alas, no. Even if you *could* fit everyone into your house, it wouldn't work. The plant only protects as many people as it has flowers in bloom. It has five right now, which will suffice for you, plus those currently living in your household."

"But my granddaughter – she turns eighteen at midnight. She's the most vulnerable, and she's not in that house," stammered Michael.

"Ah, the one born with difficulties? Yes, I was sorry to see that. But I would argue you're equally vulnerable, the pair of you. You're an ex-convict, Michael, and you just finished serving a life sentence."

"So?"

"It's kind of in the name, isn't it? Felons' letters tend to come pretty quick after they're released."

"How quick?"

"Put it this way: there's a reason I gave you the plant on your first day out of jail."

"So, you're saying I have to choose? Between protecting myself and my granddaughter?"

"I'm afraid so."

Michael's shoulders slumped. There was so much he wanted to set right, so many relationships to mend after being away for so long.

"There is one thing you could try... But it's risky," mused Clarkenwell.

Michael perked up.

"Anything!"

"You have to understand, I have no idea how likely this is to work. I've only heard about it through the people who gave me the plant, and that was a long time ago. They'd only heard about it from others. None of us dared try."

"What is it? Please! I *have* to protect them all. After all the hurt I've caused. I'll try anything, just tell me."

"This is gonna sound weird but... You gotta go to the grave of a loved one. Specifically, the one you lost youngest."

Michael thought for a moment.

"But... my father doesn't have a grave. My grandfather, though? Or Kelsey?"

"Not the person you lost when you were young; I mean the youngest person you've lost. You see, this method only works for people who lost someone younger than themselves..."

Michael's stomach churned.

"You're talking about the boy?"

"The boy you never knew, yes. If you want to do this, you have to go to his grave."

"Why?"

"How should I know? I'm just relaying what they told me."

"What would I do - at the grave?"

"It's something to do with the mixing of grounds. Apparently, you take some earth from your home, and mix it with the earth at the grave. Then you 'tether' the plant. Not my wording, before you ask."

"How do I...?"

"The plant already has two roots, OK? The primary stem goes in the ground, the other one fuses to your mailbox. I told you it was weird. I think there's some kind of nutrient exchange through the enamel, who knows? Anyway, at the grave, you just stick the big roots in the mixed soil, and the other one against the headstone."

"But how will the Ministry know which other household I want to protect? The dead boy has no ties to my granddaughter."

"Soooo... you might not like this bit so much. Then again, you did hack your own arm off, so maybe it'll be right up your street. The final step is called confirmation. Or maybe it was calibration? I can't quite remember. Something beginning with 'C'..."

"How does it work?"

"You need a blood sample from the most vulnerable person in each of the two homes you're seeking to protect. Like I said, it's an acquired taste, this whole thing. Apparently, the blood-soil-location combo is what the Ministry's after."

"That makes no sense at all!"

"Hey, I'm just telling you what they told me. Take it or leave it."

"You're sure this is the only way?"

"Unless you can find a whole new plant, which I

guarantee you won't be able to, then yes, this is the only way I've ever heard of. Fair warning, though, there's a chance the blood might contaminate the plant. In which case, it would lose its protective qualities and die. Apparently."

"OK, but if the 'calibration' were to work...?"

"Then the plant would grow a bunch more flowers and you'd all live happily ever after."

"And if that were the case, could I do it again? Add more homes – with blood?"

"Oof, er, *hypothetically*, I guess... But you might never have that chance. Let me reiterate, Michael, messing with the plant is high risk. You'd be throwing away the certainty of your own future."

"But with the potential to save my entire family. How could I *not* take that chance?"

"It's the decision every gardener like us has faced. What do you think of 'gardeners' as a nickname by the way? My predecessors called themselves the 'flower stewards', but I think that's kinda dumb. 'Gardeners' is a bit more street, right?"

"The plant - how old is it?"

"From what I was told, it's as old as the city itself. But bear in mind that's the 'flower stewards' talking. They said those plants were the reason our ancestors settled here; they used to be abundant. You have one of the last."

Thunder rumbled in the distance, and the dense rain cloud overhead began to leak. Drizzle doused the pair on the bench. Clarkenwell looked skyward and opened her mouth, letting the drops land on her tongue. She closed her eyes and basked in the sensation, as the rain grew thicker and faster.

Michael pulled his coat over his head, shielding his wrinkled scalp from the deluge. As the rain became deafening, Clarkenwell rose to her feet and faced the Ministry with a sigh.

"I think nature's giving me a hint. I'd best be off - I'll see you round, Michael."

"Wait, that's it?"

"It's my time. You of all people should know they don't take kindly to lateness."

She gave him a bittersweet smile, then limped towards the Ministry.

"Why are you doing this now?" cried Michael. "Why help me, of all people, after all these years?"

"Consider it penance," called the detective.

"For what?"

Clarkenwell turned, leaning heavily on her cane, framed against the Ministry's sweeping steps. Maybe it was the gray sky, or the driving rain, but the wrinkles on her aged face suddenly looked deeper.

"Your wife's car crash was my fault, Michael. Those final hours before her letter came must have been wrought with suffering. I've carried that shame with me ever since. I'm sorry. Look after the plant - choose wisely."

Michael watched, speechless, as she ascended the steps slowly, and steadily, disappearing into the archway of departures.

CHAPTER SIXTY-ONE

Michael hurried through the gate and knelt before the mailbox, his knees sinking into the wet mud. There it was, nestled at the base of the enamel pipe, a black stem rising from the earth.

The soil at its base was raised, but compact, no doubt bearing Clarkenwell's handprints. The plant's main stem was split as the detective had promised; part was embedded in the ground, the other half clung to the mailbox like a crawling vine.

"Michael? What are you doing out here?" cried Taylor. "Where have you been? We were worried about you!"

She hurried out from the house and thrust an umbrella over Michael's head, shielding him from the cold drizzle. Not that there was much point; he was already soaked through.

"This is it," he said, in disbelief.

"Pops, you really ought to come inside..."

"It's so beautiful."

He gazed at its translucent leaves. Bursts of spectral color shot across them with each rain drop's landing. The flashes caught Taylor's eye, bringing her down to Michael's level.

"What in the name of..."

"It's to protect us. From someone who owed us," said Michael.

"Protect us how? It's a freaky weed."

Michael shook his head, smiling, then thrust his bare hands into the soil, gently teasing up the bundled roots.

As he lifted it, the plant drooped. Michael froze. Cautiously, he peeled its secondary stem away from the enamel. It came away like tape from a parcel, leaving behind a faint residue.

As the last strands came away, the plant fell limp across the ball of earth in Michael's dripping hands.

"I need a bowl – and a plate – hurry!"

Taylor dithered, unsure how to keep Michael dry while fulfilling his request. She tucked the umbrella under his armpit then scurried into the house.

"Thank you, Taylor," he said, upon her swift return.

He decanted the fragile plant, then covered it over. Abandoning the umbrella, he rose to his feet, clutching the precious cargo, and shuffled towards the street.

"Where are you going now?" called Taylor.

"Damien's house. There's something I need from his daughter," said Michael.

"Do you even know where that is?"

"He gave me his address at the party. Don't wait up for me, I'll be back late."

Rolling her eyes in despair, Taylor hurried after him with the muddied umbrella.

"Get into my car, Pops, I'll give you a ride. Besides, they won't be at home. Hope has her weekly physio at this time; they'll be at the outreach center. Let's go."

Michael sidled through the bustling lobby. The center was teeming with excited families, checking in for appointments and socializing in the café, despite the late hour. The sound of team sports rang out from the main hall.

Michael approached the front desk and dripped over the counter.

"Hope Hadley," he demanded.

The clerk looked at him, blankly.

"Are you...?"

"I'm her grandfather, and this is urgent."

The clerk's eyes glanced sideways, betraying the girl's location. "She's in a treatment right now, sir, I'm afraid you'll have to-"

Ignoring the clerk's protests, Michael brushed past the counter and shuffled towards the treatment rooms. Taylor apologized profusely, while the clerk called for help.

"Sir, come back! Security!"

Michael fumbled with the pull-door, struggling to operate it while clutching the precious bowl. A buzzer sounded, and a Ministry automaton glided in from the sports hall. It sped across the lobby and seized him.

"Put me down, this is urgent!" cried Michael. "Taylor, do something!"

Taylor half-pleaded with the clerk, but with limited conviction. It seemed she shared the other woman's reservations.

"Look, look," hissed Michael.

He coaxed the lid off the bowl and showed the automaton the plant inside.

The machine shuddered and released its grip on Michael. Its neck twitched, like it was short-circuiting, as it stared at the glistening, clear leaves, and their hypnotic bursts of color.

Squeezing past the machine, Michael nestled the bowl in his arm stump and pulled the door open, then rushed into the corridor beyond.

"Sir, you can't go through there!"

The clerk's voice faded behind the closing door, while Michael stumbled through the treatment suite, peering into the rooms as he went. There she was!

A therapy automaton was tending to Hope. Its head snapped up in alarm as Michael burst into the room. The machine rose to its full height, about to accost him, but he revealed the glistening flower, causing it to seize up mid-stride.

With the machine rooted to the spot, he hurried to his granddaughter's side.

"Grandpa Michael? What's going on?"

Fluid tubes and electrical monitors connected Hope to a battery of instruments at the side of the room. Her frail body was suspended from the ceiling in a harness. It held her upright while a vast mechanical hamster wheel rotated beneath her legs, allowing them to move passively.

"I'm here to help," panted Michael.

He set the muddy bowl down on the counter and stared around the room. He hadn't really thought the next bit through, such was his hurry.

"Is this about my birthday meal tomorrow?" winced Hope. "I wanted you to come, but Dad said no. I could ask him again, though?"

Michael ignored her, rifling through the drawers of the therapy room, searching for a syringe, or failing that something sharp enough to pierce skin.

His hand landed on a bungee cord. The metal hook was

just sharp enough. He sterilized it with alcohol rub, then approached his granddaughter. She eyed him up, warily, as he shuffled closer clutching the bungee, with a vial poking out of his pocket.

"Grandpa? What's with the cord?"

"I only need a small sample, just stay still and try to relax," he grunted.

"Sample of what? Hey, what are you-"

He swiped the hook at her leg, missing by a fraction of an inch, as the spinning wheel carried them back and forth.

"Hey!"

Hope jerked her hips, trying to dodge Michael's swipes. Her good arm was on the opposite side, constricted by the harness, with no way to fend him off. The jolting only made her gait unsteady, causing her feet to trip and drag against the ridges of the wheel.

With her legs fixed, Michael seized his opportunity and raised the metal hook, preparing to stab it directly into her thigh.

Damien burst into the room, with Olive and Taylor in tow.

"Dad, stop!" he cried.

Damien lunged forwards, seizing Michael's hand, catching the hook just inches above Hope's skin.

"What the hell are you doing? Hope, are you OK?"

She nodded tearfully, while the others quickly shut off the spinning wheel. Olive and Taylor lowered Hope from her harness into her chair. Taylor quietly soothed the young woman, while Olive checked the machine readings for anomalies.

Damien pinned Michael against the wall, quivering with anger.

"Dad, you better explain fast or I'm calling the police," snarled Damien.

"I'm helping her," wheezed Michael.

"By trying to stab her with a bungee? Are you insane?"

"Yes, he is. And I *am* calling the police," snapped Olive.

"Don't do that, I beg you," urged Michael. "It's for her eighteenth!"

"That is the most messed up thing you've ever said," said Olive, disgusted.

"I only need a few drops of blood, that's all it takes!"

"Blood for what?" yelled Damien.

"The flowers! Taylor saw it, she knows, she understands. There's a plant, in that bowl, which can protect as many people as it has buds in bloom. You all saw what it does to the automatons, you can't deny it's special."

"You're telling us this is some kind of magic plant?" scowled Olive, peering in the bowl.

"It's not magic, it's... official. It's part of the Ministry's way. I'm a steward, now, you see? I got it from the detective. Olive, you know who I'm talking about; the redhead who took Toma's body away."

"What rubbish," spat Olive. "Even if it was from that hateful woman, there's no way it does what you think. It's a flower, for crying out loud, Dad!"

"And yet stranger things happen in your place of work each day," countered Michael.

Olive blinked, taken aback.

"You think I don't know about the wooden statue?" pressed Michael. "The waters? The clays? You may find it hard to believe, daughter, but there was a time your mother and I were like two souls wrapped in one. She told me things; prized secrets of the Ministry."

"You know about Grandma's work?" said Hope,

brightly. "I've never heard this stuff! Can you tell me about it?"

"Alas, I wish I knew more. Life pulled us apart, dear one," said Michael.

"No, Dad, you drove our family apart, which is very different," snapped Olive.

"I'm still trying to fathom *on what planet* it would be acceptable to stab a child and expect it to protect them," snarled Damien.

"Ours," shrugged Michael. "It's the world we live in. You can fight it, as I did for so many years, or you can accept it, and make the system work for you, as I am trying – for all of us."

"By cutting my daughter?"

"Barely! Like I said, I only need a handful of drops to confirm the soil, after which the stem can be separated. Then it protects both our households. Olive, if I can perfect the method, I'm confident that I can extend it to your household too. It's transactional, see? I'm speaking the Ministry's language now."

"I don't want anything to do with your insane meddling, Dad," fumed Olive. "Give me one good reason why I shouldn't report you, right now?"

"Because Hope's life depends on it," said Michael, simply.

"You really are full of it. They should never have let you out, you old psycho," fumed Olive.

"I'm begging you, let me do this for Hope's sake! You can report me after, but please just let me confirm the soil," cried Michael.

Olive stormed over to the phone and snatched up the receiver, raising her finger to dial.

"Wait!" cried Hope.

All eyes fell on the teenage girl, who shifted in her wheelchair, nervously.

"I should get a say in this, right?"

"You're a child," said Damien, softly.

"Only for another two hours. Then I'm an adult. I'm like all the rest of you. Unless I experience some seismic shift between now and then, I think it's fair to say my opinion should carry as much weight now as it will from tomorrow?"

Damien groaned, despairing.

"OK, sweetie, have your say."

"Grandpa Michael. I want you to take my blood."

Sharp intakes of breath sounded from each corner of the room.

"You do?" cheered Michael.

"You do?" cried Olive, Damien, and Taylor, aghast.

"You're not thinking clearly, it must be the stress of it all-" began Damien.

"I am, Dad, and this is my choice. My body, my choice."

"Well, yes, technically, but-"

"And I choose to give a sample of blood to Grandpa Michael, for his ritual."

Michael's heart thumped with excitement. "Yes, yes, Hope, excellent decision!"

"Aunt Olive, please can you draw the sample safely?" said Hope.

Olive looked from the girl, to Michael, to Damien, until the girl's father nodded in defeat. Cursing, she unlocked a secure cupboard and withdrew a syringe. Placing it against Hope's thigh, she drained a small vial of blood, which she unscrewed and placed in the girl's hand.

"Thank you for believing me," said Michael, extending his hand.

"I don't believe what you've been told, Grandpa, but I believe you need this to feel calm. I hope it brings you that," said Hope.

She placed the vial in his hand.

"You won't regret this," beamed Michael.

The clock on the wall struck 10 p.m. Michael slipped the warm vial into his pocket and grabbed the plant off the counter.

"I have to get this done by midnight. Taylor, I need to borrow your car."

"What? No way. I can give you a lift, but I'm not-"

"Please, this is something I have to do alone. I swear, do this for me and I will never ask you for anything again," implored Michael.

"Hell, if those are the terms, you can have my car," snorted Olive, slamming her keys on the counter.

"Thank you, daughter. I know I never got a chance to thank you enough for all you did for our family, but... your mother would be so proud."

"Thanks Dad. Coming from you, that means very little," said Olive, flatly.

Michael stowed her keys with the vial and hurried away from his baffled family. He was about to go to the one place he could never take them.

Michael rammed the car through the cemetery gates, shattering the rusty chain around them. He sped through the park, illuminating rows of headstones and sculptures as he twisted and turned through the winding estate.

He screeched to a halt mid-way up a track, as his subconscious memory nagged at him. Leaving the lights trained ahead for illumination, he continued on foot through the rows of graves until he reached the stone he was looking for.

Even with the lot number seared in his memory, he did a double-take upon finding it. Decades had passed since he last came here, and in that time the seasons had smoothed over the boy's sculpture, robbing his features of detail, erasing his vivid smile, and obscuring his withered arm. The headstone had fared no better, with lichen rendering the inscriptions barely legible.

Michael's eyes landed on the plots either side of the boy's grave; his mother and father had since passed, too. Or at least, the two people who believed themselves to be his parents, and who had dutifully tended to him for his short life.

Michael knelt before the boy's grave and dug a small hole with his bare hand. Unwrapping his overcoat, which had functioned as makeshift padding for the bowl, he tipped the wilted plant into to the cavity. It was looking even more wilted than when he'd excavated it earlier.

He covered the main bundle of roots with soil, pressing the two sets of earth together with his fingers. Carefully, he lifted the secondary black root from the ground and placed it against his son's headstone. But the feeble tendril slid down the dry stone, struggling to gain traction.

Michael plucked the vial of Hope's blood from his pocket. Unscrewing it with his teeth, he tipped it out, dousing plant and stone alike in crimson.

The plant quivered, as if shivering. The tendril straightened out, strengthening its grip on the stone. The main plant perked up, glistening in the car's headlights.

Michael reached into his other pocket and grabbed Olive's car keys, flicking open the penknife. Without a moment's hesitation, he slashed the thin blade across his thigh.

Hot blood seeped into his trousers. Dropping the knife, he prized the fabric apart to expose the wound. Squeezing the cut, he showered the soil with his blood, nourishing the main bundle of roots.

Panting, he slumped against the headstone and watched the plant, eagerly. He'd followed Clarkenwell's instructions to the letter. Assuming the plant took, both households would be saved.

If that worked, Michael would return with more blood, coming each day to protect a further household of his sprawling family. As soon as they saw that Hope was OK, they would understand; they would all give him the small droplets he needed to protect them forever.

The plant reached its apex, standing taller than ever, its leaves no longer wilted at all. Michael stared at his work and cried with triumph, marveling at the beautiful, shimmering flowers.

As his eyes moved to the secondary stem, his mouth fell. Something was wrong; it was moving downwards.

"No..." begged Michael.

But it was too late. The stem slid limply to the ground, leaving a streak of red against the weathered stone.

"Stop it, I beg you," he cried, as the malady spread across the rest of the plant.

Its strength was failing, and its stems drooping. As the plant wilted in the car's headlights, Michael realized the bursts of color were gone from the petals. Their transparency was fading too, being replaced by an ashy blackness.

He placed a desperate finger against a withering flower head, but it came away immediately. The once shimmering petals fell to the ground, blackening and curling into a crisp.

One by one, the plant's flowers withered and died. Michael watched in horror as his family's only chance of survival collapsed before him.

In despair, he wrenched the entire plant from the ground and thrust it back in the bowl. He had to get it back to safety – to the mailbox. Clarkenwell had said something about nutrients from the enamel, maybe they could save it now.

He raced across town, screeching to a halt at a crossroads. Glancing at the wilted, decimated plant beside him, a sickening feeling clawed at his stomach. The plant could only survive in one home, meaning he could only protect one family.

The turning to the left led to Taylor's home; her husband and kids, and of course, Michael's abode. He still had fifty years of real life to make up for, and like Clarkenwell had said, the Ministry didn't hang around with ex-offenders' letters.

His eyes darted right, to the route leading to Damien's family, and their daughter, Hope. Beyond them, Leon's family, and Sophia and Nina's. His head was swimming. He had to pick one.

With a cry, Michael hit the gas.

Michael staggered out of the car. Grabbing the bowl, he fell before the mailbox and clawed the earth away. He thrust the ailing plant into the soil and covered it over, watching with bated breath. No more blood, no more transplants, he whispered, placing the secondary stem against the enamel pipe.

The plant shuddered once more. Its leaves perked, but only fractionally. It was hunched over, a weakened echo of itself. Curled, black petals fell to the ground as Michael tenderly compacted the soil around its base.

"Hang in there, don't die on me, please," he whispered, now patting the soil feverishly.

Tears streamed from his cheeks as one by one, the remaining flowers succumbed to the black death consuming the plant, shedding their petals and crumpling before him.

As he sobbed, a single, glistening bud caught his eye. There, nestling between the two stems, was a tiny, transparent flower, clinging on defiantly. Color streaked across it as Michael shifted position, marveling at the lone survivor, not daring to touch it.

A light flicked on upstairs. Damien's silhouette loomed against the curtains. Michael scarpered back to the car, speeding away before his intervention was known. The family's best chance of survival rested on that plant staying hidden, discreetly clinging to the foot of their mailbox.

Michael weaved through the neighborhood, then pulled up by Olive's place. Cutting the engine, he stuffed the keys under her doormat, then withdrew, quietly. The rain had subsided to a delicate falling mist. As the library tower chimed midnight, Michael set off for Taylor's house by foot.

Dawn glinted through the top of the guest room curtains. Rising from his sleepless bed, Michael headed downstairs.

Within half an hour, the kitchen was filled with the most glorious smell of fresh pancakes. He stowed them in the warm oven, ready for the others, then watched the clock chime 6 a.m.

Raiding the hallway key rack, he stepped into the crisp morning air and approached the mailbox.

"Don't worry, old friend, I come in peace," he croaked, patting the top.

Michael reached inside, retrieving a solitary brown envelope. He smiled, recognizing the messy scribble across its front. Eighteen-year-old Michael had never been one for handwriting.

"Do I smell pancakes?" cheered Taylor, from the hallway.

Following the cold draught, she adjusted course to find Michael in the garden.

"Oh god, has the mail come? We're expecting an invoice from Ravi's piano teacher and I'm pretty sure he's hiking his rates," she began.

Taylor's eyes landed on the brown envelope and her face fell.

"Whose...?"

Her voice trailed off, nervously, as she edged closer.

"Relax, it's mine," smiled Michael.

"What? But we only just got you back. This is so unfair! I need to wake the others," she cried.

"Please don't, Taylor. Truly, I'd rather go without a fuss. Tell the others I love them. I may not have always expressed it in the best of ways, but I hope they know."

"You're going right now? Are you sure?" stammered Taylor.

"I'm done running," he smiled. "My time has come."

CHAPTER SIXTY-TWO

Wheezing and aching, Michael climbed the last of the sunset-marble steps. Swaying precariously in the wind, he hurried towards the matt black ahead. Pressing with all his strength, the mighty door creaked open.

Michael slid through the narrow gap he'd created before the door swiftly slammed shut with a resounding thud.

He stared around the vast chamber. It was an exact mirror of the other half of the building, only all of the fittings were coated in charcoal black paint. In lieu of sunlight pouring in from above, gas-lit lanterns hung in chandeliers and wall brackets throughout the atrium.

From the shadows came a pointed cough, startling Michael. The clerk was slight in stature and deathly pale. Her skin was impossibly smooth and youthful, yet her hair was thin and grey.

She plucked the letter from Michael's gnarled hands, examining it briefly, before returning it with a curt nod. The flickering gaslight above the black turnstiles switched, as the red glass filter rotated to green.

Michael shuffled through and followed the clerk's long, bony finger. Across the chamber, a bell hop awaited his arrival. She, too, looked unsettlingly youthful yet ancient, and had a glazed look about her, like her mind was elsewhere entirely.

She made no eye contact with Michael as he squeezed in to the narrow elevator, taking only a perfunctory glance at his envelope then punching in a level.

When the brass shutters reopened moments later, she ushered him out into a dark, curving expanse.

"Which way do I-" began Michael.

The shutter clanged shut and the bellhop disappeared without a word.

Save for the flames, everything in the corridor was black. A black carpet runner on black floorboards, lined by black wallpaper, hosting black canvases hung in black frames.

Flickering gas lamps offered the only illumination, but their light was second-hand, spilling out of small port holes in the black doors.

Above each door was a painted-glass symbol; either green or red, as with the turnstile downstairs.

Michael shuffled along the corridor, peering into the portholes of each door as he sought his space.

The rooms were circular and filled with slender mailboxes, as the birth side had been; only these boxes were ash-gray.

A solitary automaton removed a yellow envelope from a box, then resealed the hatch and erased the person's name from the covering slate. It stacked the person's envelope with several others on its desk. In other rooms, people were seated with their backs to him. Some were shaking, as if weeping; others were slumped, like they'd been drugged, or had passed out.

A green entry light emerged around the bend. Michael peered through the porthole, spying an automaton behind a desk. Somehow detecting Michael's presence, it beckoned him inside.

Michael entered, cautiously. The space felt eerily familiar; a muted replica of the room he'd visited on his eighteenth.

Heeding the machine's hand gesture, he took a creaky seat before the desk. His chair was at odds with the rest of the room's gothic splendor. He was sitting on a cheap, collapsible studio chair. Its pale green paint was chipped and flaking, revealing the rusty metal beneath.

The automaton opened a drawer and placed two envelopes on the table before him. One was golden yellow, the other deep maroon.

The automaton produced two blank pieces of cream paper, along with a pen. In immaculate, precision calligraphy, it inscribed a title at the top of each page, then placed them beside an envelope.

JOYS.

REGRETS.

Yellow and red envelopes respectively. The automaton held the pen out for Michael, who took it, baffled.

There were three bullet points pre-inked on each sheet. The automaton reached beneath the desk and withdrew an ornate hour glass. The brass-plated sides featured a beautiful tableau depicting humans and automatons holding up the world together. The machine set it down with a thud.

Seeing the sand drain away, Michael hastily began writing.

JOYS.

That was easy: loving Kelsey, raising their three wonderful children, his grandfather's humor.

REGRETS.

Michael's heart sank as he turned to the second sheet. For all his joys, he felt equally deep remorse that he'd squandered his precious time with those people. With great bitterness, he penned his list of regrets in a mirror image of his joys.

- *Kelsey*
- *Grandfather Amal*
- *My children*

He considered the list, then added a note below the bullets.

I hurt those I loved most, by living in fear of losing them. It is the greatest mistake I ever made, and I made it every day of my life.

A sickening feeling filled his stomach. Michael dropped the pen down and stared at the summation of his own existence in disgust.

The automaton loaded the pages into each envelope and sealed them, then returned them to Michael. Rising to its feet, the machine turned a key in an unmarked box on the wall. A doorway made of mailboxes swung open.

The machine gestured for Michael to pass through. Fearfully, Michael shuffled into the room beyond, clutching his envelopes.

The lighting changed immediately. They were in a vast chamber, with sunlight streaming through painted windows overhead. Michael shuffled forwards and peered over the edge. They were at least one hundred feet up.

In the center of the chamber, bathing in the sunlight, was a vast oak tree with shimmering, golden leaves.

As Michael marveled, the automaton beckoned him over to the side. A spiral staircase descended downward, looping in great rings to the floors below.

By the time they reached the bottom, Michael was clinging to the automaton for support. It must have taken them half an hour to descend the great winding ramp.

Reaching the base, they emerged into an earthy clearing where the tree's gnarled roots ducked and dived through the soil.

Encompassing the vast plant bed was a gold and white mosaic depicting roots. The patterning disappeared into the peripheral shadows of the chamber, which was itself encircled by coliseum-like archways.

The automaton pointed from Michael's joy letter to the expanse of soil. Michael edged forwards, allowing the mud to coat his shoes. Kneeling with great effort, he placed the yellow envelope on the ground.

The earth swallowed it immediately, snatching it from his fingers. Michael stared from the soil to the automaton, which was pointing at the grand tree in the center.

A nearby branch was shaking. The thin edge of the branch flexed, snake-like, with the motion. A swelling bead passed along its stem to a yellow bud. It unfurled into a golden leaf, which glistened in the sunlight.

Breaking Michael's transfixion, a metallic hand landed firmly on Michael's shoulder. The automaton pointed to the remaining red envelope in Michael's hand and beckoned him to follow.

The machine was gliding to the far edge of the chamber, following the mosaic roots to the peripheral arches.

Whereas the outside of the Ministry was crafted from

gleaming marble and stones which expressed the sun's full range of color, these base archways were from an ancient, gray bedrock.

Each archway was unique, and embellished with beautiful carvings; a mixture of glyphs and scripts from languages Michael didn't recognize, interlaced with carvings of humans, automatons, and mythical creatures.

Michael's automaton followed the branching roots until the mosaic delivered it to a particular archway. Beyond the stone threshold was a dark passageway, cloaked in shadow. The automaton vanished inside. With a nervous backward glance at the shimmering tree, Michael hastened after it.

He shuffled through the darkness, keeping his hand outstretched before him. The automaton's hisses and clinking gears were fading into the tunnel ahead.

"Hold on!" cried Michael.

He hurried onward, yelping in pain as his head bumped against the stone ceiling. He probed the darkness ahead; the tunnel was shrinking.

Wincing, Michael sank to his knees and crawled forwards. All fours was a difficult proposition for a man with one arm, and his hybrid shuffle was both painful and slow going.

His forehead collided with something vertical and hard. Michael's hand swiftly confirmed what his throbbing skull was telling him: he'd reached a solid wall.

Michael looked behind him; there was no sign of the chamber from which he'd come. He was in total, panoramic darkness, and fear was swelling within him. Was this it? Was this his fate?

"Help! Somebody, help!" he cried.

Michael could feel the air around him warming and

thickening with his own carbon dioxide. He spun in circles, pawing at the darkness. Stone, stone, stone...

It was all around; the machine had lured him to a tomb!

"Please, somebody!" he begged.

Something damp and grainy met his hand. He sank his fingertips into the earthy mass and pulled a chunk away.

With a desperate cry, Michael clawed urgently at the mound before him, feeling the earth cake his fingernails and crumble across his knees, layer by layer.

A glint of light appeared through a crack, but his head was starting to swim. He was growing sleepy in the dark, stifling tunnel.

He dug faster, grunting through the brain fog. He knew he was seconds from passing out; he had to break through the wall before he suffocated.

The crack expanded as greater chunks crumbled away. Something green was filtering the shards of light.

With a choked gasp, Michael wrenched a final chunk of earth away. There was just enough room for him to squeeze through. He crawled forwards, emerging from the tunnel into a curtain of ivy.

Michael collapsed forwards, plunging through the greenery to land hard on a wooden floor, gasping for breath. Fresh air cooled his flush cheeks, gradually steadying his panicked lungs. Fragments of red clay from the tunnel covered his hand and clothes, and lumps of dirt sprayed from his spluttering lips.

The room was like a shed. It had a low, sloping ceiling, and modest wooden paneling on every surface. Gloomy natural light illuminated the room via a four-pane window on one side. Rain was lashing against the glass, though Michael couldn't hear the water. The only sound was a faint a humming of an engine. Or was it an air conditioning unit?

Rising, panting, he shuffled towards the wooden door opposite. He pressed his hand against the latch and pulled; the door didn't budge. By the sounds of it, it was locked from the outside.

Michael tugged harder, railing with frustration as the padlock rattled defiantly against him. Defeated, and exhausted, he shuffled to the table in the center of the shed-room.

Taking one of the heavy wooden seats, he sat across from the locked door and waited, still gasping for breath.

Occasionally, he glanced to the rain-covered window, but an occluded gray sky was all that could be seen. As his heart rate settled, Michael's mind turned to the crumpled red envelope tucked inside his jacket pocket. He reached in with his grubby hands and pulled it out.

At that moment, there was a jangling of keys from outside. A lock clicked. A latch shifted. The door swung open. In the threshold stood a figure covered in a head-to-toe yellow anorak, clutching a yellow umbrella, and battling the watery deluge outside.

Michael's jaw dropped as he set eyes on a familiar, wrinkled face.

"Granddad?"

CHAPTER SIXTY-THREE

A mal sat down opposite Michael. He looked exactly as Michael remembered him, down to the clothes. In fact, he looked several years younger than Michael.

"Hey kiddo," Amal grinned.

Michael suddenly became acutely aware of his arm. Did his grandfather know what had happened?

Amal nodded at Michael's maroon envelope on the table and winked. Reaching into his own blazer pocket, he pulled out a matching envelope, albeit with fewer creases and no earth stains. He placed it down on the table and slid it across halfway, leaving his hand lingering on the top.

Michael cottoned on and tentatively slid his envelop forwards. Amal smiled and lifted his hand. Cautiously, like two fencers circling one another, they each took the other's envelope.

His grandfather was faster, of course, having two hands to open the envelope. Amal nodded sadly as he read the letter, before replacing it in the envelope with a sigh.

Using his teeth as a clamp, Michael prized Amal's

envelope open and wrestled the letter out. His mouth slackened, crestfallen.

Beneath the immaculately engraved title *REGRETS* were three bullet points. All of them were bare. Not a single other word graced the page.

"What's this?" asked Michael, waving the letter.

"It's what you deserve, my boy," said Amal.

Michael shook his head angrily. He felt tricked, embarrassed at what he'd shared. Tears filled his eyes as he read Amal's pitying expression, and the true meaning of his grandfather's words sank in.

"Granddad, that list is just the tip of the iceberg. If you knew the things I'd done..."

Michael trailed off, choking on his own words. Amal smiled at him softly, then rose from his chair, stepping to the door.

"Come with me, my boy."

A gust of cool air rushed in as Amal opened the door. Michael could see the rain lashing down, but the drops were falling silently.

His grandfather handed Michael the yellow umbrella, then pulled his hood up. With a glimmer in his eye, he tucked Michael's letter away, then set off into the gray.

Michael struggled to keep the umbrella up against the lashing rain. The field seemed infinite, and barren, save for a silhouette up ahead. Through the thick drizzle emerged a doorway. A single, standalone door in a thin white frame, surrounded by grass in all directions.

In the distance, a car engine revved aggressively. He cast his eyes around, but there was nothing but gray cloud and sheets of rain.

A flash of black caught his eye. Something was speeding across the field, getting louder.

"We should probably hurry," said Amal.

His reassuring smile was at odds with the firmness of his tone.

A horn blared out. The black object in the distance was getting closer, quickly. A second engine joined the melee. An orange car was coming towards them from the opposite direction, some way off.

A shimmering red beacon appeared through the drizzle, above the doorway. Michael tilted the umbrella for a better look, allowing the rain to lash him in the process. A traffic signal was right beside the doorway, and it was fixed on red, pointing towards the black car.

The black car seemed unperturbed; it was accelerating towards the interchange at breakneck speed. Meanwhile, the orange car was closing in from the perpendicular direction, with seemingly no knowledge of the other vehicle.

The engines were bearing down upon Michael and Amal, creating a deafening racket.

"This way!" cried Amal.

He stepped inside, vanishing instantly as wind slammed the door shut behind him.

Michael cried out for Amal's help, hobbling as fast as his ancient joints would allow. The uneven grass snagged his feet, tripping him with every step.

The wind seized Michael's umbrella, hauling him backwards until he released it. The yellow accessory disappeared across the field into the grayness beyond.

Both blaring cars were closing in, now just a stone's throw away. The black car could surely see the red signal by now, yet it was getting faster.

Michael grabbed the soaking door handle with his only

arm. As he turned the handle, he glanced sideways at the speeding vehicle.

As Michael locked eyes with the driver, his heart froze. Barreling toward him was his eighteen-year-old self. His eyes widened with disbelief as he processed the screaming, tearful, wheel-thumping version of his youth. The second car's horn blared. Time seemed to slow as both vehicles careered towards each other, convening on the doorway with horns blaring and engines screaming.

Without warning, the door swung inward and two strong hands seized Michael, hauling him inside.

Metal crunched with a deafening boom. Other cars skidded and screeched across the ether. Pedestrians screamed. Shards of glass and steel sliced their way through the thundering rain, which was suddenly as loud as the engines. Michael cried out as debris flew towards him. A rushing wind was growing louder, filling his ears.

No sooner had he cleared the doorway than the door slammed shut, cloaking Michael in silence.

Michael and Amal slammed into the ground, both groaning with the impact. Amal was first up, dusting himself down, before helping Michael to his feet.

A vast warehouse greeted Michael's eyes. Furnaces blazed, powering huge pistons. All around, elderly women and men were smelting, cutting, and welding hunks of metal at various stations. The clatter of hammers and saws was deafening.

"All in good time. Come," smiled Amal.

Michael followed his grandfather across the factory floor. A group of workers were huddled around a scaffold.

Suspended from the frame was the stripped-back skeleton of an automaton. A gray-haired woman in a lab coat was on a step ladder beside it, twisting a screwdriver in its shoulder socket, while others affixed gleaming new plates to its feet and ankles, covering up the intricate mechanical circuitry.

Leaving the warehouse behind, the pair entered a smaller chamber. Stacks of yellow envelopes were piled on the side. An automaton was shoveling them into an incinerator, which was powering a great steam turbine that appeared to be generating an electrical current through a huge tank of dark green-blue liquid.

Amal pressed on, leading them into a room with a ceiling so low they had to stoop. Whispers emanated from a dip where the floor fell away. Amal beckoned Michael onward, crawling to the edge of the floor.

Michael's stomach churned as he took in the scale of the drop. They were on a shelf with no rail, staring into a cylindrical chamber.

Light streamed in from the skylights by their heads. Michael was utterly baffled; he'd lost all sense of whether they were underground, outside, or, as now seemed to be the case, somewhere at the top of the Ministry building again.

In the center of the chamber was a structure so breathtaking in its scale, Michael almost laughed.

A mountain of maroon envelopes reached up from the distant ground to the heights of the vast chamber, stopping just short of the ceiling. Some looked old, and a little faded from the light, while others looked brand new, and crisp.

At the base of the pile, way down below, Michael could make out two figures, scavenging among the pile. He recognized their uniforms; they were scholars. Each had a briefcase with them; they were examining letters to harvest.

Michael had no idea what was guiding their selections; none of the envelopes had information written on the outside, but perhaps the scholars could detect things he couldn't.

Amal pulled Michael's maroon envelope from his anorak. Michael copied, retrieving his grandfather's cleaner envelope from his blazer pocket.

"What does it say?" said Amal, with a nod.

Michael teased the letter out, examining the page again.

"Nothing, it's blank," he shrugged. "You didn't write anything? Or you have no regrets?"

Amal held up his grandson's letter. Michael stared mournfully at his greatest regrets.

"To me, yours looks blank too," smiled Amal.

"What are you saying?"

"It's time to let go."

He slid Michael's letter across the wooden floor, and the pair swapped back. Amal stared at his own list for a long moment, and a tear trickled down his cheek. Closing his eyes, he took a deep breath, then stared at the page once again.

Amal smiled to himself, with an accepting huff, and stuffed the letter back into the envelope. He folded his arms and tapped the maroon package against the wooden lip, restively, while watching the scholars sifting below.

Michael turned to his own letter and felt a wave of guilt. Amal couldn't expect him to just accept the awful things he'd done? He looked at his grandfather, sorrowfully.

"Did you know you're on here, Granddad?"

Amal raised a curious eyebrow and chuckled in astonishment. "Then that makes two of us."

Michael was stunned. "I'm on *your* list? But... for what?"

His grandfather smiled at him softly.

"There was a time for those conversations, dear boy, and it's long gone. We're not here to talk about the past, we're here to lay it to rest."

Michael stared at the document and his eyes lingered on Kelsey's name. His heart panged as he recalled all the times he'd lied, not listened, or acted impulsively, in his dogged pursuit of preserving what was already there. Tears rolled down his cheeks as he comprehended the scale of his failures to his family; the time he'd wasted. The letter trembled in his hand. Michael sank to his knees as the guilt consumed him, and he hunched over, weeping.

Amal held him, tenderly, then helped Michael to his knees. Pressing the letter to Michael's chest, Amal edged back and gave him an encouraging nod.

Michael closed his eyes and steadied his breathing, forcing himself to stem the flow of tears. He thought about all he'd done in his life, and how it had led him to this moment.

As his breathing steadied, a heavy calm settled over him. Sniffing, he opened his eyes and blinked the tears away. His eyes widened as they fell on his page of regrets; the writing was gone.

"It's blank - my words have gone. Did you switch them?" gasped Michael.

"It means you're ready to let go," smiled Amal.

With Michael's letter resealed in its envelope, the two men knelt side-by-side, facing over the sheer edge. Together, they tossed their red slips onto the great mountain below.

Michael's landed on the side, dislodging several others, which all tumbled down in an avalanche of maroon. He tried to keep track of which was his, but it vanished among the tumbling pile. Slightly higher up, Amal's appeared to have settled on a ledge, balancing neatly on its side.

The scholars below had gone. The only sound in the room was the rustle of settling envelopes, and Michael's wheezing lungs.

His grandfather took him by the arm, and led him through a corridor to a muted green doorway. It had the same chipped paintwork and rusty metal frame as the chair Michael had sat on earlier.

"What now?" said Michael, as they neared the threshold.

His grandfather smiled at him with a twinkle in his eye. "Now, we meet the others."

END.

There's more.
Discover what happened to Kelsey.
Get the exclusive postscript free.
Only at marcusmartinauthor.com/ps

DEAR READER,

It's Marcus here. Thanks so much for reading this copy of *Finality*, I truly hope it resonated with you. I'm an independent author, which means I publish all my work myself, and bear all the associated costs. The traditional publishing industry is incredibly tough for new authors to break into. After my first series *Convulsive* was rejected by fifty different agents, I realized that to achieve my dream of becoming a writer, I would have to strike out by myself. So I did.

It's terrifying, but I know I can do it; I have wonderful readers like you, who send me encouraging emails out of the blue which always brighten my day. It's my sincere hope that you may be kind enough to sponsor my next book by donating at marcusmartinauthor.com/support. On the next page you'll find out why, and what a massive impact your support will have.

It took five years to write and self-publish the *Convulsive* series alongside stressful day jobs, often working seven days a week. But within six months of completion, the series hit number one in the international Amazon bestseller charts for its genre. That was the single greatest moment of affirmation I could've wished for. I quite literally danced around the room with joy. It didn't come with a windfall of cash like you might think - book margins aren't big - but it was enough for me to finish recouping the editing costs and fund an audiobook version. In fact, since starting out, I've reinvested every cent I've ever earned from my books straight back into my writing - because I know it's the only way I'll grow.

It's still early days for me as a writer, which makes each new book a white knuckle ride. In 2020 I took a leap of faith and left my job to become a full-time author, knowing I would be living off savings and reinvesting any profits to make it work. In that year I gave it my all, and wrote four new books, one of which you've just finished.

I want to continue. My aim is to write four books a year, and keep bringing bold sci-fi ideas to readers like you. I know I can do it, but I'll be honest: there's still no guarantee it'll work out. Mainly because I don't get advances on book deals like conventional authors do.

I love creating new worlds, and I'm a damned hard worker. If you believe my writing deserves a future, and would like to see more books from me each year, I would be so hugely grateful if you would support me with a donation of your choosing. It only takes a moment, just visit **marcusmartinauthor.com/support**

With the support of readers like you, I can produce more groundbreaking sci-fi. I would be humbled to offer you an acknowledgement in one of my future books, and you will have my heartfelt thanks forever.

In gratitude - Marcus.

Cambridge, England, 2021

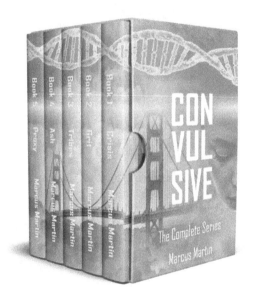

People of Change

Trilogy of standalone novels. Near future eco-lit thrillers, with fast action and dark humor throughout.

  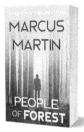

Read free samples or buy at

marcusmartinauthor.com

Don't miss Marcus Martin's next book.

Join the email list:

marcusmartinauthor.com/email

subscribers also get free advanced copies

and exclusive content.

ACKNOWLEDGMENTS

Finality was made possible by these wonderful people.

To my brilliant team of advanced readers: for your wisdom, diligence, and generosity of spirit, I am truly grateful. Adrian Bonsall, Andrew Carter, Chris Hutchings, Craig Dyson, Jan James, John Wallis, Mae Keary, and Martin White, thank you all.

James Farmer, for your honesty, encouragement, and openness, I am truly humbled. Thank you for letting this story into your heart.

To my friends, your encouragement and counsel keeps me energized between writing marathons. Thanks for always listening and being such great sounding boards.

To my cousin Oli, one of the kindest guys I know, and who brightens up every room. Thank you for buying me the professional software I needed to typeset and publish this book. You helped me get this story out of my head and into readers' hands. Thank you for believing in me, and for always making me laugh.

Lastly, to Mum, Dad, Lottie, and Tania, you are the

pillars of my life. Thank you for always believing in me. I love you all, and you are the best family I could ever wish for.

In loving memory

Walter John Hutchings
Ann Farmer
Jean Farmer

ABOUT THE AUTHOR

Marcus Martin is a British author based in Cambridge, UK. He originally trained as a composer and classical pianist at King's College London & the Royal Academy of Music, before taking a meandering route into a Master's degree in the psychology of music at the University of Cambridge, followed by a postgraduate diploma in religion and politics.

Marcus has performed at the Edinburgh Fringe Festival a number of times as both a stand-up comedian and actor. After living and working in the US and Germany for six months he returned to Cambridge where he wrote and staged his first three plays, before embarking on a career in authorship.

He's worked as a barista, a decorator, a builder's assistant, a teaching assistant, a data entry clerk, a marketing executive, a compliance officer, a pianist, a choral assistant, a musical director, a script editor for BBC Radio 4, a voice actor, and a jingle writer, to name but a few.

Alongside books and voice acting, he's host of the cult sci-fi podcast *Make It Soon*, which brings scientists and comedians together to discuss iconic sci-fi inventions that are becoming a reality. Listen for free at makeitsoon.com

Marcus is currently working on a new book series, as well as several standalone novels. He loves receiving emails from readers, and replies to each one. You can reach him at: marcus@marcusmartinauthor.com

For a sneak peak of Marcus's upcoming releases, join the email list at: marcusmartinauthor.com/email

You can also follow him on social:
    facebook.com/MarcusMartinAuthor
    goodreads.com/author/show/17601586
    bookbub.com/authors/marcus-martin

CPSIA information can be obtained
at www.ICGtesting.com
Printed in the USA
BVHW071937220221
600776BV00001B/92